PRAISE FOR *LIKE BOOGIE ON TUESDAY*

"Grosvenor brings a sense of style and quality to her prose that lifts her work out of the ordinary to secure a place as one of the brighter voices of commercial fiction."

—Donna Hill, author of *If I Could*

"Scrumtious and heartfelt, Grosvenor goes to the jugular on the uncertainties of life, elevating and inspiring us in one single stroke."

—Margaret Johnson-Hodge,
author of *Butterscotch Blues*

"In a fast-paced story textured like a delicious metaphorical gumbo, Linda Dominique Grosvenor spins a tight web of passion and desire."

—Tracy Price Thompson, author of *Black Coffee*

"Grosvenor has written a beautiful novel that touches the deepest, most tender moments of your heart. She's created characters you'll come to love and hate to leave."

—Jacquelin Thomas, author of *Singsation*

LIKE BOOGIE ON TUESDAY

Linda Dominique Grosvenor

BET Publications, LLC
http://www.bet.com

SEPIA BOOKS are published by

BET Publications, LLC
c/o BET BOOKS
One BET Plaza
1900 W Place NE
Washington, DC 20018-1211

Previously published by Sadorian Publications, LLC

ISBN 1-58314-260-6

First Printing: January 2002
10 9 8 7 6 5 4 3 2 1

Printed in the United States of America

This novel is dedicated to my grandma Cyrilene.

ACKNOWLEDGMENTS

To God, for without His truth, I would still be bowing down to worship statues, believing they could hear me. To my mom—I love you! To my son, Jamel—you know how to make a mother proud. To my sisters and brother—Judie, Janet, and Melvin—I love y'all too! To my husband and soul mate, John Riddick Jr.—"you've touched my heart in so many different places. What was love before you?" To my agent, Claudia Menza—thanks for finding *Boogie* a home. To Theresa Dawson—a fan and friend from day one. To Desiree Crawford—wherever you are, I hope you're happy! Tanya and Martina—you two are some true honest-to-God sisterfriends. I love you both (FrenzForeva)!

I'd also like to thank Timmothy B. McCann, "a constant supporter," Franklin White, Carl Weber (you are too kind for words), Victoria Christopher Murray (my big sis), Margaret Johnson-Hodge (I'm still in awe!), Tracy Price Thompson (my humble authorfriend), and Zeta Dawson Godboalt. I thank you all for always going the extra mile on my behalf. You have brought the words out of me and helped me find the courage to speak them in a room full of people!

I still need to thank Dr. Edwin McAllister and the Little Brown Handbook, BWIP.org, ProlificWriters.org, RhapsodyinBlack.com, and the support of on-line venues such as AALBC.com, RAWSISTAZ.com, and MosaicBooks.com. But most of all I thank my captive audience who patiently waited as the pages churned on this next novel.

"Love takes off masks that we fear we cannot live without and know we cannot live within."

—James Baldwin

1

Nina was the director of a newly formed company, Dartmouth. They put together the literal demographics that businesses used to decipher who was buying what product, how much they were spending on average, and the income bracket into which they helplessly fell.

Their PR and advertising department then constructed vibrant sales pitches for products and used the subliminal advertising her thesis spoke of to get people to buy items that were manufactured and sold by several companies that made up their client roster.

Nina managed a staff of ten in a small neutral-colored office across town where there were hardly any trees or a pleasant view. It was a close fit, but lawfully comfortable. Four women and six men. She oversaw the smooth operations of the sometimes hectic office efficiently. Her rose-colored Formica desk wasn't cluttered with Post-It notes, files, paper-clip chains, or rotting rubber-band balls. She was a neat freak and relied only on the daily necessities prearranged in an orderly fashion.

She had a photograph on her desk in a handmade sterling silver frame of her and Troi in Cozumel four summers ago, an oversize coffee mug that said, DON'T MESS WITH ME, YOU KNOW HOW I GET, and a red crystal heart-shaped Elsa Peretti paperweight that was given to her by her father last Valentine's Day, which now held down a few wrinkled receipts and miscellaneous papers.

Her daily planner sat neatly in the center of it all. She enjoyed being tidy. She also enjoyed the freedom of running an office that virtually ran itself, and the occasional sunshine that came in through the window to nurture the plants on the windowsill and reflect off the Ansel Adams black-and-white print that graced the wall.

She felt a twinge of guilt sneak across her conscience about that. His work didn't fully express who she was as a person. She wasn't one to get caught up in what the rave was. But, like most things in her life, she would allow it to do for now. Even a barren forest with shriveled trees in a frame was better than a blank wall.

Nina didn't date much. She hadn't dated much in college either. Romance was as foreign to her as a trigonometry and calculus high. And she hadn't had time lately for more than a cappuccino, latte, or espresso on the run with any one person in particular.

She was educated, creative, and the type of woman who could shower and get dressed in less than thirty minutes. That was a noteworthy achievement in itself. She lived alone in a huge brownstone in Brooklyn Heights.

She spent most languid Saturday afternoons decorating the upstairs apartments one room at a time, with pieces she'd siphoned from friends and family, and the remnants of which she'd discovered strolling in and out of the antique shops along Atlantic Avenue. She enjoyed finding rare treasures and castoffs in the shops at which her friends and family turned up their regal noses.

They gladly emphasized that it was used furniture, and wanted a round of applause for their insight. But Nina got a natural pleasure from browsing through the antiques with their musty smells, swollen wood, affordable price tags, rusted latches and knobs that you could polish up like new. She didn't mind the teasing; antiques were something she had relished for years while they had all only gotten hip to decorating and home furnishings by watching cable.

Nina adored the quaint little shops that transported her through time and the wares of what were left of the art and book vendors in the city. She loved soft billowy fabrics, too. Moleskin was something quite peculiar. Sort of like the kid in school that nobody understood. It's the closest you could come to that suede feel without having to worry about permanent stains and enormous dry cleaning bills, although Nina couldn't fathom dropping her lounge chair off at the cleaners and having it back in an hour.

Moleskin. She'd fallen in love with it the moment she'd felt it against her skin and wrapped it around her waist and shoulders, then draped it behind her, trailing through the fabric store like a queen making her way to her throne. A little on the expensive side per yard, but the softness of the fabric soothed the back of her hands, her neck, and her wallet.

Nina closed her bashful eyes and imagined herself sitting naked in the middle of her living room swathed in this luxurious fabric, sipping coffee that warmed her hands as she turned the pages of the book she was reading with her toes. Turning pages with her toes was a trick she had learned in college while always trying to do three things at once and realizing she only had two hands.

She had bought several yards of the supple fabric in a rich moss green hue that, on second thought, she would use to refabric her favorite chair. If she had any left over, she would make a few throw pillows to make the room even more conducive to reading. Nina liked to read with her feet propped up on several pillows, too, four to be exact.

"I'll take some fringe, too. Gold," she'd spoken confidently to the suspicious salesclerk, who hadn't been too pleased that she was dragging the expensive fabric across the dusty floor.

Nina was definitely what some might describe as a walking catastrophe or an accidental mishap, but she prided herself on being unique, and got a kick out of colorful art that grabbed you up by the collar, held on, and shook you until you bought it. It was like learning to hula. It was fun while it lasted. Not many artists lured her like that. She could name several unknowns, but couldn't have a conversation about it with the people she knew, and that was a sad fact.

Nina figured that one day she would actually be able to rationalize spending two grand on a canvas delicately smeared with a few tubes of acrylic paint. She agreed that up-and-coming artists needed more exposure and that people needed to appreciate art as much as the money-laundering presidential elections.

Most natives or foreigners couldn't name three living artists off the top of their head. Degas, Dali', and Picasso didn't count. They were overrated and dead. Nina agreed with Shelby that a house was not a home or decorated properly if it only had movie posters taped up on the walls over a four-poster bed and a leaky radiator off in the corner hissing and making a mess.

She also agreed that right here in the city, people were starving, too. Two thousand dollars could feed a whole family for months. One day she'd get something to replace that substitute that hung on her office wall, something more soothing to her spirit and reflective of her heritage. Something that had depth and had to be explained by the artist himself. Something she could relate to intellectually.

Nina also fiended for music that leaned more toward classical and jazz. She liked to tap her feet, clap her hands, and bob her head a little too much for most people's taste. Kim Burrell was a serious singing sister. Listening to her crooning melodies in minor keys was sure to get you caught in the worship of it all.

Nina also had a thing for horns. She relished the fervor with which the musicians played. She'd never been like other kids, listening to that boring music that had everyone learning the latest dance steps and forming a Soul Train line right in their living rooms on Saturday mornings.

She preferred jazz and classical to the Top 40, and she couldn't care less about Billboard. She'd lean out of her window sometimes in the evening, resting her elbows on a goose-down pillow, and listen to her neighbor across the street playing his submissive instrument like his next meal depended on it. He blew aggressively into that horn like a rite of passage, and Nina overindulged herself on it all.

His melodies were tranquil, and ivy framed his window like a trellis. She often saw the sun setting in the evening, full and rested, and she would swear musical notes were floating from his parted curtains, inviting her to dance and play footsie.

Her neighbor's comforting tunes caressed her and took her mind someplace where she felt rocked to sleep with her favorite doll and pacified with her thumb, grinning because she didn't have to answer to anybody.

She was blissful as she enjoyed a place where she had a daddy but no mother, and she and her sister could swim in the lake under the noonday sun, and Daddy would fish and catch them something that he would slather with cornmeal and fry up nice and crisp and serve with some fresh-squeezed, slightly tart lemonade.

Nina could see the seeds slowly sinking to the bottom of the glass every time she took a sip. She loved lemonade. Ice-cold. She wondered if her neighbor played in a band and thought if not, he should. His music took her to faraway places that only existed in her mind and invited her nightly to come and pretend over and over again.

Nina wasn't a difficult girl, really. She often hung out in joints like Sweet Basil, which was supposed to be New York's hippest jazz club, and the Blue Note. She loved live music and the atmosphere of it all, although she could do without the smoky haze.

She loved jazz clubs not just because they were the happeningest places in town, but because music did things to her that people hadn't managed to do thus far. Nina didn't care about friends. She often found herself desiring to be alone, listening to the sultry sound of Nina Simone.

Too often she'd press Play and Repeat as Nina Simone crooned something about dying and despising a man she once called father. Nina remembered how she would lie on her crisp powder blue sheets in the autumn breeze with her eyes closed as the large earth-hued maple leaves brushed near her window, calling her, and she'd rediscover the sound that often serenaded her as she drifted off to sleep.

Music was Nina; she had known that ever since her freshman year at Cornell. She would listen to the guys from the school rehearsing in the courtyard. They'd warm up and exercise their lips for a nonstop jam session that lasted way into the wee hours like a church revival. Everyone sat out in nearby complexes reading and enjoying the free music that helped them escape having to study or write research papers.

Nina's passion for music almost prompted her to change her major in her sophomore year, but she didn't. She refused to ruin her desire of it by overindulging in it. She also didn't want to know about B-flat and off-key; she just wanted to enjoy the sound that tickled her ears and made her believe she was sexier than she actually was. Her mother was pleased as peaches that she reconsidered changing her major, although Nina insisted, "It's my life, you know."

Nina had her dreams and aspirations, but often thought of things that she never wanted to be. She never wanted to be one of those women who read *Shape* but was never physically fit, she never wanted to be a guest on a talk show, she never wanted to become a product of her environment, and she never ever wanted to be still single at forty.

One out of four wasn't that bad. She didn't crave a man or the presence of one, she just wanted to have someone with whom she could share and communicate the little things. Things like a district-manager-of-the-month certificate, or maybe even just the regurgitated details of the annoying assistant at the office who refused to clean the food particles out of the telephone receiver when he was done munching lunch while talking on it.

She needed someone to tell, even though Nina made a silent pact with herself to deny it to the death. Having a love interest surely beat coming home and talking to her fish and plants. Heck, they could talk to each other, she thought with a laugh.

She just wanted to know that her holidays would not be spent alone sitting in her favorite chair watching her prestrung reindeer with sparkling white lights sitting in front of the house twinkling. She also didn't want to end up drinking so much thick prepackaged eggnog from the carton until she wanted to vomit, or calling up people she no longer liked just to prove that she still had someone to talk to around the holidays.

Nina could appreciate mittens, snowballs, holding hands, and having to pick up someone from the airport even on a late-night transatlantic flight. She wanted to expect a birthday card from someone besides her sister. Valentine's Day needed to find her dining at Maxim's in a red dress with a French manicure and being served like a goddess by a waiter named Jacques.

She wanted to be excited about something more than just Alvin Ailey American Dance Theater. She was elated because she had gotten tickets ahead of time. They had once performed at her school, she'd joined their mailing list, made a donation, and was now what they considered a sponsor.

She wanted things to be different this year. They ought to be. She just needed to find a comfortable place and reside in it.

2

Tim was silent. He scribbled his notes and buried his head as his classmate stood at the head of the class and acted out her dialogue within the guidelines that the professor had set forth from the textbook. His professor had written the textbook, so regardless of the fact that Tim hadn't had enough funds to purchase the book in time for the start of class, it was smooth sailing, as the professor went over each chapter verbatim. Tim was thankful enough for that. His class was made up of approximately eleven men and nine women. Age range was between nineteen and forty-six.

"Can you see how important dialogue is?" his professor asked, gesturing, then applauding at his student's efforts. She made her way back to her seat, smiling all the way.

The woman sitting directly behind Tim nudged him in the back, then passed him a folded-up piece of paper. Tim looked over his shoulder and smirked as he unfolded it and read the words. The letter made him feel like a grade schooler with some girl diggin' him, too shy to say it. The note read *Let's do dinner @ my place.*

Tim turned around and eyed the woman, then leaned back in his chair and ignored her. He knew it was just a matter of time before some woman would be overeager and hit on him. It never failed. From time to time he had to take inventory, check himself, and make sure he wasn't sending mixed signals by staring too long or trying to be overly helpful. He wasn't. Women were just a trip.

His hair cut close, his silk sweater courting his muscular frame and baggy khakis assisting, he was being smug, and he knew it. She leaned forward, put her lips to his ear, and whispered, "You looking good, Tim, so when?"

"Dialogue makes our scenes come to life." The professor paced the floor.

"When what?" Tim spoke over his shoulder.

"You, me, dinner and . . ."

Her words left him hanging.

"C'mon, Tim, we can work on our projects together," she said, ignoring the professor's gaze.

"This is important, and you both need to be paying attention." The professor glared in their direction.

"Go over your syllabi this weekend to see when the project is due and make a note of it. There will be no late papers, no makeups, and no exceptions. Class is dismissed." The professor nodded.

Tim lifted his bag onto his shoulder and hurried out of the classroom to his comfy ride, old faithful. He tossed his books in the backseat and headed over to the beauty shop, looking behind him only once to make sure his classmate wasn't hot on his heels.

Rochelle needed a ride home because Carl was working late. He hated the thought of going into that hair place, because women always sat around gossiping about nonsense. When he walked in they'd glue their eyes to him as if he were their last supper. He could think of better things to do than fighting to keep those man-hungry women off of him. He could go by the fish place, get some takeout, kick back, and listen to some tunes, or stir his creativity by toying with his Magnetic Poetry set. He enjoyed sliding the magnets around on his fridge, discovering new phrases and being prolific. It often gave him fresh thoughts and a new direction for his ideas.

Tim grudgingly pressed his way into the salon anyway and offered smiles all around as he spotted his sister near the back of the shop and made his way to her.

"Good evening, ladies." He eyed them one at a time.

"Oooh, good evening, young man. What can I do for you?" A middle-aged woman with clothes two sizes too small squirmed in her seat, rearranged her breasts, and got comfortable.

"I'm here to pick up Rochelle." He slowed his pace.

"Oh, umm, uh-huh, I see." Another woman eyed Rochelle over her specs.

"That's my brother, if you all must know." Rochelle smirked.

"Good-looking young man," the old woman agreed.

"Yeah, he needs a date, some love in his life, though." She shoved her brother.

"So does my sister," Troi interjected while making change for Rochelle, counting out singles.

"Tim, this is Troi Singleton. She's been doing my hair forever."

Tim nodded his head and acknowledged her.

"Don't pay your sister any mind. She's always trying to set someone up." Troi waved her hand at Rochelle.

"I'm trying to help him, Troi. He does need love. We all do," Rochelle added.

He couldn't believe his sister was practically saying that he was desperate in front of all these strange women—women she had to know had granddaughters who they were probably eager to pawn off on him.

"I need a little love myself." The woman with the tight clothes and protruding breasts pursed her lips.

"You ready, Rochelle?" Tim spoke impatiently.

"Yes. I'm coming." She gathered her things up.

"Nice meeting you, Tim." Troi smiled.

"Likewise." Tim nodded.

Rochelle waved and tripped out of the salon. Tim held the door open for her and gave her an icy glare.

"What?" she asked.

"You know what . . ."

"If I knew, I wouldn't ask, Tim."

"You know I don't like that."

"It was innocent. They didn't mean anything by it."

"I didn't mean them, I meant you."

"C'mon, Tim, lighten up."

"You're always telling me to lighten up."

"That's because you won't listen."

"I'll find someone when it's time, Rochelle." He slid into his car.

"How do you know it's not time now and you're not just blocking it out or something?" She pulled the door closed.

"Because when it's time, I won't need you to tell me, I'll know for myself."

"Fine then. End up old and gray with no one to tuck you in at night." She raised her hand toward him.

"I'm sorry, Rochelle . . ."

"No, you're right. It's your life. I can let you wither away if you want. I just thought that I was helping."

"You're my sister. Your love is help enough."

She glanced over at him, not sure if she wanted to accept the truce.

"I love you, too, Tim."

"I know you do." He smiled. "I know you do."

3

Nina Madison was a nonaggressive Pentecostal woman in her midthirties who observed Easter and Christmas in the more traditional sense. Not that others didn't; it was just that she had managed to incorporate the spirit of it all into her celebrations. She'd deck her halls, but she didn't offer chocolate bunnies or give into the blasphemy of Santa Claus, not even for the kids.

She never could get the correlation of Christ to a bunny rabbit, and ho-ho-ho was hardly the same as Noel. She did, however, enjoy the luxury of jelly beans, though it had absolutely nothing to do with the holiday itself. She had a sweet tooth. Jelly beans were her sugar of choice.

Nina took frequent pleasure in giving to the homeless by volunteering her time at a local soup kitchen on Thanksgiving, Christmas, and other nonoccasions in between with her sister, while others who were abundantly provided for sat around, ate like gluttons, and beached themselves like harpooned whales in front of the television, watching football and being thankful for nothing more than clear reception.

She imagined that most people normally felt compassion for the homeless in their hearts; they just didn't take the initiative to get up and do something or otherwise show it. Volunteering made her feel useful, needed. There was much to be said about those who were selfless enough to give.

As of late, Nina had been in and out of the halls of sanctification and wore no labels that were perpetuated by mere men. She wasn't estranged from her faith; she still prayed, and she was even more comfortable now without the accusing look-who-decided-to-come-to-church stares.

Her face was fuller, although her lips always were. She had matured quite handsomely and was often told that she was mentally stimulating and energetic.

She loved laughter and paid close attention to her weight, which was now teetering between 190 and 195. She didn't care who laughed at that. She was as content as a kid in a double-feature matinee with a large popcorn and a family pack of Milk Duds.

Nina was comfortable being a size fourteen, sometimes sixteen, and dressed modestly unless it was one of those rare occasions that brought out the diva in her—for instance, when she'd take in an evening performance at the Met dressed in sequins or a stunning bugle bead number with a slit that bared a little thigh.

Renditions of *La Boheme*, Elgar, or Chopin were equally entertaining, although her enjoyment of it all mattered more on who was performing than what she was wearing. She led a rather voluptuous life.

Nina's family, on the other hand, was something she was less vocal about. Her father was a melancholy man nearing sixty who had left the contracting company that had drained his entire life and sucked the fabric out of his family bond and started a small contracting company of his own.

Remodeling kitchens was one of the rare things he enjoyed. Nina could swear that when she'd stop by a job and find him working without a lunch break and trying to meet his deadline, she saw the residue of a smile every now and then. Her mother had reluctantly agreed to take out a second mortgage on their house to fund his construction company idea. It was a long time coming and barely thriving. He was too smitten to notice.

Nina's mother was a head nurse at a Mount Sinai in the city and had made financial plans to retire in two years. It was straining watching her parents disagree and circle like vultures above the carcass of what they'd managed to scrap together and still call family. She loved her father, though Nina and her mother had never really been close. Mother would tend to smother her creativity by criticizing everything Nina adored. Nina often resented it out loud and made vain attempts to be as flamboyant as she could be without being considered ridiculous.

Nina's sister, Troi, did hair. Troi did wraps, scrunches, finger waves, box braids, goddess braids, Senegalese twists, and any other style in *Black Hair, Style Q* or *Hype Hair* magazines. She had her own shop and spent endless hours in her haven listening to the chatter of the unfulfilled lives of women as far away as Jersey and Connecticut.

She attended the Beauty, Barber & Supply Annual Convention, the Big Show Expo, and the Summer Madness Hair Competition faithfully, to keep all of her customers up on the healthiest and most stylish alternatives for hairstyling. Troi was content. She always doted on her husband and child. They were staples in her life, along with God. The shop just fit neatly into the equation. All she needed now was a tidy red velvet bow so she could peel off the backing and stick it right on top of her gift-wrapped perfection.

Owning a beauty salon had been Troi's dream since she was a child. As far back as Nina could remember, her scrawny little fair-faced sister had said, "I'm gonna have my own shop. I'm gonna do every style there is and I'm gonna do it better than everybody."

"You've got to know what you're doing, or you'll be out of business in a heartbeat," Mother had chided.

Shangrila had materialized just as if Troi had spoken it prophetically into the wind.

Nina remembered how, growing up, Troi would style her doll's hair just like hers. She would go to school every morning with a newly created hairstyle that would be the envy of every girl in her homeroom. She'd have all the girls staring at her all day long and then running home anxiously trying to imitate her latest coiffure.

Troi would come home, plop down at the kitchen table, whiz through her homework, mix a noisy glass of chocolate milk, and then pull out her worn drawing tablet. She'd sketch up hairstyles that she envisioned a sleek model would wear on the fashionable Paris runways or at a brightly lit photo shoot on location in the Caribbean. Whimsical thinking. It came rather naturally for Troi.

Twisted locks fastened with colorful barrettes, loops, pins, woven braids that looked more like a hat than a hairstyle, and fanlike Patti Labelle things swaying more than the hips of the woman for whom she fantasized she had created the style. She was only fourteen years old then. She was curious and creative, an interesting combination. Mother had resented the fact that Troi chose hair styling as her profession. "She'll grow out of it," everyone had said.

"Doing hair? It's so limiting and common, child," Mother had said, never once taking into account what desires her children had stirring inside them or what dreams fueled them to breathe.

As a mother, she could have been more supportive, but then, their mother wasn't your run-of-the-mill June Cleaver type. There were no kisses, hugs, or congratulations. She didn't bake brownies, and they were never Girl Scouts, but she was their mother, like it or not, even if she was barely tolerable.

Mother lived to voice her opinion and could cut you down to the nubs with her words, gag you, and then cast you aside like a mule that was too useless to cart a load. Mother hadn't necessarily seen what Troi did for a living as talent, but Troi's career was definitely paying the bills now. The family felt safe.

Nina, on the other hand, wore self-imposed labels from her past. She thought from the inside looking out that she was boring, a little too chubby, and had a lisp that was slightly noticeable only to those looking for something to criticize.

Nina remembered the school functions where she was always the one standing in the corner, leaning on the wall, waiting to be asked to dance. She'd drink watered-down punch until her tongue and lips were bloodred. In junior high she was jokingly voted most likely to become a wallflower.

The kids had thought it was funny, but they didn't know how deep wounds buried themselves. Labels peel off, she often thought. But with her self-image, her mother's concept, and everyone else's thoughts about her buzzing around all the time, no wonder she was a walking mishap. She just wanted the peace and quiet to live a fulfilling life.

Nina had become a compulsively private person over the years and kept to herself more as she got older and wiser. She had maybe three friends, if you counted the one who barely called her. She shredded her mail, even the sweepstakes.

She refused to put return addresses on envelopes, made sure to blacken the address label on all of her magazines before she lent them out or gave them away, and denied her heart the overwhelming joys of love. She'd never love someone who would eventually end up leaving. That would be absolutely too much for her jaded heart to bear.

Nina was a rule queen. She had tons of them. She never argued in public. She locked the doors and windows and checked them again before she turned out the lights to retire for the night (although her therapist warned that that type of behavior bordered on compulsion). And although Nina lived alone, she still went to the bathroom with the door closed and the flap from the roll of toilet tissue facing out.

She was paranoid by the "what ifs." Always creating scenarios in her mind of a masked man with green teeth running through the house and surprising her on the toilet or in the kitchen. He'd probably tell her that the door was open so he just came in, but she'd know he was lying. She could spot a liar at least half a block away.

The fear of the unknown kept Nina a virtual prisoner the majority of the time. Friends who made futile attempts to try to get her to lighten up also offered that she needed to enjoy life, open up, and feel free. It was easy for them to say. They blossomed like ripe tulips in the spring breeze, with the sun beating down on them and releasing the fragrance of who they were, while Nina felt more like a weed that a passing dog lifted his leg to pee on.

Nina wasn't svelte and she was always self-conscious, especially since her mother found it necessary to remind her that she was fat every chance she got. In school, Nina had been teased about her butt being big, fat, and hanging over the chair. Some of her classmates had been way past fat, but they'd joined in with the name-calling to take the focus off of themselves.

The kids would say Nina sounded like King Kong coming down the hall. They'd embarrass her by holding onto their lockers as if there were an earthquake and they were trying to save each other's lives. She'd swallowed one too many doses of pride and sat on one too many tacks.

It had been because of those episodes in school that Nina had always acted out at home, releasing all of that repressed hurt and anxiety. This was no surprise. Home was the only place she felt she had any power. Her father let her have her way most of the time, and it was more fun than a roller-coaster ride. She relished the attention of being heard. She felt invincible for the most part, although she was growing more and more uncompromising, like her mother.

"It's expected of a child," people had said, but she didn't know how her father put up with such behavior from her mother.

Nina had a calculating personality. She was always up to something, if not with her hands, then in her mind. The preacher stood on the pulpit and said, "Woe unto them who let an idle mind rule them."

But even Nina herself was glad when she outgrew her mean streak.

"It's useless and self-defeating," a counselor at school had told her parents. "It may stem from feeling estranged from your mom," the counselor had added to Nina. "How is your relationship with your mom, Nina?"

That was the last appointment Nina remembered them ever having with that counselor.

"I don't need some high-heeled diploma-toting woman with a razor-sharp tongue interfering with how I raise my kids," Mother had spat.

Nina was a little girl then, she hadn't a clue, but she understood what her mother was now. Even then, with continued weekly counseling visits that eventually became monthly and a therapist they all almost agreed on, Nina had been allowed to realize that her anger wasn't so much a part of her personality as it was rage directed toward her mother.

"You need more interaction with your children, Mrs. Madison."

Mother hadn't liked this new therapist either, but Daddy had refused to go scouting for another one. It was always like a tug-of-war with Nina and her mother from birth. When Nina was a knee-high child of almost ten, people couldn't help but chatter, "Watching you is like looking at your mother, child."

Nina would stand hand on hip, as children should never do. She would plug her ears with her fingers, tired of people telling her the same thing over and over again.

"Stop telling me that, I can't take it," Nina would say.

I'm nothing like my mother, she thought. She wasn't useless. In hindsight, she realized that her mother had stolen enough from them. She was such a clumsy thief.

"Cut it out!" her father would yell when her mother would go on and on about Miss Nina being too fast with her mouth. "She got it honest." He'd frown.

He didn't take sides. He just ruffled the paper, folded it over to the sports section, and refused to get involved. He demanded peace in his house. Occasionally he got it.

"You can't say everything that comes to mind, Nina," he'd plead. "You have to respect your mother," he'd request, his arms extended like a pauper in utter despair.

Nina hated when her father scolded her. Nina would nod as if she understood, her head full of beads with aluminum foil at the tips, shaking her head wildly and rolling her eyes, making the beads jingle. Her bell-bottoms always made her feel dangerous. Girl power was nothing new. She was a child and was supposed to be rebellious. It was what was expected. It had never been her intention to disappoint.

Nina was a homebody. Even as a child, she enjoyed the time she spent at home more than school. Home was more than four walls closing you in and warding off evildoers, home was where her music was, all shiny and vinyl. She loved some of the songs from back then when she was growing up, too young to know all the words or apply them. The *Daily News* was a dime, and the songs, they were more like anthems for life.

She was just a baby, so "Love the One You're With" was hardly something she could live by. Nevertheless, she loved to ignore people and get under their skin and stay awhile, especially people who wanted to teach her lessons. She would hear her father go on and on about how she needed to try more with her mother. But her mind drifted consciously to more musical thoughts. Thoughts like how she could convince her daddy to start giving them an allowance again so she wouldn't have any problems getting those new 45s she wanted so badly played in her mind.

"I won't tell Mother, I promise," Nina had convinced him.

She didn't purposely manipulate people; she was a kid herself. But those who she couldn't manipulate, she'd ignore. Antisocial was an understatement. She hated everyone in her school, every single teacher and even most of the nosy fashion-tragic people in her church. On the rare occasions that her father took her mother's side, it made Nina want to hold her breath and count to three hundred.

Her mother would feel as if she won any little debate she and Nina were having once her father put his two cents in. Her mother would smirk like a spoiled-rotten child, pushing her chest out and chin up, being sure to keep her upper lip stiff, as if to say, *I told you so.* Nina would mumble something under her breath that only her mother could hear, pretending she was singing it. It was always a game to her.

"See, she's starting now, Charles. When I finish with her, she'll be sorry, hear?"

"Sadie, you can't be so sensitive. She's a child. Quit acting foolish."

Her mother would huff off to a secluded part of their yard-sale chic house when she didn't get her way. Nina manipulated her daddy because she was his favorite, although she denied it every time Troi insinuated that. Her mother would sit at the tiny lopsided kitchen table and lose herself in a choice of a gray haze, a game of solitaire, or three shots of vodka.

Mother would sit with a lit cigarette dancing on her bottom lip, licking the rim of a shot glass. The careless cigarettes burned holes in the peeling contact paper that was supposed to cover up the fact that they were long overdue for a new kitchen set. This had gone on as long as Nina could remember. Bickering and family outings that never were as perfect as they appeared to those on the outside looking in.

"What pretty little girls you have, Sadie," friends, neighbors, and church members said.

It sounded lyrical when they made that statement. It made you think that Nina and Troi should be on top of music boxes. Ballerinas. Twirling.

"They're absolutely adorable."

Her mother would give them dry dirty looks, only half-masking the statement, *you want 'em you can have 'em*, as she nudged them forward.

Nina often wondered if Mother would really let them pack up and go, and possibly salvage some of the life they had left. Snide remarks like that cut right through little children and made them feel like they had grubby hands. Never feeling wanted, needed, or good enough to sit on what Mother considered the good furniture was all either of the Madison girls remembered.

Nina couldn't even imagine hugging or feeling her mother's warmth. Nina had held a snake once, down South when they had spent the summer with the only living relative that remained on the Madison side. She wondered if Mother felt like that.

Nina remembered vividly when she'd made her mother an ashtray in the third grade. She'd painted it royal blue and green because the plaid sofa had green stripes in it. She had pressed down on the clay when it was soft, making sure that it had more than enough spaces for mother to rest her cigarettes. Nina had missed recess that day because she'd wanted so badly to finish her gift for her mother. She'd felt revived, almost yearning.

She'd been attempting to be more useful. In her mind, she'd seen her mother's joy when she unwrapped the gift. Her mother would give her kisses for the first time ever and hug her so tightly that Nina wouldn't be able to breathe. She'd imagined that her mother would say that she was sorry for everything and wanted them to be like normal families. Nina would ignore the stench of alcohol that seeped through her mother's pores, leapt off her breath, and lingered in her clothing, and they would be on their way to something good. Finally.

When Nina had actually brought the ashtray home, proud and willing to try being nice as Daddy had asked so many times, Mother had laughed hysterically.

"What is that?" She'd pointed at the ashtray as if it were a creature.

Nina had swallowed hard. The lump in her throat wouldn't move past her chest. She'd fought the pain and dared not let it lead to tears. Mother had rejected the truce.

"Please get that contraption off my living-room table, Nina! You don't think I'm gonna display that, do you?" Mother had been falling over with laughter, and had waved Nina away when she'd tried to assist her to her feet.

People on the outside looking in didn't know how much of a joke it was being one of Sadie's kids.

4

Sharon bought Tim delicate silk shirts in brilliant tropical hues. Fuchsia (which he probably would never wear), lime green, aqua, and a pale yellow. Michelle had been paying Tim's overpriced tuition for his continuing education classes faithfully for the past year and a half. It was too expensive, and he knew she only did it to show him that she didn't care how much it cost. It was the name that he was paying for more than anything. It was the best. She wanted him to have the finest, so she provided the means even if it cost her everything short of breath.

He had met them both right after he'd found out that he had been accepted to college. Now he was enrolled in New York University's film school. It had been two days shy of a month since he had spoken to either one of them. He tried not to allow women to distract him. He needed to focus on his screen plays and completing his film assignments in a timely fashion without being interrupted by someone craving attention—unless it was him who was craving, he smiled slyly to himself, licking down the corner of his mustache.

Getting his films to stand out and catch the eye of major studio executives was the priority on his list. He was weaving a plot so tight that it would snatch them within the first ten pages, and slap them in the face with the last. But it seemed that the two things he was most passionate about often clashed. Filmmaking and women, in that order. Filmmaking always came first, but women hardly ran a distant second.

Women always admired Tim's towering height and muscular frame.

"He can change a lightbulb without standing on a chair," he once overheard a sister say.

He was six feet even. His smoldering complexion and dark eyes left women claiming that he was exotic looking.

"Where you from?" they'd ask.

His eyes drew them in, they said. So, it was only inevitable when they fell for him.

"You know what you do," an ex-girlfriend once told him. "You set women up for the kill."

He smirked. It was almost true.

Women adored Tim's sleek sideburns and mustache that always had a slight sheen, and he had to curb their constant urges to touch his face. He had sensitive skin, and women were always putting their hands in his face. They wanted to prove that he was theirs. He didn't like that.

"Love is a game," Tim said, "and I don't want to play it."

He was talking to his reflection again, brushing his goatee and checking between his teeth, doing that little thing with his tongue.

He wasn't vain. He just didn't have time for love, a relationship, or someone who would be there in his apartment trying to get him to eat what they thought he should eat, playing wifey, planning his weekends, and making smug attempts to redecorate his urban suite.

They called him a pretty boy, but he was pretty tired of the game is what he was. He wasn't God's gift to women. He wouldn't allow himself to believe that. He was charming, intelligent, and most women just believed they needed someone, namely him. He'd been told more than enough that he was pleasing to the eye, captivating even, and granted, he loved women, but his head wasn't up to the emotional game of tag that usually ensued shortly after becoming involved with them.

He believed that men limited themselves by dating exclusively.

"If you aren't married, then you're single," he was famous for saying.

Most women walked around with a leash dangling from their clutches, and as soon as they found someone whom they'd remotely consider, they'd chain him up and walk him home. Tim said it and it was true; he had seen it happen.

As a single unattached man with a vivid imagination, he found that he could swing with a theory that was founded on moral truth. Women wanted to possess men. They were beautiful and came in various shades and ethnicities, but he wasn't buying.

He imagined that eventually he would settle down once he was established and possibly do the family thing, but he reneged on the thought of it for now. It was a far-fetched notion that for now was only feasible in the way too distant horizon. He was concerned that his love of filmmaking would be hindered by any type of relationship that he'd try to cultivate, and something had to give.

Women didn't want some of your time, they wanted all of it. They didn't take no for an answer, and they interpreted *I'll call you* to mean, *tomorrow morning I'll be there for breakfast, eggs over-easy.* He didn't play that money game with women either. He didn't have any. He was living grant to grant, and if he did come into any cash, he wasn't about to blow it on hair, nails, or Nine West. Women had to learn to support their own habits. The minute you started giving women money to shop, they relied on it, and worked it into their monthly budgets. He was sweet, but he wasn't about to be anybody's sugar daddy.

Tim didn't have a harem of women, but he wasn't a loner either. He thrived on the constant feedback from women he labeled "friends." They hated that term. If you called a woman a friend they'd get indignant.

"What do you mean *friend?*" they spat with snakelike attitude.

They wanted another label. *My boo, my baby, my woman,* or *my girl.* Even *my stuff* was better to their ears than *friend.*

The constant drama that the women in his life provided stirred his ideas. He loved the female perspective, and he knew exactly how to portray them: merciless. And that wasn't necessarily a bad thing. But he had surely enjoyed the time he had been alone for the past few weeks. He could focus, and that was a marvelous thing. His thoughts were clearer and his dialogue flowed from the tip of his tongue right onto the paper. He was pleased with his progress.

Michelle was out of town on a promotional tour with a group she was managing. She believed that they were destined for the big time, like so many other four-guy groups that were but a flicker. They crooned and woo-wooed, and she shopped for them and spent hours rehearsing the poses that were most photogenic. She had a life besides Tim, and that was cool. He dug that. He was too busy prioritizing anyway.

He had spent the past few weeks dodging Sharon's answering-machine messages, sorting out storylines, and doing background research for the characters in his script. He loved the fact that like, women, a filmmaker could give birth to something extraordinary. A creation that had been fed by their ability to conceive an idea, carry it to term, and bring forth life. His dream had always been to make films. He was barely surviving on the small stipends that he had been given to complete at least one of his amateur films. The money they gave wasn't enough to produce an episode of *Mr. Bill*, but he made it rubber—it stretched.

Sharon kept calling and calling, sunup to dusk. She wanted to come over and lounge in the newness of his personal space, and she always used gifts she had bought Tim as bait. It was no secret that he liked nice things. All you had to do was look at his shoes, his apartment, and his fingernails.

But he didn't want any woman taking care of him. He refused to be a kept man. Women's money and gifts came with strings attached that rendered you a puppet. He wasn't about to be strung along.

Women were creatures bent on instant gratification, always wanting their desires fulfilled immediately. Michelle was a prime example.

She was always too occupied for him, but when she wanted Tim in the middle of the night, she expected everything on earth to stop and succumb to her. And it did . . . he did. But it wasn't a forever thing. He figured he'd leave it at that. It wasn't a constant struggle in his mind to think of something other than Michelle.

He preferred her to Sharon, that was true. She wasn't needy. Her voice sent him to near hyperventilation, though he tried to be nonchalant about it. His sweaty palms always gave it away. Most of the time she pretended not to notice. She was the only woman who did that for him. But if he had to leave her alone, he could. He wondered if she knew she had an edge, however slight.

Tim didn't have time to date exclusively, or go out much, but women all but insisted. Men had to keep in mind that anywhere you appeared with a woman in public was construed as a date. They wanted him to drop them off, pick them up, help them move, drive them to the mall in Jersey, help them do research, put up shelves and bookcases, or program their VCRs.

And when he resisted and all else failed, they offered their cleavage while leaning over reaching for something imaginary. He was raised to be the perfect gentleman; women loved it and hated it at the same time. They were attracted to the gentle courteous nature of a man who had enough willpower to compliment without overwhelming, but not the gentleman who refused to take advantage of a situation.

Women had their tricks. They wanted to buy Tim things and feed him like he was new to the neighborhood. Their motives were fueled by the old adage that the way to a man's heart was to feed him to death. Women showed up with crumb cake, oxtails, paella, peach cobbler, pastelles, curried shrimp, and a host of other dishes that decreased the amount of time he would actually have to spend in the kitchen.

Michelle's specialty was braised lamb chops with wild rice, but with her constantly traveling, he hadn't savored the taste of that in awhile. He did miss her cooking, though it was her presence he missed more. He'd never tell her that. Then she'd really have the upper hand and manipulate him into submission or beyond.

Sharon, however, was a take-out kind of girl. She knew all the best places in the city where you could get mouthwatering takeout that left you licking your fingers and digging your teeth under your fingernails. Dallas BBQ, Cabana, Jerk Chicken House, Sabrosura, Wedge Inn, and Gonzalez y Gonzalez. It didn't matter how far out of the way the restaurant was, as long as she didn't have to mess up her silk-wrapped fingernails to cook.

Many women came in and out of Tim's life, each equipped with their own talents, and although he had never met a woman who had come to his door wearing only a fur coat and a pair of black patent leather stilettos, he knew that it wasn't long before someone acted out the tired scenario.

Tim was doing a good job. He was balancing. He had to fight to make time for himself. Working at school, needing a better place to live, trying to work at odd jobs to fund his ideas, and going to the gym kept him strapped for personal time. He didn't work out obsessively, but his body was prime. He was twenty-eight and still young. He lifted weights when he was kicking around with friends at the local health club, but he knew that he needed to do it more often. Especially now that he was getting older.

Besides, it was a mental release. Exercise stimulated the mind and started the creative juices flowing. He needed some creative juices. Things had been going well, but a dry spell was inevitable. He knew this was like the pseudo-cool after the torrential rain—the sun would come out and dry up every flowing drop of juice. He hated when everything he wrote began to sound like something he had written before. He hated being redundant as much as he hated having to repeat himself, which was the same thing, but not technically. Tim made a mental note to call up his boy Justin to see if he wanted to do this workout thing on a regular basis. Two heads were better than one, he imagined. If Tim made a commitment, he knew that Justin would hold him to it. Always did, always did.

Tim ate voraciously, and though he wasn't a vegetarian, he did limit his meat intake and ate lots of roughage. It wasn't his fault. Women showed up at his door with food. Tupperware, aluminum pans, and pots from their own kitchens just so they'd have a reason to come back. He knew the deal. But he was entertained by eating. It was his favorite thing to do besides creating memorable scenes and overindulging in women.

He favored pasta, and was especially fond of garlic. He ate it raw. It was good for a lot of things, healthwise. He laughed to himself, thinking that it also kept the vampires away. His mother had taught him early on to nourish the inside with food and knowledge. Read. He didn't read nearly enough. He had been focusing on school for the past year and change, and was desperately trying to develop his own niche. He'd get there eventually. He saw himself a household name in less than five years, surpassing Mr. Clean and the Ty-D-Bol Man.

When the phone rang, Tim closed his eyes and scrunched up his nose. Flashbacks of him faking excitement played in his mind. He knew it was none other than Sharon attempting to leave her sixth message. He wondered what she found so fascinating about him, and he smiled, figuring that she hadn't had a man treat her like much of anything. He did feel privileged to give her a standard by which to measure other men.

She was pretty, just a little abrasive for his personal taste. It was unfortunate that some men treated women like a gooey wad of gum that they couldn't get off the bottom of their shoe. But it made it that much easier for the brothers who had a little finesse to get a fair shake or the time of day.

Women loved attention. When they had a man, they felt like they were on stage. Sharon was lonely and desperate; it was obvious by the way she couldn't let a day go by without calling. Their affair had been in its final weeks for months now, but she didn't have a clue. She wasn't budging. She had left five consecutive messages and was attempting to leave her sixth. Tim listened to half of his outgoing message before snatching the phone off the hook and telling Sharon he was busy.

"Oh, so you don't want me to come over?"

"I'm not saying that," Tim said.

"I picked up a few nice things for you and I just want to drop them by, that's all."

He could hear her prerehearsed sexiness emanating through the telephone. He wished she was that feminine all the time and not just when she was trying to get her way.

"You can come by, Sharon, I'm just working on something for school. It has to be completed by tomorrow though."

"So, Tim? Can I stay the night?"

"I don't know, baby. Do you think that would be a good idea? You know I wouldn't get anything done with you looking good sprawled all over my sofa. You know how you do," he teased.

He didn't understand his incessant need to lie to her.

"Uh-huh, I see."

"Seriously . . ."

"You sure you don't have someone else coming over, Tim? Because you know I can find out."

"Baby, when do I have time for that?"

"Uh-huh."

"You know how serious I take my work."

"Yes, I know."

"Tell me where I would fit another woman in my life?"

"I know, I know." She laughed. "I was just testing you, that's all."

"Still playing games, huh, Sharon?"

"No games, honey, you know me. But I'll be over with some Chinese. Shrimp chow mein?"

"Sesame chicken for me, with plain fried rice. Thanks. And no MSG, okay?"

"I'll be there in less than a half."

Tim placed the receiver on the hook, looked around the room, and began to prepare himself mentally for another evening of playing grin-and-bear-it with Sharon, who would taunt and tease him into performing how much he really cared. Tim never had a problem getting women, but it had become a bit unnerving at times trying to get rid of them.

His only major rule was that no one spent the night. He had broken that rule twice with Michelle. He didn't label women trash or objects that needed to be discarded, but they just needed too much. They wanted your time, your money, and sex in compromising ways that was supposed to convince them that you were theirs or vice versa. He didn't have a dime or a flashy car, but surprisingly enough that hardly mattered to most women.

Tim had the look, and he had been getting by on that for years now. Women had been a mental challenge for Tim since he was thirteen. They had a knack for weaving themselves into every aspect of your life. They would do your homework, buy you lunch, sneakers, and pay your homeboy's way to the movies if you told them you left your wallet home. They'd tell their grandmother that you were coming to the family reunion before you even knew a thing about them or their grandmother.

They wanted you to meet their gigantic older brother who drank a gallon and a half of milk everyday and was a quarterback at the local college, as if it was some sort of collateral measure that would assure them that you wouldn't break their heart. The Nina, the Pinta, and the Santa Maria, they just wanted to rush off of the ship like Christopher Columbus and stake their flag deeply into you marking you as conquered territory. Claiming something they hadn't discovered. It was like a game of tag, and Tim was the one being chased.

Tim agreed that his life was promising but wasn't without its fair share of tragedy. Some women literally brought the devil out of you. He wanted to be kind and generous, even a gentleman. But they wanted you to take everything they were and ravage through it. They threw it at you and made you take it and then lay helplessly declaring, "Look at what you've done to me." They wrote songs about it, told their friends about it, and even wrote books about it. You'd think they'd learn something by now. Sisters didn't need rules, they needed boundaries and scruples.

And from a brother's point of view, Tim would offer that "it takes more than a plate of collard greens and some ham hocks to get a man." Each woman he encountered spent her life pretending to be a glass that she demanded was full and then tried convincing you that you drank from it, when she knew she was half empty coming into the relationship.

Estella was a prime example. She was psychotic and possessive. She got a kick out of showing up unannounced and rifling through Tim's medicine cabinet and dresser drawers, counting condoms and searching for a reason to cry and become hysterical. She was famous for working herself into a frenzy.

When Tim had decided to move from 135th Street and sublet his brother-in-law's apartment on 62nd Street, he'd told Estella that he was relocating to North Carolina to stay with his ailing grandmother. His grandmother needed him. She had raised him in the absence of a mother, and he needed to be there for her. She was all alone and had no one to lean on in her final years. He could help her with odds and ends around the house, shop for groceries and help her keep track of her bills so she didn't end up in the dark burning candles for light. It had hurt him to make up stories about his grandmother. Women made men lie.

Tim was tired of the never-ending auditions he constantly encountered with women. Estella hadn't been pleased in the least when Tim had said he was leaving. She had mustered up all the theatrical drama she could and insisted that the real reason he was leaving was because she was too skinny, her breasts weren't big enough, and she was too short. True, he fancied a thicker woman, but she'd insisted, "I can get implants, baby, tell me what you like."

Tim didn't have time to nurture a woman with low self-esteem. He wanted a woman who had goals and didn't wait for a pat on the head. A woman doing tricks to keep a man brought him no gratification; it only gave him the urge to toss her to the lions and out of his life. He wanted a woman who could stand on her own without toppling over and getting distracted the moment he said something that she couldn't look up in one of her self-help books. Estella had a one-track mind. She wanted Tim, but he wasn't about to become her life preserver, or anybody else's for that matter.

From the moment Tim had said he was leaving New York, Estella had begun harassing him daily. He'd been working at a local video store labeling videos and eking out a living that he was sure would bring him closer to his goal.

Estella would show up and wander around the store for hours, rearranging the videotapes and trying to persuade Tim that she was the woman he had waited for his whole life. The thing he remembered most was her mannerisms changing. She developed a nervous condition where she kept rubbing the left side of her face with the palm of her hand as if she had an addiction.

She'd been drawing attention to herself, and their nonexistent relationship, but she hadn't cared. Integrity had forced him to quit his job there. One, because his manager hadn't been too pleased that Estella created a daily scene and constantly distracted the customers whenever she came by; and two, because as long as he was working there, she'd always know where to find him.

Tim had wanted to make a clean break. And although ruthless wasn't a word that characterized his nature, he and his boy Justin had packed up his room full of things—mostly clothes and records—and put them in the U-Haul while Estella stood curbside making a fool of herself, pleading, "Baby, you don't have to do this. We can work it out. I need you, Tim."

"I'm not one for scenes," he'd said, as he pulled her arms from around his neck and threw them down at her sides.

She'd been persistent, clutching for any shred of hope. He'd rolled the window down, pried her fingers from around the driver's-side door handle, driven off, and left her weeping loudly on the corner of 135th Street and 8th Avenue.

He had decided shortly after settling into his new apartment to apply for the film school. He was three days away from missing the deadline. He'd been accepted a month and a half later and enrolled in a summer 101 course. Finally it seemed that his future had direction. He never saw Estella again.

5

Mornings always found Troi deep in wonder, helplessly daydreaming. She had a thriving business that she adored, a husband who was in for the long haul, a healthy baby girl, and God as the head of her life. She felt in sync with the hum of the refrigerator, the second hand on the ticking clock, and mentally punished herself for even conjuring the thought that something was missing.

God was supposed to fill the void, but honestly, sometimes she felt incomplete and unsure. It was those nooks and crannies that had her bothered. She thought that things were perfect, but often felt as if there was more that she couldn't see. A door marked number two behind which would be a fabulous prize to tempt her to trade in what she already had. The myth of the greener grass wasn't going to catch her out there.

Troi shuffled around the bedroom in her fleece robe, trying to snuggle her toes deeper into her slippers and get a few minutes to herself before Dakoda woke up crying for cereal. She definitely needed to do the heap of smelly laundry today, but she knew she wouldn't have time.

Saturdays were the busiest days at the shop. *Hair* and *Saturdays* were synonymous. And Vaughn was still asleep. Besides, he was busy. He was always busy. So the pungent two-week-old pile of laundry that was almost up to the doorknob wouldn't get done. Not this weekend. She didn't know what time he had managed to come waltzing in last night. He was always light on his feet. They had been married for three blissful years, one thousand one hundred and twenty-five days, and she didn't find it too hard to compromise or learn to share her world with Vaughn.

He was attentive and giving. She just wished that he'd dedicate more time to the things that needed to be done around the house and take the initiative with doing the mounds of laundry or sink full of dishes and not just sit back and wait for her to do it all. She had spent her whole teenage life playing house and cleaning up after grown folks. She was dog tired.

Troi took a deep breath and let out a long exaggerated sigh. She made a conscious effort to be open and receptive to Vaughn's needs. He was a man. "Yes, he is," she said aloud.

Personal space and time to himself were part of that, and she understood. He needed to be around his friends, not cooped up in an apartment every day just so she could keep an eye on him, making sure no one else was sinking her teeth into his heart. Male bonding, he needed that. It was some tribal thing, her father said. She didn't see why he had to go out with friends during the week and every other weekend, and she wasn't too enthused about it, but she let it go.

The last things she wanted to be were possessive and jealous. Women everywhere had been batting their eyes at Vaughn, but Troi wasn't really the jealous type. She had the ring, a firm tug on his heart, and he paid the bills. Furthermore, they respected each other. It was a rewarding relationship. Vaughn was giving, and she was grateful.

He loved his little girl. She was his princess, Koda. He took her to the circus, balancing her all the way there and back sitting atop his shoulders as she spent the entire adventure smacking him around and playing patty-cake with his head. *He's an ample husband, too,* she thought aloud, covering her sly grin with both hands.

He wore his wedding band prominently on his third finger, and didn't offer excuses about the ring being too tight just to get out of wearing it, like some men did. All it took was an absent wedding ring to set the process in motion for a man to forget he was married. But they were open, honest, and fair with each other. She told him when she wasn't pleased, what she was thinking, and tried to always put herself in his shoes when they had a disagreement. Being fair was important.

Troi vowed going into this marriage that she wouldn't be the proverbial ball and chain that weighed a man down and made him feel in his heart that he had made a mistake marrying her, so she wasn't. She also said that she wouldn't nag him. That was a hard one. She had to literally bite her tongue more often than not. Her tongue was her best defense. She had inherited it. It was a Madison trait. She was working on it.

She began her morning routine by making coffee, putting on a worship tape, and sitting cross-legged at the breakfast nook in the kitchen to read the Word. She liked grinding her coffee beans fresh; they tasted better than those freeze-dried tasteless crystals. The flavor of the Brazilian blend would dance on her tongue and make her feel like she was really drinking something special, instead of a mouth full of decaffeinated wash water.

Troi flipped the pages over to Proverbs, as the coffee made itself and soothing music confirmed what she already knew—she was blessed. Spiritually, some never got it, some managed to fumble and lose it, others never thought they would have it so they didn't. But she had it, and although a frayed thread got loose every now and then, she and Vaughn both managed to tighten it up quite nicely.

Troi thought back to a childhood where she was raised with so much negativity and criticism, and wondered how it didn't affect her more obviously. Why wasn't she insecure, fearful, or one of those angry black women that men always wrote in to relationship magazines about? Her father only swept everything under the rug or glossed it over, never getting to the root of what the problems were in the house.

She vowed that she would never be like him. She would deal with issues head-on; but she knew she had seeds from her childhood planted in her. She refused to water those seeds and all the negative things she grew up with. That was the key. The hard part was destroying the roots.

Troi also mentally relived the fact that her mother was unbearable, and she knew for a fact that it was only her dream of one day owning her own beauty salon that had sustained her in that depressing house of torment. She never let the things her mother said affect her, never. Her sister Nina always did. Nina let words plant themselves in her, creep into her blood, and mar her personality.

Mother would water every seed, causing anger and strife to flourish and bloom. Troi thought that Nina's level of tolerance was the only way she was glad she wasn't like her sister. One day she knew for sure that she'd conquer that Madison tongue. She just refused to take on any of her mother's other traits.

Mother was an alcoholic, to put it nicely, or alcoholically challenged, to make it politically correct. Troi had to face that fact finally. She had to look it in the bloodshot eyes, see it, smell it, confess it from her own mouth, and swallow it. They all had to. Enough of the charades and pretending that her mother just needed an occasional drink to calm her nerves or help her relax.

Her mother was 151 proof 98 percent of the time. The other two percent of the time, Mother was in transit to get a drink. And the fact that she had managed to keep her job for as long as she had was a miracle in itself, like the parting of the sea. Mother said that she was planning on taking early retirement, but Troi had overheard Daddy talking one evening late after she and Nina both should have been deep in REM sleep.

Mother had confessed that it wasn't so much wanting to retire from her job as a nurse as it was the higher-ups giving her the choice of taking early retirement or facing the consequences of her slipups. Slipups that included falling asleep at the nurses' station, nondocumentation of progress notes, mixing up patients' medication, and mishandling equipment. The job should have been held accountable long ago for allowing Mother to work in that condition. Spare the patients the trauma. But no matter where you worked, there were always those who found a way to get around the administrators, directors, and their own job descriptions. There were those who could make a single task last a month and a half, and then there were those who didn't even bother pretending. They just preyed on the kindness of others to cover up for them long enough to sign the back of their paycheck, cash it, party all weekend, and then come in to borrow twenty bucks first thing Monday morning from one of their more responsible coworkers. Her mother's job and life with Daddy were just the fuzzy little culprits that enabled her mother to stay intoxicated. Whenever her father was around, all Troi remembered him being was either too tired, too bothered, or too zoned out to care. Pretending was his modus operandi, and the whole family suffered much longer than any normal person should have had to.

But, in spite of that, Nina adored their father, flaws and all. It had been a mystery as to why for years. Troi, no matter how disillusioned, did thank her mediocre parents for giving her roots in the church. Hallelujah! It was the only remnant of sanity that they had managed to offer her dismal and pathetic existence as a Madison. Troi had always gravitated toward truth, so she gladly held on to the promises of God. It was all she had. She grasped His truths tightly and clutched them with bloody hands as if they were a rope hovering over a ravenous crocodile's pit, because she knew her deliverance was coming. She could see His hand in the midst of their situations.

When it came to faith in God, whether it was borderline malnutrition, twice handed-down clothes in September for the first day of school, or no oil to heat their ice-cold feet in January, Troi believed. Mother didn't get it, her father was too far removed to get it, and Nina acted like she got it sometimes but she didn't really. Troi felt that God had been more reliable than her own parents. Truly he was Lord, for only the Creator of life could sustain it.

Troi never thought that anything was worth doing halfway. If you were gonna go to church in the snow and rain, smack around a tambourine and scuff up your new shoes, you might as well receive what was being said and apply it. Make it manifest in your life. Don't just sit there and wait for a tragedy and then call on Him with a snotty nose and tears. That's how too many people she knew were. Seasonal. But then, going to church didn't make you a Christian any more than going to McDonald's made you a hamburger.

Troi remembered vaguely how distraught she had been when Nina had prepared for and finally gone away to college. When Nina had left, she'd been what Troi longed to be, free. Like a field slave in the underground looking back only to motivate his feet to move faster. Nina had packed up every memory that had been acquired since childhood that day. She'd taken with her the reminders of warm milk with too many marshmallows, shiny red apples only around Christmas time, and details about how Troi said the cute boys kissed with their mouths open.

Nina had tried to comfort Troi with a hug that day, but it had been rushed and awkward because of the anticipation of the moment. It was Troi who'd begged her on both ashy knees to stay. Troi had given Nina ten unsurpassable reasons off the top of her head why she should stay. She was her sister, she was the oldest, she cooked better than Mother did, she'd allow her to play her favorite song all day without complaining, she needed her, her daddy needed her, everything she learned she learned from her, she loved her, she missed her, she appreciated her, and dozens of other reasons. Troi had really needed God then. Before the door had closed behind Nina on her way out into a world that welcomed her with open arms, Troi was already missing her sister, who was more like a mother to her than anything.

Sure, Troi had spent a few sacrificial weekends with Nina on campus in her septic and sparsely decorated room, but she hadn't wanted to interfere with her studies, especially when Nina had an exam and was adjusting to being on her own and finally, for once in her life, making a few friends. Selfish was something Troi never was. Being alone. It was all so new to her. Novel yet painful at the same time. For both of them.

So, Troi had prayed, cried, and travailed until she felt a release that allowed her to know that it wouldn't be long before it was her turn to leave. Her turn to escape the hell that so many thought was limited to the afterlife. She wouldn't be in that house forever. The stench of melancholy wouldn't last always. She'd needed to believe that with her whole heart. She'd just needed a little more faith to believe that far. Enough faith to believe past the front door.

Troi had been especially devastated with her home life since, in Nina's absence, she had now become the focus of everything that her mother was angry about. Every dirty dish, every overdue bill, every empty bottle, and every argument her mother and father had. She'd been alone in that asylum of family madness that seemed to leave her no room for a crisp clear thought. She was, however, never one to let a situation overtake her. So she'd had no choice but to recognize when God's hands had definitely stroked a few situations that found themselves brewing in the Madison home, like the college fiasco.

A few years after Nina's departure, Mother had told Troi that it was never too early to start looking at colleges. Troi never wanted to go to college; she just wanted her shop. She thought that if she did go to college like Mother wanted, she would only be wasting money and precious time, both of which the Madisons had only in short supply.

"Who goes to school to open a beauty salon?" Troi had asked.

"Ladies, please," is all Daddy would say when the bickering started.

He was more interested in anything that was going on outside of the house than anyone who actually lived there. It hadn't mattered that she'd been the only child left at home. Troi was convinced that Daddy had other shapely interests. It hadn't mattered much, because once she was eighteen and got a loan, she'd be gone, too. History.

It was a strange, unnatural feeling to be ignored. At one time her father had participated in their well-being and carefully cultivated their minds to utilize the thought process. But the more Mother drank and their marital relationship deteriorated, the more Daddy cast the whole family aside like damp shoes that made your feet itch.

He skimped on time and created situations that would keep him away from home for hours on end.

He and Mother both had already become like the seasonal saints who only came to church on Easter and New Year's Eve decorated from head to toe in overpriced, low-quality clothes. Troi didn't understand how Mother thought that those women in the church couldn't smell her coming around the corner. The alcohol oozed through her pores and discolored her lips, stripping them of pigment and muscle control. Her daddy, on the other hand, was too passive for his own good. Mother's loud mouth demanded a balance. Her daddy often said that he didn't know what all the fuss was about.

"I'm a hardworking man," he'd say, sounding more ridiculous than he looked. As parents, her mother and father were one major disappointment after another, after another, after another.

For instance, Troi, being a stickler for details, remembered the time when Nina almost died of heartbreak. She had graduated from junior high and prepared her walk, bow, smile, and speech three weeks in advance. She had saved her record money to buy stockings that were a shade lighter than coffee. She'd been pretty in her fluffy dress, polished shoes, and Easter gloves. The parents, friends, and family members in the audience that day had eagerly applauded every child as each made his way across to the podium.

When Nina had walked across the stage and looked out into the auditorium, all she'd heard with her heart's ear was her sister clapping, proud and alone. It had been as if Troi's presence wasn't enough. Nina had felt shortchanged. Daddy had been unable to make it to the graduation. "Overtime," he'd said. Mother hadn't made it either, but that hadn't mattered as much to Nina as Daddy's presence. Nina had bawled the whole way home, tossing her things to the ground as Troi watched helplessly. First she'd tossed her gloves, then her diploma. Her nose had been running, her ears hot, and her head . . . Troi was sure it had been throbbing, too.

When Nina had gotten home to her room, Troi remembered how she'd begun screaming and throwing things around like a crazy girl. She'd thrown books, dinner, her collection of 45s, and her favorite Archie jelly glasses. They'd crashed on and around the wall, leaving nicks and scratches that were telltale signs of the misguided childhood they'd both had. Mother had stumbled up the stairs to investigate the commotion, and she and Nina had literally gone at it in a verbal tango. Nina'd gone on boisterously about how other parents knew how to love their kids and how they respected them enough to show up to their graduation. Nina had made a fist, pounded the table, and demanded respect but Mother had said she'd have to get a job and pay some bills first.

When Daddy had come home, he'd just stood motionless and devoid of feeling. He'd stared at the food on the wall, shards of glass on the floor, and directed Troi to clean it all up. He'd been disappointing them all ever since. He'd tried to make it up to Nina for weeks after that with a record here, a package of silver hair beads there, but by then it was as if her heart had become icy and cold enough to disown him.

Nina hadn't eaten for almost a week, and she'd stayed in her room listening to music all day, staring at the ceiling as if it were the sun and refusing to go to school or even take a shower. She was never the same really, especially about trusting people. It seemed from that point on Nina just hung on to her perfect idea of Daddy in her mind, because she knew he'd never actually live up to it. Deep down, Troi hoped that Nina knew he was no longer that man she idolized; she had to know. Troi prayed she did.

Growing up, Troi was a different child altogether. She wasn't disrespectful, although any child might have been, given the circumstances. She wasn't promiscuous either, but she sure was elated when she met Vaughn. He was like a chocolate sundae with extra caramel syrup dripping down the sides, bidding her tongue to catch every drop. Vaughn was delicious-looking and had courted Troi for all of six months and then proposed. Everyone thought it was sudden, but for Troi it had taken way too long.

"Child, you don't even know this man," Mother had said. "What does he do for a living? How much money does he make?" Mother had gone on and on.

"Mother, I love him," Troi had said, "so just be happy for me for a change, okay?"

All the women in the church had turned their noses up at Troi, as if she thought she was better than everybody because she'd unwittingly caught the most sought-after fish in the sea. She couldn't help it if her lure caught big fish and theirs just sat there dragging the bottom of the ocean, snagging uneaten pieces of chum.

"Don't hate me because I'm Mrs. Singleton," she'd said out loud.

The Hallelujah Girls hadn't thought that was funny, but she'd sure gotten a kick out of the way they'd expected her to follow Vaughn's every move. She wasn't that kind of woman, and wasn't about to become that kind now. The less attention she paid to what

Vaughn was doing and who he was doing it with, the more he became hers.

They all needed to know that true men of God wanted a woman who had a genuine love for God. Every woman in the church wanted to become a preacher's wife, so they performed and acted out their faith in God openly like women in a beauty pageant trying to win a crown that, for all they knew, was made out of papier-mâché. Some of them hallelujahed their way down the aisle to the altar only to shuffle their way into divorce court a year and a half later.

Vaughn had been watching Troi from the third pew for months. Troi had been a member of Zion Missionary for several years then. She felt led there. She was a down-to-earth sister, and didn't feel the need to wear big fancy hats or have a loud mouth to amen everything the preacher said just to be noticed. Vaughn told her that he really did cherish that about her. "Girl, I know that's right," and other religious lingo were not phrases Troi uttered to prove how religious she was. They called her stuck-up and pious, but the truth was that they didn't know what to make of her, so they talked about her instead, she thought, sitting at the breakfast nook sipping her coffee.

There were times in their courtship when Vaughn had been rumored to be messing around. Several people had told her that he had a baby on the way by another woman that lived across town and that the woman attended his mother's church. It was humorous how all of a sudden they'd found it necessary to look out for her best interest. By the time the rumor had circulated around the entire church twice and made its way back to her, Troi had been negotiating a lease for the space that was soon to be christened Shangrila. She'd been determined that she wasn't going to get pregnant to keep him, and she wasn't about to give in to sex just to woo him into marrying her. If he wanted her, he would have to wait or hit the road just like all the rest who had tried before him.

She hadn't believed the rumors being whispered about him, and wasn't about to try retaliative tactics either. They'd wanted to see her squirm, so she didn't. The Hallelujah Girls wanted her man, the man God had promised her, and if they couldn't have him, they didn't want her to have him either. But Troi and Vaughn had a connection, and he was a provider, she'd known that much about him. Endless nights they had spent together in his little beat-up ride talking . . . those discussions had revealed to her that in a million years he wouldn't let his seed lack. So the lie about him having a baby that he was keeping a secret had to go back from where it came: the pit of hell.

"Mah-meee, ceweeal," Dakoda mumbled sleepily, stumbling into the kitchen with her favorite Winnie the Pooh blanket dragging and tripping her up.

"You want cereal, baby?"

Dakoda nodded and raised her arms for Troi to pick her up.

"What kind of cereal you want, boo-boo, huh?"

Dakoda pointed to the Fruity Pebbles, and Troi shook her head in disbelief. All the artificial coloring and dye. She knew Dakoda only ate that cereal because she knew her daddy did. Vaughn was hooked on Fruity Pebbles and Cocoa Puffs. Sometimes she wished he'd grow up. Sometimes he just had too much kid in him for her.

Troi's day began slowly as she sprinkled the cereal in a red bowl, added some milk, and flipped the worship tape over to the other side. Since she was feeding the baby, she thought that Vaughn needed to dress Dakoda and take her to Virginia's. Mrs. Singleton spoiled Dakoda rotten every chance she got by giving her everything she ever pointed at in a store or a supermarket.

Vaughn was still asleep, but he usually got up and played ball early on Saturday, while Troi prepared for a day of women craving to look like something in a magazine.

"Can you do this with my hair, CeCe?" they would ask her.

"Girl, you ain't got no hair." She'd laugh.

"Why you gonna dis me like that?"

"Girl, please, you know it's true."

Troi popped some waffles in the toaster and caught the milk that was running down Dakoda's chin with the spoon.

"No, mahmee . . ."

"Yes, Dakoda, I'm gonna feed you," she said, smiling at Dakoda, who would take too long if she fed herself.

Troi wanted to be dressed and out of the house by ten o'clock. The phone rang. Troi glanced at the wall clock that was struggling on a dying battery. It was about ten minutes after nine. On the other end of the phone was lame Sofie calling in the sickest, most pathetic voice she could conjure, telling Troi she couldn't make it into the shop today because she had an emergency, which sounded more like a hangover than anything else.

"Girl, you know I'm stuck, right?"

Sofie apologized profusely and Troi imagined Sofie's dilemma. She probably just rolled over into the arms of the man who was the dish she'd served the evening before. She hadn't changed.

"These women need to stop letting men come between them and their money," she yelled.

By the time Troi hung up the phone and made a mental list of what she'd have to do in Sofie's absence, the waffles were cold and hard and Dakoda had milk all over the place. Troi poured Vaughn a cup of coffee. Black, one sugar.

"Vaughn, can you help me?" Troi asked, barging into his sleep. She flipped on the lights, holding Dakoda with one arm and rummaging through the dresser drawer for something for the baby to wear with the other.

"I'm sleeping, CeCe."

"Come on, Vaughn, I have to go in early, Sofie's not coming in today."

"Why don't you fire her?" he mumbled from under the pillow, peering at her like a one-eyed zombie who needed just an hour more of sleep to be fully reincarnated.

"And who's gonna do hair in her place, you?"

"Okay, okay," he grumbled.

"I'm sorry to wake you, baby, but don't you have to get up anyway? You usually play ball with Anthony on Saturday," she smoothed over with a hint of sympathy.

"No, not today, he's on lockdown."

"Coffee's done, Vaughn," she tempted.

She hoped he wouldn't be in a bad mood because she'd woken him up. She sat Dakoda on the bed. The baby fell back on the bed, smiling and contorting her body because her daddy was playing peekaboo with her from under the blanket.

Vaughn threw off the covers, stretched loudly, spread his toes, arched his back, rubbed Dakoda on the head, then shuffled into the bathroom. He came back with a damp washcloth in hand. He undressed Dakoda, then wiped off her face first and saved her toes for last to play the counting game as he always did. Vaughn always looked sexy without a shirt. Not too much hair or muscles, but just enough cuts in all the fashionable places. He was mouthwatering, like succulent fruit you took your time to peel and placed delicately on your tongue. He always left Troi feeling as if she had honey on her palate.

"What?" he said, catching Troi's eyes undressing the rest of him.

He always slept with his pajama pants, and sometimes Troi wore the top, but not often. He had on the blue satin ones. They clung to his rear and his lips were as thick and irresistible as the liquid in a chocolate-covered cherry. She never could curb the urge to kiss them, not even with Dakoda sitting between them on the bed mumbling, "Ma-ma-ma-ma."

Morning breath didn't matter; after three years she was used to it. Their kiss lingered and he smoothed down her braids, which were always shiny and neat, and looked her in the eyes, taking her to that familiar place in her mind; then he whacked her on the butt.

"Come on, girl," he said. "You said you had to go, didn't you?" He grinned.

Troi was confident that the shop could manage an extra thirty minutes without her.

"Come on, Vaughn, don't do that to me." She frowned.

"Do what, girl?"

"You know," she pleaded, pulling him closer to her.

"Tonight, CeCe."

"I don't want tonight, I want now." She pouted.

"No."

Troi sucked her teeth long and hard, rolled her eyes, then got up and rummaged through the closet for something to wear. Begging was beneath her. She pulled out a green T-shirt and a pair of faded jeans.

"I need the car, baby," Vaughn said, "so I'll drop you off, then Dakoda, and come back for you tonight, okay?"

"Sure, whatever, just be back by nine to pick me up, I don't like spending money for cab fare when we have a car, Vaughn."

She was obviously agitated. Vaughn admired Troi's facial expressions. He always got a kick out of her frowning and trying to be nonchalant. He smirked as Troi disrobed, kicking off her panties and twisting her arms behind her back to unhook her bra, and made her way into the bathroom. She reached through the curtains to turn on the shower. Vaughn knew that men were always expected to be in the mood. He wanted his wife to be content. They had issues that arose, but he wanted to make his marriage stronger, not weaker.

Vaughn buttoned up Dakoda's jumper and placed her in the playpen, gave her her favorite toy, and turned on PBS so she could watch the blue fuzzy thing that ate cookies. He slipped out of his pajama pants and strode into the bathroom, thick and tall, determined to give his wife a scene she would play back in her mind all day long. The bathroom was damp. The mirror was clouding over with steam;

it moistened him, too. He startled her as he parted the shower curtains to enter. It had been too long, he thought, as the warm water beat down on his back, calling not only his name but hers, repeatedly. Troi's eyes said *thank you*. Vaughn's body said *you're welcome* and his arms assisted.

Her shoulders glistened under the hot streams of water and her soaked braids spread apart and clung to her back as he worked her favorite soap into a rich frothy lather. He slathered her with a bubbly fragrance, smoothed it slowly over the contour of her hips, her knees, and her toes, then patiently made his way back up again. The water soothed them both as he moved her hair to the side of her face and sought a spot where she'd never been kissed.

She managed his name as unidentifiable words followed, escaping her and allowing her mind to reassure her that she loved her husband more than anything. Eyes closed and water that would have obscured their view dripping from their noses, they faced each other, gasping and allowing the moment to remind them both that they had each other and that, despite what people said, there was truly beauty in submission.

6

Nina had a magnificent green thumb, which her mother sarcastically suggested she must have inherited from her grandmother. Nina never knew her grandmother. She hardly even knew her mother, but she couldn't help but think that her mother did suck the life out of anything she came in contact with. A tile hung on Nina's wall in the foyer insisting that MARTHA STEWART DOESN'T LIVE HERE, but Nina's window boxes were always full of exotic flowering annuals. Begonias, chrysanthemums, sweet Williams, carnations, pink coreopsis, black-eyed Susans, and the like.

They often brought butterflies and neighborhood children with itchy fingers who wanted to show their mommas what they had found blowing in the wind. She didn't need gardening shows on HGTV to know what she was doing. The array of colors from the flowers comforted her each time she peeped out of her window, looking onto the streets where passersby were always agitated and in a hurry. She believed that tending to nature was a way of feeling closer to God, although she didn't necessarily believe gardening or appreciating it was a replacement for a relationship with Him. Birds singing, clouds wafting, and the sun beaming just made life more bearable, was all.

Nina could sit in her window and hear the rapturous bells chime from the church that was four blocks over. The air was damp and the birds chirped, fluttered, and played hopscotch on and off the trees above briskly moving cars that, by day's end, would be a traffic jam on Nostrand, Atlantic, and every other major street in Brooklyn.

A slow-moving station wagon tossed the *Daily News* wrapped in plastic into the yards of the same six residents and hurried through the block, making a slushing sound on the wet street. The bus at the corner stopped as it did every morning around seven forty-five, letting two people off who, arm in arm, shared more than normal people should at seven in the morning. And although it was still early and half the neighborhood was probably still curled up comfy, a roaring plane overhead tried to convince Nina that she should be on a tropical island somewhere seeing her world through hot pink lenses, fantasizing and digging her toes in the sand.

Nina opened the front door and squinted in the sun's brightness, which hadn't given her a change to adjust. She squinted as she often did when people thought she was frowning. She picked up the paper, which had made its perfect landing in the large clay flowerpot at the base of the stairs, took the plastic off, and unfolded the slightly damp paper.

She waved at Junior, the neighborhood vagrant who actually didn't even live in the neighborhood, but rather just roamed up and down the street looking for something to get into. He was dressed in his everyday gray polyester work pants with evidence of static cling and cat hairs skimming the hem. His sneakers had Velcro flaps and he was sporting an Afro mustache. He gave a semitoothless grin, tipped his oily red hat, and was on his way.

The newspaper headline read HANG TOUGH—FIRST LADY URGES BILL NOT TO CHANGE STORY. Nina thought how she never wanted to be in the president's shoes, or his wife's. Their lives were too public, too showy, too theatrical and dramatic, and Nina craved privacy. The limelight truly wasn't for her. No one ever had to worry about her stealing the stage.

"Morning, Nina." Martha waved with an overused broom she was using to sweep down her scantily littered steps.

She wore a pink paisley housedress, blue striped tube socks, and brown men's house slippers.

"Hey, Martha, girl, what you got planned today?"

"Just some shopping. What you got planned?"

"I have to pick up Shelby. We're gonna take a ride up to Shangrila. Just look at this mess," Nina said, pulling off her navy bandanna and running her fingers through her hair.

"Yeah, I know, I have to do something with mine, too, but not today."

Martha had plaits sticking up all over her head, and Nina thought, *That girl better come and go with us now!*

"I have to take Glenda to her dance class at eleven. What's doing tonight?"

"I don't know, maybe going by the country club with Shelby, I'm not sure. I'll call you?"

"Don't you have to be a member or something?"

"Martha, you know if you wanted to go, you could get in with us," Nina said, almost scolding.

"Child, that's okay, I don't have a babysitter and Gerald might come by. And besides, I don't have a thing to wear." Martha made excuses, as if she wanted Nina to run out and buy her something quick.

"Well, let me know if you change your mind."

"I sure will," Martha said, still fixed on sweeping the debris down to the last step.

Martha and Nina had gotten friendly mostly because they were the only women who lived on the block who weren't shacked up or married. They hung around on Saturdays and talked a bunch about nothing. Married people became reclusive. Nothing existed for those codependent couples except their world of marital bliss, a world she thought people fooled themselves into believing was a never-ending honeymoon. Martha was great company. Open, honest, and never bit her tongue. Always said what she felt. Didn't matter whose feelings she hurt.

She made Nina laugh often. She would tell stories about the men who came in and out of her life. Nina lived her life vicariously through Martha's, just as she had done through Troi's her entire life. Martha would tell Nina about the men who wanted to be a part of her life so badly they'd do whatever she said.

They'd arrive with groceries, bootleg videos, jewelry, and money, expecting to sleep over and get a little something extra. If she felt like it, she let them, but only after Glenda was asleep. She didn't want Glenda to get the wrong impression or end up like her, though she couldn't care less what the nosy neighbors thought. Everyone had bones in their closet. Skeletal remains. Some people had so many they couldn't open the closet or their mouths for fear of an avalanche.

Martha and Nina would chat for hours and just sit looking out the window, seeing who was doing what with whom. They made plans of things they wanted to do with their lives once they either found someone significant enough to share them with or made their first million; both were sure the million would come first. Martha liked to talk about all this New Age stuff, which Nina explained to her was really Old Age stuff since it had been around since before Jesus came.

Martha would go on and on about feng shui's negative chi and what a harmonious life you could have through the arrangement of furniture, mirrors, and such. *If her life is so harmonious, why can't feng shui bring her a husband, a job, and a father for Glenda?* Nina thought, trying not to sound too judgmental.

People wanted answers right now, Nina imagined as she lit her honey-colored twenty-wick candle sculpture. It had taken almost two years to burn halfway down and was too big to hug. She always spent Saturday mornings lounging in her newly upholstered moleskin chair.

Nina enjoyed the natural oils that wafted from the candle and mingled with the April breeze that blew through the sheer muslin curtains. Her door was slightly ajar. It excited her senses. The wildflowers on her windowsill danced a little in the sway of the morning air. She sipped on café vianetta, watched the sun reflect off of the wood floors that she was accustomed to walking on barefoot, and played a little jazz to clear her head of déjà vu clutter until it was time to go uptown to Shangrila.

Troi had promised to twist Nina's hair or do something to it that would make it more wash-and-wear. Nina required maximum potential with minimal effort, and didn't have time for pin, curl, and wrap. She had outlived that preoccupation with her hair in her twenties.

Nina was hungry. The marble tiles in the kitchen were cool on her feet, so she tiptoed over to the counter, toasted a slice of cinnamon raisin bread and buttered it, then took a bite. She puttered around the closet, deciding what she would wear today. Something comfortable, she thought, pulling out her favorite pair of jeans and a belt. Any top would do, so a navy acid-wash tee did. She didn't want to get too dressy. That was Shelby's job. And far be it from her to upstage Miss Shelby.

Nina wasn't hard to please; she was just determined. A friend had once called her cold-natured, which may have been true, but the only fact that bothered her remotely as much as that comment was that she was never as hard on men as she should be. It was a fact. Kevin, for one, had never been reprimanded. He'd trampled on her, leaving footprints that were noticeable and dark, yet she'd taken him back countless times until she swore off men for good a few years ago.

She couldn't deal with the distractions or the bitter taste the masquerade left in her mouth. Nina had always been a strong-willed child, but like a horse being whispered, she'd mellowed considerably. She was still vocal about everything except men. She allowed them to come in and rob her blind. They stole her self-esteem, which was flimsy to start. Sure, she came on strong and tough, but everybody knew that once they got past the icy exterior, she was Silly Putty.

Growing up, it was a constant that Nina had an opinion about everything.

"She'll grow out of it," her daddy said, but she wasn't buying it, even if it was on sale.

"Never talk about politics or religion," she remembered hearing in a multicultural America course.

"People have opposing views when it comes to religion and politics," the professor had explained, "and it's not worth the debate."

"Politics and religion are crucial issues that should be discussed," she demanded. No one would refute that fact with her. They might have labeled her a wilted wallflower or even a Wall Street bore, but she always had her say. Nina had many beliefs, though they nearly consumed her in their contradictions. She had things that she didn't believe in, too. She didn't believe in the skinning of animals for the beautification of man. And although she had since graduated, was working making more than enough, and could waltz into any thrift shop and purchase one, she didn't own a fur coat.

The fur coat issue was a controversial topic, especially in the church, where outdoing and upstaging was the prerequisite for acceptance into the religious cliques. There was the fur coat clique and the "I've-got-the-latest-hairstyle" clique. There was also the "I've-got-a-brand-new-car" clique, but they didn't really count because the repoman could come just as quickly as it took for them to say, "Fill 'er up." It was senseless, she thought. A sick society of people who wore all the money they had on their backs or on their fingers and then lived somewhere reminiscent of a crack den. Many people offered that her antifur campaign was her opinion, and they were right, it was.

She wasn't an activist or anything remotely obnoxious. She was however, peculiar in a sense and determined to have her say. She was almost novel, in fact, and found herself leaning more toward eclectic than cool on the popularity meter. Her friends didn't care, they swung their pelts about as if to say, *look at me, see me, envy me.* They couldn't care less about the torture and bloodshed it took for them to wrap themselves in fur that was skinned off an innocent animal foraging for food. It was like stealing the covers from a malnourished child in a third world country on a blustery cold winter night. Trifling.

Nina often thanked God that she was nothing like her friends. She didn't know why she thanked Him, she wasn't much like God either—something that she vowed to rectify each New Year's Eve. Her friends with their opposing views were a constant distraction. She had grown to care about them, but she hadn't picked them; they chose her.

Her friends wanted to know the boyish girl who seemed unafraid to say what was on her mind. They wanted to observe her when she went head-to-head with the dorm mother, who was fighting to shorten the curfew, and the dean of students, who was eagerly going along with the program because he didn't want to be responsible for any promiscuous teen girls in New York City after eleven P.M. on weekdays.

"We're women," Nina had reiterated, and, clipboard in hand, she'd started a petition fighting to stay the current curfew.

"We're all over eighteen years old, and we pay to attend this college, it's not free."

Five thousand twenty-three signatures and a board meeting later, the curfew had been stayed and Nina had become a hero of sorts for initiating the fight. Neighbors, store owners, the man in the cleaners, students, and their parents had signed the petition, only reinforcing the fact that there was strength in numbers, and that the pen was indeed mightier sometimes.

These friends that Nina had acquired were so different from her and the life she was allowed to lead. They crowded their weekends with faceless men whose names were never remembered, for the sole purpose of not appearing to be dateless. Nina never understood their dating dilemma or the urgency. It was as if they had an imaginary deadline to meet. There was nothing barbaric about not having a date. It didn't make you less of a woman. If that were the case, Nina thought, her femininity would have been shot from day one. "I can do bad all by myself," came to mind. But the men she knew were just as tired as that old cliché.

She never really meddled in the love lives of her acquaintances and scattered friends. But she still couldn't relate to these people. It was like comparing airplanes to boats. They both got you to your destination, but one glided through the air unscathed and the other sort of dredged through tepid waters against the current.

The only person Nina had to confide in when she was growing up was her sister. It's why she and Troi were tight. There was no parade of schoolmates in and out of the house; Mother didn't allow that. Mother had to keep up her royal front. She wanted to be held in high regard. She played numbers, chain-smoked, swore relentlessly, belittled only those directly related to her, and drank like a fish in purified water, but sure, she still wanted people to see God in her. It was the longest stretch of the imagination.

If Mother didn't go to hell for sinning, she'd sure go there based solely on how she treated her kids. But looking back, Nina was sure it was God's doing really, because Nina and Troi had been there for each other in ways that only strengthened the bonds of sisterhood.

"Family business stays in the family," Mother said quite often, as if either of them wanted to pull out a chair, get on a bullhorn, and broadcast their family life.

Nina and Troi had relied on each other for everything. They were each other's confidants and worst critics. Boys never came between them, although Troi was the prettier one and the one with the endless suitors. But if it ever came down to a boy or each other, they knew that they were stronger than that.

As adults, their lives were aligned differently. Troi had run to the church and the saving grace of God, and although Nina had followed, Troi practically lived there. She had consumed herself, immersed her heart in redemption and salvation. Shelby was considered part of the family, too, but she'd run as fast and as far from the church as she could, which wasn't a surprise.

"I have more entertaining things to do," she'd said, dismissing the women as frumpy and plain.

Martha, on the other hand, allowed the theory of reincarnation to comfort her into believing that if she didn't get it right this time, there'd be other lives to try again. Troi had said of Martha, "Maybe she'd come back as a guest in a hotel and get a wake-up call." Troi seemed so confident in her beliefs.

"Girl, I wish I had your faith," Nina had commented one evening over three-cheese lasagna.

"In God?"

"Yes . . ."

"It's something that comes in time, Nina. It's a process. You know how we were raised; I am a miracle, a testimony. I mean, even if salvation were a hoax, I'd rather be safe than sorry."

Nina had nodded, wishing she was more like her sister.

And so, Nina sat in her favorite chair that matched her fondness for nature and watched the weekly visitors file into the block. The Jehovah's Witnesses were like teenage boys with raging hormones begging for sex. They kept coming and laying the pressure on, telling you how good it was for you, and how you needed it. Paradise, bliss, they named it to lure you in. They didn't take no for an answer.

They opened her gate, trespassing, and walked patiently up the stairs. They nudged the little girl ahead of them. She was their sales gimmick. A mile away you could spot them with their plastic cases.

"Just tell them politely, no, thank you," Mother slurred whenever she overheard Nina complaining about it.

Troi understood. But everything seemed simple from the seedy haze in which her mother was perpetually vacationing.

Nina opened the window and rested on her elbows as she dug around in the window boxes, propping up her flowers and discarding fallen leaves, squinting again in the sun. She managed a smile and shook her head no, as they approached the top step and began to tell her something about good news. She refused to hide behind her door like a guest at a hooky party. This was her house, and they would just have to respect that. From the smallest to the tallest, they had to learn that they couldn't just come probing and prodding around in her space.

Nina watered her plants more sufficiently than the morning mist had and pondered how she would spend the day. She thought about how people didn't respect each other or relationships. "It'll be okay," she said to herself, realizing that some plants got more faithfulness than people. She still hadn't decided if she would go riding with the girls tonight at the uppity little country club that allowed them all to become members. In clubs like those, it wasn't about having money, just about having enough.

Shelby loved it. She fit right in, poor little rich girl that she was. Shelby didn't care if she was token. Nina wasn't looking forward to the facade. It wasn't what she'd call an enchanted evening. Shelby was caught up in the prestige of it all. When the valet smiled and took Shelby's keys, she would saunter in like royalty, plop down poolside, and snap her finger for something cool that would slide down her throat and give her a slight buzz. Nina wasn't amused.

7

Relationships took too much time and effort. Dinner, flowers, and extra-polite nonoffensive woman-friendly conversation. Tim often didn't know why he bothered. But he knew. He knew exactly why he bothered. He loved women. Too many of them. Late-night phone calls and unannounced visits that were sometimes pleasant surprises. When he held a woman close, touched her softly, and pressed into her with his lips lingering by her ear, attempting to say something that made her gasp, shudder, and pause, allowing an all too familiar sigh, he knew. He knew why he bothered. He got off on the feeling he evoked. The innocence of a kiss was a commonplace that fear could not deny.

One day he figured he might settle down, but not yet and not now. No games, and no promises. He owed himself that. He didn't have the heart to lay all of his cards on the table. Heck, he wasn't even emotionally playing with a full deck, and he couldn't risk his entire future for a quick lay. But in the back of his mind, he sure wanted to see where it could go for a change without either of them ending up angry and hurt in the end.

He was green. There was so much that he still hadn't learned. Like what prompted men to write poetry that revived jaundiced hearts and chased shadows in gypsy clothing through several continents. Men and women appeared to be from two different planets. That whole trivial Mars and Venus thing, if it was true. Other than that, there was no explanation as to why so many women claimed that he had hurt them and even more women waited for Tim as if he were their only chance at happiness. He believed that just as the sun was destined to rise and line the anticipating sky, he, too, would one day understand why the magnetism of a woman's scent lured him so, and why, when soft eyes with lips to match lingered on his, it made him want to give in voluntarily.

He needed to know why, when he closed his eyes, in his mind he didn't touch her or her honey-hued hair, but there was a connection. He just gave in, submitted, like a nursing babe with his lips slightly parted, anticipating sustenance. Some women made him feel this more than others. But he'd never tell. Michelle did stir these feelings in his steaming caldron, which he playfully referred to as his heart. Mostly late at night, after she'd flown back into the city sometimes at one A.M.

A charcoal-gray cloud collage would waft through the sky and the stars scattered across the East would be barely visible in the city's haze. The phone would ring as if it were purring. "I'll be there in thirty minutes." And there wouldn't be any other word spoken between them once she reached the apartment and filled it with her essence. It was an ongoing sensual pleasure that defied all of his rules, especially the one about no one spending the night.

Sharon, on the other hand, didn't trigger this cosmic feeling in Tim. She was predictable, dictating, and aggressive. Men didn't want to be dominated, at least not on their feet. But Sharon was still new to this game. He didn't know where on earth women had gotten the notion that men wanted women to act like men. Show a little ingenuity, yes; act like men, no. Someone had written a book assuming to know what men wanted in a woman, and women had read this book cover to cover, picked up the ball, and run with it. Time out.

Tim wasn't most men, but he knew that he did want a woman who was soft, flowing, and feminine, but never weak. Sharon was none of the above. She was a definite turnoff, and although his body responded to satisfy itself, there was never even the remote thought that there would be a long-term anything with Sharon.

Michelle had potential for permanency, but she only had one flaw. She was unavailable. She had her nose to the grindstone and spent more time en route than anyplace else. She was also a little too thin for him, but that wasn't a major dilemma. He could get over that, but he wasn't going to play the waiting game. Nah, that wasn't him. Whenever he made an effort to arrange something that would overshadow the moral wrongs in his meandering life, she had an appointment or another urgent engagement. They'd make plans, only for her to call at the last minute to overapologetically cancel.

She'd stop by whenever she could, and always smelled exotic, like a country girl who bathed in garden scents or something like a fruit salad with molasses, which made him lick his lips. She had warm brown eyes that were slightly slanted and lashes that made up for her unavailability when she looked at him. Her eyes spoke volumes, even when they were intimate and breaking down their attraction to the core of animal magnetism. She was sexy. Slinky. Her voice was like the ocean at night that played and got a little rough.

Such a seducing quality, it undressed you head to toe, naked. He fought not to let Michelle distract him from his thoughts, his work, and his purpose. She opened him, most definitely, but he couldn't wait for her, and he wasn't about to play cat and mouse.

"Never give a woman the upper hand," Justin said.

He was young to be so wise. He had more sense than Darius, Charlie, and the rest of those knuckleheads.

Tim honestly didn't want to give the impression that he was using any women, but since none of them were getting what they wanted out of the deal, it could hardly be looked at in any other fashion. He didn't have a long-term interest in any of them. He couldn't. Sharon was in a training school and had an opinion about everything, from why they should move in together to what types of films she thought Tim should make. Michelle, meanwhile, lived and breathed the groups that she managed, which left her little time for friends or relationships. Tim wasn't satisfied with any of the arrangements, and although his eager intentions were to acquire more attention from women, he wasn't necessarily willing to give more. So, like justice, it balanced.

Tim had been convinced years ago that passion alone wasn't enough reason to share the rest of his life with anyone. His major focus in life now was to smash the myth in Hollywood that stereotyped black men as being abusers, lowlifes, and unemployed. Though he wasn't employed and possibly fed right into making the myth a reality, he was not a drug dealer, although he had more tenacity than the average street thug. He believed that movies hadn't done right by him. They still failed to portray black men in a positive light, and the ones that did make a feeble attempt had fallen short. A black man as an occasional lawyer or doctor wasn't enough for him. He wanted a blockbuster film. He wanted to be the next F. Gary Gray, Forest Whitaker, or Carl Franklin. He wanted his name in blinding lights, luring the entire city. The whole shebang, before he was forty. And women were only a distraction.

"I am an intelligent, attractive, athletic SBF, mid 20s, 5'5", 125 lbs. I have a great sense of humor, nonsmoker, light drinker. I live in New York. I am seeking a SBM with similar qualities to correspond with."

All of the ads sounded the same. Snobbish and boring. Great sense of humor probably meant, "I'll laugh at anything you say," and light drinker meant, "I'm an alcoholic if you're buying."

Tim didn't know why his sister was so dead-set on getting him hitched.

"I'm not looking for anything serious, Rochelle." He tossed the magazine onto the futon.

"Yes, you are."

"Besides, one hundred twenty-five pounds is skin and bones. I like a bumpy woman," he said.

"Please, never mind that. You can always fatten her up. The point is that you need a wife bad."

"I need studio backing is what I need."

"You'll get that, just wait, first things first." Rochelle shook her head and reached for the curled-up magazine, intent on shuffling through the New York personals to find someone suitable for her long overdue brother.

"I'm older than you, Tim. Trust me, I know what you need."

Tim nodded, almost surrendering.

"Look, do whatever you want to do, but I'm not going on a blind date. I'm not desperate."

"Well, I know a girl who is single, no kids, and works as a secretary at the law firm Carl interns at."

"Yeah, and . . ."

"And what?"

"Well, what does she look like? What is her name? Tell me something . . ."

"She's cute."

"Only cute?"

"Okay, she's beautiful."

"Red light!"

"What?"

"If she's beautiful and single there's a problem somewhere. That's an oxymoron."

"What about next Friday, Tim?"

"Hold up, I'm trying to get past the cute versus beautiful part." He motioned with his hands.

"Leave that to me, Tim."

"I don't know. Are you sure she won't embarrass me, eating with her fingers, or . . . I mean . . . picking her teeth with a matchbook or some other nasty habit?"

"Please, what are you, a king?"

"Nah, I'm just particular, you know that." He smiled, nodding yes.

"Her name is Fawn. I'll call her, Tim, and I'll let you know when she's available."

"Fawn? You're kidding, right?"

"I'll call her, Tim."

He shrugged, getting past the woman's comical name.

"You know what I want, right?"

"Yes, I do."

"I want someone who knows what my work means to me, and won't try to interfere. Someone who can hold an intelligent conversation," he bellowed.

"Do you think you are the only one who can read, Tim?" Rochelle frowned. "For someone who isn't looking for a serious relationship, you sure are picky."

"I'm picky, but I'm not . . ."

"Yes, I know you're not desperate. But give everyone a break, will you?" She sucked her teeth and folded her arms.

"C'mon, Rochelle, don't be like that."

"Be like what? You act like I'm gonna hook you up with a hunchback."

Tim lowered his head and snickered quietly. "Now you're exaggerating, Rochelle."

"I mean, anything has to be an improvement over Sharon. What do you see in her anyway?"

"She's a friend." He paused.

"Friend?"

"I don't have time for much else."

"Make time, Tim. You can't stay cooped up with this scary-haired woman and think that you're content with that."

"Who said she has scary hair?"

"I've seen her, remember? She was not a pretty sight, trust me."

"Well, I'm leaning more towards Michelle," he said.

"Michelle doesn't want you, she wants her job. I'm sorry, Tim, but it's true and you know it's true." Rochelle spoke hand on hip and neck rolling.

"So, who do you suggest, oh mighty Queen Rochelle?"

"Stop playing, Tim, you know I care about you. That's why I'm doing this."

Tim had always thought his sister was pushy. She wanted him to be happy because she was, but you couldn't force someone into your ideal of happiness. Happiness for Tim would be his name in neon lights and positive reviews in the trade papers. Not everybody had marriage and commitment in their future. He assumed he did, though it may have been more like an obscure fog.

Show me how to get the attention of some people at New Line Cinema and all I'd need was some interesting dialogue, not a woman, he thought.

Tim wasn't a bad boy. He was cultured and had exquisite taste. African sculptures sat on his coffee table and three hand-painted tribal masks from Zimbabwe hung in a row on his terra-cotta walls. A student he had met at NYU had them sent from Africa for next to nothing, in exchange for some toiletries. The earth tones made his pad look lived-in, comfortable, serene, yet masculine. For now he was comfortable with that IKEA appeal. The studio apartment was barely big enough for him alone, and his sister wanted him to meet someone who'd want to spend the night, subscribe to all those female magazines, and have them coming to his apartment to ward off evil spirits, namely other women.

"Hmm . . . I see somebody who claims to have no money has been shopping up a storm." Rochelle dug into a glossy shopping bag, past the tissue paper, pulling out and waving a soft navy silk sweater from the tip of her finger.

"It was a gift, if you must know." Tim flashed a handsome grin.

"Gift? I wish someone would buy me gifts."

She folded the sweater neatly, wrapping it back up in the white crinkled tissue paper.

"You've got a husband, make him buy you whatever your heart desires, Rochelle." He laughed.

"That's not funny, Tim. You need to stop using those women, that's what you need to do. You're gonna get it. One day, Tim, that's all I'm saying, one day . . ."

Tim had a thing for silky cotton-linen blended fabrics. He loved the way the texture soothed his skin, baby soft, and made him feel like he was sleeping on warmed flannel sheets in November. Sharon enjoyed when her man looked good. At least that's what she said. She undressed him, so she figured she might as well dress him, too.

"I'm not using anybody, I'm just welcoming the blessings." Tim waved his hand forward.

"Well, what are you giving them? You keep playing, you'll be in hell talking about, 'Can I p-l-e-e-e-a-s-e have some ice water?' " She shook her head, not believing how desperate her brother was.

"Let me just say something for men everywhere. If I go to hell for this, it'll be crowded down there, 'cause women have been doing it for years. Using men to pay their rent, buy their groceries, and feed kids that aren't even theirs."

"I can't believe you said that!"

"I got it, maybe they'll have stores down there and the women down there will be asking the brothers in the lake of fire, 'Can you buy me these shoes I saw on sale, I can pay you back when I get my check?' "

"Okay, Tim . . ."

"Listen, Rochelle, I'm just saying, I'm not using anybody, they give of their own free will. I don't promise them marriage and kids. No house on the hill either. They just buy, buy, buy, thinking they're gonna get something, and that isn't my fault."

"Okay, Tim, but you don't have to explain to me."

"C'mon, sis, get down off the horse, this is reality. Hell is for people who don't recycle. Besides, if I did tell them I didn't want to be bothered, they'd still come around trying to convince me otherwise."

"And you know this because?"

"I've been there, remember?" he said. "I lived it. Remember Estella?"

"Let's change the subject please." Rochelle raised her hand, instructing Tim to stop. "The last thing I want to remember is that psychopath. I think Fawn would be perfect for you. She's tall and . . . color-coordinated . . ."

"Don't fix me up, Rochelle, I can find my own date. Besides, I'm not looking for anything serious. I have enough to deal with now with school and paying my bills."

"Tim, don't let pride get in the way. You know Carl and I can help you out financially if you need a loan. Anyway, you need some excitement in your life. Meet new people and get rid of that tired circle of morons you hang out with. Think of it as fresh new experience that could make for good dialogue."

Rochelle had a point, Tim thought; it would make for good dialogue, even if the date didn't go quite right.

"Hmm? What do you say?"

He eyed his sister intently, as if it were a childhood prank.

"Please, Tim, just go out with someone nice for a change. I want you to be happy."

"I have my work, I am happy."

"You know what I mean."

"You're always trying to set me up. What if I don't like her? I don't want you coming back asking me what I did to your friend."

"First of all, I wouldn't fix you up with any of my friends."

"That's refreshing, Rochelle."

"C'mon, Tim."

"All right, I'll go. But I'm not putting on a front for anybody."

"Great, it's settled."

"And if she is uncouth, I'm gonna tell her about herself."

"You'll like her, Tim, I promise."

"Well, what choice do I have? A cheesy personal ad? I'm not desperate."

Rochelle grinned, feeling her mission was accomplished.

"I'll call you from work." She hugged him.

"This is a hectic week, it probably won't be until next week when I can go out with her."

"Well, don't tell me, tell her," she said.

"Well, maybe I can squeeze her in this week. I'll see," he said, tumbling his schedule around in his head.

"Sounds good, bro." She laughed.

"Thank you for being genuinely concerned about me, sis."

"I worry about you, Tim." Rochelle held her brother's hand.

"I'll be fine, I have enough to keep me busy."

"Like Sharon?" Rochelle asked, raising one eyebrow just a bit on the way out.

Tim and Sharon weren't exclusively a couple, although Sharon hung onto the notion that they were. And maybe he did lead her on a bit, but he wasn't up to the trauma that ending the relationship would cause. If he ended it, he would spend hours and endless midnights explaining to Sharon on the phone in a fatherly baritone why it wasn't going to work between them.

And she'd cry, and he wouldn't get any sleep. And she'd cry, and he'd let her come over. And she'd cry; then he'd console her and they'd end up right back where they are now. Together but not. He just didn't have the time or the patience to try and convince her of anything, so he let her believe it was a monogamous reciprocated kind of love affair they were having. It was entertaining, and although he wished he could give more, he usually couldn't, so he didn't. Nobody said life was easy, and those who insinuated it might be lied.

8

Troi had a raunchy crowd of noisemakers outside of Shangrila. People were standing around under the green awning shucking, jiving, smoking cigarettes, and drinking too much caffeine too early in the morning.

"You coming in or out?" she asked, waving her hand to ward off the smoke she didn't want to get inside. "First we pick it, now you smoking it," she said, shaking her head at the woman who was tipping the trembling coffee cup up to her lip and simultaneously dragging on the cigarette. Troi imagined it to be a nauseating combination.

She thought that if her hands could reach, she would ring Sofie's neck for sticking her like this. Mostly because it was a Saturday, but also because it was classic Sofie behavior. Passing the buck.

Every hair dryer had a head under it, and Carmen had been working it all by herself. The unnerving music was blaring and women in all conditions were still their usual talkative selves, each one talking louder than and upstaging the next.

"Girl, I'm gonna hook y'all up!" Troi said, mustering strength, taking a deep breath, and marching into the shop swinging her arms, ready to whip some heads into shape.

"Too early in the morning to be yelling," an elderly customer complained, with her bottom lip poked out, her brows wrinkled, and her eyes squinting like she needed to put on somebody's glasses.

"She must have gotten some last night," a younger girl hiding behind hair that wasn't all hers tried whispering to her friend, who was picking at her pastel fingernails, disenchanted by the whole moment.

"Too early for all this loud music, that's what it's too early for."

Troi brushed past them all, twisting the knob, turning the radio station to something more soothing and lowering the volume a bit. CD 101.9. Smooth jazz. Nina had her hooked on that station.

"Aww, come on, that was my jam!" The girl with the pastel nails came to life momentarily.

"Your jam? Girl, please, there's more to life than Puffy, okay? Besides, Shangrila is a beauty salon, not a beauty parlor. Peace and serenity needs to be up in here, not Puffy, Mase, and the Dogg Pound," Troi said, rolling her eyes and proceeding to hum along with Anita Baker's "You Bring Me Joy." She paused only to smirk, nod her head in their direction, and say, "And honey, I got some, but it wasn't last night, it was this morning. So, talk what you know."

"Peaches, you want your head wrapped?" Carmen asked, making a circular motion atop her head.

Peaches was flipping through an old magazine. An issue that had shirtless, bulging bronzed muscle men slicked down with an oil base that appeared to be dripping from the cover.

When Troi saw stuff like that, she always thought of her husband. He was as golden as an Indian summer, with lips that held the strength of an ocean. And his thighs? She thanked the Lord she didn't have to run around fiending after another brother's body. However, it was still a difficult issue to part with. Peaches nodded yes, and Troi waved her over.

"I'll do her and you can do those," Troi said, pointing and flicking her hand at the fresh-mouthed girl and the rap fanatic.

Peaches was Troi's best customer. Not because she was consistent, but because she brought her own stuff. Troi never had to ask her what she wanted, and she never wanted anything special. "Wrap it," she'd say. She still wasn't working, but faithfully came and got her hair done every other week at the expense of her noncommitting man.

"My man likes to run his fingers through it," Peaches said, grinning and showing her gold-framed tooth as if it were a novelty.

"Every single time she comes into the shop, it's like she the only one who have a man," the rap fanatic mumbled to her friend.

Troi had a mind to toss them both out and send them down the street to the Beauty Shack.

"Girl, I have to clip your ends." Troi hesitated.

"Oh, no, don't clip it, it's fine." Peaches twitched.

"Girl, you got some hair now, if you want to keep it you gotta let me clip it."

"Okay, but only a little bit, he gets mad if he thinks I cut it."

"Well, you better tell that man of yours not to worry about the hair, enough of that shackin' time to get the pie in the sky."

"He said we gonna get married next year." She grinned, believing it herself.

"Well, let me know when, girl, I'll do everybody's head in the wedding party. I'll even hook up your momma for free. Him, too, don't he need an S curl?" she kidded.

When Troi had started with Peaches's head, the child had had a bad perm, her hair had been uneven, and she'd been near bald. Although bald wasn't necessarily bad. Some women looked good in fades and lower sculpted cuts. Peaches just wasn't one of them. Doobies did for women what fades and baldies did for men—made nothing look like something special. People didn't come to Shangrila because they liked the atmosphere or even because it was affordable. They came because they could hook some hair up!

This was going to be a long, drawn-out, "are-we-there-yet" day. Troi could feel it already. Attitudes creeping, beepers vibrating, and cell phones playing "Für Elise." There were too many people up in the shop, and they just kept coming, like she was giving away shampoo samples at a hair convention.

She saw heads that looked like someone had galloped through them, tangled Afros that looked like they should be in the barber shop getting sawed off, and all kinds of sisters who looked like they wanted to torture her by having their braids taken out and now wanting a perm and conditioner.

"Half of your hair is gonna come out," she told one girl.

"Nuh-uh, why?" The girl pouted.

"Because you didn't comb out the ends. All this is dead hair, girl. What you think I can do with this?" she said, picking through the girl's head, annoying herself more than the tenderhead.

Other women in the shop, with their oversize eavesdropping dog ears, giggled at the woman's misfortune. Troi didn't care. She disliked when people wanted to look like a *Cosmo* cover and only came in with about enough hair to be a Chucky doll, then tried to convince everyone in the shop otherwise.

The bell on the shop door jingled and Troi looked up as she always did.

"Hey, hey." Carla sauntered into the shop with her high-heeled boots, short skirt, and a multicolored scarf trailing behind her.

Some labeled her as one who hadn't fully come out from among them, but Carla was Troi's girlfriend from grade school. She defied every statute ever set by a congregation or denomination. She and Troi went to the same church. The girl loved God. Night and day their lifestyles were by comparison.

Carla was the nontraditional Christian girl who had managed to break every man-made rule in the church handbook simultaneously. She wore her skirt above her knee, was known to show a little cleavage, and the music she listened to wasn't anything like Donnie McClurkin or Fred Hammond. Some said it bordered on blasphemous, but God was in her heart, and her only judge.

The last time Troi had heard from her best friend, she'd been asking for her unadulterated opinion of Christians and tattoos.

"Tattoo of what?"

"Something like a cross on my thigh," she'd said.

"I don't know. Who you expect to see it?"

"That's not the point."

"That is the point," Troi debated.

"We are human, and we can have our own personal likes and dislikes," Carla had argued.

"Yes, as long as they don't go against His word," Troi had reasoned. "And I'm not saying that it is against His word, but you have to seek Him for your own answer concerning this." She'd smiled and hugged her sisterfriend.

"Thank you, CeCe."

Troi had looked Carla square in the eyes during that discussion. "I wouldn't do it, you know, I wouldn't, but the final choice is yours."

She'd love Carla no matter what, and they'd remained friends. Troi looked up and grinned as her friend approached her.

"You neva call me, CeCe."

"Back at ya, girl."

"Where you been?" Carla asked, playfully shoving Troi.

"Well, where it looks like I been? Here." She laughed, thinking the girl must be blind, retarded, or both.

"And just where are you going, Miss Shopaholic? You never stay still. Always going and coming. But mostly going, of course."

"You must have ESP. I'm going shopping, girl." Carla grinned. "I gotta buy something to wear for the concert tomorrow."

"For what? We're wearing robes."

"Yeah, I know, but you never know who'll see you. I might meet my husband, child," Carla whispered. "You never know."

"Husband? Girl, in that tight little getup you workin'? You better praise God for not sending down lightning."

"Relax, relax, relax, I know what I'm doing. I've been doing it for . . . five years now," Carla said, squinting and taking a moment to calculate.

"Okay, I see, you got it covered, huh?"

"Yes, Miss Troi, I got it covered. Just wanted to say hi to my sisteren. Let me go before there's nothing left on the racks. Then I'd really have to repent. I wish you could come with me though."

"Look at this crowd, now you know." Troi shook her head.

"I know, do what you gotta do. I'll give you a call later," Carla said.

"Okay, yep, do that. Peace and grace, sister." Troi grinned.

"Well, you be blessed and walk in his mercy," Carla exaggerated.

Troi waved Carla out the door into the arms of the salespeople in the department stores. The girl was a walking fashion statement with an exclamation point. She was also the epitome of forgiveness. She never had an unkind thing to say about anybody. She was giving, too. If you were broke and she had a dollar, you knew you had two quarters to rub together. And if she had a sandwich, you knew you could have more than a bite. Carla was a sister in the true sense of the word. Made even blood relatives pale by comparison.

Carla, like Troi and Nina, was a survival story, too. She literally defied the laws of nature. Her mother and father were heroin addicts, chasing that white horse and galloping all the way into the twenty-first century on it. They'd been addicted her entire life, from what she'd been told, and odds should have held that Carla get addicted to something, too. But the predestined spirit that God had claimed her as His own had given her a new start. She often said that if it weren't for the church and Troi, she didn't know where or what she'd be.

Carla had been on her own since she was nine, and had done things for a meal that you could only think about with your eyes closed tightly and fear strangling your throat. She'd lived in abandoned dilapidated buildings that she'd sneak into when the streets were barren and most kids her age had gone inside for dinner. She'd made her bed on a soiled bug-infested cot and snuck around in the night, avoiding men who crept about looking for sexual prey. By day she'd boosted clothes that she would never have been able to afford otherwise. But she'd always managed to keep everything she owned clean, lint-free, and well pressed.

Carla often said that her only vision of her parents was high. They were always slumped, staggering, dragging, or nodding. She had never once heard either of them speak with any genuine concern for her. She didn't blame them though. They only did what they knew to do: nothing.

"If their only purpose was to give me life, I praise God still," Carla said.

People said that it was her daddy who'd turned her momma on, but the thing was that as far as she was concerned, she didn't really have a momma or a daddy. At least not in the normal everyday sense. She'd been like a baby bird perched high in a tree, and the minute she'd shown signs of independence, they'd pushed her out of the nest, teaching her to fly and fend for herself. Almost like a mercy killing.

Troi remembered how she and Carla had met. The kids had made fun of Carla in grade school because her mother never came to PTA or open-school night. Foul-mouthed little buppie kids wearing watches and playing tennis, and they couldn't tell time or keep score.

"Where's your momma at?" the kids would ask Carla, as if it were any of their business.

"She's busy fighting for world peace," she'd scream.

"Well, she's always busy," they'd teased, giggling, pointing, and making fun, although there was nothing humorous about a child not able to find a role model in her own house. Their parents would come to school wearing a look of genuine concern for their child and clothes to match. Carla had always envied that, but compensated the only way she knew how, by doing the best she could in school and studying hard enough to get financial aid and tuition assistance, despite what her parents were or had become.

Troi hummed, struggling with unkind memories of her own. She recalled the shame that had flushed over her as her inebriated mother stumbled into her fifth-grade class for a visit with her math teacher wearing her Sunday hat with a pair of sweatpants and a T-shirt that said SMILE, GOD LOVES YOU. Kids had lined the hall, pointing as if the circus had come to town. At that moment, Troi had known Nina's plight. Troi had cried the entire way home, and she'd been teased for months and greeted every morning with the infamous "smile, God loves you," and cackling laughter that was as relentless as ten-year-olds are known to be.

Teachers had done all they knew to do: nothing. Shortly thereafter, she fell right into a lifelong friendship with Carla. There was nothing like a common experience to solidify the bonds of friendship. Other than Nina, there was nobody remotely as close as they had become. They forged on through high school, becoming more popular and much sought after by the boys, putting to rest their not-so-glamorous childhood memories, or at least concealing them very well.

Carla was street-smart. But she wasn't naive where God was concerned either. Ask her and she'd tell you. She knew firsthand that God didn't hold your past against you. She'd be the first one to tell you about the second, third, and fourth chances you always got with God. She was a walking testimony. A prophecy, even. But to some people, your labels always stuck. If you'd been a prostitute then, you were a prostitute still in their minds. A sick society of judgmental heathens. *They have more faith in the wind than they do God, and they can't see neither one,* Troi thought.

But she thanked God that He alone had the keys. If she'd wait on the Hallelujah Girls, she'd have a reservation in hell with first-class tickets to get her there. She fought not to care what people thought. When they heard the name Madison, Troi wanted people to envision Shangrila and her sister's Ph.D, not her mother's ongoing not-so-concealed bout with alcoholism, stumbling, tripping, and falling. But like oil in water, rumors always surfaced after a while.

Luther was on the radio singing one of his lush love songs. All Troi wanted to bask in was the recurring thought of this morning with Vaughn. Many ideas of marriage were conceived by people who either had married the wrong person or were so boring themselves that it sort of rubbed off on their partner. They exhausted the possibilities. But her ideal was spending the weekend with Vaughn making stir-fried something and sitting on his lap watching a movie of which neither one of them would ever need to see the end.

She knew life didn't come with guarantees. She'd lived a life of broken promises, with love and affection being only things she saw on television or heard blindly glamorized in a song. But she had waited and her reward was handsome. And tall, she thought with a smile. She was more than glad that she'd lowered her electric fence, the imaginary wall. She praised God every morning that she hadn't ended up blowing him to the corner with all the other little dust bunnies in her life.

Vaughn knew what she needed. He'd clasp her hands in his and tell her that she was the most intelligent and sexy woman he knew. She believed it was true. Like a banana, she had peeled off the protective layers and exposed herself to him for the ripe fruit she was. The supple yet succulent woman she knew was inside, almost too ripe. She had given herself freely to passion and her living was found in laughter, and her heart and soul in Vaughn.

Troi's mind was somewhere near Puerto Vallarta, honeymooning with her thoughts that proved love lingered. Troi imagined that the lengthy strokes of her brushing somebody's hair were the gentle brushing of his lips grazing her back. She wasn't even marginally curious to make out the features or the face. Only one man had ever evoked such pleasure.

Troi, almost totally submerged in reverie, had just surfaced into a conversation that the women around her were having about life. There was no other topic that held enough stimulation or such a debate.

"Girl, let me just say that life is a never-ending learning experience, okay?" Carmen interjected.

"Yeah, well, life is growing, knowing, sharing, and a whole lot in between, too," Troi said, grinning as if she had just fallen in love seconds before.

"Life means different things to different people." Peaches leaned back in the chair as Carmen sculpted her eyebrows into wicked drive-the-men-crazy arches.

"Life is being able to experience joy." Troi smiled and motioned like she had sugar on her tongue and couldn't describe the taste.

"Life is also sitting on his lap reading the Sunday paper. What joy little things bring," Troi continued.

"That's what I'm talking about," Peaches chimed in.

"Ooh, Mami, I know what you mean," Carmen said, looking down and shaking her head.

"Well, you know that love is also accepting others, regardless of their situations and circumstances," Peaches said, obviously quoting somebody or something that she had read in some overrated cult literature.

"Who said that?" Troi asked, wondering since when Peaches had gotten all philosophical.

"I just did."

"No, she didn't." Carmen giggled.

"Yes, she did." Troi nodded.

"Alrighty then." They laughed.

9

Vaughn shifted his brown Yankee cap and checked his features in the rearview mirror. The traffic in every lane was at a standstill. Cars bunched up like a bouquet of overblooming roses. He despised traffic, as much as he hated the glutton who always took the last piece of pie. He sat still. His lips twitched as they always did when he was agitated. He drummed his fingers impatiently on the dashboard, waiting to merge onto the main expressway. The bridge to Jersey was hideous this time of the morning. Kids whined, music blared, and people took one too many liberties when driving. He never understood why they called it a rat race when everyone moved slower than turtles.

He didn't know what he'd been thinking waiting until midmorning to make his way over the bridge. If he hadn't gotten in so late last night, he would have gotten an earlier start. He fiddled with the radio and tossed a couple of Dakoda's colorful toys into the backseat. The steady crawl of cars finally quickened to the point that they were doing almost twenty mph. After crossing the bridge, he pulled off the highway at the first exit and took the local streets. He groped under the seat to pull out a CD from the case. He needed some music in the car. Nothing too preachy, he got enough of that on Sunday. He put on something soothing and instrumental that Nina had given Troi. He had too much going on in his head now. He just needed to chill.

Vaughn did feel a twinge of guilt that he wasn't spending the day with his daughter, but he thanked his mother for graciously babysitting again. She seemed to be doing more of that lately, but hardly seemed overwhelmed. Older people enjoyed the company of children, he rationalized.

Troi was so busy at the shop and refused to hire more staff, he grumbled to himself. And he was on his own journey to self-discovery that he couldn't help thinking should have been completed before he had asked Troi to marry him. He was more lenient than he should have been with himself, but eventually they both had to deal with these issues.

Vaughn's momma wanted to cook him breakfast, and Dakoda was crying for Da-da to stay, but he had things to take care of. He had to turn down French toast, bacon, and grits. He wouldn't be good company today, couldn't promise tomorrow either. His mind would be wandering to a place where things made sense. He had things to figure out, decipher, unravel. His dad sat in his chair, guarding the television, reading his newspaper, and groaning as if nothing around him mattered except current events and the injustices of the black man.

Vaughn was glad that his momma wasn't the pushy type that kept pressing him for information on where he was going. Sam. He said he was going to his brother Sam's. Sam was freshly divorced and spent a lot of time trying to fix things around his house and in it. Sounded like a well-thought-out alibi.

"Bye, Pop." Vaughn waved broadly, heading toward the door, lingering only for his father's response that he knew would come eventually.

His father peered over his reading glasses like a college professor grading midterms and nodded approvingly. He wanted to shake his dad sometimes. Participate, look alive, something. This was a different era. He needed to put all that black pride and those balled-up fists to better use, like on a shelf. Save them for someone who cared.

"Son, don't let the white man keep you down."

Vaughn brandished a fist now. His father hardly ever made sense . . . life didn't.

Vaughn eyed the second-, fifth-, and tenth-grade school pictures of himself that lined the wall. The same hard dented wall with the peeling floral wallpaper that his brother had convinced him was edible when he was seven. He hated that wallpaper, the wall, too. He remembered how Sam always used to tackle him into it. Then they'd get in trouble whenever a picture fell or a shoe left a circular scuff mark. Vaughn had always taken the rap.

"We are black men, we are not savages," his father would always say, taking one of them by the arm, speaking directly into his ear.

Vaughn straightened out the picture his momma had taken of him when he won the spelling bee in third grade. He was holding a ribbon in his hand, missing a tooth, and grinning sillily.

"Tell Sam for me that he can call his momma. It won't kill him, you know. I may not be around much longer, he'll be sorry then." She shook her head and pointed her finger before Vaughn hugged her tight and walked out the door with his head hanging low and his heart even heavier for having to lie.

He had to remember to call Sam and ask him to cover for him if anyone called or asked if he was there. Not lying really, just smoothing things over and keeping the peace. He did feel kind of guilty that he would be in Jersey and not visiting his brother. His only brother. They used to be kind of close until he married Brenda. She was the genius who'd moved him all the way out there to Jersey, when she knew that his entire family lived in the city.

She'd pursued him, bedded him, married him, and left him, in that order. Maybe Vaughn would make time to check up on his brother, he thought. Then he wouldn't have lied to momma or anybody else. But then again, Sam always had company. It was like a harem at his place. Women flocked to his brother, who looked both collegiate and athletic, with the physique of someone who could have been a lifeguard.

"Save my life, save my life," Troi's friend Carla had said on one too many occasions.

But he said he wouldn't get married again, and that he was content enjoying the fruits of the departure of his wife. Just dating was fine.

Vaughn stopped at the minimall strip right off the main road and walked past the video store that was tempting him to rent something. But he went into the corner deli as he always did and picked up a half pound of tuna salad, a six-pack of Pepsi, and the Jersey edition of the *Daily News*. He thought that maybe he should have rented a movie or something else he could lose himself in for the afternoon, but figured that he'd be better off just relaxing and watching the game. He wanted a stress-free day. No questions, and no pressure.

Today Vaughn noticed the trees. The trees surrounding the area were tall, sheltering, and reaching up with colorful foliage. Vaughn was inhaling the faint scent of burnt leaves. It made his nose tingle, almost burn. It always reminded him of Halloween, although they never celebrated it.

He remembered growing up in a house where going to church wasn't a question. It was as natural as going to school. They just did it. When he and Sam were eight and nine, they'd have kiddie church in the basement and most times they'd mock the adults dancing and shouting, putting napkins on their heads and jumping around until they fell off.

"Oh, hallelujah, glory, hallelujah," they'd say, stomping their feet and smacking around a tambourine. Sam as the preacher. He loved to play that part.

"Now, y'all know that Jesus is coming. I said, you know that Jesus is coming, look a' here . . ." Sam was a natural.

Those were the days that Vaughn enjoyed remembering about church and life. After he turned sixteen, his life, along with his feelings toward a lot of things, changed.

His momma kept pestering him back then. She wanted to know when he was gonna meet a good Christian girl, a clean girl. A girl who would submit to her wifely duties without complaining or go into the marriage already contemplating half. Vaughn had known a few girls and talked the panties off all of them. He realized that it was no reflection on them, people just did strange things for love. Sex being one.

But it was when he'd met Debbie that he'd known. They had been kickin' it for almost a month. Going steady, they called it. She was a cute little thing. Tall and tight. They had gone for a long walk with the evening sky playing chaperone. It had been three days before his eighteenth birthday, and they'd been sitting in the back of her momma's house under the awning, contemplating kissing and touching, which was almost enough back then. She had made a big deal about why he hadn't kissed her yet, and he had promised that tonight would be the night. It hadn't been spontaneous. It had been deliberate and planned, but he'd been game.

On that night their lips had drawn closer as their hands motioned and groped for any kind of physical contact that they could run back and tell their friends about. But he hadn't felt anything. She'd tried to coax him, tease him, excite him into submission, but he hadn't even known if he actually liked her. Friends had pushed them together because everybody had somebody and they hadn't know him to be dating anyone they knew. He'd assumed he did like her—he *was* sitting in the back of her momma's house. But it wasn't good to assume.

"Why you kissing me like that, Vaughn?" she'd said, forcing him away.

"Like what?" Vaughn had defended.

"Like it disgusts you to kiss me." She frowned.

"I-I-I'm sorry, it's just that . . ."

"Just that what?"

He'd reached for his baseball cap, feeling cold and strange.

"Maybe you should go." She'd stood with her arms folded and her lips twisted up until tomorrow. He knew he had injured her pride, and he was certain that it was Debbie who had started the rumor, although it didn't really matter now.

Vaughn looked around the streets curiously. Traffic was flowing onto the avenue. He saw an old man who was letting his big-footed dog walk him down the street on a blue leash, and approaching him was a mother and father holding the hands of their vibrant skipping kid. Vaughn wasn't new to this neighborhood, he was comfortable here. He knew where the closest mailbox was, and he knew the woman at the dry cleaners personally. He made a right onto the main street, went two blocks down and made another right, as he always did, and pulled into the parking spot for apartment 22.

Tracie had said it was urgent. Which didn't necessarily mean emergency. It was just an adjective that was descriptive, in that it said *no, not today* would not be an acceptable answer. From the cell phone Vaughn called up. The phone rang four times.

"I'm outside," he said to the voice that sounded out of breath but only responded, "Okay," in a low hush.

He preferred to be expected. He let out a long exaggerated sigh that was more relaxing than it was a sign of apprehension. He thought about his morning tryst and how he really wasn't in the mood now for Tracie's grandstanding. He didn't want to spoil their day, but this was becoming too demanding, he thought. He put his key in the building door and smiled at a woman who Tracie had introduced him to a few months earlier.

He didn't want to meet anybody. He had no desire to know these people. He didn't need familiar faces passing him in the city and his mind struggling to figure out which part of his life they were from. He was lost in his abyss of pleasure, and although he wanted to stay there, he also wanted to be what people expected him to be. Honest. Sincere. Faithful. He wasn't about to spoil that for the world, or his momma either. Not that people didn't make mistakes, but on the other hand, Tracie wasn't a literal mistake. It was natural. It felt that way. Even if it was wrong, he couldn't stop now. Vaughn was caught in a noose on a bridge that was crumbling. That was his equivalent of a rock and a hard place.

If someone had told him six months ago that he would be spending the day with someone who wasn't his wife, and diggin' every minute of it, he would have called them more than a liar. Troi. Talk. They needed to talk, he thought. He'd make every effort to be at the shop by nine as Troi had asked him to be. Made no sense adding fuel to the fire that was probably already simmering in her because he'd come in late last night. Although he figured she should be in a better mood after his performance this morning. He didn't want to beat himself up about it though.

There had to be some kind of way that he could explain what was happening here. Stolen moments. Encounters that he wasn't ashamed of, that had in fact become habit. He had what any man would want: an attractive woman who had goals, ambitions, and her own business, which still left her with time to be a mother and a good wife. *So, what's my problem?* he questioned.

Here he was sharing his mind with someone other than the person he had vowed before God to love and cherish until death did them part. The person with whom he had walked down the aisle and whom he had taken as she was given away by her father in the church where they both worshipped was not in his thoughts now.

He thought back to the day the bank had sent him to the main branch. Such a twist of fate. He had had no idea that a casual meeting would turn into something that needed to feel so permanent. Someone who heard what was unsaid and the uncertainty he felt without him having to verbalize it, and then accepted him as a whole package anyway. Over lunch they'd confessed to each other, "Something is missing."

It wasn't a premeditated statement. It had slipped out while they shared a tuna melt and fries. The coffee had been bland, but Vaughn still remembered the conversation word for word. "Come by my place, we can talk if you'd like," Tracie had propositioned. When he'd accepted that offer, little had he known it would take him someplace where the sheets were pulled off and he would be revealed for what he was.

In the newness of it all, he guessed he hadn't taken a moment to think long-term. He didn't know what he would tell Troi, if anything. He knew it felt right with Tracie. He couldn't leave his wife or baby. That wasn't one of his current options. But he did know that it was only a matter of time before there was some evidence that surfaced and showed him to be guilty.

A receipt, or a purchase on the charge card. He hadn't felt this much guilt since the blackout of '79, when he'd bolted out of the sporting goods store with several pair of sneakers dangling from their laces. He'd had to run for his life not to get caught, only to end up with several pairs of sneakers that were two sizes too big and none that had a match.

Life wasn't easy. When Vaughn looked at Troi, he was appreciative. Her eyes said she was faithful and her smile said she'd marry him all over again. He wished he could convey the same. The baby she had given him and the way she compromised and didn't mind doing the dishes or laundry for her man made him love her all the more. But was love enough to make him stay? He couldn't help it. He was caught up and his head was hurting from thinking so much. His mind wasn't talking, his body was, he was sure. He didn't want to fake his way through a marriage though. Satisfy his wife and desire another?

Although brothers liked to brag, they hardly had the stamina. And he didn't see the need to tear his family apart. In time he hoped this thing with Tracie would pass, wither, die. But for now it was a raging and consuming fire. He didn't want to think about leaving either one. He couldn't do it. If he left Troi, his momma would cry, but his dad would probably still be sitting in front of the television trying to read a newspaper and watch CNN, yelling that it was a conspiracy to keep us unemployed, pausing only to interject another militant outburst, but otherwise reacting as if nothing had happened. He didn't want to think about it now. He wanted to kick back and relax. No pressure from either end.

Tracie was 5' 11", a little on the light side, and stood at the door draped alluringly by a plush burgundy towel with a gold crest like the kind they lent you in posh Beverly Hills hotels. Tracie welcomed Vaughn with a warm smile, clutching the towel that inadvertently revealed more than it concealed. They hugged each other as if it had been years. It had been seven hours, to be exact. He had crept home at three in the morning, stripped down, put on his pajama pants, and slid into bed next to Troi. She hadn't questioned him, so she had no clue.

He had called in sick at the bank yesterday and spent all afternoon getting his fill of Tracie. Weekends hardly seemed enough anymore. He'd had to run a few errands yesterday morning, and hadn't wanted to go home afterward. He'd been feeling like that a lot lately.

He and Tracie were spending more and more time together. They were an item in some respects. Vaughn grinned and made his way into the apartment. With his lips, he backed Tracie away from the doorway, which was inconspicuous, but he wasn't taking any chances. Vaughn had become leery of their public displays of affection.

"I miss you," Vaughn said.

"Show me," Tracie murmured, and, as if timed for a director on cue, the towel that was draped so attractively fell to the floor, exposing Tracie's manhood.

Vaughn's breath quickened and he thought that it was moments like this that were always utterly unpredictable. In an instant, he was in the mood.

In the back of his mind he couldn't help but feel overwhelmed with guilt. Not just now, but his entire life. He was nursing wounds too hidden to notice and too deep to comprehend. He faked and tolerated his way through situations with women. He avoided playing football with his brother and his friends for fear that some urge that he was trying to suppress would arise and demand attention. The last thing that Vaughn needed was a distraction while holding a football.

He thought of all the women who had laid in his bed unaware and told him how they were attracted to him because he was so nurturing and sensitive. Women. They needed him, but he didn't necessarily need them. Not in the same way. He'd had to think long and hard of Tracie and the moments they'd shared to perform for his wife this morning. It made him feel as if he was holding her whole life hostage. His heart had tied her up and his actions set a roaring fire to her feet.

He tried to remember when it had started. It always went back to high school. He remembered vividly. He'd tried to stay out of the tales of conquests and bragging sessions that the guys went on and on about first thing Monday morning. They would talk about cars, money, and technology, but the conversation always came back around to women. He would say that he had dates, but no one that any of them knew. Always far enough upstate to disguise. The truth was that Debbie had almost shot his reputation. She'd thought he was gay because he hadn't wanted to kiss her. It could have been a million other reasons why he hadn't wanted to kiss her. Her breath, for one, her bushy eyebrows, too. But none of them would have been quite as accurate as the guess she'd made.

The first thing everyone would insinuate if they found out that he was gay was that he wasn't a man. Being gay didn't make him a woman. He was still a man. He always would be. His head was still bald and he still had to shave. He had to pee standing up and still had enough testosterone to pump up and flex those biceps while making his wife giddy enough to brag about him to her friends. It wasn't his fault that women did absolutely nothing for him. Their games didn't turn him on; their tricks didn't persuade him that he was straight. He didn't even like that stereotypical term, because technically he wasn't crooked.

Vaughn remembered spending the night with a close friend in high school. He'd been almost like a brother. His friend's mother had gotten a new job, they were moving out of state hundreds of mile away, and he had extended the usual weekend invitation to Vaughn. The night that they'd spent reminiscing had been emotional, cautious, but never physical.

Vaughn had stayed up all night and watched his friend sleep as the sun rose delicately in the background. Vaughn's leg had purposely brushed against his friend's all night, making contact with a world where he wasn't even sure he wanted to go. The next morning they'd woken to say good-bye forever. And Vaughn's undisclosed feelings had stood still stiff and pent-up inside him. They'd embraced after breakfast and cried, too, but not for the same reasons. Vaughn remembered not wanting to let go. He'd wanted to hold him in his arms forever. He remembered wanting to kiss him gently on the mouth. Vaughn had struggled with thoughts like that in college, too, but thoughts like those in a modern yet uncompliant society had left him terrified that he would spend the rest of his life labeled an outcast.

So Vaughn banished his thoughts of other men almost immediately, praying, rebuking, and focusing on his studies. He graduated only to move back home and pursue a career in banking. His momma convinced him that it was because he'd been away from the church so long that he was feeling so miserable and melancholy about life. How could he tell her the truth without breaking her heart? So he pretended that his feelings didn't exist. He had met lots of girls who were happy to be dating a college graduate, but none of them had even stirred a knee-deep interest in him, until he met Troi.

Silly of him to think that marriage would be the cure-all, although when he met Troi he'd been smitten. She was intelligent and sexy. Made him contemplate that he was bisexual. He'd meant no harm. But that was then. It was Tracie who kindled something like sparks in him now. It was Tracie who unleashed something that taught Vaughn it was okay to care this way and proper to feel what he was feeling. But his upbringing hadn't dictated that. His upbringing had told him that fire and brimstone were waiting for anyone who believed these thoughts were normal. He had seen the shame and ridicule projected at people who tried to sort these types of feelings out, and he couldn't help but think that a blind rabid dog got better treatment.

10

Nina reluctantly drove uptown through watermelon-sized potholes to pick up Shelby, who was decked out in an orange shantung silk bustier with matching capri pants, an orange and white polka dot scarf knotted around her neck and turned to the side, and big rectangular shaped frames resting on her head. Shelby spent the whole drive blowing her nails dry and gushing over a corny guy she had met last night at an A-list dinner party.

"You should have been there, Nina, there were two doctors, a lawyer, a promotion person from a music label, an advertising executive, an artist, two authors, and a psychic." She paused only to take a breath. "He told fortunes, girlfriend." She waved dramatically as if someone was about to kiss her hand. "'Girl,' he said, you vill meet somevun tonight that vill change your life,'" she mimicked in a dramatic Russian accent.

"You can't be serious, Shelby."

"Sure I am. I refuse to sit at home alone waiting. You can wait all you want. I deserve to be a little optimistic, you know, half full. I, unlike you, would like to have an idea of who I'm waiting for."

"You have seriously lost your mind, Shelby." Nina stepped on the gas. The faster she got Shelby to Shangrila, the faster she'd be out of Nina's hair and into somebody else's.

Shangrila was always crowded, Nina knew that. She always had to prepare herself mentally two days before venturing up to Harlem. Finding a parking space and having African women trying to snatch her into those little hole-in-the-wall shops to braid her hair so tight it pulled out her follicles was tiring. She couldn't believe that there was that much hair up in Harlem. It didn't really matter one way or the other, because Nina and Shelby never had to wait when they went there. But she just didn't do crowds. It was the principle. People made her feel claustrophobic. It wasn't her thing.

There was a mixed class of people who visited the salon, which was impressive, even if Mother wasn't remotely moved by it. A room full of women. They all had hair, and their sole purpose was to get it done. There were patrons wearing gold sandals with toes painted in even more glittery hues, straw hats that were reminiscent of the Caribbean shores, bags full of hair rollers, schoolgirl knapsacks, bags from Saks and Pier 1 Import. There was one woman who looked like she didn't want to be anywhere near Harlem or the dirty little ghetto hoodrats. She sat in the chair as stiff as a sardine in oil, as if she didn't want that ebonics and other slang rubbing off on her or a broken crack vial getting stuck to her Ferragamo shoes.

No matter where you went, there was division. Even up in Shangrila. Each group sat as if in their own world. Imaginary class lines. Some had headsets with music that was too loud while reading books by Donald Goines and chewing big wads of artificially flavored gum that they'd crack and pop annoyingly through their teeth. Others preferred to read only what the *New York Times* said was a bestseller, check their appointments periodically in their electronic organizers, and inquire about where the best eateries were in the immediate vicinity.

Some didn't feel that they should have to succumb to the societal pressures of reading, because every effort was made to keep our ancestors from learning to read. So they were illiterate by protest. The thing that they all had in common was the black conditioner stacked behind the register. The women swore by that stuff. It was all over the place. In boxes, on the floor, in the display cabinet, and stacked in a pyramid on the glass countertop.

"Hey, Troi." Nina waved frantically.

Troi had on an army-green T-shirt that said BABY PHAT, snug-fitting jeans, and multicolored flip-flops.

"What's up, Nina? I'm running around like a chicken," Troi said, trying to carry a carton of relaxer to the front display cabinet. "One of the girls had an emergency, and you know Saturday is my busiest day. I could lay hands on her," Troi grunted, balancing the carton.

"Hi, Troi," Shelby sang.

"Hey, Shelby, how ya doing?"

"I'm in love, child . . ."

"Please don't get her started, she's always in love." Nina waved her hand, dismissing her.

"Who's the lucky guy, Shelby?" Troi humored her.

"Ooo, girl, I met him last night . . ."

Nina wandered around the shop, mostly to ignore Shelby, but also to inspect what Mother labeled Troi's urban jungle. You would think Mother wasn't proud.

"Troi sure loves herself some Harlem," Mother always said, shaking her head as if the girl was doing hair on the sidewalk in an old kitchen chair. It paid the bills. You'd figure that's all she'd be pressed about.

It was warmer than it should've been for April, but the shop wasn't stuffy. There were hanging plants, all green and thriving, resting on glass shelves that were connected to the wall. The fan was on, the air conditioner buzzed on low, and Najee was playing on the radio now. There was a sign done in calligraphy that was framed in gold that said, JESUS SAVES. Troi loved calligraphy and Jesus. There was a palm leaf woven into a cross that was attached to the mirror, and a picture to the left of black women in all shades with hair color that varied from cranberry to yellow. Nina was impressed with what Troi had done.

Troi had finally ordered the aromatherapy products as Nina suggested. She felt trusted when her sister took her advice. Cute cobalt-blue bottles with aromatic scents lined the shelves and made the shop look more upscale. Maybe she'd give in and sell candles, too, Nina thought. Loud hysterical outbursts of laughter echoed from the front of the salon. Nina turned to observe the hee-haw cackling and words that shouldn't even be used in the presence of decent people, let alone children.

A woman with yellow nails, which were long and uncoordinated, went on without shame about how she'd made her man beg last night, and then she'd told her man that if he didn't pay the rent, she would put all his things in storage and move in with her sister.

"Girl, for real? So, what did he do?"

"He paid the rent, what you think?" The woman snickered. "Train 'em, I'm telling you, you gotta train 'em," she told her. "He had the nerve to say 'Boo, why you gonna do me like this?' " she told the woman in her best baritone imitation.

"What you say?"

"I told him, 'Because I love you, baby, I'm making you a man.'"

"Girl, stop!"

"I'm not playing, you know me." She sat with her bright-red glossy lips twisted up and her hands self-consciously covering her bulging belly.

"You too much, girl."

"Well, what I say goes, and that's it, period," she said, licking her fingertip and making an imaginary period in the air.

Shelby was bending Troi's ear about this new beau of hers, and all Nina could think was, *I'm glad it's not me*. He could belong to anybody. She had only met him less than twelve hours ago, and here she was, in her mind moaning and groaning from the sex they hadn't even had yet. She always fell so quickly. Nina thought about how ridiculous Shelby looked in orange. She thought about how she wished that she was rich and didn't have to work anymore. Maybe she'd go to school just for fun, like Shelby had. Use a book for a coaster. Maybe she'd wear orange.

In the mirror Nina observed the slight darkening under her eyes. They were a little puffy, and she looked like she could use at least a makeover. Nina spent entirely too much time sitting up at night dwelling on a life that was going on without her. She always figured that pondering "what if" was better than nothing. The fear, it vanished, but nothing changed fate. She didn't want to sound like those women obsessed with having a man, but she needed to be lying next to someone who would sing her to sleep. Even if it was off-key. She must have been dreaming.

You didn't necessarily have to sleep to dream though, and she knew that all too well. Nina loved escaping into literature. For now it satisfied her dream quotient. Her belt was digging into her waist. It was too tight. She undid the buckle and loosened it over about three holes. She felt like a sausage in her jeans. She was hungry again. She wondered if she could get a fried fish sandwich and some fries over near 125th Street. Nina only managed to think about food when she was bored.

Troi wrapped Shelby's dripping hair in a thirsty green towel that matched the awning out front, and sat her down in the pink fancy salon chair. Nina thought that if Troi could sell something like fish and chips in this diva of a salon, then customers wouldn't mind waiting so long. But the nauseating smell shampoos, relaxers, and fish grease conjured in her mind made her rush right into the little toilet stall her sister called a bathroom and confiscate a wad of light green tissue.

"So, do you want to go, Troi?"

"Girl, please, you know I don't party, that's not my style."

"It's a country club, c'mon," Shelby insisted.

"I have choir rehearsal early in the morning, darling, and I ain't missing that for nobody."

"Nina, are you going to the club?"

"I don't know, I just want to crash. I can't stand the snobbery."

"Snobbery? Please, you're always by yourself, gimme a break. Get your hair done and let's go to the club," Shelby demanded.

Troi rolled Shelby's hair, pinning each curl in place, tied on the hair net, put her under the dryer, and motioned for her next customer.

"Nina, just let me wrap her hair, please. I'll do you next, I promise," Troi pleaded, trying to move the crowd of happy-go-lucky hair divas along.

Nina observed Shelby sitting fidgeting under the dryer, which Nina hoped was burning her ears and drying out her forehead. She'd already lost half her mind, so it might as well shrivel up what little bit was left. Besides, it was Nina's own business if she wanted to stay home rather than meet a horny Russian guy at a neighborhood snortfest. Shelby waved Nina over. Nina tried to pretend she was staring at something else, but Shelby started yelling. Typical.

"Ninaaa!"

Shelby had caught Nina like a mouse with his teeth still in the cheese.

"So, guess which one he is, girl." She twitched most excitedly under the hood.

"Lower your voice, Shelby." Nina folded her arms. "He who?" She frowned, trying to slow her down.

"Guess which guy it was that I hit it off with last night."

Nina didn't have a clue, but she guessed correctly that it was the starving artist. It was something about the desperation of being an artist that she was sure would've attracted Shelby. Shelby nodded.

"How you know?" She grinned just as she had when she'd gotten her new town house off campus.

She felt special. He was her new toy and, as any friend would, Shelby wanted Nina to find someone to play with, too.

"You'll meet someone at the country club, Nina."

"Shelby, please, I'm not going."

"You've gotta go, destiny awaits."

"Listen, destiny knows where to find me if he's looking."

"Okay, well, answer me this. Have you ever heard that artists make the best lovers? I guess it's because they've mastered their paintbrush, right?"

"Spare me, Shelby."

"It's true, Nina," Shelby whispered and grinned like a little girl who'd let a boy lick her ice-cream cone.

"On the first date?"

Shelby mustered a throaty chuckle and threw her head back so hard it shut off the hairdryer.

"Shelby, you're one sick chick, and nasty, too!"

"Don't judge," Shelby said with her finger in the air, reminding Nina of those quiet posters in the old hospitals, where the nurse had her finger pressed to her lips so you wouldn't make noise.

"Don't judge you? Listen, don't worry about me judging you. You better get a job so you can get some health insurance."

"What are you trying to say?"

"I'm not trying, I said it. You probably didn't even use a condom, did you?"

"What's your point?" Shelby fiddled with the dryer hood.

"The point is, I can't believe that people still have sex without condoms, or sex period. You know better."

"Shhhh," Shelby said, having the nerve to be embarrassed now. "But, Nina, he's an artist, and his paintings sell for thousands, girl." Shelby widened her eyes.

"You just don't get it, honey. Daddy's money can't save you."

Troi walked by and flipped the button on the hairdryer. "Yeah, only Jesus can!"

They had all gotten a good laugh at Shelby's expense.

Troi guided her sister to the sink, washed, conditioned, and relocated her to the pink salon chair closest to the back of the shop so she could blow out her hair and they could gab about how Mother hadn't changed and Daddy was still evading issues.

"How's Mother, Troi?"

"She's fine, I guess. I haven't spoken to her in a couple of days," she said over the hum of the blowdryer.

"I'm starving, sis. What you got up in here?"

"Nothing." Troi laughed. "I thought you were on a diet anyway?"

"Not really," Nina said, lowering her head.

Troi neatly divided and twisted Nina's hair a few strands at a time back into a bun while the two robust women still went on about how her man better check himself.

"How's Daddy?"

"He's fine. I'm trying to get him to have lunch or something, but he's been so consumed with the business."

"Is business still slow?"

"Yes, still slow, he can't find reliable help."

"I know how that is," Troi said, thinking back to this morning when Sofie had called in sick.

"How's Vaughn?"

"He's good." Troi blushed.

"And my niece?"

"She's still trying to be independent. You know, got that Madison blood in her."

"You know she does. Got it innocently, too."

"And what about you, Nina? You still hanging on, huh?"

"Listen, I ain't going nowhere. I'm working, got my little brownie in Brooklyn. Unless, of course, Shelby drives me crazy. She's gonna drive us both to drink," Nina kidded.

"Is there a man in the city she hasn't dated?"

Troi said sheepishly, "I understand that single women want sex. I know about wanting, but these times are different. You can't go pulling down every pair of Hilfigers you see. Something might come crawling out of 'em one day."

"Ewwwww, you nasty, Troi."

"I'm serious."

"Well, you know that something could come clapping out of some married drawers, too." Nina giggled.

"Not mine, but I get you, just not mine," Troi said seriously.

Troi patted Nina's hair. "Okay, I'm done. Do you like it?" She spun Nina around and gave her the big round mirror so she could observe what was going on in the back.

"Yeah, it looks good," Nina said, staring into the mirror and touching her hair, hating that her sister always gave her those young-girl styles.

"Just tie it down tight at night so it doesn't frizz up."

"How long is this gonna last?"

"About a week, two if you're really good and don't sleep too wild."

Nina folded up three twenty-dollar bills and pressed them into Troi's back pocket. Troi motioned for Shelby to come on over, and Shelby click-clacked across the floor like a duck trying to balance the oversized tote on her lap and the extra large rollers on her head.

Nina unbuttoned the top two buttons on her silk blouse, which felt so wonderful against her skin and especially her shoulders. She thanked God that she didn't have the constant urge to prove that she was exciting and fun to be around. She had an opinion about everything and did tend to whine, but Shelby and the girls still enjoyed her company just the same. They thought she was real and down-to-earth, whatever that meant. She had convinced herself that normal was a myth. They teased her and called her a virgin, in the drinking and drugging sense, as if drinking were a prerequisite to having fun. They nagged her, saying, "One drink won't kill you, just have a sip."

Although it was exactly one drink on a Friday night almost twenty years ago that had her sitting here wishing she was really pure and virginal again.

Full of wine, like holiday fruits soaking for black cake, she had given in to some chipped-tooth fly guy in high school. With her lips pressed firmly against her clenched teeth, a putrid smile had suppressed the bile that rose in her throat. He'd been trying to get another notch, while Nina had grasped aimlessly for comfort in a world that constantly rejected her. She had spent two whole years trying to get his attention, anybody's attention. And when she finally had arrested him, he'd found her worthy only of the backseat of his father's beat-up burgundy Cadillac, with her skirt crumpled around her waist, sipping on a warm wine cooler at ten P.M. on a school night.

She'd tried to prolong the experience like an ice-cream cone you ate slowly although it dripped. She'd wanted to cuddle and feel the warmth of arms that might not want her tomorrow but sufficed today. She'd wanted what all the other girls claimed to have gotten from guys they labeled their boyfriends. She'd wanted to feel more than just the pain of rejection, the shudder of disrespect, and the pointing finger of mockery. After their tussle in the backseat of his father's car, she'd known it was over when loverboy mumbled something about how he'd call, but he never did.

She ached to hear something. Any explanation at all would have soothed her. He had used her like a slimy dishrag and left her hanging to dry. She'd felt like a flower that was fragrant and ripe until he had come and plucked the petals off and left her wilted in the breeze. She could never give another soul the gift she had given him. Unworthy little devil that he was.

He'd ignored her in school, pretending she was invisible unless he was making fun of her hand-me-down clothes right along with everyone else. He'd teased her mostly to avoid the shame, Nina had found out later. He had told everybody about what she'd done in the backseat of the car, and she'd thought he was bragging until she'd overheard several people indiscreetly whispering and giggling in homeroom about how he'd done it with the fat girl.

Boys that young had no sense of loyalty. A tongue unwise enough to bite the breast that fed it. They said what they had to say to get over and then they moved on. It wasn't until she was an adult that she realized grown men with careers and bank accounts acted the same way, too. No loyalty.

Nina had gone on to become the valedictorian of her high-school graduating class, had made her speech from the podium, and never saw any of those self-absorbed fashion victims again. She'd never quite fit in high school. With her mouth she said it didn't bother her, but it did, deep down inside, where she was alone with her thoughts. It especially bothered her since Troi didn't seem to have any problem at all making friends and drawing the attention of the boys. The cute ones. Nina pretended that it was just because she was not cheerleader material that the boys had ignored her. She wasn't fully convinced.

Nina remembered back to when the girls had been trying to see who was the most popular and had dressed alike in matching angora sweaters and Lees with permanent creases. She'd sit at home alone reading, watching international news and culture and snacking on marshmallows, Vienna sausages, and potted-meat sandwiches. She didn't need school. She hated the fact that the teachers spewed their opinions at you and made you eat them like a mouthful of spinach they demanded was good for you, while you gagged and mentally hurled obscenities at being force-fed. They didn't know much themselves, if you really thought about it. All you had to do was memorize their bogus facts long enough to get promoted to the next grade, then surrender it like a sponge that was squeezed out for the next load of dishes.

Nevertheless, Nina had gone to school everyday and gotten good grades. But the capital A's had been more for herself than a submission to her mother's demands. She'd known that if she got acceptable grades she could get out. She could go away to college, move onto a campus, and be out from under her mother's hairy thumb and the pathetic house of cards that always came tumbling down the moment the blinds were pulled and the front door was closed. Life had never given Nina what she expected, so it was for that reason and that reason alone that she thumbed her nose at it.

Nina didn't know why she'd agreed to go along with Shelby. Shelby could talk a horse out of his shoes and into ice skates. Nina felt displaced at the country club. She felt like furniture that didn't quite go with the color scheme. It was light and airy, but she didn't match the citronella candle stakes that lined the greens, the slight hum of the automatic bug zapper, or the white wooden folding chairs that pressed into the grass ever so gently. There was a casino with flashing lights summoning you to empty your pockets on a whim, but Nina didn't gamble, it was against what little religion she had left.

The lawn was brightly lit and drinks were floating by on balanced hands. She took one and hoped it wasn't something too strong. She nodded her head to the peculiar music and watched Shelby acting seditty. A tall Caucasian guy who mistook Shelby for white sat and offered borderline conversation. Nina smiled, got up, and walked away from the whole scene.

She noticed from afar the silver spoon that made contact with the nostrils of the couple sitting behind the pool house and how they took such regal delight in it. She knew she was in the wrong place. This couldn't be what being rich was all about. But then, she figured, statistically speaking it wasn't us that the drug kingpins supplied anyway. Just more evidence of the miseducation of not only Lauryn Hill but all of us. Rich. After they'd bought two of everything in the world, Nina assumed that they just snorted some drugs to heighten the whole experience.

Nina was pacing now. She was ready to go. She had been ready when she'd arrived. She folded her arms and admitted it to herself. She was just stalling until Shelby had enjoyed herself enough to be ready to go home, too. Nina was wearing a silk blouse over a floral dress that was summery, feminine, and inviting. She looked like something out of a seedy romance novel, but she wasn't as interested in finding romance as she was a good book or a Marsalis tune. It was getting dark. She checked her watch several times and thought of all the things she could be eating. She walked over to where the couple near the stable were high on more than intellectual conversation.

"Wanna ride?"

Nina turned and looked at the dusty figure.

"No," she said.

He smiled and shied away at her initial response.

"You sure?"

"I don't even know you."

"I'm sorry for being rude. My name is Derek, and yours?"

"Yes, that was rude." She paused. "I'm Nina," she said, extending her hand, taking two steps forward, then one step back.

Nina observed Shelby, who was consumed with the man of the moment. She was tossing her hair, flashing her newly bleached teeth, and sinking her claws into this unsuspecting man. She hadn't even noticed that Nina was gone. If this man kidnapped Nina, tied her up, and put the toe tag on himself, Shelby wouldn't have a clue. She was *parlez vous*-ing on cloud nine.

And Nina didn't know what this stable boy here wanted, but she was not going to entertain stupidity. She could envision a dozen ways to warm her bed if an unrelenting chill came on an April night other than to fill it with a sex-starved player. There was nothing attractive about a gaudy man who always appeared to be sweating and never left home without his red silk shirt, big clunky gold-nugget rings, and so many gold chains that they got tangled in his chest hair. A man who snagged her sheets with the jagged edges of his toenails was equally uninviting.

Nina wasn't choosy, and she wasn't antihomeboy either. She could swing with a brother who could fit in anywhere, a chameleon, someone versatile. She didn't want shiny and bourgeois. She couldn't do anything with a man who was so high, mighty, and decorated with etiquette that he'd try to reserve orchestra seats in heaven. She just wanted cultured and personable. She underestimated how difficult that could be to obtain. But the Lone Ranger here was pushing his luck. She wasn't Tonto.

Her life was full of theater, art, and social issues like homelessness to notice. Except on nights like this, where the wind told stories and convinced you that tonight was your night for romance. The wind lied. She eyed this Derek character from his boots to his eyebrows. She'd admit Derek wasn't all that bad, if fate would stop tempting her. He had shared that he was more self-educated than formally. It didn't bother her. College men were overrated.

Nina was making him over in her mind. All he needed was a nineties style and he'd be good to go. She observed the worn blue jeans and his scruffy fingernails, which weren't as neatly manicured as she was used to. He wasn't extremely attractive, but his body made up for that. He was muscular, not to mention alive and breathing. She figured that she could use a little mental exercise. She imagined what she could teach him and the kinds of things she could expose him to. She brushed off the thought that there was something strange about Derek. She was always jumping to conclusions.

11

The street wasn't as peaceful as it should have been at six A.M., and the sounds that he rose early to avoid were annoying him. Garbage trucks and soiled garbagemen tossing aluminum cans haphazardly to the concrete. A yapping dog small enough to be a cat, and the quiet laughter of two voices that must have just ventured home from last night after spending themselves on each other. He frowned because he couldn't concentrate. The air was heavy and a noisy car blared by, thumping some loud uncoordinated rap tune. Tim was, however, thankful for the occasional breeze. It was the type of weather that prompted him to sleep in the nude. He rubbed his hand across the stubble on his head and his bare chest.

He needed a haircut and a shave, breakfast, too. He sat at the table he used to designate the dining area wearing red plaid boxers, scratching himself now and then and reading ads in *Backstage*. He liked to keep up on the buzz in LA and New York. He browsed through the callboards to see who was working on projects similar to his and what types of funding they had available in the grants section. Anything would do, really.

Company seeks plays, writer-performers seeking movie scripts, 16mm shorts, nonunion, send resume.

He circled a few. He figured that his options were limited, and time was, too. He'd probably have to end up as a model, hoping to get recognition as something that would pay the bills if no finances made themselves available for him to fund his own films in the near future—near future meaning three to six months. He was bordering on starvation financially and didn't dare ask his sister for another loan that he knew he couldn't pay back this year.

He was definitely going to send out his writing résumé and a few treatments today. He had to stop procrastinating. "Procrastination is the art of keeping up with yesterday," he recited out loud. He needed to have money to live on today. And there was so much of it floating around out there. He just had to acquire the knowledge to access it. He was tiring of living in such a cramped space, and he'd like to travel back home to Belize one day. Get a little sun, some real culture. When the stew of life simmered, it all boiled down to the fact that he wanted to be comfortable financially. Being comfortable would afford him the time to be leisurely about his writing. Then he could write because he wanted to, not because he needed to do so to live.

He interrupted his own thoughts, reminding himself to run by the post office to get the necessary envelopes and stamps, and check his post office box. He would make a commitment to send off one of his works to at least four companies he had circled in *Backstage* and two he had seen in Scr(I)pt. He thought seriously about acting, too, part-time. Maybe a gig as an extra or a nonspeaking part in a low-budget college project. A commercial. The lunch and carfare alone would come in handy on some days. But he debated the fact that it might take away from his creative ability. Then again, he really needed the money. It all came down to money. It shouldn't have, but it always did.

The nippy spring wind was blowing through his studio now. The trees outside were waving honey and cranberry leaves. *Hello*, they were saying to flings and possibilities. The African violet his sister had given him as a housewarming gift blew off the windowsill, spilling its soil all over the floor. The papers piled so deliberately on the table were flipping off onto the floor and around the room like a madman in his tails directing an orchestra. Tim weighted them down with a glass half full of orange juice. The skies clouded up and gray hungry masses wafted across the sky, consuming the sun. He watched the sky as if it were a motion picture.

Every scene morphed into the next. Each frame the only thing in existence until the next one was clearly in focus. The glare of light through his curtains, which had been there since the sun had risen this morning, now was gone. The sound of rain tinkled down from heaven. It sounded like the static of an overplayed record. Tap-dancing ants. The rain was soothing and cool; the memories weren't. He wondered how long he could repress the distasteful thoughts. He tried to think about anything else but the past.

He tried to think about how he wasn't looking forward to dinner with a stranger, but the other alternative was listening to Sharon trying to convince him all night that they should move in together. He chose the lesser evil. He refused to get any deeper with Sharon than he already was. He contemplated breaking her heart. She would label it that, but men didn't want to be smothered. Tim went for the number that was tacked onto his bulletin board.

He dialed the number that Rochelle had given him and remembered that she had asked him to "please be nice." He still wasn't sure about a blind date. He debated whether or not to call this woman at work and possibly interrupt her doing her job. But when she answered she sounded pleasant, and Rochelle had called her to let her know that he was her brother and that he was hardworking and open-minded. He was able to forgo the small talk.

"Indian is fine," she said, sounding as new to this blind-date game as he was. She worked in the city.

"I'll meet you at seven?" he cued.

Tim had nixed his initial thought about people who placed personal ads. They weren't for those who couldn't get a date, but rather for those who led busy lives, which made him instantly eligible. Some people, he agreed, had no time to case the bars for potential mates. He thought that Rochelle was right: He needed somebody. Momma would be proud. She wanted grandchildren to bake ginger cookies for. She wanted family vacations at the Grand Canyon, which Tim was sure would lead to someone getting arrested for throwing rocks just to see how far they fell and if you could hear them when they landed at the bottom. People, he knew, always liked to push their luck. Momma loved the holidays. Snowball fights, Christmas Eve eggnog, and carols by the fire.

He remembered so many times when his fingers would be almost numb and Momma would bring hot chocolate down to the kids who played with him and Rochelle in the snow. Momma would always get in one good lick while everyone was warming their hands around a mug and licking melted marshmallows off their top lips. Momma had good aim.

But that was then. Reminiscing was gruesome. It had been almost five years ago when Tim and Rochelle had gotten the news of the accident. He'd been only twenty-three, Rochelle had been thirty and a just-married should-be-blushing bride. Momma and Dad had been driving home from a leadership convention in Buffalo one November evening. It had been raining heavily, and the roads had been slick and icy. Black ice. They'd been driving at a moderate speed; the torrential rain had beaten down on the windshield, blinding Dad's vision temporarily. He'd always been such a careful driver, but it only took a moment to change their lives forever.

The car had skidded off the road, the brakes had locked, and they had hit the dividing rail. Their car had flipped over the highway divider and landed smack in the center of northbound traffic. The compact car had been struck by an oncoming minivan. Crushed into a metallic heap. It had only been recognized by the license plate and the color of the now-demolished vehicle. They had both been wearing seat belts, but it was Tim's life that was mangled now, and his parents' lives that were erased forever.

Tim had been angry with God for years. Had raised more than a fist to heaven. How could a good God allow death to overshadow all that his parents had done? There were murderers, child molesters, and thieves out there. Why couldn't God have taken one of them? For five years he'd wrestled with the thought of why bad things happened to good people. It was the proverbial question. Rochelle had assured him that Momma would be more proud of him if he left the drinking and drugs alone.

"Those friends of yours are dragging you down, Tim."

"Yeah, but they're my friends!"

"Real friends wouldn't let you do that to yourself."

"What am I supposed to do, huh? What am I supposed to do?" Tim had asked foolishly.

"In my mind I'd rather see Momma and Dad in heaven, painless, than lying in a hospital bed a vegetable, how about you?"

"Whatever, Rochelle." Tim had shrugged. He was an orphan, just like Annie. He couldn't help but think that.

"We can't understand God, Tim. We can only allow His will to be done in our lives." Tim had refused to take the time to refute this. So, he'd made like a duck and let all of the fine-tuned words of wisdom roll off of his back.

God, God, God. Tim thought that was a lot of mumbo jumbo and proof texting. He didn't want to hear how God's plan was to make him stronger, he wanted his parents. Warm oatmeal and hot cocoa. He needed his parents and their advice, which was administered with kindness and compassion. These were the crucial years of his life. He had held his mother and father in such high regard. They were moral people. If parenting needed something to define it, they were it. He'd always loved the way his momma folded his sweaters and placed them neatly in his dresser. He'd always known where things were when she was done. His clothes had smelled clean and felt soft. Everything his momma had done was done with care, and you could photograph the enjoyment of it all on her face.

Tim would secretly like when his momma would insist that he wear a hat and gloves the day the temperature dipped below forty degrees. She'd grin, convincing him to come on over and let her put his sweater on, even though he was thirteen and it was only October. He'd insist that his friends weren't wearing sweaters or jackets yet. He had nobody to tell him that now. He'd walk down the street with traces of the on-again off-again weather blowing down the back of his neck and nobody to tell him to zip up his jacket as he shook his head no. He was rebellious anyhow.

As the older sister, Rochelle assumed her position and frequently insisted that Tim attend church. It was never a question of "would you like to come to a service?" He had to go. She wasn't being bossy, it was more because she didn't know how else to help him.

"Go to church for what?"

"Because it's good for you." She would sound just like Momma trying to get him to take some nasty-tasting medicine.

He was already feeling alienated from society after the death of his parents, so he went along with Rochelle's plan that God could solve everything. He slept through most of the services and smiled at the neighbor he was directed to turn to when he was awake. He'd nod and repeat, "Devil, you can't steal my joy." But he did steal it, it was gone. He had lost the two most deserving parents on earth. He'd ride out the theory about God for a while because he didn't want to lose the only person in his life that he had left, Rochelle. But he wasn't making any promises. No promises.

Rochelle and Carl were good to Tim. He figured he could at least admit that. And he did. Rochelle would come over regularly and help him cook up something other than chicken fried in re-used grease and clean up the dilapidated room he was staying in at the time. It smelled like mildew and had dingy green walls that he guessed hadn't been painted in over a century. It made him itch thinking about it now.

Carl loved Rochelle. Tim was pleased that someone loved his sister. Carl had been around for years and was more than helpful. It was Carl who'd tried to find Tim another apartment and a job. He loved Tim like a brother. Carl had known their family for five years before he married Rochelle. They had all gotten along well enough for their father to grant Carl their blessings, and Dad, in his old-fashioned manner, had nodded as Carl had asked for Rochelle's hand in marriage.

"You can stay with us for as long as you need to, man," Carl had offered after the death of Tim's parents.

"I can't do that, man, it's too humiliating. I don't want my sister and her husband taking care of me." Tim had gazed at the wall, then the floor.

"But it's not like that at all, you know that," he'd attempted, to no avail.

"I have to stand on my own," Tim had defended, although Carl had managed to help get Tim a job as a clerk in a video store and then encouraged him to pursue his dream, be it filmmaking or whatever.

"Just do something, man, you know your sister worries about you."

"Yeah, I know, I need to get myself together." He'd nodded.

And Tim had been working diligently for several months until that crazy girl Estella had slithered onto the scene in a nightmare dream sequence. In hindsight, she'd been more a motivation than a distraction. She'd forced him to get up and do better. He had managed to scrape together every extra dime he had made stocking, labeling, and alphabetizing the videos. His mood had been for the most part melancholy during that period of his life, and women had just sort of taken his mind off of things long enough for him to realize that he was still alive and that in life he could do more than eat and sleep.

Tim had moved into a studio apartment in Harlem, cut loose the leech that had found herself helplessly attached to him, and moved on. He had saved up enough for a few months' rent. Three, to be exact. The reality of it was that he couldn't share a bathroom in a rooming house with other men who were at various levels of hygiene awareness for a moment longer. Nobody had cleaned, washed, scrubbed, or known any uses for disinfectant or a sponge.

The last thing he'd wanted was athlete's foot or an antibiotic-resistant fungus. He didn't even play sports much. He couldn't grasp how people made up in their minds to live like that indefinitely with no immediate goal in sight or a hint of one in the distant future. He'd been tired of feeling sorry for himself. Tired of hearing himself say what he was gonna do. He'd been tired of his soap being used up. He'd been tired of funky smells and the flies grazing the dishes in the kitchenette. So he'd moved.

He had some space that was his now, every inch. He'd furnished his studio space with easily assembled furniture until he could get something better. For now he had a futon and a small dining table with two chairs. He had made a silent promise to himself and his mother that he would make something of himself or die trying. There was more to life than getting green at the gills and crashing on Justin's love seat every Friday night, only to wake with some sticky woman stuttering and telling you she had a slammin' time and asking you what you were doing same time next weekend.

Tim tried to purify himself by washing the lingering scents of the past out of his mind. He focused on the darkening sky, which normally preceded a thunderstorm. Outside of his window the clouds were still smothering the sun. The wind was a tad warmer now and blew feverishly, shoving his drapes inside. The heavy drops of rain had started off modestly, then increased to such a degree that innocent bystanders could drown waiting for the bus. It was constant, steady, flushing the early birds and noisemakers out of the streets and off the sidewalks. He thought that maybe this would give him an excuse to cancel his blind date.

Women didn't like to get dressed up to go out in the rain. A lump of sugar is what they thought they were, dissolving to sweeten the melting pot of the city. He had heard Rochelle complain about it often enough. Rain messed up their suede shoes and made their hair kink.

He didn't know what he was afraid of. Maybe he was afraid of finding someone for whom he just sort of settled. He never wanted to get married unless he felt that he could care for the woman forever. She had to be a very special creature, he thought. Something like his momma. She had to have levels.

Thunder grumbled in the sky like a bag of microwave popcorn doing its Friday-night movie thing. He could feel the trembling in his chest when the thunder struck. He saw the lightning part the sky and counted one . . . two . . . three. Three miles away. He lowered the window and watched the raindrops run down the windowpane and off the side of the building, pouring off the fire escape. Helpless but happy, each drop connecting to the next drop until it was too much to contain. It trickled down. He saw the lightning invade the sky again with more force than the previous intrusion, and he took a breath and counted again. One . . . two . . . three . . . four. The storm was leaving. He hoped it would take the rain a while to dry up. He loved the freshness this sort of drenching left behind.

Tim thought back to when he was a child and his momma told him that raindrops were the tears of God. He hadn't believed it then and dared not believe it now. With all the crime and waywardness on this earth, God would have to be crying all the time. From the window Tim saw a tall man in a blue sweatshirt running with packages that were soaking wet. Tim broke his gaze and rationalized to himself that he really didn't have the time to mail anything today. Especially not in the rain. He figured sending out the manuscripts could wait another day or two, maybe even a week. He didn't want the ink to run or the pages to get stuck together, smudging, marring the documents. He wasn't going to let a watercolor mess be a representation of him. After all, the two bits of money he had he needed for dinner tonight. He didn't necessarily want to impress this woman, but he didn't want her to think he couldn't hang.

He wore a brown crushed velvet shirt and matching shoes, with steam-pressed black gabardine pants. Tim hoped that she'd wear a neutral color so that she didn't clash with him. "And please, Lord, no weave." He didn't like gluey, knotty hair or the false sense of beauty it gave. And he cared less for those ugly tiny platinum curly things. Everyone wanted to be somebody else. Men wanted women who were headstrong and independent enough not to go chasing fads. Keep it real, baby.

Tim's friends often told him that he could probably have any woman he wanted. People never really understood what an undertaking in itself that was.

Because he could have any woman, it drew all kinds, like annoying flies to the dung pile. He got women with missing teeth, women with too many teeth, chunky king-size girls, anorexic girls, girls with no jobs, girls with platinum cards, girls who couldn't read, girls who believed they were what they read, and a mix of everything in between. Single or married, it didn't matter to them. He had never considered dating a married woman though, because he couldn't respect a woman who didn't respect her vows. It was that simple . . . he wasn't desperate.

"Fawn?"

"Tim?"

"Hey, good evening . . ." He balanced his umbrella and reached for her hand, trying not to overdo it on the flattery or first impression but to make a good statement nevertheless.

"Were you waiting long?"

"I just got here . . . just got here," she said, wearing a flimsy brown suit with a beige lace top peeking out from underneath, black shoes worn one too many times, a print shawl, and a fragrance that he couldn't identify. That was her calling card. Her hair looked stiff but neat. He couldn't keep up with hairstyles, but he figured it was a product of her creative genius, whatever she decided to call it.

If she was anything like him, she'd probably had to toss to see if it was heads her hair or tails her nails that got done for this date. Must have been tails. Her legs were long but not too skinny. He didn't like skinny or hairy legs. Her nails were done in a neutral color and he nodded, thinking that he really enjoyed a color-coordinated woman. He was also proud of himself for being prompt. "People have better things to do than sit around waiting for you to show up," his momma had always reminded him.

Meeting near the restaurant was a good idea. It was a central location for both of them, and he joked to himself that he could make a run for it if he got cold feet. If she wasn't appealing from afar, he could stare into the restaurant window and pretend he was window-shopping or reading the lunch menu. The rain had dissipated, but there were still puddles on the sidewalks that yelled *splash in me*. They stood, chilly, under a green awning, making small talk and eyeing colored coffee mugs displayed decoratively in the window inviting you to come in, buy one, and get a free refill.

Businessmen armed with killer briefcases elbowed their way past without so much as a "pardon me," and people who didn't realize that the rain had actually waned still maneuvered their umbrellas and packages through the midtown crowd. The restaurant was a block away. They had to be careful crossing the main thoroughfare as the cars swooshed by and tended to spray. There was nothing worse than being wet and cold, unless you were hungry, too. There was a chill in the air, and her shawl rested delicately atop her shoulders, so he helped her wrap it more snugly around herself. He got closer than he'd intended. Her hair smelled greasy. Strike one.

The restaurant was spotless. The soft chanting of Hindu music echoed throughout the room, which was decorated throughout with vibrant red and gold. It wasn't particularly busy, but it was cozy and isolated enough for a blind date. A short man with a white shirt and black vest bowed slightly, seated them, and handed them the red-and-gold menus.

"Good evening, welcome to Bali," was what Tim thought his waiter said.

The walls were decorated with beads and lots of mystical-looking artifacts. There was a statue of a jeweled goddess on a mantel and handcrafted works on display.

This blind dating game was a new thing. They both pasted smiles on their faces like contestants on a game show who were waiting for a question to which they obviously couldn't know the answer. It was awkward the way they sat with their eyes fixed on the menus, avoiding each other's gaze. His growling stomach bit him and reminded him where he was.

"What's good here, Tim?" his date asked, breaking off a chunk of silence.

"I, uhh, usually have the chicken curry. They serve that over rice. I get mango chutney and paratha to go along with that." She smiled, knowing exactly what he was saying.

"Indian is my favorite," she said, considering the tandoori chicken.

"Okay, I'll have the chicken curry and paratha."

The waiter nodded.

"And I'll have the tandoori chicken, with a Diet Coke, thank you."

"Water for me."

The waiter took their menus and Tim pledged to enjoy himself. He smoothed down his mustache with the palm of his hand and thought of things he could talk about, like television shows, new movies, and books. He asked his date what she liked to do.

"I don't do much, just work and I do a little crocheting."

Strike two. He tapped his fork and grinned. A woman who lived in a void was a turnoff.

"I like to see a movie now and then and read," she added. "What do you like to do?" she questioned before he could ask her who her favorite author or actor was.

He volunteered that moviemaking was his life, he lived it and breathed it.

"Everything in life is material for a movie. Life is a soap opera," he said, smiling as she noshed on the abundance of dry noodles.

She kept reaching for the noodles, as if just noticing them.

"That's hot pepper," he cautioned, thinking she must be starving.

"Don't worry, I can handle it . . ." She smiled, dipping the noodles in the pepper sauce.

Her eyes began to water and she gasped for air, reaching for a glass of water, gulping it down, and refilling it on cue.

"Are you okay?"

She took a few deep breaths.

"Yes, thank you, I'm fine." She smiled weakly. "It's hotter than I remembered."

There was silence as he visually calmed his date, who was now looking slightly embarrassed. He nodded as the aroma from the curry tickled his nose and invited his appetite to dine.

"Chicken curry?" the waiter announced.

"Yes, looks delicious."

"Tandoori chicken?"

"Thank you," she said, as her waiter served them and hurried back off to his kitchen post.

"I don't mean this the wrong way," she began, mumbling with a mouthful of food, catching a few rice grains before they fell. "But how can you focus on a relationship with anyone if you are obsessed with filmmaking?" she asked, pausing only to chew. "I mean, it takes months to dedicate yourself to something like film, and then there's no guarantee that you will even get recognition." She had said a mouthful.

"I realize that," he said, savoring the flavors that were tantalizing his tongue. It was she who was barely palatable. "I'm just getting started. In a few years I hope to have something with maybe even a limited engagement showing right here in New York or at the Urban Film Festival."

"Yeah, but, I mean, your first attempt at a film would have to be stupendous to get any attention, and then you'd probably need at least a million to produce something remotely close to what we actually see or appreciate in the movies nowadays," she shared sarcastically.

"Not necessarily," he countered.

"Do you realize that nine out of ten films are flops?" she added. "Unless you get a box-office star for your movie, who would actually want to see it?"

Who was this opinionated demon? he thought.

"Do you have a more realistic dream?" She smiled at the obvious uneasiness the question posed.

Strike three. The imaginary red balloon of hope that hovered above their strained but cordial conversation burst. This date was over.

He couldn't believe this country mouse was taking stabs at him. "Can you excuse me?"

"Sure," she said, looking more helpless than he hoped she was.

He went to the men's room and glared at himself in the mirror. Was he desperate? He paced back and forth, waving his arms wildly like those guys in the wrestling ring. He wanted to leave her sitting there at the table, choking on pepper sauce.

"She sits home and knits, how exciting, and now she wants to tell me I need a more realistic dream?" He spoke to the mirror. "She wants to tell me how to crochet a movie? Ain't this a trip?"

His irrational side wanted to sneak out the back door of the restaurant as they did in the movies. Run through the kitchen and snatch up a piece of bread on the way out. He hoped she only had a token and a quarter in case of emergency. He hoped the rain poured down on her and left her walking home in sopping wet shoes that made noise all the way home. Who was she to analyze him? To pick him apart? To judge him? After all, she didn't have a date either. If she had other more realistic prospects, then what was her eagerness all about? "Indian is fine, Indian is fine."

Rochelle was definitely going to pay for ruining his evening with her unsolicited suggestions about how he needed to get out and meet people, especially after he'd told her that he wasn't fond of this blind dating game thing anyway.

Tim was always good at putting on a happy face, a master of disguises. So that's what he did. Cool mack pose. He returned to the table, chuckling at the fact that she probably didn't even know any better.

"You know . . . I'm really getting the sniffles, so . . . umm . . ." He couldn't believe he'd actually said *sniffles*. "I got wet earlier. I can call you later in the week and maybe we can reschedule this." He motioned, instructing the waiter who was standing guard at a nearby table to wrap it up.

"Was the food satisfactory?"

"Very satisfactory," Tim said, peeling two bills from his wallet, smiling quickly, and not making eye contact.

"Is something wrong, Tim?" She lowered her head and whispered. "Was it something I said, did?" his date inquired, noticing his hurried manner.

It's too late for all that now.

"No, I'm fine, I had a great time, fabulous time, Fawn," he lied. He could feel the devilish horns pressing through his freshly shaped-up crew cut.

He escorted her out of the restaurant, barely touching her elbow, and hugged her good night as she clutched the doggie bag that would probably be lunch for her tomorrow. He stood pleased as her yellow cab faded down the busy New York City street into nevermore.

Tim had managed to find a parking space in front of his building, and Sharon had conveniently found herself on Tim's doorstep, like a package begging to be returned. She sat in front of his building like a helpless victim who was conditioned to keep coming back for more. Her first words were, "I don't know why you've been acting funny lately."

She must have thought this whole film thing was a pipe dream of his or something concocted to get rid of her on weekends. She apparently figured that she would stand there until he decided to come home, either alone or with someone whom she figured he'd have to explain to her later. Another reason why he hardly ever took women back to his place.

"I had a business meeting," he responded to her questioning, rushing into the building, brushing past her. She quickened her step to keep up with him. He didn't fully understand his need to lie to her.

"Why didn't you return my call this morning?"

"I've been busy, Sharon, I told you that before."

It was almost eleven P.M. He was frustrated, tired, and it seemed that tonight she was intent on breaking his house rule. She wanted to spend the night. He didn't have the energy to debate, rationalize, or break it down to mere semantics. After the rude display of ignorance by his blind date, boredom had ensued. Tim was up for anything remotely close to routine, and figured that with Sharon he could be particularly thankful for someone familiar, predictable, and non-judgmental.

12

Troi got up early, quietly stretched, and played tag with her mind. Her routine always began with ground coffee beans and a tape with which she hummed along, accompanying the instrumentals. She didn't want to be late for the preconcert rehearsal. She loved to sing, it was obvious. That's why they nicknamed her CeCe. She was no Winans, but she could carry a tune. And when the anointing fell, Lord. She'd have them bobbing and weeping, like the resurrection was every Sunday, because she knew that they could feel her deliverance in the song. She turned on the coffeepot, turned up the volume on the CD player a little, and waltzed into the bathroom to gargle. Troi swished the blue minty stuff around in her mouth, through her teeth, and spat it out before it burned a hole in her cheeks. "Please meet me downstairs," she had told Carla last night. It was 7:36. She pushed down two slices of toast and woke Vaughn, who needed to get ready since he was always like the slow-moving traffic he hated so much.

"No, no, I'm not going," he mumbled.

"Vaughn, I'm singing this morning and in the two concerts this afternoon."

"CeCe, I'm not up to it this morning. Really. I need to rest if I'm going to work tomorrow." He squirmed.

"Can you at least stay for the morning service, Vaughn? Please?"

"CeCe, I said I'm not going," he spoke harshly, pulling the thick fleece blanket up over his head. "And can you close the door, please?" He motioned.

His dissatisfaction was evident, but she wasn't about to let him ruin her mood.

"Well, I'm sorry to interrupt your vacation, Vaughn." She snatched the blanket off of him. "But you need to drive me to the church, because you know there'll be no parking," she said, walking over to the window and parting the curtains to let in some deep penetrating sunshine, which his pale attitude needed right now. "And you keep the baby with you. I have to rehearse, and I'll be in church until at least eleven o'clock tonight. I can't keep her with me that late."

"Why can't she play with the other kids?"

"Because in the back of my mind I'd worry about her all day," Troi snapped. "Why can't you watch your own child? All you're doing is sleeping. You gonna sleep for twelve hours straight?"

He let out an exaggerated sigh, snatched the sheets back onto his body, and laid still momentarily before flinging them off again and stumbling into the bathroom to throw cold water on his face. He gave Troi a look that said *you're really trying me*.

Troi gathered that Vaughn wasn't too pleased with having to get up out of the comfy bed and drive her to church, but that was his problem. The baby was made together, and they would arrange their schedules to accommodate her together. Once you had kids, you couldn't afford an attitude. Your children dictated what you did and how and why you did it. Troi wondered what went on in that head of his. Sometimes Vaughn didn't seem pleased, and it annoyed her, because she knew that she had always given the full hundred percent.

Troi mapped out in her mind that Vaughn could drop her off at the church and come back home and try to sleep. But he'd have to baby-sit and entertain Dakoda, along with the other thoughts in his head, because Troi was sure that, of all people, his mother was in church or on her way to one by now. He needed to be in church, too. She didn't know how all of a sudden Sunday was deemed a sleep-in day for Vaughn. She didn't get what was going on with him, but she couldn't worry about it now. It was a trick. The enemy wanted her mind. He wanted her to worry and get wrinkled in the brow. It wasn't gonna happen. She looked lovely in navy.

Clad in gray sweatpants and sneakers with no socks, Vaughn pulled up to Carla's building and beeped the horn.

"Did you tell her to meet you downstairs?" he asked, beeping the horn several more times.

"Yes, I did, Vaughn, what's the problem?"

He drummed his fingers on the dashboard while Troi was fiddling with the radio. His lips twitched.

"What's wrong with you?" Troi said, glaring at Vaughn.

"I'm tired, CeCe."

"So, why you have to take it out on me?"

"Look, I'm tired, that's all, okay?"

She hoped that Carla was ready and would come bolting through the door as she always did. Troi wanted to get into the tabernacle and hear from heaven. People let the enemy manipulate their moods. Troi thought, *I'm not even having it.*

Carla came sauntering out of the building with a turquoise scarf with mint-green swiggly lines swaying behind her, and clutching her bible as if her life depended on it. She was smiling and waving her open palm when Vaughn revved the engine like he was going to take off without her.

"Morning all," she chimed, touching Vaughn on the head and playing with Dakoda, who was fastened safely in her car seat.

Troi couldn't help but think that Carla had come a long way. She remembered that as a teen she'd been kind of awkward and shy, but then she thought that mostly everyone she knew had been. From big red plastic glasses to funny hairdos. They had all managed to peck their way out of their shells; they had all literally come full circle.

When Troi thought of Carla, she thought of someone tough, who didn't ask the world for a thing, but who always tried hard at whatever she did. She never used her upbringing as an excuse for anything that she didn't have in life. Her mind was set and her destination clear. Troi and Carla were tight. They had a connection on a spiritual level, which was the best level on which two beings could relate. Their needs weren't always verbalized; when Troi was bothered, bored, or bogged down with the trying compromises of marriage, Carla knew.

"Let's go shopping, girl," she'd say. And when PMS allowed Carla to sit on a pile of dirty clothes in her bathroom with the bathtub overflowing, the phone would always ring and it would be Troi. "I'm coming over to do your hair, girl."

They were the same, yet different in some respects. Carla was honest about one thing: She said that she could only care for someone who could care for her. Which is why salvation and Christ wasn't the most understandable option for her, especially since He wasn't as tangible as people would like Him to be.

Carla's parents had subconsciously instilled in her mind that all she needed was herself, nobody else. Troi and Carla were friends because Troi had made Carla's plight her own. She'd single-handedly defended a girl she didn't even know. A girl who could have ended up making her as unpopular as her sister, Nina. But when the kids would start teasing Carla, Troi would say, "This is my cousin. If you mess with her, you mess with me."

Carla was cute. Surprisingly enough, even the boys said that. She always had a smile embracing her face, even when some people thought she was being fake. "Nobody's that nice all the time," a Hallelujah Girl mumbled under her breath once. But Carla, she was the epitome of niceness. Troi cherished people like that. Even in elementary school, Troi always thought that Carla was the prettiest dark-complexioned girl she had ever seen. Her skin was radiant, like the edge of night, with a glow that invited you to be her friend. And as friends, they meant so much to each other, words didn't always suffice.

Carla taught school. Fifth graders now. It was ironic. Her pain had been her cure, but she loved children. She was enamored with them. If the doctor was right and Carla couldn't have any, Troi hoped that the Lord would bless her friend with a man who either had children of his own or wanted to adopt. That way they'd both go into the marriage knowing what to expect. Yes, Troi and Carla would always be friends. They had always been honest, although when Troi had gotten pregnant a little over two years ago, she hadn't known whether to tell Carla or hide it until she was showing. But with the power of discernment, Carla had come to her door unannounced with a supply of disposable nursers and a Winnie the Pooh crib set. Dakoda still draged that old blanket behind her like a lifeline.

"What's this?" Troi had asked when Carla had giggled and pushed the packages wrapped in green pastel paper with baby blue and yellow umbrellas on it into her trembling arms.

Troi had tried to cover up a fact that had obviously already been revealed.

"Congratulations! I know I'm the god-momma."

"Who told you?" Troi had asked with her mouth hanging open and her hand instinctively rubbing her belly.

"Don't put nothing past God."

Troi had looked at Vaughn, who'd shaken his head and raised his hands, surrendering. "It wasn't me."

"I'm so happy for you, I'm so happy, girl," Carla had said. She had been the most extravagant godmother Troi had ever known.

"Okay, but don't spoil my child," Troi had said.

"If I don't, who will?" Carla had giggled.

"You know I'm sorry, Carla, it's just that I didn't . . ."

"Girl, I'll be fine, I never know what God has in store for me. Babies one day, maybe. Until then"—she'd rubbed Troi's belly—"this one will do."

Vaughn pulled up to the church doors and Carla tapped Vaughn on the shoulder.

"You all right, brother?"

"Me? Yeah, I'm fine."

"All right now, 'cause you sure are quiet this morning." She smiled. Carla grabbed Dakoda's cheek and pinched it. "Drive carefully, Vaughn," Carla said.

Vaughn simply nodded. Troi got in the backseat, adjusted Dakoda's clothes, and picked up her pacifier, which had fallen.

"Mommy will see you later, Dakoda, okay?" she said, pulling the hat down on the baby's head to cover her ears. Dakoda kicked her feet as if she understood what *later* meant.

"Hi, Vaughn," a group of girls from the church cooed in unison, totally disregarding that Troi was there and that she was his wife. Vaughn raised his hand and waved without breaking so much as a smile. He knew she was already upset. He didn't need to fan the flames in word or deed.

"Eleven o'clock, Vaughn," Troi said without so much as a goodbye, slamming the car door. She looked away and walked toward the church. Vaughn sat unsure, knowing only that his decision not to go to church this morning had started it. He should have just gotten up to go and hear his wife sing. He hated the silent treatment. He leaned his head on the steering wheel and rocked it back and forth. Troi observed his plight.

Her change of heart prompted her to turn around and go back to the car. She tapped on the window and Vaughn looked up. Unlocking the doors, she got in and scooted over next to him, as close to him as she could get without the emergency brake getting in the way. Carla stood over by the church entrance, engaging someone in conversation.

"I love you," Troi told Vaughn.

"Me too, CeCe, it's just that . . ."

"We'll talk about it tonight, Vaughn, okay? Pick me up at eleven, I should be done by then."

"Okay," he said, pressing his lips to hers and pulling her into a moment where she wished they were back at home and could start all over again.

Troi had to be thankful for what she had. Nothing came easy, especially to the Madison girls. It was Nina who had told Troi to make her career something that she loved, and then it wouldn't feel like a job, but a hobby . . . and it did. She was thankful for Shangrila, Dakoda, Carla, Nina, and anything else she was blessed with and forgot to mention. She thought about the old her, who would have marched into the church and totally disregarded Vaughn's feelings. The old her would have left him sitting out there tormented, and probably wouldn't have spoken to him until at least Thursday. But she was trying. It was a daily struggle, but she was in for the long haul.

Carla grabbed Troi's arm.

"Are you all right, girl?"

"Yes, never been better." She smirked.

"Okay, okay, that's what I like to see," she said, hugging her sister-friend. They waved at Vaughn, turned around, and headed toward the church.

"Morning, ladies," Rochelle said.

"Hello, sister."

The older women in the church prided themselves on being friendly; it was the younger ones who hadn't learned that yet. Although it depended on where you fellowshipped, because sometimes you could get a look from a sister who acted like she was defending her salvation and your sole purpose for coming to the church was to steal her joy or her man.

"I knew that was your car, Troi! Who you know in Jersey, girl?" Rochelle asked, louder than she should have on the sidewalk outside of the church on a Sunday morning.

"Jersey? Oh, Vaughn has a brother out there."

"CeCe, I'm gonna hold two seats." Carla pointed to the door and motioned that she was going inside.

Troi nodded.

"Oh, okay, maybe that was it," Rochelle said, not particularly convinced.

"It what?"

"No, I just saw your car in my neck of the woods."

"Teaneck?"

"No, Patterson."

"You sure, Rochelle?"

"Yep, Vaughn was driving and he had on a brown cap. I'd know that gorgeous husband of yours anywhere," Rochelle said, looking around to see if her own husband was within earshot.

Troi was never one to be jealous. But little green feet tiptoed across her brow until she was frowning and suspicious. Today wasn't her day. Sam lived in Teaneck, not Patterson. She didn't want to assume or jump to conclusions. He could have been shopping. He could have been banking, going for a drive, or straight-out cheating. She had been giving. So giving, in fact, that she had given him enough rope to hang himself if he chose to. She thought she knew everything there was to know about her husband. He didn't drink alcohol and he didn't smoke. She knew all of his friends. Maybe one of them lived in Patterson now. She had too many questions, and she wasn't about to sit sulking in denial. She wanted answers. And she wasn't going to let his "you don't trust me" statement guilt her into feeling that she wasn't being committed to their marriage by inquiring. Space or no space, they definitely had to talk. Vaughn had too much time on his hands.

13

Vaughn choked on his own thoughts, which slid down his throat like a raw egg. He didn't know what tomorrow would bring or what he'd do if he had the option to relocate, get delivered, or die. He had no clue. He was like a child who spaced out because something had caught his gaze and held him there, drawn to the uncertainty of it. He was trapped. Confused like a kid in a candy store that had dozens of options, from gummi bears to bubble gum, when he had no money. Balls of lint and rice grains in his pocket were all. He knew that he should have come clean and been honest months ago, even years. But he couldn't handle it. He thought he could. He wished he could. But there was nothing left for him to face now except the truth.

Vaughn was soothed by the pacing of his own footsteps. Nothing made sense. He was a man, he wanted to deal with his own situation his own way. Bottom line was, when it came down to unmasking the situation, he didn't want to see it. He didn't dare stare his secret in the face for fear that it would glare back. It was a raging monster, a giant that had been there as long as he remembered. Raising its head whenever he wanted it to sit quietly in the corner and go unnoticed. He wished that he could adore and appreciate only his wife in all of her feminine charm. He wished that he could touch her without thinking of his fingers draped across someone else, anyone else. He would give anything if he didn't need the fantasies in his mind to sustain himself in the increasingly infrequent moments that he and his wife spent together as a couple. He wished that he was attracted to everything that her sex represented and everything that it was supposed to do for him.

Women called this the ultimate betrayal. Not catching you cuddled up spoon fashion in the wet spot with their best friend, but another man. It was unfair, he supposed. A woman couldn't compete for a man who desired another man. It didn't matter what she did or what she wore. Looking at his wife in a lace teddy still left him needing something extra to get him going. It wasn't about wearing the pants or the mustache, it was about familiarity. The body of another man was familiar to Vaughn. He was giving himself headaches thinking about this whole thing day and night, sunrise, sunset. Gazing out the window of regret. His mind was never where he was, and when it was, it wandered through the possibilities of what if.

His fingers itched to dial Tracie's number. He clasped his hands together to diminish the urge. He needed the comfort of a voice that understood him. A voice that had called his name so many times that it was almost as familiar as his mother's. But Vaughn figured that Tracie would only coax him into coming over to his place for a little private time, and although Vaughn wasn't living quite right by Christian standards, he wasn't about to take his baby girl into his uncertainty. He may have been straddling the fence, but the fact remained that he would not introduce his child to that world. He would not snuggle up in the bedroom with Tracie while his daughter was being entertained by a purple dinosaur or a big yellow bird. He could never do that to her.

He thought about growing up, and all the fickle friends he'd had who had made it their purpose in life to get the girl.

"Come on, man, let's double-date."

"Hey, Vaughn, man, this girl's got it for you bad."

But it hadn't been his thing. It was never his thing. He had known how he felt since he was seven. He hadn't had a wild fascination for dolls or played tea party. He hadn't dressed in his momma's shoes and saggy pantyhose, tripping around the house either, but he'd known that there was something that a boy did for him that a girl never could. Sure, women excited him, but keeping him there was another story.

Vaughn had had girlfriends. Lots of them. Tall statuesque types who'd had men at their beck and call. They'd wanted commitments, rings, corsages, and foreplay in the backseat of anybody's car, once in the woods. His whole life had been spent performing like a show dog at a pageant for people, with a total disregard for his own desires. He had pushed himself so far back in his mind that he didn't know who he was anymore. He couldn't recognize himself, and he was so far removed from his desires that he was making a sandwich of his life, and he was stuck in the middle, oozing out of the sides like a condiment. He didn't want to hurt anybody, but that anybody had to include himself. He felt as if he was in a world that didn't want him, and living in a skin that rejected him.

He knew the names that men like him were called. Homo, butt buddy, fudge packer, rump ranger, rear admiral, pansy, cakeboy, fruit, and queer. Sounded more like a salad or a birthday party. He'd heard people say that gays and lesbians would bust hell wide open. So would liars and thieves, he thought. But people tended to overlook the obvious. A lie was acceptable, so was stealing if you were hungry, and if passion caught a woman and a man in a moment that allowed them to let their hair down, along with everything else, well, then, forgiveness had their name on it. But gay? Homosexual? They were the modern-day equivalent of witches. Society wanted them burned at the stake. They didn't want them near their kids for fear that their tendencies would rub off on the backs of their hands. But they were out there. They were grandmothers, doctors, priests, accountants, athletes, and veterinarians. The problem wasn't them. Vaughn didn't want to justify the whole situation. The dilemma was what he was going to say to Troi.

He'd thought constantly of exiting this world when he was in his teens. But suicide would only solve half of his problem, not the eternity part. There were days when he felt that he could go on, and others when he felt like he was being forced to wear something that wasn't his favorite color. Tracie made Vaughn feel comfortable. There was just a confidence that Tracie had that made everything seem like it would be okay eventually. They had met up several times after work. On those occasions he had called and told Troi that he was going out with friends from work. Technically, he hadn't been lying.

He would have never been able to pull it off if Troi weren't so trusting. That was the thing that hurt him the most. He was betraying her trust. She'd given her trust to him, and he'd laid it on the ground and walked all over it. He knew about her upbringing. He knew that her older sister basically raised her and that her mother and father were just shells of human beings who never actively participated in their lives much, aside from dictating what to do or not to do. He knew how family life was extremely important to her because of that. But nevertheless, here he was, telling her one thing and doing another, making love to his wife in the shower and allowing her to think that they were just as devoted to each other as on the day they married.

Vaughn had been disillusioned long ago. He had watched women try to mold him into something that he wasn't. He'd smile and pretend that he enjoyed it, but all he'd wanted to do was find a pair of strong hairy arms and open up. He'd wanted to spill all of his emotions out to someone who wasn't going to judge his preference, just love him unconditionally. Troi was a strong black woman, he knew that much, so there was no way she was going to take his revelation sitting down. He would give it standing up.

She wasn't a weak woman, so she would cry, but she wouldn't fall apart. He wondered how those pious women in the church would react if they knew. They'd probably rub it in and tell Troi, "Sorry to hear about your husband's preference." Vaughn had been learning recently not to put so much importance on what people thought. It wasn't working. He thought of writing his wife a letter and leaving it on her pillow, or attempting to drop some subtle hints. Watch reruns of *Ellen*. Maybe she knew but was just in denial. Maybe he could expose himself to her and then go and stay with his mother, then come back when Troi had calmed down and was ready to talk rationally. He didn't know why he'd allowed Pandora's box to be opened in the first place. Just because you had a thought didn't mean you had to ponder it. Just because an idea surfaced did not mean that you had to act on it. But he had, and now it seemed that there was nothing he could ever do to suppress his feelings. How would he explain to his wife the pleasure he got out of kissing another man? How did you stop a three-alarm fire?

They'd argue about it for sure. Troi would yell and Vaughn would be forced to hold his tongue, partly because he was the one who had betrayed their commitment to each other, and also because he had been keeping a secret from his wife that had existed since long before they were married.

"What do you want me to say? That I'm gay?" he'd yell back.

"No, I know that already!" she'd scream.

She had a sharp tongue, but all he wanted was for people to understand him. He was more than gay. He was a man, a father, a husband, an American, a Democrat. He could predict Troi's response.

"That's rhetoric, and you know it, Vaughn."

Vaughn sat his baby girl on his lap and smiled. "Dakoda, Daddy loves you, you hear me?"

She drooled, flashed four razor-sharp teeth, and nodded her head like she understood, but she didn't. He didn't know where he was going with this entire situation, but he did feel how hard it was for him to stay away from Tracie, and how much harder it was to pretend. Faking wasn't benefiting him or Troi. Vaughn figured he'd better get used to it being him and a cat alone in an apartment in SoHo, because when the church got wind of this fiasco he would be the outcast of Zion.

His affair with Tracie took his thoughts to another level. Beyond legal limits. His affair gave his thoughts depth, another dimension. It had been innocent at first, but now this whole situation with Tracie meant that his feelings were no longer abstract fantasies, they were real and actualized.

Vaughn thought about Sam. He didn't want to disappoint his brother, who loved enough women for both of them. He didn't want to disappoint his father, who would think that the white man had brainwashed him while he was away at college into believing that he was gay so that he couldn't reproduce further and extend their family tree. He didn't want to disappoint his momma, who was always telling all of her friends about how her boy Vaughn was a good, strong, hardworking man. He didn't want to disappoint Troi, who he knew for a fact could have had other suitors. There were men waiting to snatch her up like a twenty-dollar bill on the curb. He never wanted their marriage to be thought of as a complete waste of time. But it was. It had been.

Now all he wanted was to be left alone. He didn't want to be looked upon as freakish, evil, or perverted. Television made light of the whole situation. What he felt inside couldn't be explained on a sitcom with dialogue for cheap laughs. He had feelings inside of him crying, aching, struggling, and demanding to come out. Feelings that everyone let on shouldn't exist. Feelings that would mess it up for everyone. But he was tired, it was hurting, and he was in pain. He didn't think that Troi would be able to forgive him for the shame that he would cause their family, and, deep down, he truly didn't think he could forgive himself for disappointing everyone either. Namely Dakoda. She didn't understand now, but one day she would, and she might resent him for the rest of her life.

One way or another, he would have to bring this whole issue to a head without it spilling over like a draft beer into the rumor mill of his meager yet sacrificial existence. He had to brace himself with both hands, close his eyes tightly together, and take it on the chin. He had made his bed, tucked in lies, deceit, and masquerades; now he had to crawl right up in there with them and snuggle up as he did on the sofa almost every night, trying to stay awake, flipping channels to avoid Troi approaching him for sex.

14

It was a brisk and still six A.M. It smelled of rain. Nature and its freshness wafted through the house, bidding Nina to open every window and dust off the proverbial welcome mat. Not a soul was on the street. Barren. Except for the man who always walked the tiny shih tzu with the limp. Parked cars for rows and rows of city blocks, as far as she could see. They looked like dominoes, except for the colors. Nina was half-dressed in an extra large T-shirt and barefoot as always.

"I'm fine, child," Shelby said when the phone call interrupted Nina's morning relaxation.

"I'm glad to hear it," Nina consoled.

She played the role of the all-knowing dorm mother well. Especially since she knew that Shelby had a tendency to spend the night at the apartment of whomever she happened to meet the night before.

She was like a child who was orphaned, a kitten without a home, putting on her best face, faking contentment and rumbling purrs at every passerby, trying to convince someone with her eyes to take her home. It was a nasty habit that most women simply overlooked in their quest for a diamond solitaire. Shelby was one of them. But she always made sure she checked in to let Nina know that she was still in one piece.

"So, Nina, who was that guy?" Shelby whispered.

"No big deal, Shelby," Nina said, breathing out all the air in her lungs.

"No big deal?"

"No big deal, I said. Who was that clown you were with?"

"I can't say right now. Can I get back to you on that one, Nina?"

"Girl, you better hope he don't beat you and leave you for dead in an alleyway somewhere."

"I can handle this one . . . he's a pussycat."

Nina was amused.

Shelby had been Nina's snotty and slightly overexposed roommate since their sophomore year at Cornell, and they'd been acquainted ever since. Shelby wanted Nina to confide in her, but there was nothing to tell. Her life was about as exciting as a picture pop-up book. Shelby said that she needed to know if Derek was a member of the club or the help. Nina offered that it didn't matter to her. Her father owned his own construction company and her sister owned her own salon, but it hardly made her a member of the elite. She reminded Shelby that the rich did it all the time. Ice cubes dangling from their fingers and face-lifts that made them look like they were permanently surprised.

They had summer flings with the pool boy, the bellboy, or the pizza boy, it happened all the time. Shelby's parents were rich. Not filthy, just a little grimy. They had bought stock over a decade ago, which had literally gone through the roof. They'd moved Shelby to a costly apartment masquerading as a town house off-campus in her junior year at Cornell. Though Nina couldn't afford to join her, she had spent at least every other weekend there kicking around and realizing that the stories from Shelby's life were better than watching television. They had remained close and had gone through a myriad of episodes together, from cheating boyfriends and the head cheerleader to unaccepted marriage proposals and unreturned engagement rings. The marriage proposals had been Shelby's.

Nina thought back to last night. She had been quite intrigued by Derek's interest, although she'd tried hard not to show it. He'd appeared for the most part totally enamored with her, which was sufficient for a change. She needed the pleasure of her phone ringing off the hook for a spell, and someone deep and mellow on the other end begging her to come by and see him. Derek was thin and thievish looking, as Mother would say. Mother said that a skinny man either drank too much, did drugs, or couldn't make enough to sustain himself.

Mother wasn't one to talk. She was the textbook case of a worshiping woman, and alcohol was her god. She bowed down to its throne and made it her reason for waking, sleeping, existing, and had she died, it would more than likely be her reasoning for coming back to life.

It was Nina's job to collect the dead soldiers. It always had been. Mother would stash her empties anywhere with a crevice thick enough for a palm-sized slim. The sock drawer, the Tupperware cupboard, the medicine cabinet, the Betty-the-teddy-bear cookie jar, and countless places that you'd never think to look unless you had the spontaneous urge to go there. There they would be. Lying down, drained, emptied, wounded, snitching. Mother was a textbook case all right.

Nina tried to think of something more pleasant. So she thought to herself that Derek could do. If she took a moment to think long and hard about it, he really could. It wasn't geometry. He was a man. A vocal one. Derek liked to be heard, and when he wasn't pleased, everyone knew. She appreciated a man who had a little confidence about him.

At dinner last night he'd sent the waiter back to the kitchen several times until his dish appeased his palate. Shelby had dragged Nina to this posh club before, so Nina agreed that the service was always mediocre enough to complain about. Derek had said that black men had suffered enough, and that when they went out to dinner, they should get exactly what they asked for. She dismissed the notion that he was one of those men who lived their lives on an "I'm a black man" tirade. She didn't want to date anyone like that. She wanted someone to whom she could relate, but someone still gentle enough to recognize her as someone of the opposite sex.

Derek had dined à la white T-shirt, jeans, and added a spare dinner jacket that he kept in the pool house for good measure. She hadn't cared. She tried not to judge the corn by its husk. She had done that in the past, and it hadn't done her heart any justice. She was still lonely and denying every excruciating moment of it. She nursed the image of him that she had made over in her mind. They were arm in arm at the next fund-raiser. He looked transformed fabulous in a tux. That was definitely something to look forward to. Nina had looked at him last night as, with a crooked smile, he'd taken her hand across the table at dinner. He'd been straightforward, making a gentlemanly attempt, so she'd appreciated the gesture. She was long overdue for a random act of kindness.

He'd immersed her in what he liked to do when he wasn't doing odd jobs, and although the things he suggested weren't Nina's ultimate idea of a fun festive evening, she'd agreed. Moping got boring.

She could enjoy spending some time with a man until something good was sure to follow. She didn't think he was bad-looking. He needed a close shave and a manicure to even his nails, but then most men did. She'd be happy enough if she met someone who had a job, could read the *Daily News,* and knew a little about music. She didn't ask for much in life, not even a man to support her, but she didn't want to support one either. She figured a compromise was in order. She'd see what developed.

Relationships were tricky little misconceptions. Like a raffle almost. If he was a tasty-looking type, then for sure there was a void in some other area. Some of the most gorgeous specimens she had ever seen were lacking in the chivalry department. Romance usually eluded them, too. She didn't believe that all the good ones were taken or waiting to be born; they just didn't make teachers the way they used to, that's all.

Older men usually refined those rough bristly brothers until they were safe enough to engage, but lately the elders were displaced, noncompliant members of society themselves. Each one teach one, but when there are no teachers, then we all lick the wall. Nina's life was stifled. Theater, functions, country club, theater, functions, country club. Cultured was one thing, but she never wanted to be uppity like Shelby. Shelby was so high on herself that the thought of it made Nina dizzy.

Derek had said he'd call, so Nina would wait and see what gave. They'd exchanged numbers after what he'd said was a promising encounter, but if he didn't call her, she wouldn't call him either. She wondered if he could have thought that she didn't like him. Sometimes men and women could be on two totally different wavelengths. She could have given off signals that meant the exact opposite of what she'd been feeling. She hoped she hadn't. Sometimes it was hard for her face to remain expressionless. Her face always confessed thoughts her lips never had. Nina had been tired at dinner last night, that was all. She had been out since early yesterday morning sitting up in a beauty shop half the day. By the time they'd had dinner, it had to have been half past midnight. Then again, Nina thought she might call him. It wouldn't be right away if she did decide to call. She was one of those dawning millennium women, and although Troi always emphasized that "a man findeth a wife," Nina figured that her options were few and, unlike what the Weather Girls thought, it wasn't raining men.

Nina sat on the bare floor with her arms over her head, stretching her arched back slowly. She was looking forward to spending the day with Martha. Whenever Nina would hang out late on Saturday nights, she was always too tired to make it to church for the early Sunday service. She hated to fall asleep in church and, unlike her mother, she wasn't the disrespectful type. It was an excuse, yes, and Troi occasionally let her live it down. She hoped that this morning was one of those times. Besides, she enjoyed Martha's company, and she could use a good strong dose of catching up.

Martha and Nina had met accidentally one afternoon when the mailman delivered Nina's mail to Martha's house. It was junk mail, nothing confidential or crucial, but Martha had felt obligated to rectify the mailman's mistake.

"You didn't have to come all the way over here for that," Nina had said politely.

"It's no problem at all." Martha had introduced herself as friendly.

Nina had offered a freshly brewed cup of coffee. Martha had been making regular stops by Nina's little java hut ever since. Their lives had become intertwined.

The brownstone Martha lived in had belonged to her grandmother. Martha said that it was the only thing the woman had ever owned. When she died, she left it to Martha. Martha was unregrettably the only one in her family who wasn't married or settled down. She had had a child out of wedlock and her prude family, with the flamboyance of the West Indian Parade, disapproved. They weren't religious, they just thought they were better than everybody, Martha confided. Her momma and Nina's, they both cared too much about what everyone else was doing. Mirroring the Joneses and couldn't even see their own reflections.

When Martha had gotten pregnant with Glenda and her family had realized that they couldn't finagle the poor gent into wedding a woman who he had the hots for but didn't want to wake up gawking at every morning, they'd wanted her to give her baby up for adoption. Even though she'd been more than old enough to make up her own mind to keep it. She'd kept her baby, her flesh and blood. They hated her for stigmatizing their family. Her grandmother had adored her all the while, which is probably why she had chosen Martha as the one to leave the house to.

"Don't listen to them, baby. You're gonna be just fine, darling," her grandmother had told her. Martha hadn't been the happiest child growing up. But owning this Brooklyn brownie sure gave her a chuckle or two.

Martha never smiled when she talked about her family. She said the high-school diplomas and college degrees on her momma's living-room wall were a shrine. Her momma labeled all of her children according to the degrees they had, her favorite child being Martha's oldest sister, who had a Ph.D. in micro-something, and her least favorite, Martha herself.

"All of my children made something out of themselves but you," Martha would mock her mother in a pretentious yet familiar condescending monotone.

Martha would say, "Rumor has it that the neighbors still whisper about how one of the Frasier girls got knocked up." She couldn't believe that nothing more exciting had happened in all this time.

Martha also remembered that there hadn't been any congratulations, cards, streamers, balloons, piñatas, or wishing wells for her when her momma had made her go down to the clinic to find out if she was pregnant and she'd come back positive. Her family didn't believe that anyone needed to be praised and given gifts for having premarital sex and bringing a child into the world who would have no father.

"What are you going to do with your life, Martha?" her momma had asked at least every other day since Glenda had been born.

"Live," she'd said, quite surprised by the insinuation that the question posed.

Life was so complex, and family didn't make it any easier with their lies, secrets, and subjects that were taboo. That much they agreed on. So Martha kept her issues mainly to herself, as did Nina. Nina didn't need an apartment full of friends or a telephone ringing off the hook with people trying to get into her business then telling it. Martha had moved onto the block just as quietly as her grandmother had died and been removed, stiff and unnoticed. Martha had painted the apartment a brighter shade of periwinkle, but everything else she'd allowed to stay the same as her grandmother had had it. She loved her grandma's furniture, always did admire it as a child. They didn't make furniture like they used to.

Martha and Nina had done the movies, the theater, and Martha had accompanied Nina and Shelby to one of those dreaded charity fund-raisers, which left her vowing never to do it again. It wasn't Martha's bag, that whole glitz and spectacle. Martha said she didn't like feeling that just because she was a mom and didn't have a career she wasn't worthy of conversation. Nina agreed, and was glad to meet someone as afflicted as she was. She thought to herself that not even education prevented you from avoiding dysfunction. Nina thought about how her own family ticked and realized that what others did was no reflection on her individually. And though it soothed her to believe that, it wasn't absolutely true.

Nina ground up some fresh Brazilian coffee beans and set the coffeepot to brew. The drip timed her as she laid across her bed listening to CD 101.9. Her feet were cold and dangling off the side, and she fought with the blanket, which wasn't big enough to cover her and her feet. She wondered when she would get to the good part, the fruit on the bottom of life. All she ever asked for was more love. She wanted it to take root in the corridors of forever as images stirred inside and made her daydream about piggyback rides and holding hands. She didn't know what would be enough finally to make her mother proud of her, or if her mother would even notice long enough to be proud. Minutes ago the sun had been rising, and now the skies had the subtle look of death. She hoped life wasn't trying to tell her something.

The last thing Nina or her love handles wanted to do was bore a man, she thought as she watched the rain wash the streets, cleanse the filth and debris that lingered, and scatter the people who hung out near the corner. It had been raining on and off since yesterday.

"What do you think, Martha?" Nina said, running down the whole scenario from last night to her.

"Girl, if he helps you pay the bills, keep him! I've had my fair share of mediocre, and it's not all bad. The fine ones only think about themselves. You don't need that. You can't eat fine."

Nina chuckled.

"When you're fifteen, you want to date any boy on earth just to say you have one. When you're eighteen, he's gotta be the finest, and a car is a plus, a definite plus."

"True," Nina agreed.

"By the time you're in college, mediocre and trying to get an education, even if they don't have a job yet, is good enough, because one day they'll have a degree and have at least the high end of a five-figure salary."

"Yep."

"By the time you're twenty-eight or twenty-nine, you'll take someone who has a job and one free weekend every other month. But of course, by the time you hit thirty-four or thirty-five, man, if it's got two legs, almost all of its teeth, and is still breathing, sold!

"True," Nina said. "Your priorities change."

Martha nodded.

"But I'm still holding out for a man who has all of his hair," Nina said as she tied the curtains back at the window and enjoyed the freshness of the mist that wet her face.

Nina and Martha had spent so much time just peeping into the lives of others through this window. They'd pull chairs up to the window, nibble on crumb cake or nut bread, and watch the teenage girl across the street when she should be in school or in a book but wasn't.

The overdeveloped girl had the body of a twenty-year-old but was probably eleven or twelve, and wouldn't cover up her belly to save face. She still sucked her thumb, which was ironic, because these young girls wanted to be grown so badly, but still hadn't managed to kick that oral phase.

Even without Martha, Nina would always observe the girl, standing in the doorway of the brownstone directly across the street, tongue-kissing the boys, several, in fact. Nina wondered if all this time she was really just envious. She imagined the girl's thumb still wet, just waiting for the boy to finish feeling her up to stick it back in her mouth. He'd grab her behind and hold it like it was a prize. It was his because she had given it to him; he was just trying to figure out what to do with it. She was young and she couldn't help that, but she was stupid, too. The boy's friend would always tag along as friends always did. He'd lean on a car the whole time and laugh at the fact that the girl would put on such a show.

"C'mon, man," his friend would say.

The girl would pull on his jacket, asking, "Where you goin'?"

"I'll be back," he'd say and kiss her again.

"You ain't leaving!"

"I'll be back, a'ight?"

"You always say that."

"Don't I come, tho'?"

"C'mon, man," his friend would insist.

"Beep me," he'd say to the girl, walking away, nodding his head as if he had accomplished a noteworthy feat.

"A'ight, but you better call me back," the girl's voice always trailed off after them.

Nina and Martha observed everything from the tall windows of the brownstone. That's what her life was reduced to. It was just Nina, Martha, whatever they happened to see outside that pane of glass, and, of course, an occasional meeting with Shelby.

"You're probably right; besides, it's not like they're lining up at our doors. You know?"

Martha shrugged. "Mediocre is underrated, Nina. If a mediocre man wanted to come into my life, buy me furniture and clothes for my baby, shucks, I'd take it." She grinned.

Martha spent her nights teaching her seven-year-old daughter, Glenda, how to play the piano and speak anything other than Ebonics. Martha had plans. She had entertained a few gentlemen, one of whom she hoped one day would assume the responsibility of being a father to Glenda. She had men floating in and out of her life like leaves being tossed about in the fall, but she never neglected her child.

"It's all in how he treats you, not what he looks like. Broke don't pay no bills, you know."

"I know," Nina said, "fine don't either."

"'Cause please, girl, men don't sit and stress over us like this, they just go on about their merry way."

"Ain't that the truth," Nina said, watching the flowers get drenched and beaten by the now-persistent downpour.

Her muslin curtains blew around her window frantically and she refilled their coffee cups and sliced the nut bread that Martha had brought over to share. With nothing but silence and the tick of the clock between them, they enjoyed the moment.

"This is delicious, Martha, as usual." Nina squeezed together the fallen crumbs. The bread was still warm and the aroma was throughout the house now that Nina had opened the foil.

"It's my grandma's recipe. She left files and all sorts of things packed away in that house."

"Well, share, I'd like to make a few for Christmas or Thanksgiving." Nina smirked.

Martha was wearing a simple navy velvet dress and her house slippers. Her hair was brushed back and her face was clear and glowing. She was smiling happily.

"So, where's my little girl today?" Nina asked.

"I left Glenda with my upstairs neighbor. She likes to play with her daughter."

"That's nice, how old is her daughter again?"

"Five. I'm glad to have them right upstairs, Nina. You don't know how easy it is for me to run a few errands without having to dress her and take her with me."

"Thank God for modern conveniences, huh?"

"That's the truth."

"So, umm, how's your love life, Miss Martha?" Nina asked cautiously, giving her the lowered eye.

"Fine," Martha said, not totally enthused.

"How's Gerald?"

"He's Gerald," Martha said with a straight face, then started giggling.

"Girl, you're a mess. Are you gonna get serious with this guy or what?"

"I haven't decided. I can take my time making up my mind, can't I?"

"Sure you can."

"All I want is peace."

"Yeah, and unspeakable joy," Nina ribbed.

"I'm not pushing it." Martha grinned. "I'll settle for a little peace."

15

Tim didn't need an overzealous woman trying to psych him out with her feverish pitch and legs so long they spanked her as she walked. He had dated women who made lots of money, and they were no different from the normal, everyday, minimum-wage working girl. They just drove better cars. Their education gave them a leg up on everything except relationships. He remembered getting excited about a woman when the fascination was new, but somehow found himself glad now that the blind date hadn't developed into anything serious. She knew too much, or thought she did. Rochelle definitely would not hear the end of this, Tim thought, looking out of his bedroom window at the overcrowded city that bragged at how it had so much to offer.

"Wouldn't this be perfect . . . waking up like this every day?" Sharon said, pawing all over Tim's chest and interrupting his thoughts.

That's why he couldn't live with a woman. Tim didn't need a woman trying to move into his apartment. No pantyhose, no toothbrush, no tampons, no T-shirts.

"I guess so," he said.

"I could make you breakfast and make you lunch to take to school," she offered.

She had watched one too many episodes of something that was probably canceled now.

"Sharon, I have an appointment this morning, I need to get ready." He pulled away from her and got out of the bed half-naked, brandishing only his boxers and abs that were saying, "Here I am, touch me."

"Go on then, I'll just wait here for you." Sharon wiggled contentedly under the sheets. She was making herself at home in his crib. Impersonating someone who belonged there.

Tim's patience with this girl was surely down to the last grains of sand. She was wearing him thin. He had one nerve left, and she was tap dancing on it by tossing and turning in his sheets, marking her territory and trying to leave her scent.

"When I come back I want to start working, so I don't think it's a good idea for you to stay."

He didn't know how to tell her no, but that's what the answer was. He should have never broken his house rule, but she was clever. Tricky even. He didn't like people playing games with him. He paid the rent, and he was in control here.

"You telling me I can't stay?" Sharon posed with a fixed stare that felt like it was peeling back layers and exposing things about him that he wasn't ready to share.

He wasn't intimidated.

"Look, Sharon, I'm not playing games, okay? You know I have to work. I need to concentrate. How many times do I have to tell you that?"

"So, it's like that?" She frowned.

"It's like however you want to take it. I have business to take care of and business comes first," Tim said, icing the mood and wrinkling his brows, which were almost touching now. He reached for his robe.

Tim didn't have time for mind games. He had been through that whole Eastern religion phase. Worshiping the mind and knowledge. To be enlightened, they said, when, for the most part, everybody ended up more confused than instructions in Chinese. He'd even tried karate for a while, until he'd realized that the lessons indocrinated you in the religion itself. You had to count from one to ten; then you had to say a prayer and meditate on nothingness, was the way he saw it. His hopes of receiving a black belt were nil, because there was no way that he would ever throw away the little faith he had in God and surrender it to some pseudo-enlightening being. Although he was currently nonpracticing, he could attest to being Christian. He believed in God, but he wasn't going to let a woman perplex or manipulate him, nor let those Eastern religions fool him.

He smirked, because every time a woman thought she had played him, in turn she had actually played herself.

Sharon bounced out of Tim's bed, slipping her big feet down through her wrinkled pants, which she had shed so easily last night, trying to warm Tim into submission. She was making every attempt to make Tim more commitment-oriented, when what she needed to do was find a place for herself. He wasn't it. He knew he needed to level with her. Lay all his cards on the table and tell her that it was fun, but she wasn't the queen of hearts, and it wasn't going to happen. The air was thick, and it was hard for Tim to swallow. His room had the faint scent of puppy dog.

He knew he was guilty. He was keeping Sharon's hopes up, and she was trying to reinforce what didn't even exist between them by buying him gifts and bringing dinner over for him when he was working, concentrating, and couldn't pause long enough to make a cheese sandwich.

"I'll call you," Sharon said, rustling her bags, making as much noise as possible, then slamming the door on the way out.

Those three words that women dreaded hearing: "I'll call you." They didn't mean quite the same thing to him.

There was definitely enough drama in Tim's life. He couldn't elude it if he had a magic escape hatch. Life. Having to live through such an existence was probably why cinema had become a very popular hobby. It wasn't a hobby for Tim. He was film, and film was him. Everything he said, did, dreamed, and saw was material for a script. He was trying to master his craft. His spring schedule was kicking his butt. His new classes were several intricate projects woven together, each one a prerequisite for the other. He had one advanced editing course, a level three writing course, a film analysis course, and an introductory class that was packed with high-heeled boots and plaid micromini skirt-wearing wanna-bes that flaunted *yes, I'm not wearing panties,* right out of the script of a B movie.

Those weren't the ones that got in his nose though. He had had enough of them. There were about six of them on every bus, and at least twenty on every train. They were predictable, and they all shopped at the same department stores, looking like clones right off of a factory assembly line. They studied film for the glamour of it all, not the art itself. And he didn't want to end up with a woman who was unoriginal, or didn't really have a point to anything that she did or said. Sharon was both. Michelle was neither, but she was unavailable, so she was eliminated by default. He wanted a woman who was fashionable, articulate, and not too laid-back. He'd be better off praying for rain.

Tim was digging a woman who made it a point to hold her head up and could discuss something she'd read since high school. He wanted a woman who would make you want to roll out the red carpet and knew the difference between a dinner and a salad fork. A woman who knew art, stood behind at least one cause that benefited something other than herself or her tax return, had read the biography of W.E.B. Dubois, and didn't just fake her way through life. He wanted a woman he would never find, because she was on a pedestal in his mind. He wanted his momma.

Tim surrendered his attention to the telephone and the doorbell, which rang simultaneously. He never had time for himself. Never.

"Hello?"

"So?" Rochelle paused impatiently.

"So, what?" Tim said, walking over to the door to look into the peephole, then opening the door for his boy Justin.

"What's up?" Justin said, giving Tim a pound and a nod, leaning his umbrella up in the corner, and heading straight for the refrigerator.

"Rochelle, the girl was corny. She tried to come off like a . . ."

"Tim, you need to stop, you know you didn't even want to go out with her."

"Well, that may be true, but she didn't help the situation any by running off at the mouth," Tim said, frowning and motioning for Justin to get out of his kitchen.

"I can't believe you would set me up with someone who sits around on the weekend and knits."

"How am I supposed to know what she does for fun?"

"You could have asked. I'm your brother."

"Okay, Tim, I'm sorry, but she's not the only woman I know. I know more exciting women who . . ."

"No, no, no, Rochelle, I don't wanna hear it. Just keep your quilting group of women friends away from me and my ideas."

"You've got a problem, not to mention an attitude, brother dear."

"Well, sister my sister, if you had to sit there last night and listen to Glinda the Good Witch and what she was saying about me and my films, you would probably feel the same way. Besides, she's lucky I didn't leave her sitting there to foot the bill."

"How kind of you, Tim," she mocked.

"Seriously, I started to, just like the scene out of a movie."

"Boy, calm down."

"Look, Rochelle, no offense, but we just didn't click. She probably can't carry a tune, let alone a conversation."

"I see," Rochelle responded.

"Listen, Rochelle, Justin is here, can I call you back?"

"Fine, good-bye, Tim." He hung up.

"Man, you had a blind date?" Justin elbowed Tim, obviously humored. "You must be crazy. What's up with Sharon and Michelle?"

"Look, mind your business, man, and stay out of my fridge. I don't have groceries to feed you."

"Oh, so a brother can't have a Pop-Tart?" Justin laughed.

"It's not funny, man, I get women, you know, I get women. I just don't want to spend my life chasing skirts and not wanting to come home at night or being frustrated because I'm alone. I've got needs. I mean, player is tired, you know?"

"So, what are you saying, that a woman is gonna rescue you?"

"I'm gonna rescue myself. A woman will just be there, that's all. It's not about skins or money either, man."

"Listen, Tim, you need to relax, you're taking everything so seriously."

"Life is serious, this ain't no joke, this ain't no rehearsal. That's the problem now, nothing means anything to any of you."

"Look, don't get all philosophical on me. We are in the same boat, so let's just row together." Justin motioned. "I'm here for you, man." He rested his hand on Tim's back.

"Yeah, yeah, I know, Jay. Sorry, man." Tim sighed. "Sharon is stressing me, you know, that's all." He massaged his temples. "She showed up on my doorstep last night and then didn't want to leave this morning." Tim's head had a truckload of thoughts ramming through it.

"I told you not to let a woman sleep over, man. Haven't I taught you anything?"

"Yes, yes, I know, and I made a mistake letting her spend the night, but this morning she was talking about waking up next to me every morning, scared me to death."

"Yeah, a scary thought, man. Michelle is more your speed anyway." Justin stroked his chin. "She's more . . . cultured, shall I say?"

"Yeah, but she's not here now, is she? And then my blind date was a horror."

"What did she look like?"

"I don't know, man, I was fumbling my way through the date because she knew Rochelle. I couldn't care less what she looked like. I like to pick 'em, I don't like being set up, it makes me feel like a vic."

"Yeah, a victim, been there, I know what you mean."

"I don't have time for drama, Jay."

"But that's what you do for a living, man. You film drama, you write drama, so what are you talking about?"

"You know what I mean. You remember Estella?"

"Oh, man, what ever happened to her?" Justin's eyes widened.

"Don't know, don't care. I'm just not trying to repeat that."

"I hear you. Listen, I just stopped by to give you a shout-out, shoot by my place tonight, we can vibe. Some of the fellas will be by the crib later."

"Yeah, that's cool," Tim said, embracing Justin, gripping his hand, and patting him on his back. "Thanks, man, 'cause I feel like I'm losing it."

"You'll be fine, trust me," Justin said as he headed out the door. "I got your back."

Tim figured that a woman would want a man to be a balance of compassion and strength. So if a man met a woman in his film who said, "What can you do for me?" his character could reply, "Everything." He jotted down some notes and points he wanted to touch on in his current project, then reached for a lightweight sweater in his closet. He couldn't fold like his momma. His drawers were a sloppy mess. Most of his socks didn't have a match and weren't folded. His shirts were just balled up and stuffed down inside any random space, the same way he used to hide his crayons when he was nine.

He pushed both arms through the sleeves of his sweater and then popped his head through. His dad used to put his sweater on like that. "Men put on their sweaters like this, son," his father had demonstrated when he was a youngster. "I don't want you putting your sweater on the girlie way, son. You try it now," his father had said, handing him his favorite little red sweater with the white snowflake. The sweater was wool and itched him to death, but he'd never tell. He could bear it with the best of them. "Good job, son." His dad would pat him firmly on the back, even though the opening for his head in the sweater was too small and always ended up dragging his lip and his eyes down all scary-like. He missed his dad. It was always the little things that mattered.

Realigning his thoughts back to the present, he rationalized that going to the post office would only take twenty minutes max. He needed to finally get these applications out, or else he would be broke, homeless, and dependent on either the state, his sister and her husband, or Sharon and Michelle. He'd never let that happen. He tried to focus and stop procrastinating. *Film* was the first thing he'd written on his to-do list for Monday. *Go to the post office* was the second. Tim was eager to be off and doing anything that was even remotely more tempting than standing in line waiting for a disgruntled postal worker to assist him, but he had to do what needed to be done. The phone rang again. He smoothed down his mustache at the corners and licked his lips. Calm and subdued, like a rustling of the wind through the trees on the perfect evening with someone he'd come to revere as special, it was Michelle. She'd flown into LaGuardia last night. She said she'd be in town for the next two days. She didn't say she wanted to see him, she said she needed to.

16

Troi sat in the last pew, closest to the drafty door. She looked up at the stained-glass windows, which were now devoid of sunlight. She smiled at everyone as they left, making their way home to merriment and preparation for the work week. She was stacking the bibles to put in their places, separating the black ones from the burgundy. She momentarily forgot where the extras were kept. There was a door, a knob, some shelves, that much came to mind.

She was distracted, preparing her thoughts for when she got home. She couldn't take it if it were true. Hours had slipped by, but not quickly enough, and this whole deal had her contemplating never returning to the apartment, where Vaughn could possibly make her eat her words or worse. Everyone felt pain in this lifetime. There was no getting around that. All she knew was that if she had been honest with Vaughn throughout their relationship, rejected any advances, innuendos, or flirtations ever made by another man, and he had betrayed her, she didn't know what she'd be capable of doing. She had given him space, attention, time, and didn't question him nervously about his comings and goings.

The thing was that she trusted Rochelle, unequivocally. Not that her word was flawless or gospel, but if she said that she saw their car in Jersey, then she must have seen it. It wasn't like she was one of the fanciful Hallelujah Girls, who'd doomed her marriage with Vaughn to failure before it began. Rochelle had no ulterior motive. She came in love and peace. Rochelle had always thought that women needed to learn to stop being unduly suspicious of each other, so in attempts to rectify that, Rochelle had extended her home, finances, and, on occasion, her car. "We need to trust and care for each other. Bear each other's burdens," Rochelle said. That was an understatement.

After the soul-stirring concert, which had electrified the church, left runs in stockings, and brought members of the congregation to tears, Troi couldn't wait to sit face-to-face with her husband, look in his pupils, and dare him to lie to her. Looking around the church, Troi focused on something familiar, Carla talking to a guy and waving a wave to Troi that meant *good-bye*, not *hey, I see you*. Troi, Rochelle, and Carl exited the church. Vaughn was parked outside with Dakoda in the backseat, just as she had asked him to be.

"Call me, girl," Rochelle said, embracing Troi and walking off toward her car as her husband embraced her waist and kept in step.

"Yep, I will, take care." Troi made her way down the stairs and smiled to mask the pain that was devouring her inside. She couldn't believe that her husband hadn't even come to hear her sing. What was his real reason for not showing up? His absence only made her more suspicious. Rochelle's husband was there to support her, even if he was nodding off, and Carla's admirers sat front row, waiting for a pause in the program to run up and greet her. Troi thought that Vaughn must surely be up to something. He had to be.

Troi got into the car, reclined her seat, kissed her sleeping baby's dumpling hand, and put her bags in the backseat on the floor. Vaughn reached over and kissed Troi on her cheek, but she didn't lean into him as she usually did. She was wearing attitude.

"So, how was the concert?" Vaughn tiptoed around her mood cautiously.

She was smug and indifferent. "It was a concert."

She had always been able to hide her anger very well. But after Rochelle saying something about seeing their car in Jersey and now sitting next to Vaughn and not being able to tell if it was true or not, she was burnt, hot under the collar, fuming, upset, vexed, and angered, just to name a few. It was noticeable. Her nostrils flared and her breathing quickened. She was more confused by the fact that she thought she was giving him what he needed than the thought of him feeling the need to step out on her. Men needed space, they needed time to process information and make decisions. She thought she had followed the rules, and the rules had turned around on her and made her look like an idiot.

She fought the urge to say, "My momma ain't raised no fool." Now she knew how Nina had probably felt when Daddy hadn't come to her graduation. Betrayed. Not that this concert was the most important night of Troi's life, but the fact that she had a husband and he should have been by her side but wasn't bothered her. Especially since he found time to be every place else except the designated place at the appropriate time. Dakoda's empty bottle fell from her hand. Troi reached for it and pushed it down in her bag.

"So, what have you been doing all day, Vaughn?" Troi asked with bitterness dripping from her tongue and partially covering her clenched teeth.

"Nothing much, just watching the game."

"I see," she said, convinced he was lying.

Their drive home was silent, aside from her clearing her throat to get him to look in her direction. She couldn't believe how she was allowing her mind to be a playground.

She had sung like an angel. They'd let her sing another song, not the one that had her nicknamed CeCe. People said that her song gave them goosebumps, and that they could feel the spirit moving. It could have been the fan they felt. It got awfully hot in that old dusty building. And now here she was, she didn't know whether to laugh out loud or be a crybaby.

She knew firsthand that God had put her here to do more than be intimidated by the unknown.

"He comes to rob, steal, and destroy," she repeated aloud, from the sermon she had heard earlier.

"What?" Vaughn said.

Troi ignored him and focused on the fact that she wouldn't get mad or even, she'd just accept whatever it was and move on. It took a strong woman to do that, and, being raised in the Madison home, she had to be a survivor.

Walking through the front door of the apartment, Troi tossed her bags on the floor near the sofa and held the door open for Vaughn long enough for him to come through carrying the baby, then allowed it to slam quickly behind him. His eyes darted around, trying to make sense out of what Troi was feeling now, but she wasn't telling. Her eyes didn't convey and her lips hadn't spoken a word since she'd mumbled something about *steal and destroy.*

She'd been fine after they had made up in the car this morning. He laid the baby on the sofa and unzipped her jacket, which startled her, and she instinctively reached for a bottle that wasn't there. He didn't have a clue as to what was going on in his wife's mind. Playing the guessing game wasn't high on his list of priorities. He wanted an answer, but figured it would be much safer to play along. In the game of charades, he always found that it wouldn't help to ripple the waters.

Vaughn hesitated, and it was his turn to clear his throat.

"What's wrong, CeCe?"

"You tell me." She smiled, inviting his betrayal.

"If I knew, I wouldn't be asking. Can't you just tell me what's wrong? I don't read minds." He frowned as she walked over to the telephone and dialed a number.

"Who you calling at this time of night? Put the phone down and talk to me."

Troi turned, facing him with her ear pressed to the receiver and her lips pursed like she had a secret that she dared him to guess. Her eyes were lowered, adding a hint of mystery. He noted that she dialed eleven numbers, which meant it was long distance.

"Hey, it's CeCe," she said, momentarily taking herself out of character.

"Hey . . . CeCe," the familiar voice said. "Long time no hear, I ain't seen neither one of you in months. How's that brother of mine?"

"He's fine."

"So, when y'all coming out here? Let me whip you up something nice for dinner or something . . ."

"Well, I'm off tomorrow, planning on making some of that homemade cheesecake and peach cobbler that you like so much. Wanted to know if you'd be home late in the afternoon, maybe Vaughn can drop some by you."

"Mmmm, oh, yeah, girl, you know I love that good home cookin'."

"Okay, so it's a plan," Troi said, clothing her eyes in disappointment. "I'll talk to you soon."

"Sure thing, sis. And, uh, tell my brother to call me?"

"Sure will. Later."

Troi carefully placed the phone into its cradle, walked over to the baby, and lifted her slightly to put her in the playpen. Troi was ignoring Vaughn's persistent gaze.

"Go to sleep, baby," she cooed, using her hand to pop the cap off of the baby bottle she placed in Dakoda's mouth to satisfy her through the night.

Troi was livid. She turned, faced Vaughn, and spoke harshly. "We need to talk."

He was sitting by the window, looking over his clasped hands, either trying to discern what was going through her head or praying.

Troi searched the room, grappling for words that would have the impact she wanted them to have. Words that wouldn't intimidate but would show that she wasn't about to play who's-sleeping-in-whose-bed.

"Where were you yesterday?" she blurted out. "And don't lie to me, Vaughn," she said, twisting her face up into an unrecognizable scowl.

"I was just . . ."

Calmly she spoke. "Vaughn, before you try and use your brother, Sam, as an alibi, I want you to know, that was him and he ain't seen you!"

Vaughn panicked, thinking that he had forgotten to call Sam. He'd been so consumed with what was going on in his secret life that the here and now apparently had eluded him. There were going to be major changes in his relationship with Troi. He had played out the scenario with the myriad of endings long enough. Logic told him that he'd better just own up to what he was doing. Common sense told him that he was a fool. Women loved the truth. They always begged you to tell them. But Troi didn't look too happy, or forgiving, for that matter. She might not see the truth as a gift.

Troi winced as her father's words haunted her. "You've gotta let a man be a man. He pays the bills and he needs his space." Her father was never the man of his own house. Funny of him to give advice. She was patient, and pacified Vaughn with her silence. She could wait until he formed the words in his mind to confess. But she didn't.

"Why was our car in Jersey? What is the real reason you didn't come to the concert? And I've noticed that you have been a little preoccupied lately. Who is it, Vaughn? Is it someone I know?" She paused. "Now, you just feel free to answer the questions in any order you like, just answer them!" she spat.

Troi didn't have time for games, rhetoric, or anything like it. If you care, act like it, if you want someone else, leave. There was no time for talking it out, no time for "baby, I'm sorry it won't happen again, I promise," and there was absolutely no time for counseling. She wanted no part of a man who couldn't stay faithful and found it necessary to slip up with every sway of a hip. He'd wanted a baby immediately after they were married. They'd hardly had time to bond with each other, enjoy each other's minds and spirits. She'd initially wanted to enjoy his companionship and love him for at least the first few years of marriage. Just he and she taking vacations, dining in cozy restaurants with soft jazz playing and tempting her. But he'd insisted on a baby. And she'd allowed herself to get fat, stretch marks and morning sickness. Now the family he had been so dead set on building was crumbling and falling apart, and he wasn't doing a thing to salvage it.

She remembered how he would go on and on as if he were sensitive. Doing for her and showering her with undue affection, telling her "that's what husbands are for." She didn't want guilt flowers, or lovemaking first thing in the morning prompted by his infidelity and thoughts that it would keep her suspicions at bay by tossing her a bone to throw her off the trail. Mercy sex. She wasn't a charity case. There were brothers who would love her for real, out in the open, not just in private with the curtains drawn and eyes closed.

Either he cares or he's out the door. I'm not a booby prize, she comforted herself. *I am a woman. A good one. Any man would be glad to whisk me off to an island and love me until dawn with the waves breaking all over us, virgin Mai Tais in hand. Men approach me everyday, in and out of church, so what's that about?* she thought. Her parting words would be "I love you and I will miss you, but I don't need you." But it was a lie. She didn't understand herself why she felt it so necessary to need him or lie about it. She tried to convince herself that he was anything other than what he'd smugly claim to be, her first love. He was her husband, but she wanted to protect her heart, a heart that no longer belonged to her. She had given it to him, sacrificially.

Although it appeared that he wasn't completing her, he was. He was the milk in her coffee and the lemon in her tea. He was special in the way that he cared for her and allowed her to be herself without judging her about being too open, too emotional, and too free. She wanted the freedom to love someone for a change, without being badgered about why she tolerated such dastardly deeds from a man who was supposed to be committed to loving her. He was special in his own right. He made life for her exciting, and she always felt safe and provided for. But loved? She never felt she could give enough. She was mentally drained by his constant need lately to have space. She had second-guessed herself to the point that if she had to exert an ounce more energy on this man, she'd lose her already confused mind. What space did he need? The space to sort out another life that didn't include her or her things?

She thought about how she had never been able to love two people at the same time, and hoped that he felt the same, provided that she was the one he adored. She doubted that he could love two. Men weren't that complex. So she was stepping into the upper hand the situation gave her. It was Vaughn's turn to show her due compassion now. It was his turn to explain and prove what he felt, giving the justifications and ramifications of each emotion. She didn't want to hear it; she wanted action. She wanted him to act them out and mime them for her. He had her to the stage where she had evolved into a monogamous being; she couldn't feel the need of anybody else but him.

Flirting in overdrive. She remembered trying to flirt just to see if she still had it, and she did. She'd always have it, she just didn't want anybody else. She bade no other hands to speak sign to her mind and no other lips to dare touch the ones that were familiar with his kissing pace and technique. Why were emotions so hard? Maybe she was overreacting. Love should come with rules. A book chock-full of usefulness. But something still small enough to roll up and stick in the pocket of your skintight jeans on a Friday night. We needed rules. Something that wasn't man-made, just spiritual. Something that showed you in advance how your actions would affect your life, with a love clause that said *pull here in case of emergency.* She felt like a victim before she had even weighed the evidence. She shrugged her shoulders, because she wasn't going to let her emotions ruin her. She wouldn't allow them to control her life completely.

Troi had spent the past three years of her life working and making things comfortable for her family. She'd saved, she'd compromised, and she'd swallowed one dose too many of understanding. She wasn't about to let some freshman come with her g-string antics and swipe her husband's affection. It was hers. She belonged to him, and he belonged to her. She knew how he liked his eggs, she knew which tie was his favorite, and if his special tie was soiled, she knew which one he'd choose instead. She knew him. She wanted nothing more than to continue to wake up next to her husband for the next forty years and occasionally give him reassurances about why he'd married her. She wasn't the most fashion-conscious woman he knew, but she knew how he liked his coffee. She washed his dirty underwear and she knew that when it all boiled down, she wanted him to stay because, without question, he loved her. She didn't know why she was jumping to conclusions. Just like her mother, she was always jumping to conclusions.

She tried to convince herself that it was probably nothing, and that she was just being oversensitive again. But she wasn't. It wasn't even near that time of the month. She knew that Vaughn worked in the city, and there was no reason for their car to be in Jersey. No reason at all. She'd hear him out and figure out once and for all how the competition weighed against the foundation that they had built. She looked over at Vaughn, who appeared emotionally still.

"I'm waiting, Vaughn," she fumed with her arms crossed and her foot patting to some imaginary rhythm.

"We'll talk about this in the morning, CeCe," he said, turning his back and walking into the bedroom without so much as a second glance.

"Vaughn!"

"We'll talk about it in the morning," his voice echoed.

Troi plopped down on the sofa, leaned her head back, and listened to the hurried caged frenzy of the ambulance in the distance getting closer, the flutter of the ceiling fan overhead blowing her hair slightly, the gurgle of the toilet that Vaughn had just flushed, the infantile groans of Dakoda restlessly fighting sleep again, the switch of the bedroom light that had now immersed her pillows and sheets in darkness, and the thick silence, which was more a humming than an audible sound. She'd loved with her whole heart, she would regret nothing. What we want isn't always good for us. She fought with her mind as her curiously curled lips pressed together and she held back tears.

17

Women. Always an emotional tidal wave that made you lose your footing. Vaughn was apprehensive, but he'd known that this day would come eventually; he didn't know why he was surprised. He had spent his whole life feeling scrutinized, misunderstood, and threatened. Marriage hadn't changed that. If anything, marriage was a hibernation, a shelter, a crevice in the dark that disillusioned him. But when he came out, the same dilemmas faced him and stood waiting for him to confront them. Didn't really make sense to pretend. It was always there waiting for you like a noonday shadow.

His sexuality was not something that he readily discussed. He'd heard the rumors and questions and, for the most part he'd ignored them. To say that his sexuality was none of their business was just like raising his hand and volunteering, "Yes, I'm gay." The best defense had been to say nothing at all. It had taken all the bravado he could muster to put off the confrontation with Troi. She was dragon-breathing angry and ready to burn somebody to a crisp, namely him. It was all so novel to him. He was still processing the information himself. A collection of random mishaps? Nothing happened by accident. Then he thought about Tracie. Tracie wanted the end of Vaughn's marriage to come sooner than Vaughn would ever confess he did.

In Tracie's mind, Vaughn knew that he already had a condo picked out for the two of them with one of those new picture-frame-thin televisions on the wall and a leather recliner that they would take turns sitting in, allowing each other to be in charge of the remote control for hours at a time. But it wasn't so much about ending it with Troi, as it was about Vaughn's not being ready to face the changes that his revelation would pose. Vaughn didn't want to think about divorce. He didn't even know how he really felt about Tracie, other than the fact that the situation allowed him to remain indefinite. It had only been a few months.

Vaughn's revelation would come with ultimatums. He didn't want some judge sitting up high with a gavel slamming it down, piercing his eardrum, telling him he wasn't a good father because he didn't conform to society's ideals. He wasn't about to negotiate his ability to see his child, a child he'd helped create. A child who was flesh of his flesh and beyond that. Vaughn clenched his eyes and pondered how he had kissed Troi on the cheek and she hadn't leaned into him as she usually did. Instead of giving and submissive, she was as stiff as a wall of stone. Sometimes he had felt that way when they were together.

She'd never know. He wouldn't hurt her like that. He felt in some ways that he was as giving as she was. She gave time; he gave of himself physically, even when he didn't want to, even when he dreaded it. But it wasn't like Troi to be cold, even when they had disagreements. He had stepped outside of himself countless times, trying to make her nights something about which she could brag to her friends. He thought he had been on his best behavior all this time. When their baby was born, it put an end to some of the rumors that lingered after Debbie. Surely Troi couldn't know.

With that, he had gotten used to the idea that it would be he and Troi forever, so he'd accepted what was and shelved his cravings. The addiction that created numerous scenarios in his mind had been willfully extinguished. He'd tried not to look or allow himself to enjoy, with eyes closed, the thoughts of another man. A man who would reveal his deepest desires and manifest the nature of him, which always came under scrutiny. To him, his desires felt as natural as breathing a sigh of relief. There was nothing that she could say or wear that would make his thoughts wane. Tracie was the key. He had opened Pandora's box, unleashing a multitude of festering suppositions. They had been a part of him long before he had loved Troi.

He'd tried to look the other way when a fashion-conscious brother with thick eyebrows, strong shoulders, and flawless skin approached him for the time or directions. He had often dined alone in restaurants and made it his business to sit in a particular waiter's section. That was before Tracie, too. Vaughn would grin at the waiter and the waiter would acknowledge Vaughn. They would smile at each other and nod approvingly. It had to have been something that he was giving off. He knew that he knew and he left it at that. For years the pleasure of viewing had been enough.

He would window-shop, observe and concoct scenarios in his mind. He dreamed of being touched, explored, and forced to face whatever it was that he was so fearful of. His desires had been off-limits for years. He'd pulled away, as from the radiant glow of a smoldering charcoal bit covered with ash, which coaxed you to think it held no threat. He had never known anyone who was openly gay. He knew the tight-pants-wearing types who giggled as he passed them on the street, but none of the ones who could fit right into the corporate world without a hint of the connotations of homosexuality. Something inside of Vaughn was fighting to escape the confines of society. But what if she was able to pick up on it? She didn't know. She couldn't, he convinced himself.

But what he was sure of was that this was the first night in all the years they'd been married that Troi had been hellified enough to make her bed on the sofa. It had to mean something irreversible, a turning point even. She was unapologetic. He thought to tell her that they shouldn't let the sun go down on their anger, but if he quoted Scripture, she was likely to throw something more powerful right back at him. He wasn't taking any chances. Things were always better when the anger waned. Torment. How could he show her without destroying her that his desires weren't a reflection on her? It didn't mean that she wasn't sexy, beautiful, or strong. She would take it as a blatant rejection of who she was as a woman, for sure.

He didn't know why he felt what he did, and he didn't know how to convince her that it had nothing to do with her being unappealing or not feminine enough. The unflattering reality of it was that no matter what she did, it wouldn't quench the fire that raged in him whenever a brother stood about 5'10" or taller and was masculine enough to warrant the attention of any woman in the room. Even he didn't believe that he could control his feelings now. It was as if he had been kept prisoner, and now, finally unlocked from the tormenting abyss, he had been presented with a banquet, a bevy of beauties. There was no way he could go back to that dungeon. That dank vile place where your thoughts cuffed you to the four posts of the bed and dared you to squeal bloody murder.

There was something missing in the way he cared about Troi. He knew that. He wasn't caring for her with his whole heart. And he'd have liked to think that he married Troi out of affection, but the truth was that he was more than likely hiding. Yep, it was all coming to him now. Like with blurry vision at four A.M., he'd rub his eyes with his fist and blink to capture the image. He was making the picket fence a reality for his mother, his brother, and everyone else except himself. Now the paint was peeling off of his perfect confines, and pretty soon the photographs would fade, the trophies and awards would tarnish, the heart would break, and the song would play its final note.

Troi walked into the bedroom's darkness. He observed her silhouette. She pulled off her stockings and slipped her dress down over her hips. Vaughn eased out of bed and walked up behind her, reaching out, trying to touch her shoulder and kiss her or exude some type of affection, but she took one step forward, turned to face him, and pushed him off forcefully with both hands. He stumbled back onto the bed. Making love wasn't the way she ever liked to make up.

"Don't, Vaughn," she said.

"CeCe, I'm sorry."

"No, you're right, we'll talk about it in the morning." She headed to the living-room sofa, dragging two pillows and his fleece comforter off of the bed.

Relief rested on his brow. He didn't feel like pretending. His goal was to make Troi feel secure, not make her second-guess her womanhood. It was a constant battle to suppress his desires. His rabid hunger was released, and now sought a place to come alive and run rampant, consuming him and making everything he adored about his wife a lie. The way he touched her was a fallacy, because in his eyes she still didn't stir nearly as much passion in him as Tracie did. It was naturally inviting the way Tracie made him feel that to be a man who needed a man was okay, especially when the world told him, in several octaves, "*no.*"

Vaughn had been living Christianity loosely for months. Especially since the emphasis seemingly took on an antigay theme. What's the big deal? he'd said often, but not enough to stir suspicions. He didn't want people putting him in a closet or even in their minds placing him in the same category as a drag queen or a pre-op transsexual. He had issues, but for the most part, if he didn't tell, no one would know. He knew it was the world that he should be wearing like a loose garment, but it was far beyond that now. He didn't know when it had happened. Soon after the baby he supposed. He thought of myriad reasons why relationships didn't work.

Research had shown that incompatibility was one of the major reasons. The lowest divorce rates did occur between people who shared the most in common. But he and Troi shared race, religion, and economic class. Those weren't enough. Although he efficiently camouflaged it, he had lost the sexual desire for a woman years ago. It wouldn't have mattered so much if it were just any old woman who was turning him off like a mealymouthed trickster, but it was his wife. *Forever, until death do you part.* He had to admit that he hadn't surrendered totally to Tracie or his flesh, but he didn't know how much longer he could pretend that Troi was the one turning him on.

Vaughn just wished that he could go to sleep and wake up in a different frame of mind. Wake up and be totally intrigued by a woman with firm breasts, shapely hips, pouty lips that longed to please him, and a tongue that assisted. He wasn't one to play games or the field. He had to tell Troi tomorrow. If he put it off any longer, he might end up chickening out; then they'd spend the next ten years of life making each other unforgivably miserable. Vaughn didn't want to live like that. He just wanted to live. In his mind now, Diana Ross had grabbed the microphone and was singing, "I'm . . . coming . . . out." It wasn't the remix.

18

Nina had always maintained a close relationship with her creative counterpart, Troi. Troi had helped Nina through her heartbreaking crushes and endless Valentine's Days that went without so much as a red frilly-laced card from a distant friend or ex-lover. They were sisters who hardly fought because they really had only each other. They would consider each other best friends if they'd ever conceive that the title *friend* needed rank. There was no parade of acquaintances in and out of the house when they were growing up. Mother didn't allow that. Their childhood was far from ideal, just a slew of don'ts. "Everybody you meet is not your friend," was one of them. Last week the therapist asked Nina why she still felt like she was a child when she was clearly thirty-five years old, successful, and independent. She figured her mother had programmed her to always be a child so she could maintain control. She told her therapist that she didn't know why, but wondered why she was paying her to answer life's questions herself.

As a teen, Nina had hung out with Troi's friends and met boys who she couldn't decide whether or not were cute. They'd hang out in the schoolyard and Nina would pretend she was someone she didn't even like. It was always a constant struggle to fit in. Troi's friends had thought that she was funny and entertaining, and so had the boys, but the boys had wanted a girl who did more than just make them laugh. They'd wanted a prize. Nina didn't know who that was, but she'd known it wasn't her. Besides, they were probably only being nice to the fat girl because she was Troi's sister.

Nina had tried everything to be popular. Hair color, mahogany lipstick, and cutting up in class. She'd learned all the latest songs, ironed her name going down the side of her blue jeans in pink velvet letters, and started smoking joints, too—which, for the most part, just left her feeling hungrier than usual, and tired. Daddy was always gone, Mother was impossible, and Troi fit in the cliques perfectly, which left Nina feeling impotent and as useless as wet leaves clumped together blocking the gutter. When Nina's grandiose idea of being popular bit the dust, she'd tried effortlessly to mend the frayed relationship she had with her mother, believing that it was the reason that her life wasn't as happy as people often said life was supposed to be. It hadn't happened.

She was always going from one extreme, then volleying to the other. By the time Nina was ready to go away to college, her quasi-relationship with her mother had dwindled to an occasional grunt at the breakfast table with a mouth full of Corn Pops and a stifled good night on her way up to her bedroom to listen to music and write in her journal. Sarcasm may not have been productive, but it sure made Nina feel better. Her mother fought every attempt Nina made to reconcile or extend a truce, so she obliged her and let her sleeping mother lie.

What Nina did recall most from her youth was how her daddy had constantly chosen work over his kids. At her graduation, Nina had had to say a speech. She'd practiced for four weeks in front of the mirror for the monumental occasion. She had never felt so important in all her life. She received an award, she was the valedictorian, and she had made a speech all in the same day. She'd smeared her teeth with petroleum jelly as they did in the beauty pageants, and been more eager than if she were unwrapping her one toy at Christmas time. But he hadn't shown. Forty measly bucks was what her daddy had sacrificed her happiness for. Overtime didn't mean a thing to a child. Besides, for someone who'd wanted children, he didn't cherish them the way the fathers on television did. He let Mother do and say whatever she wanted. He hardly came home, and when he did, he was glued to the television like somebody was gonna come through it and show him how the parenting gig was done. He said he had goals and dreams. But from where she was sitting, he was trying to accomplish the feat of doing absolutely nothing very well.

Nina's life was one string of disappointments after the other. It didn't make sense to take herself out of character now. Confusion had set in. She didn't know whether she loved her father or hated him. He had tried to educate them, however little. He wanted them to know about different cultures, Brazil, Ghana, and Zimbabwe. Mother never saw the need to learn about places so far away. "They ain't ever going there, so what's the point, Charles?" Her vision for the kids was limited; Daddy's was hopeful, but implementation was his major flaw. He'd insisted that they read the *New York Times* out loud on Sundays and had taken them to the Bronx Zoo once on a Wednesday because it was free. There were always museums and libraries with lectures and films, but time was something he sorely lacked.

"You keep putting them on a pedestal and they gonna fall off!"

"Sit down and shut up, woman, you're drunk."

"I ain't drunk, Charles, just listen to what I'm sayin . . ." When Mother got a little sauce in her, she'd ramble on like that forever.

An intellectual idiot. "How could I marry a woman who would always try to undermine me so?" he'd pleaded to his wide-eyed children. He couldn't be asking them why he'd picked Mother for a wife. If they were on a fishing trip and they had baited the hook, cast it into the water, and gotten a bite, reeled it in, tugging and thrashing, and found out that they had caught Mother, all Nina could think is that she'd beg them to throw her back. She was a complaining, nagging, foulmouthed, obnoxious human being for whom mothering itself was a rusty science.

Mrs. Sadie Madison had no qualms about slapping her kids to get them to respect her. All it did was make them more defiant, but she was too under the influence to care. And Mother always had something for her girls to do. When they were done with the menial household tasks of dishes, garbage, and making liquor store runs, it would be time to sit down, be quiet, and read. Nina loved to read, except when her mother made her do it. "Stubborn child. You think you know so much, you don't know a thing." Her mother would whip her something awful when she didn't obey. She'd have extension cord whelps on her legs for weeks. You hadn't been beaten until you were beaten by a drunk, Nina thought. In an inebriated state, people had no aim, and no compassion. It reminded Nina of the young girl who lived down the street from them, who'd started having babies when she was eleven. She would beat her kids all day every other day and twice on Fridays. Always yelling and screaming at them to "shut up."

She beat those kids so terribly they had welts that hadn't gone down before she let in on another round. "These my kids," she would say. "Whoever don't like it, don't look." Dirty dingy T-shirts that were too small and full of holes, bellies exposed, skin drawn-looking like a Somalian on a hunger strike. They wandered around in those filthy clothes for days, playing with broken pieces of wood and aluminum siding that had fallen off their now-dilapidated house, which miraculously still had a door. Old milk crates, cardboard boxes, and rocks were toys for them, as they'd plead for permission to come over to your yard to play tag in the hopes that it would be nearing dinnertime.

Kids made fun of them because they had mosquito bites that had turned into sores and left unattractive blackened blotches all over their bodies, mostly their legs. Mothers were supposed to love their children. What a shame you couldn't pick your family. Nina wished she had a receipt; she'd surely take her mother back or demand that the cashier at least give her the sale price. Nina knew that her mother had never wanted children; her daddy was the one who had. Mother had no choice, she had taken his ring, so she was confined to whatever he created for her. It never made sense to Nina why Daddy loved a woman who couldn't show emotion if the sun's rising and setting depended on it, or show empathy if it came in a box and all she had to do was add water.

Nina saw right through her mother from the beginning. Hypocrite. She demanded that her children call her Mother, not Momma, Ma, or Mom. "Call me what I say," she'd scoff, pushing away her already ostracized children. Her voice was annoyingly raspy, and everything she said was followed by a threat and the evil eye that normally made wild children fall in line, but not them. They were used to it. Mother was famous for "or else." Nina religiously observed her mother sprucing herself up in the mirror and marching off to church virginized on Sunday mornings with her lopsided hat and a two-step shuffle, after drinking bargain whiskey and playing spades and poker with her unwitting comrades all Saturday night.

Sunday mornings were always quiet around the Madison home, for which Nina was thankful. Mother made them attend church, smiling "yes, ma'am" and "no, ma'am" all the way there and back. She would primp the girls with ruffles, tights, and lacy pink dresses that were so neatly pressed they had to be kin of royalty. Nina hated tights. They were itchy and wrinkly. She hated ironing. Nina hated everything. On the mornings that Mother felt she herself would be nodding off on Daddy's shoulder in the middle of pastor's sermon, embarrassing him, she'd send the kids off to church without her. Nina was thankful for those Sundays. Skipped all the way there and back. Nina would stuff a pair of socks down in her little white patent leather purse, and couldn't wait to get to church to run down into the basement, snatch off her scratchy tights in a nearby stall, and make giant holes in them so she couldn't wear them the next Sunday. Nina thought she was too old to wear tights. She was twelve going on thirteen then. Besides, they always sagged in the middle, and that annoyed her.

After a while, Nina remembered Daddy stopped going to church altogether. He said he was too tired and that he worked hard and needed some rest. Troi would always mock that when she got married she'd be doggoned if she was gonna let her husband lay up in the bed when she went to the house of the Lord on Sundays. "I want a man who loves me and loves God more," Troi would say.

"Be careful what you ask for, God might send you a missionary or something; then you'd be lucky if you saw your husband once a month," Nina would caution.

On the Sundays that Mother did stumble into church two sips shy of legal intoxication, Nina remembered how they'd all come home after a moving sermon and the kids would pray that pastor had made an impact that would change their lives for the better. But Mother was rotten and festering to the core. She'd only pick up where she'd left off and start ranting all over again. "Pastor said 'what's in you comes out of you,'" Nina had reminded her at age twelve.

"You just shut up, you silly child! This is my house," her mother had spat, with a Virginia Slim dangling from her lips. She'd lit a match, pressing it to the tip of the cigarette, dragging deeply, and exhaling as she spoke each word, her lazy right eye squinting, avoiding the smoke that was getting in it.

Troi ignored her mother her whole life. She worried more about her hair and the boys than anything else. She'd take up the bathroom time primping herself and make everybody late for church, school, or wherever they were going. Mother called it pimping, though she also thought that it was good that at least Troi took such an interest in her appearance. It was one of the rare comments bordering on a compliment that she'd ever given either one of them, but then, Mother only managed to compliment one of them if she was putting down the other.

"That's more than I can say for you, Nina. Why don't you do something with yourself, meet somebody, won't you? I know, I know," her mother had said, raising her hand like she was in class dying to give the answer to a question. Nina had sighed. "Nobody wants the fat girl, right?" her own mother had taunted. Nina had learned eventually that ignoring her mother worked best, so she'd turned a deaf ear. Nina hated the memories. She remembered how she'd yell, simultaneously pounding on the French doors with the painted-over panes. She and Troi had each etched their names in them with a safety pin so that if either of them was ever forgotten, at least their names would remain. "What are you doing in there, Troi? Come on now, you ain't even using the bathroom."

"Aren't," her mother had said, walking by, correcting Nina's ghetto grammar. "I spend too much money for your education, girl, for you to be saying 'ain't.' "

"Well, you say, 'be saying,' and that isn't proper English either, Mother," she'd reiterated with a gyrating neck and pursed lips. Nina was always up for a challenge. "I can't wait until I'm eighteen!" she'd threatened since she was thirteen.

"I can't wait either," her mother had said calmly, blowing smoke purposely in her daughter's direction and batting her eyes like she was still young and agile. Not the fondest of memories, but memories nonetheless.

Martha had stopped by Nina's for her daily dose of early morning chitchat. Martha was staring out of Nina's window, keeping a close eye on Junior. She thought out loud that one day she was gonna force that man to bathe and wash those greasy clothes.

"Especially that hat." She chuckled, observing him following some young girl down the block, trying to get her to say how she was doing today. "They're gonna lock that man up for child molestation." She noticed his streak of gray and his dry hands. She giggled. "He looks like that head gremlin from the movie, what's his name again?" Martha asked, as the phone startled Nina and she readjusted herself in the chair and answered in her infamous sultriness.

"May I speak with Nina?"

"This is she." She anxiously recognized the voice as the one that had tried to charm her the other night at the country club.

"So what's been going on, lady? I haven't been able to think of anything else but you all night," he said, without hesitation.

"Well, I'm just doing my morning routine," she answered, as her voice took on a hint of mystery.

"Yes, and a good routine that probably is," he said. "So, lady, I know this is short notice, but do you have plans for this evening?"

"This evening?"

"Yes, I wanted to shoot by."

"He wants to come over tonight?"

Nina nodded, looking starry-eyed at Martha and pointing to the phone. "I don't know, Derek." She paused intentionally.

"I won't stay long. Listen, unless you'd rather I come by tomorrow evening. Maybe we can go out for a drink or catch a movie or something?"

"Well, I don't drink, but . . . umm, that sounds good. Tomorrow sounds fine."

"Excellent, excellent," he finalized. "And I just wanted to say that I've never been this preoccupied before, so count it as a plus."

Nina smirked as Martha looked on, puzzled.

"I've had to restrain myself from calling you at dawn."

"He was gonna call me at dawn," Nina mouthed.

"What time?" Martha motioned, pointing to her watch.

"Well, what time are we talking, Derek?"

"What's good for you?"

"I'm off on Tuesdays, so any time tomorrow is feasible." She bit her tongue, thinking she should have just said *fine. Feasible* sounded so professional.

"Great, I'll be by about four?"

"Sounds like a plan."

"All right, babe, see you then, ciao."

Martha ran the whole deal down to Nina in her anxiety. "Don't go getting too dolled up. Let him see that you're versatile. You don't want to wear your Sunday best to the movies. Don't smile too much, it looks fake. Just relax and let him dominate the conversation if he wants. Keep the conversation simple."

Nina definitely wanted Troi to meet him, but Martha first. So, they devised a plan where Martha would go home and wait for Nina's date to arrive, then come by to pick up something that she'd conveniently left earlier. Now all Nina had to do was go slow, figure out if she really liked him, then get him to meet Troi. In her mind, she held him like a delicate piece of china. This could be it.

Nina sighed, overwhelmed mostly by the preparation that needed to go into a date. She wished that she could forgo the lathering talk and the orange-wedge smiles.

"Okay, let me get ready for work, or I'll never get there," she said to Martha, who was still tangled in the images of Junior being illegally offensive to the neighborhood girls.

"Spike, the head gremlin, that's his name," Martha recalled.

"I'm not even gonna ask," Nina said, walking through the house with a gray skirt suit on a hanger, holding it up to the light.

It looked larger than she remembered. The skirt appeared as if one and a half people could fit in it, and it was god-awful short. She had gone shopping with Troi and Carla. Carla had picked it out, telling Nina she needed a little pizzazz. Next thing she knew, she'd have her wearing a harlot toe ring.

Sifting through her closet for her white cotton shirt, Nina wondered if people really thought she was fat fat, or just fat.

"Yes, okay," Martha interjected. "Let me get Glenda up and ready for school." She headed for the door.

Nina was thankful that she had the kind of job that she was often able to do from home. She had a computer notebook that the company had bought and a spare phone line with built-in conference calling in the extra bedroom. Her office manager always handled things efficiently enough that she didn't have to worry when she was away.

"Nina, I'm going. I'll give you a buzz later, and I want details. Full details." She smiled.

"Will do." Nina grinned.

19

Michelle had done her disappearing act as always, made her entrance and exit without so much as a lingering scent. Strands of her light brown hair still slept on the pillow next to him. Tim would think she was a figment of his imagination, if it weren't for the grin she left behind that now found itself wrapped across his face. At four A.M. she'd slid out of bed, trying not to wake him or hint at her pending departure. He'd watched her put on each earring, fasten on her watch, and pull on her stockings one sensuous leg at a time, then slip on her shoes.

Her shoes had laid next to his all night. It was as if they belonged together. His, large and strong, and hers, resting delicately on their sides. She'd wrapped and buttoned her dress, then reached into her bag for her compact. She'd licked then colored her lips slowly and purposely. Then she was gone, without so much as a good-bye, *sayonara,* or adios. Tim needed a little affection, and Michelle had sufficiently supplied that. He leaned over, avoiding the sunlight, and tried to scribble a few thoughts onto his pad. He needed to spend more time out of the house. He wrote that on the pad. He underlined the word *more.*

A girl in his film class had invited him over for dinner. "You need to be having dinner at my place," she'd said, most self-assured. He had been contemplating it since last week, but thought that he would go. She'd claimed that they could work on their assignments together. That was the oldest trick in the handbook. He knew she had other plans, namely him, but it was solid. He was looking forward to getting a home-cooked meal and some much needed conversation.

He didn't want to get tangled up in strings. Women figured if they cooked you a meal, they'd gotten you at least halfway down the aisle to the altar. That wasn't even remotely warm to the truth, but his stomach refused to let him cancel.

Tim hadn't been spending nearly enough time honing his craft. He was angry with himself for that. So, the last thing on his mind was dating. He knew that if he was trying to prove himself, he needed more discipline, more drive, more ambition. And he also needed to wean himself off the lure of a woman. Women. Plural. They required everything short of blood. He'd never become well known in the film industry by chasing women and focusing only on getting his sexual needs fed, then coming back for seconds. That was the pastime of enough men he already knew. He wanted to soak up the industry phrases and be privy to information about film scouts and nightly parties along the beach, where making contacts was frequent and life-changing. The words *West Coast* would probably become popularized and overused in his city-boy vocabulary.

He reached in the closet for a light jacket, which he might not need with the warm May winds prompting residents to shed it all. But he needed to get some indirect feedback regarding Michelle and his constant craving for her. He was trying to rationalize it, but he wouldn't make it appear that he was needy or ravenous. He didn't want Justin or anybody else to think that someone had him strung. He'd hint at the subject. Justin would set him straight, he always did. Granted, it was no secret that Michelle and Tim had a magnetic attraction, sexual even. He didn't know if that was a good thing. He didn't know when or how they could finally coordinate the things in their lives to allow time for each other if either of them wanted more.

It was Michelle who was unavailable more than it was Tim. All his friends took pleasure in calling Tim a player, but it wasn't like that. He was searching, seeking, and waiting for something to stir him up. He had tried to tell Michelle how he felt without sounding weak. He wasn't gonna sell his manhood short for a skirt. Never that. And not for a woman. He tried to be open and communicate, but her needs took precedence; she wanted to be held without question. She wanted to silence him with a kiss whenever he began to ask about her job and how little time she spent in New York.

"I adore my job, Tim. It's a once-in-a-lifetime opportunity. Don't you know how hard it is for a woman in the business? I have to prove myself. You know those old boys won't take me seriously otherwise."

He understood. He was trying to do the same thing. A black man in film definitely had to prove that he could write and direct a movie about something more than players, pimps, and drug deals gone bad. So they were in the same boat, sort of. But he was a man. He'd never allow a woman to manipulate his feelings. He enjoyed her, it wasn't a lie, but when he needed someone, it would have to be a woman who would be there when he needed her to be. He wasn't looking for much. Just reciprocation. Fair exchange wasn't grand theft auto.

Tim rang his study partner for the evening to find out if they were still on. He knew they were, but he just wanted to hear her say it. He shook his head, thinking how other women in his life had always been predictable, but never Michelle. That was probably the dilemma. He wanted her because he couldn't have her. His thoughts skipped back to his date for the evening. He forgot what she looked like. Short skirt, knee-high boots, they were all the same. He had everything in his mind straight. They were going to study and work on the film project, that was it. They'd toss around a few ideas and maybe even get a head start on next week's assignment. If she made a pass, he wouldn't let on. He'd pretend that he didn't notice her checking him out head to toe, or right there.

He'd try to convince himself that this woman was attracted to his mind. He was sorely misled. He knew that but he'd bask in the ear candy and enjoy whatever came of the evening. He was a well-dressed black man, and he liked to indulge in the pleasantries of passion. It was a struggle to abstain, and his body fought him every step of the way. But not yet, not now, and absolutely not with this woman that he hardly knew, his conscience retorted. To be in the presence of this woman who desired him would be the reassurance he needed after Michelle had left without a word. Michelle was a seductress; everyone wanted her but no one could have her. She'd lure you to the flame like a moth and, before you knew it, your wings were scorched, useless. She couldn't be faulted though, because she gave just as much pleasure as she received. And Tim was nothing more than a willing participant.

"Are you ready?" she asked impatiently.

He was reassured that his study partner's motive was to get him to her place as quickly as possible and then dance the dance. There was an urgency in her voice that extended a finger and motioned, *come here*. He was certain that she would call up her fellow classmates and ask them to guess who was coming over to her place.

"Do you need me to bring something?"

"No, I've got everything you need," she clarified.

"Yes, I'll call you when I'm on my way. Apartment 7C, right?"

He smoothed down the hair on his chin and scribbled on a yellow pad. She was definitely forward, taking no shorts. He was not looking for a relationship, and he hoped this girl didn't think that he was just because he spent the evening with her. He was hungry, that was all. He didn't need any demands on his time now. He couldn't afford to lose any more focus than he already had.

"Man, what about Michelle?" Justin asked.

"I really dig her, but I'm not trying to go out like that. Chasing skirts ain't my thing. I just want to be me."

"What does that mean?" Justin chuckled.

"I want to work and get my stuff out there, be recognized as one of the new up-and-coming filmmakers."

"I hear ya."

"I'd like to have someone there by my side to share my joy." Tim shrugged. "But I'm not stressing that now, you know?"

"Yeah, I know. But you have to get out there, meet people. Go out with several women. Aren't you the one who said if you aren't married, then you're single?"

"Yeah."

"Well, live by your own motto, man, stop letting this woman hem you up like this. She's not available, get over her, man. You could have women falling out of the sky right into your lap. You can have any of them you please."

"Yes, but I'm not desperate, Jay."

"I realize that, man, but check this out, if you were less available, Michelle would surely come around."

"I know. But it's just that . . ."

"No, man, stop, don't let yourself go there. Does she care what you're feeling? Sneaking around at night, flying into JFK at two A.M? What's that about? Have you ever thought that she might have a man here, there, and everywhere?"

"She's not that kind of woman, Jay."

"They never are, huh?"

"You right."

"You can't be her puppet, man. You know this stuff, you taught me. Where did you put it? You need to recall this information that you shared, man." Justin tapped his temple. "It's what got me through my thing with Pam."

"I know, I know."

"And you need to leave that Sharon alone, too. She's trouble, man. She's trying to get you to the altar, might use all kinds of voodoo to get you there, too. You better check your closet. She might be burning candles, putting roots under your bed. You know how women do, 'by any means necessary.' Seriously, don't play and don't sleep."

"True enough. I gotcha." He nodded, still not satisfied with the fact that Michelle had left without so much as a kiss on the forehead.

Tim kicked around with Justin for a bit. He went through Justin's cabinets scrounging for food. There was only an onion, half a gallon of milk, and a box of Cheerios in the fridge.

"Where's the food, man?" Tim joked, waving the onion. During the day, Justin mostly slept to get ready for his night gig and mixed a few sounds.

He deejayed a lot, but mostly for himself, or private parties.

"So, how's the job situation, man?" Justin asked, unrolling a brown paper bag on the counter and handing Tim a bagel.

"It's cool, I gave my brother-in-law my résumé; he's supposed to hook me up with something. Answering phones, Xeroxing, or something. I need money for tuition, rent, telephone, and some gear, man."

"So, the ladies still spending the money, man?"

"You know that. Sharon lost her mind, just bought me a hot pink shirt. Now she knows I'm not all colorful like that."

"Man, bring it over here," Justin said eagerly. "You know a brother wears everything."

"It's yours, man." Tim laughed, spreading whipped cream cheese on his bagel. "'Cause I don't do pink."

"Oh, yeah, party this weekend, man. I'll bring a couple of ladies to help get your mind off of Sharon," Justin ribbed.

"Sharon's not the one you have to worry about, it's Michelle," Tim blurted out.

"So, what, you think you love her, man?" Justin asked, with his eyes fixed on Tim's hands and facial expression.

"Nah, it's not even like that. You know I don't swing that love thing. I just want to do my film gig and chill, you know. I'm not trying to get tangled. I've got bills to pay. A little company now and then, that's it."

"You sure, man?"

"Positive. Rochelle keeps trying to fix me up like I'm starving for affection or something."

"That's how sisters are, man, you know that."

"Yeah, but I'm not a charity case. I want to do what I want with whomever I choose."

"I hear you. So, what's up for tonight?"

"Nothing, dinner with a friend."

"Friend?" Justin smiled.

"You don't know her, she's new," Tim said, shaking his head at the thoughts he assumed were going through Justin's mind.

"A classic situation."

"She's from film school."

"She got money? A sister?"

"I don't know. And yes, she's a sister."

"Can she cook?"

"I hope so, I'm going over for dinner. A brother is starving like Marvin."

"I hear you, man."

"So, let me jet, man." Tim slapped his thigh. "I have to mail off some applications, try and get some ends."

"True, true."

"So, tonight?"

"A home-cooked meal, man. You know a brother will never go hungry." He laughed.

"I trust you will handle Sharon."

"No doubt, man, no doubt. And good looking out."

"Not a problem. Be safe."

The line in the post office was longer than it was at tax time. Labels and papers scattered all around the countertops and people carrying parcels, complaining to each other because the pens chained to the counters for use wouldn't write. There were only two Plexiglas windows open, until one clerk pulled down his shade and put up his indignant CLOSED sign. The woman at the other window was moving in slow motion. *Women. That's why they cause so many accidents when they drive. They're too slow,* he thought. He counted the people on the line. Forty-seven. There was no way he was going to have time to wait for forty-seven people to be serviced, find the closest ATM machine, and then make it downtown for dinner. He was hungry. Starving. He opened his knapsack and pushed the envelopes down inside his bag, drew the string, and slung it over his shoulder.

He needed an ATM machine and a meal. Seven-C. He kept her apartment number in the forefront of his mind.

He knew that this woman would greet him at the door wearing something that surely would be considered lingerie. Jay had always warned him that women thought less was more. He knew the drill. She'd tell him how intelligent and handsome she thought he was and say that she admired his work. She'd also ask if he wanted seconds. She'd play on words and inquire whether or not he wanted dessert. Women were a trip and a half. The trip wasn't that bad; it was that half you had to worry about.

20

Troi woke and began preparing her daily java jolt. Coffee beans churning and toast popping always set her mind in motion. Vaughn's "good morning" was greeted with an icy silence that made her have to repent in her mind as she buttered her bread. *Lord forgive me, but I hate him right about now.*

"CeCe, we need to talk." Vaughn stood, not looking her directly in the eye.

"About what?"

"You know what, CeCe."

"It wasn't important enough to talk about last night, so . . ."

"We were both too upset to talk, and you know it." She looked through him, realizing that she probably didn't know him as well as she thought.

For years his love had been liquid; she'd just drunk it, bitterness, sweetness, and all. But she loved him, although she deserved to be excited about something for a change. *I'm too young for the pasture,* Troi thought. She closed her eyes as her eyelashes tickled her face. Vaughn grew closer and took the bag of coffee beans from her hand, rested it gently on the countertop, and pulled her into the bedroom behind him, as if he was ushering her in there for a surprise.

Vaughn sat her down on their bed. Troi searched around the room for something that she could hang onto as a reminder of the life she'd once had if she decided to throw him and his things out after this most troubling revelation. Her eyes were curious and childlike. Her lips curled, and in her mind she whispered, *be gentle.* He didn't know what he was going to say, she could tell. He hadn't rehearsed anything. Vaughn was pacing again. His nervousness was evident as he tapped his fingers on the dressing table, biding time until the words formed complete sentences.

"CeCe, I don't know how to say this," he began, with his praying hands resting against his lips.

"Just say it, Vaughn," Troi encouraged. "Just say it," she whispered.

He let out a sigh that wasn't even beginning to release the tension this conversation was sure to create. His back tensed as he continued, "Now, you know I love you, right?" Vaughn's voice echoed into a hollowness, like the aftereffect and ringing sensation you got when you were smacked in the face with a cold wet hand. Tears started forming as she fought to hold them back with sheer will alone.

Troi didn't know what to expect. She nodded, twiddling her fingers, thinking that she wasn't as sure of herself and her marriage as she was a week ago. Seven days, 168 hours. There was a time when she could swear up and down any street that no other woman could take her man or make him want to leave her. After all, she did the laundry, she cooked, she kept herself looking presentable most of the time, and she was compromising to the point that Vaughn almost always got things his way.

"Well, I didn't go in to work on Friday." He paused.

Her gaze was fixed on something on the dressing table. She thought about throwing it square at him if she didn't like what he was about to say.

"I spent most of the day with a friend." Her silence egged him on. "This friend lives in Jersey." He paused. "That's why whoever told you they saw me, saw the car out there . . . our car." She nodded. "I've been visiting this friend frequently, and at first it was just friendship but . . ."

"But what?" Troi gaped, her mouth full of fear, her bottom lip trembling, and her fingers curling into unsteady fists.

"But now it's a little more than that, and I don't know what to do. I mean, I didn't mean to disregard your feelings or make you cry," he said, noticing the tears that were fighting to be released but were held back by her Madison pride.

"What is this friend's name, Vaughn?"

"It's not important, CeCe," he dismissed.

"It's important to me, Vaughn, I need to know." She lowered her voice as it trembled in an almost inaudible whisper.

He sighed and ran his hand across his head. He took a deep breath and slowly hissed every ounce of air out of his lungs.

"Tracie . . ."

"Tracie, huh?" She nodded. Troi stood up, face-to-face with Vaughn.

"Yes."

"And how long have you been violating our relationship, our marriage vows, and our child's future sneaking around and having an affair with her?" Troi was yelling now. "How long, huh?"

Vaughn captured the expression on her face, which he was sure would change any minute. Vaughn hesitated as he held Troi's face, embraced her rigid body, which no longer pressed into his. He looked into her eyes and spoke deliberately.

"Him. Him, Troi."

"Him? You're kidding, right?" She smiled weakly, stepping backward. "Stop playing games, Vaughn!"

"I'm not playing games. This is nothing that I would joke about." He raised his voice and his hand for emphasis.

Troi's mouth hung open, her lips lost their function, and she heard the mocking, thigh-slapping laughter that shook her.

"Noooooo!" Troi yelled loud and long, vibrating her lungs, pulling at her hair, and making vain attempts to throw anything that was within reach.

Glass didn't shatter, but she was hot enough to chase demons in hell and angry enough to blend in.

"You have got to be kidding me!" Her mind raced, instinctively thinking what she had done wrong. "Okay, okay. This can't be happening." She paced. "Wait, wait. Okay. Stop." She looked Vaughn in the eyes. "Gay?" She turned her head to the side, examining him from an unfamiliar angle.

Vaughn tried to touch and reassure Troi, but she shrank away from the sight of him. She didn't want to talk to him. She didn't want to see his lying face telling her that he loved her and their baby girl. Her hands were trembling, holding each other, and she prayed silently for something to grasp onto that she knew wouldn't leave. It was then that she was clothed in disgust and repulsed by this situation, his presence, and their steamy shower scene that she had practically begged for the other morning. Gay? It wasn't what she'd thought she'd hear. A sorry maybe, but *gay*? She closed her eyes momentarily with her head to heaven. She wanted to scrub any part of her body that Vaughn had touched.

She tried to purify her thoughts. He had undressed for a man. A man. The same sex.

"Vaughn, how could you do this to me? I mean, really, how could you?" She fought the dramatic urge to release her anger by crying, beating his chest, and falling to her knees.

She felt ashamed for not knowing. Madison women had always blamed themselves. It had to be her fault. How could she have not known? She wasn't stupid, and naive was a nondescriptive adjective where she was concerned. She questioned herself, then him.

"Are you telling me that you are gay? Seriously gay, Vaughn?"

"I have these feelings, CeCe, I don't know what I am."

Cautiously she asked, "Well . . . have you acted on these feelings? Sexually, I mean?"

He paused, then nodded yes.

She could feel the bile rise in her throat. Her hand instinctively clasped her mouth as she stumbled into the bathroom. Hanging over the toilet, her life was replayed like a bad film with a one-week run. She thought of the love she had given this man, who had just taken her dignity away with a three-letter word. She turned on the faucet and soaked a washcloth under the force of the water. She wiped her mouth and rested the warm cloth on her face. "I will not be a doormat, I will not be a doormat," she repeated to herself.

"CeCe, you have to know that I never ever meant to hurt you," Vaughn offered, walking into the bathroom.

"But you did, Vaughn," she said, excusing herself past him and making her way to the bed. "Do you think this makes me feel glad?"

She poked her chest. No word could describe feeling as if she had just undergone an emotional lobotomy.

"My God, I can't believe this!" Troi fell back on their bed, slapping her head.

"CeCe, wait a minute."

"Wait what?"

"I wanna tell you something."

She sat up, glaring at the man who should have never uttered the word *forever*.

"No, I wanna tell *you* something, Vaughn Singleton." She pointed. "I gave you everything I had," she said. "I put all I was into this marriage. I cooked, I cleaned, I did stinking laundry that was mostly yours, so tell me, exactly what do you want me to give now?"

"A chance, CeCe. Give me a chance. I'm confused, that's all. I still care about you, you know I do. I want this to work."

"So, what am I supposed to do, Vaughn? Move him in here with us?"

"I just want you to hear me out, CeCe. I married you because I saw something in you."

"Oh, really? What? A man?"

"That's not fair, I'm just being honest. I could have lied."

"Look, I can't deal with this or you now." Troi brushed past her husband again, purposely bumping him.

"No, don't run, CeCe."

"Don't run? What am I supposed to do? Stay? Wait until you figure out what you want and be astonished at the fact that it isn't me?"

"I need you, CeCe. Please don't leave me like this," he said, grabbing her by both arms and holding her close.

"I don't want no mercy sex! Don't feel sorry for me, don't give me nothing. I can't believe I didn't know!" She pulled away.

"CeCe, please."

"I tried to please you." She emphasized her words with her finger. "But you can't please me." She turned her back and motioned him away with her hand.

"I need you, CeCe, you're the only one who . . ."

"Need me to what? The only one who what? What about what I need? What about our baby? I need honesty, and I need to be able to trust you to please me and only me, and right now you can't do either."

"I just need to figure some things out, CeCe."

"We've been married three years. You're twenty-eight years old, you had twenty-five years to figure you out!" she bellowed, waking the baby into a screaming frenzy. "I just want you to go. Go live with your boyfriend or whatever position he's assuming in that godforsaken relationship that the two of you have concocted. I really can't look at you now."

"No, I'm not going." Vaughn reached for Dakoda, picking her up and hugging her tightly. "We live here together," he said, standing like he was staging a protest. "For better or worse, remember, CeCe?" He bounced the baby to lull her back to sleep.

It was times like this that Troi should have been able to call her father, but he was so far removed from his family right now that she knew she couldn't.

"Take her with you, Vaughn, I need to be alone."

"But I'm running late."

"I don't care if you have to quit, I need time alone. Take Dakoda to your mother's, just like you probably did every time you went to see your man in Jersey. And please stop whining, it's pathetic."

Vaughn wasn't too big on groveling, but he figured he'd better perfect the art if he wanted their relationship to work.

Troi stared at Vaughn, imagining what he had wanted from her for the past three years if he was so insistent on making these new sexual discoveries of his a natural manifestation.

"I'll be back," Vaughn said, interrupting her silence.

The front door slammed as it always did on his way out. Troi crawled into the center of the bed with cold dirty feet. She rested on her side and drew her knees up to her chest. The sheets were cool, it was almost 8 A.M., and she couldn't sleep. She stared at the ceiling fan, which she figured should spin around and chop her head off. It couldn't hurt any worse than what her husband had just told her. All she could imagine were the laughing faces of the Hallelujah Girls, smiling and taking more delight than her situation should have brought.

She was sure if they got wind of Vaughn's revelation that they'd spread it like a brush fire in a dry unkept forest, and the story would get so distorted that it would come back to her that her husband had run off and left Troi to join a gay midget circus. She held her knees tightly to her chest, covered herself snugly under the blankets, and gazed out the window at the noisy city, trying to block out the men submitting their bodies to each other in her mind. She didn't want to know what he did. She didn't want to visualize it. She didn't want to hear the pleasure that another man was able to give her husband.

Troi thought she had found Eden. Her husband's voice was so strong and deep that it alone could bring her to a spontaneous orgasm. But now fear decorated her face as she realized that her feelings could no longer be trusted. He did the dishes, for goodness sake. How many men did that? He had come into her life with his colorful college phrases; she'd been floored by his forward nature. After they were married, he had pierced his ear; surely that should have told her something. She laughed. A sexual mispreference. No woman deserved that. The problem was that when your heart ached, you felt an emptiness in your stomach. That wasn't hunger, and nothing satisfied it, nothing.

Troi remembered when she was little how Nina would sit in the kitchen and drink hot chocolate with more than a handful of marshmallows melting over the sides of the mug and listening to Nina Simone. Whenever Nina was in deep thought or had a crucial decision to make, a steamy mug of something and blues aided her. Troy would find the CD later, but there was no way she was going to stay married to a homosexual. Troi thought about Sam and wondered if he knew about Vaughn's desires and had just willingly failed to tell her.

Maybe Vaughn's mother knew, too. Maybe Troi was the sacrificial lamb. The dedicated wife. Maybe her life had been offered while Vaughn was still in the process of trying to figure out which sex he preferred, and everyone was just going along with the program. They had always gotten along so well, the both of them. Their marriage had been open and reciprocal, until recently. She dared not tell Nina about her marital hoax, for fear that she'd feel sorry for Troi. She definitely wouldn't tell her mother either. Troi was the only guest invited to this pity party. She didn't have the energy for Nina Simone.

Troi was always pleased that she was never considered the impulsive one, but she was feeling so out of her element. She was secretly being summoned by a drink that would numb her senses and make the world she lived in vague enough to trudge through this moment.

God knew everything. He had to know that this would happen to her. What had she done wrong? Of course that would be her first question. God had to have known that she would feel stripped of everything that made her a woman. When your husband left you for a man it rendered you useless, leaving you to wallow in despair.

At this moment she didn't feel sexy. She felt like an old wrinkled bald woman, with a mustache and no breasts. She thought now of how many times she had hated her mother for making a highball glass with three ice cubes more important than her kids. She remembered her mother's requests for more ice, splashing something overproof on it, and giving it that swirl. The liquor had hugged the ice, comforted it. She needed comfort now. She didn't want to numb her maternal instincts, although she did need to feel less of something. Less rejected. Less unworthy. Less tortured. Less unfortunate. Dakoda needed her. She wanted to feel loved, and if she couldn't, then intoxication would do. It could do. But she also didn't want to spend her life being too wasted to know when her daughter was in pain and needed to talk, as her mother had.

Troi closed her eyes. She refused. She wasn't about to become her mother. She couldn't spend her life wrestling with that generational curse. Her life and dedication to her beliefs had broken that chain, and she was satisfied with that. It just didn't stop the devil from trying to bring your past back to your memory or tempting you to reclaim it. And right now he was trying to convince her that one sip to put herself to sleep and allow dreams to follow wouldn't kill her or make her an alkie.

Everyone kept alcohol of some kind in the house, and if they looked hard enough, it could be found as close as the cooking sherry or the cough syrup. Troi got out of bed and walked into the kitchen, looking down at her cold dirty feet. She reached in the cabinet behind the molasses and took the cooking sherry down off the shelf. The bottle was sticky. She searched for the Bay Rum that she knew was up there because she always added it to the holiday cakes. Behind the vinaigrette and cans of salmon stacked atop each other, there it was, tall and slim, the color of cognac.

She unscrewed the cap and took a whiff, inhaling so deeply she could taste it. Surely it would burn going down and leave a warm feeling in her chest that would cue her to stick out her tongue, gasping for air. It would provide her the closeness and comfort that nobody around her could supply at this very moment. This second was what mattered. No one knew the hole Vaughn's betrayal left in her. Here she stood with the shrapnel of despair his confession had left behind. In their bedroom was where he had made his confession; her heart was lying wounded somewhere near the dust ruffle on the floor.

She was still partially numb to the facts right now. The strength of the bottle would help her sleep, and she would dream of a life closer to perfection than what she was living. She wasn't completely sure though. She knew that she needed all her wits about her to get through a situation that demanded that she deep-six the love she and Vaughn had, and that was on the pretense that he had ever loved her in the first place. She didn't believe what was happening. Maybe he just wanted another woman and wanted her to think that he was gay. She couldn't make heads or tails of a solitary thought. She placed three ice cubes in the glass, poured the rum, filling it almost to the top, turned on the tap, and drizzled in some cold water. Nobody had ever needed to teach her how.

Her mind went back to her mother, nodding off at the breakfast table when Troi was nine and again at twelve, then sixteen. That was her whole life. Her mother would talk with a cigarette that was shedding ashes dangling from her chapped lips, never making sense. Troi couldn't bring herself to mirror her mother. Even though she was emotionally dying, she knew with all that was righteous that she had to be sober for her baby. Dakoda was her gift, and there was no second-guessing that. With sharpshooting precision, Troi tossed the glass into the sink, sending shards of thick broken tinted glass and ice chunks flying about. She reached for the statuesque bottle, too, gripping it with every ounce of authority, making it surrender, tipping it, and slowly poured temptation down the drain.

21

Vaughn sat quietly with his mom in the dank kitchen that was devoid of natural color. The sun didn't shine and the city sky was never blue from their house. The whole feel of the table, the window with the curtains that matched the pot holders hanging on the hook by the stove, brought back memories of intimate childhood discussions. He remembered sitting at the table with his brother, Sam, and his mother telling them both that they had to bear with their father and that he was only doing what he thought he had to do for his people. She'd make them breakfast and they'd listen to her justify his rantings and ravings about a conspiracy against the black man. "Your father wants to make sure that when you both grow up you get a fair share of the financial pie, babies."

"We know, Momma," Sam would say, always ready to speak for them both.

Now, twenty years later, she was making breakfast for Vaughn and his baby. Pancakes. She made them thick, just the way he liked them as a kid. He smiled, reminiscing about when he was eighteen and having his last big home-cooked breakfast before going off to college. He'd topped six pancakes off with butter, whipped cream, and warmed blueberry syrup, savoring each bite. With his belly full and still licking his lips, Vaughn had loaded his beat-up ride with the necessary college essentials, while his momma had wept and packed Tupperware containers full of leftovers in his trunk simultaneously. "I'm going to college, not a third world country, Momma."

"It's okay, baby. I don't mind doing it. Anything for my babies," she'd said, making sure everything fit without spilling over.

"You better be lucky your momma's sending you off with a care package," his dad had interjected. "You know, they give black men scholarships and then get them way out there in Kansas somewhere and starve them to death so that they don't make the grade. The plot is getting you off focus, your GPA falls, and then they're anxious to revoke your scholarship and give it to someone they feel is genealogically superior. They're always out to get us. Hidden racism is the worst. At least when they were burning crosses we knew what was coming. It's a conspiracy. You have to know these things, son."

"I do know, Dad," Vaughn had pleaded.

But Vaughn was experiencing something completely unrelated now. He couldn't tell his momma that he preferred a burly man with a baritone groan and a five o'clock shadow to his wife. A wife who had taken him for better or worse but dared not assume the latter. He couldn't risk telling his authoritative father either that he had a fetish for a black man with smooth skin, unblemished and unmarred by tattoos and cryptic messages. Skin that invited him to caress it, a mustache that tickled his. Melanin that was maybe a shade or two darker, but preferably lighter than his own.

"So, how's Sam, Vaughn?" his momma asked.

"I don't know," Vaughn mumbled with his mouth full.

"I thought you were gonna stop by him the other day?"

Vaughn sighed as he rested his fork on the side of his plate and reached for his orange juice. He had not only betrayed his wife, his God, and his marriage, but running around his momma's house was an innocent child whom he possibly would not get to see grow up into womanhood. He didn't feel as guilty as he thought he should.

"I didn't make it over there, Momma."

He didn't understand why something he felt so naturally could destroy the lives of everyone around him. If he had kept his feelings on the hush, he could still count on white Christmases, cheery Father's Days, and boisterous family reunions where Sam tackled everybody to show them all that they missed a good thing when they didn't recruit him into the NFL. Vaughn's mind was racing. His eyes wild like someone under a bit too much pressure.

"What's wrong, baby?"

"Nothing, Momma."

"Now, you know I'm your momma, I know when something's wrong. Tell me, son."

"I said it's nothing, Momma."

"Is it Troi, baby?"

"Momma, I really don't want to talk about it."

"Okay, well, I'm here when you're ready."

"I know, Momma." He managed a smile.

He just didn't want anyone trying to pry into his mind and help him deal with something that he didn't even know if he wanted handled. They'd talk him into giving up a part of himself that he didn't necessarily want to relinquish, at least not yet.

Now his momma was mixing something in a pot and muttering about how his daddy had a meeting early this morning and would be sorry that he didn't get to spend the day with Vaughn and the baby. Vaughn walked over to the window, gazing out at a couple of schoolkids walking with notebooks rolled up and pushed down in their back pockets.

He had missed a couple of days from work; he'd never get a promotion that way. Dedication was what they looked for in a managerial candidate. He just wasn't sure that he was ready for any other form of undue stress, even if they were paying. He could only dedicate himself to one thing at a time. And right now that one thing was his blossoming feelings.

His thoughts drifted back to this morning, the vile hatred in Troi's eyes, and her despising hands that had pushed him away deliberately, making him wonder if she'd ever loved him. But he knew that she had. Probably still did, even after he had violated her womanhood in the most unforgivable manner.

"You know it'll be okay, baby, you just need some time apart, you and Troi, if that's what's bothering you," his momma said, resting her hand on his back and comforting him with small circular motions. "Your father and I fight. All couples fight."

"Momma, don't."

"Okay," she said, throwing up her hands and reaching for the baby, who was playing hide-and-seek from the sofa.

He didn't want to leave his wife. Although he had issues, she understood him better than anybody. Better than his own mother.

He cared what Troi thought and felt, but he couldn't honor her request to go and live somewhere else. That was his home, too. They had made it together. They didn't go half on a baby; they genuinely loved each other. That was, until temptation had reared its ugly head and shaken their once-firm foundation, knocking over a few things in the process. If he left, there would be a wedge between them forever, a male wedge with a mustache. He needed to be with Troi and Dakoda; they were what he considered his family. He understood that *sorry* wasn't a Band-Aid that made everything go back to normal. His new discoveries didn't change anything. He was still married and Troi was still his wife.

Vaughn had admired Troi's structure from afar, thick as those Madison girls were. When she'd sung her solo in church, his heart would always leap, and he'd known that he'd marry her one day. Their time together had been as melodic as two hearts beating in tandem. There were so many women who deliberately flaunted themselves in Vaughn's face, but he wasn't buying. Their love came marked down, almost given away free. Obvious wasn't his thing. He wanted new and unrehearsed.

He loved the way Troi fumbled trying to find the Scriptures and the notes that she jotted down in the margin of her bible. She was attentive to the Word, and had only missed one Sunday since he had come home from college and joined the church as an active member. He often helped out with the sound system and printed up programs for special events on his computer. He preferred Zion Missionary to his momma's church because at his momma's church he felt like he was always under the watchful eye. He didn't attend church to be observed, he was there to be fed, and he had gotten tired of going home hungry.

Vaughn remembered back to when he'd asked Troi out for the first time. She'd been sitting in a pew next to her friend Carla after service. They'd been gathering the bibles from their slots. He'd cleared his throat and begun with, "Troi, can I ask you something?"

"Sure."

"I'd like to know, I mean, if it would be possible that we can go out sometime. That is, if you aren't spoken for."

She'd said, "No."

"No, you aren't spoken for, or no we can't go out?" He'd rubbed his hands together.

"Both." She'd been rather polite about it. "I just don't have time to date right now."

It had caught him off guard. He'd never gotten a chance to utter his smooth line, "I'll pick you up at eight."

"No offense, Vaughn. I'm just not ready yet. I mean, it can get sort of distracting, you know?"

"Yes, I understand," he'd said. "By the way, I loved your song this morning," he'd said, smiling as she grinned.

"Thank you." He'd licked his wounds and let about three more weeks go by before he was determined to approach her after the New Year's Eve service that had their small church bursting at the seams and onlookers peering in from the streets.

There had been green and gold holiday festive decor meticulously mapped around the church since before Christmas. The pulpit had had poinsettias prompting everyone to sing carols. Vaughn didn't have a problem with being rejected. He didn't have low self-esteem or a complex about being told no. Someone telling him no just made his go after what he wanted with a vengeance.

So, he'd figured that he'd devise a plan that would bring the need to help out of Troi. She'd been wearing a black skirt suit with a silver blouse that evening. Black shoes, too. One of those psychedelic scarves like her friend Carla wore. Her hair had been rolled up and pulled back in a bun thing with sparkly glitter all over it.

He'd taken a deeper breath than he normally did that night. There was something about Troi that demanded respect. He had to muster tact to approach her. "Hey, Troi, can I ask you something, if you have a minute?" Carla, who had always been aware of what was going on around them both, had nudged her in Vaughn's direction.

"Sure, what is it?"

"I need help."

"Whatever I can do." He'd smiled, glad that she'd offered her services before she even knew what it was he needed.

"I need to take some things to my brother, who lives in Jersey. He and his wife are having problems, and I figured that it would do him good to have some company to cheer him up a bit."

"And?"

"And I wanted to know if you'd accompany me."

"To Jersey?"

"Yes, I know that you don't really know me, but I'm a God-fearing man, I haven't missed any Sundays in two years, I work in banking, my favorite color is blue, my favorite Scripture is John 13:35, and I'd really like to get to know you . . . as friends," he'd added quickly. "I know you said that you didn't want to get distracted, and I promise, I'm not here for that."

"Okay," she'd said.

"Okay?"

"Yes, I'll go, but when?" The shock of the unexpected response had made him pause longer than he should have.

"Now . . . right now, if that's good for you?"

"Yes, it's fine."

"Great!" he'd said.

"Okay then," she'd said, tossing her scarf over her shoulder, reaching for her bag, and winking at Carla, who'd been double thumbs-up when she'd glanced back at her.

They'd driven to Vaughn's house and picked up the pies that he'd had his momma baking all weekend just to pull off the stunt. He'd wrapped them up, set them on the backseat, and driven off into the future with the soon-to-be Mrs. Singleton riding shotgun. He'd known then. She'd been hard to get. He'd known she wasn't acting; she was really not giving up without a fight. He could respect that. It made it all the more fun. He hadn't thought about Debbie and the kiss on her back porch in years. He hadn't even thought about how certain thoughts prompted his body to respond without permission.

He'd known he loved Troi. When he'd thought about places that he wanted to go, he'd imagined them sharing them together. Greece, Venice, and Acapulco. Water all seven shades of green and tropical scents like mango chutney imposing themselves in their nostrils. He'd tell her what he'd read about the places that he wanted to visit, and she'd pretend to be the tour guide, making up stories and fables along the way. He'd thought he wouldn't mind having separate rooms. He'd respected her that much. Soon enough they'd share one. Troi was one entertaining woman. It hadn't necessarily mattered what she was saying; he'd loved to hear her speak. "Don't let her get away," his momma had urged. He had made up his mind to propose after six months of exclusive dating.

Leaning over a local day bridge in White Plains, looking into the peaceful serenity of the water and the grassy area lined with succulent magnolia trees, after doing some summer shopping together in the Galleria, Vaughn had asked Troi what she thought about tomorrow. She'd thought it an awkward question. "Tomorrow is the future, it's not promised, Vaughn." She'd thought he was being spiritual.

"Well, today is, Troi. Will you promise me today?"

"What?"

"Promise me today and however many tomorrows God allows us. Marry me?"

She'd dropped her purse and squealed a high-pitched shriek, flapping her arms and jumping up and down as the ducks flew away, birds scattered, and curious parkgoers catching a few rays eyed them to make sure Troi was delighted and not in danger. "Are you sure,

Vaughn?" she'd asked, as he'd held her hand steady and slipped the ring on her finger.

"I want to do the right thing," he'd said, noticing that she was out of breath and could have been a shade of crimson, but he couldn't really tell.

Troi had been everything to Vaughn then; she still was. There was nothing like a couple that prayed together. But as the excitement of their marriage had waned and his vision had blurred, he'd begun pressuring her for a baby. He'd been merely creating substitutes, he thought in retrospect. "As far as I know, I can have kids, Vaughn. What's the rush?"

"No rush, I'm just curious. My brother's wife got pregnant on their honeymoon." With the eat, sleep, smooch of their own honeymoon, Troi should have been pregnant, too, but she hadn't been.

She hadn't worried about it, either. She'd wanted to enjoy her husband and their new life together before she got distracted with kids and extra mouths to feed. She'd wanted to shave him as he sat on the toilet and feed him while he read the headlines from the *Daily News*. "Kids are a blessing, CeCe, and after Brenda's miscarriage, I know a baby would overjoy my mom."

"I know that, but don't we need to relate on a few levels before we bring a baby into our life? That baby will demand attention, Vaughn."

"I know."

"That means you'll get less."

"I don't mind that, CeCe, I want us to have a complete family."

Four months after they were married, CeCe's pregnancy test had come back positive. Vaughn had watched his wife go from a gentle God-fearing woman who found joy in reading and other quiet activities to a knife-wielding chef who practically ate them out of house and home, leaving crumbs in her path and sneaking around the kitchen like a bandit at night. She'd often come to bed with her breath smelling like tuna and onions, then want to kiss of all things. His momma had said things would be okay then, too. Even when Troi would cry for no reason and think that she was fat and getting blacker by the minute. And he and CeCe had been getting better, but he didn't know what to make of it now.

His life was anything but ordinary. "I want him," Vaughn had whispered out loud to himself across the table while he'd been having lunch with Tracie that fateful afternoon.

"Excuse me?" Tracie had asked.

"Nothing." Vaughn had blushed. Those words gave his feelings life. The minute he'd spoken those words, he'd made them alive. He believed them. He made them exist. He was aware you had to be careful what you asked for. He was aware that a single word could level your life to ruin, but he was up to the challenge; he was in it for the long haul.

22

Nina picked up the phone and buzzed Troi at the shop, but she wasn't in. Nina had forgotten it was Monday. Sometimes Troi still came by the shop anyway, but Carmen said that she had called in and said that she wasn't feeling well. Nina tried to call her at home; she hated answering machines. She wanted Troi to meet Derek. She wanted to know what her sister's impression of him was. He wasn't fabulous, as Troi would say, but he was a man. There had to be someone who was close enough to make Nina want to consider matrimony or some other form of togetherness, she thought as she sipped her coffee and stared out of her office window. She thought about how Tuesday was her day off. She would spend tomorrow pleasing herself and preparing for Derek. Something non-Shelby related to look forward to for a change.

She wouldn't tell Shelby a thing about him until she was sure he was for keeps. Shelby got overexcited, and would want to give pointers on how to keep him interested, in check, and in limbo, and still keep the cash flowing . . . even though her advice never worked. Nina felt rescued. She had almost reached the point where she had adjusted her mind to accept the fact that she might always be alone. This man had shed rays into her life. He was almost a savior, only he didn't know it.

She had created a mental wall where love was concerned. Brick by brick, over the years it had slowly been built. This weekend had found her on the other side, with her head sticking up and hands waving, saying, "Hey, I'm in here, don't lock me in." The construction crew in her mind had halted production and apologized for the fact that they hadn't seen her standing there. "What was she doing behind that wall?" they whispered to each other. She ignored them because it had been each man who'd come into her life as a brick that slowly trapped her behind the wall. That and the fact that she never cleared out the debris when the previous man left before she made way for the new one to enter.

Accounts slightly overbudget at work and clients more than pleased to overlook it. At work, Nina had begun putting herself in the mood for tomorrow evening. The best dates were the ones you got when you weren't even trying. No frowning, she reminded herself. She had even caught those one o'clock rays as she held onto the window in her office and closed her eyes. Everything had looked red as she'd tilted her head back and enjoyed the penetrating heat from the sun. It had made her smile. She had dozens of scenarios kicking around in her head, but preferred to indulge in the real thing. She could wait, she imagined. She'd held out this long.

Tuesdays always left Nina wishing for another day off. When Nina came home from running errands, the first thing she did was check for messages; then she showered, changed, ground coffee beans, and was now staring into the mirror, applying her lip liner around the perimeter of her lips and coloring them in generously. She had planned on spending Tuesday afternoon unwinding for tonight's rendezvous, but instead had been lured by the call of bills and statements marked NOW DUE. She reached for her perfume, sprayed it near her hair, and sauntered into the living room, and sprayed some near the sofa.

Nina was brewing some hazelnut coffee and listening to that Dawkins & Dawkins CD she found so catchy. She picked up the Sunday papers, which were still scattered around the floor, and stuffed them under the sofa cushion. She smoothed down her powder-blue microfiber blouse, which was hardly keeping her breasts in place. She surveyed the living room, went to the bookcase, and removed a book from the shelf, placing the copy of *Love* by Leo Buscaglia on the coffee table. She had only skimmed it, but they could discuss it if he was deep enough.

Deep. She didn't necessarily want a man who was deep. She wanted someone who could sit next to her in church and listen to a sermon on single life and how it was better to marry than burn and feel inspired by the whole moment. Provided he was a believer. She'd like spontaneity, even. She wanted someone whom she didn't have to struggle to figure out. She didn't like riddles. She wasn't saying he should be weak, but he should just make sense. She needed to pray. Her life was evidence that she didn't do it nearly enough.

She also didn't want someone who said the right things deliberately. She didn't have the patience to spoon-feed a man her love, and she dared not dress up and play the fool for him either. She remembered how Troi always told her that sarcasm wasn't productive, but it sure made Nina feel ten times better. So, in anticipation for tonight, she had to take a deep breath and set up her radar. There were certain things for which she just wouldn't stand. She was getting older, true, but she wasn't ready for wrinkles and hormone replacements.

Derek was supposed to arrive at four P.M., and it was 7:20. *He's late,* she thought when the doorbell rang. She thanked God silently that at least he had shown. She greeted him with a ladylike kiss on the cheek, and he in turn held her face and planted a big sloppy one on her lips. *A bit presumptuous,* she thought.

"Long time no see," he said, as Nina took his bag and he made himself comfortable on the sofa.

"What's this?" she said, lifting the bag, imagining what made it so heavy.

"Just some things," he said, taking in the scenery, but mostly her.

He looked over at Nina, then pulled her to the sofa. "Sit here with me," he said.

"Okay."

"So, what do you want to do tonight?" he asked.

"We can go to a movie or something I guess," she said, "or just get something to eat. I know this little café . . ."

"I think it would be better if we just stayed here and got to know each other a little better, don't you?" he convinced, moving in closer, bringing them almost face-to-face.

She nodded. "I guess we can do that, too." She wondered why he'd asked her what she wanted to do if he already had his mind made up. She bit her bottom lip and tried not to be petty.

"So, what you got to eat?" he asked, rubbing his hands together as if she had made a turkey with all the trimmings.

"I didn't cook. I thought maybe we'd be going out or something," she said.

"Well, I hope you're not one of those women who think that a brother has to wine and dine you or starve to death."

"No, that's not it at all," she defended, "I just didn't know we were staying in. I have no problems cooking."

He grinned, reaching for her and pulling her close again. "I just want to make sure I know what I'm getting into, that's all. You're not offended, are you?"

"No, I'm fine," she insisted.

"The woman I marry will have to be able to tempt more than my body." He grinned. She found the analogy repulsive, but she shrugged and figured it was his idea of charm.

When the phone rang, Derek appeared as if he wanted to answer it.

Martha was whispering. "Is he there yet?"

"Yes, I can say that's correct," Nina cued.

"So, should I come now?" Martha pried.

"If you'd like to, that would be fine. Okay? I'll talk to you soon."

Nina hung up the phone and turned to find Derek skimming her book collection.

"You read a lot?"

"Not as much as I should," she confessed. "I mostly buy books that I'd like to read and, if I get a chance, I usually do."

"Is that right? I think I've read almost every book here," he bragged.

"Would you like some coffee?"

"That would be grand," he said, flipping through the pages of her copy of *Our Bodies, Ourselves for the New Century*.

Nina returned from the kitchen, balancing the steaming coffee cups on a tray she had been saving until she moved to a nicer place. He was sitting on the sofa now, and didn't budge a muscle to assist her. He just watched her saunter across the room and set the tray down on the coffee table.

"I didn't know how you liked your coffee, so here's the cream and sugar."

"Light, three sugars. Remember that." He smiled and glanced at her out of the corner of his eye. "So, baby, I mean, I know it may seem forward of me, but I've got to ask you this. Why are you single? A strong black woman like you with your own place and a job that pays well," he said, drawing attention to her home furnishings.

"I'm single because I'm selective."

"So, what does a man have to have for you to consider him worthy to be in your presence?"

"No, I'm not saying it all like that, I'm just saying that if he has a mind, is a gentleman, and knows how to treat a woman nicely, then I'd consider him a prime candidate."

Derek nodded and seemingly agreed with what she was saying. She wondered if he always twisted people's words around.

"How old are you, baby?"

"I'm thirty-five."

"I see. You're not as young as you used to be, you know. And I'm sure you've put on a little weight over the years."

"Yes."

"Yes, I can see you've got a little something happening around the middle here," Derek said, pinching the fold that hung slightly over her waistline. She pulled away from him. "But I like it," he said, smiling and pulling her back toward him. She couldn't fully fathom his idea of flattery.

The doorbell startled Nina. Martha stepped into the apartment, rushing and seemingly out of breath. The girl was instant drama in a can.

"Nina, oh, girl, I didn't think you'd be home yet, I just wanted to stop by to . . ."

"Martha, this is Derek. Derek, this is my neighbor, Martha."

"A pleasure to meet you, Martha," he said.

"Likewise, Derek," she said, holding his hand in hers only momentarily. "Well, I'm not staying, I just wanted to drop off this nut bread I made; maybe you could have some with your coffee or something," she said, pointing her chin toward the cups resting on the table and taking note of the music playing faintly. "I have to pick up my baby and start dinner. I'll see you tomorrow, Nina." She waved, making an about-face and heading for the door.

Nina excused herself and walked Martha to the door.

"Not bad-looking, but I don't like his karma."

"His karma?"

"Yes, he's strange."

Nina thought that Martha was the one who was strange. Always conjuring up something. Nina dismissed all of Derek's minor offenses. She wasn't blissful, but she was content that at least now she'd have someone calling.

"Girl, you can do better than that."

"What are you saying?"

"Nothing, I'm just saying . . . okay, what does he do for a living?"

"What does that have to do with anything?"

"I don't know, I'm just making conversation." Martha giggled. "But, I mean, it's your call."

"He's a gentleman."

"So, where is he taking you tonight?"

"We decided to stay in."

"We? Okay. But make him take you out in public every now and then and pay some bills. Should have told him you lived with a relative, because the next thing you know, he'll want to move in."

"I have this under control," Nina teased.

"Sure you do," Martha said, "but can you really handle it?"

23

Tim's vision was blurry; his short-term goals wouldn't yield him any gains if he kept goofing at this pace. He never wanted to be labeled a loser, but he hadn't done squat lately. He couldn't; there was a weighted feeling that wouldn't allow him to move forward, yet it didn't want him to stay put either. He had faxed his résumé to several temp agencies because he desperately needed a cash flow. He really wanted something working in film, even if it was researching. But at this point he knew he'd take anything that materialized. There was too much entertaining going on in his life and not enough creating. He was being pulled in several different directions, and feeling like everyone wanted some of him. He needed to get away on one of those writers' retreats in those colonies, but he couldn't afford that.

Everything had its place, and Jay was right, Tim needed to let Sharon go so she could find someone who wanted what she wanted out of a relationship, and mostly so he could take care of his business. He felt tangled, caught up. He hated that feeling. He had been avoiding it most of his life. And he needed to stop being so open for Michelle, too. Women were a distraction. Eventually he'd believe it; then he'd act on it. He didn't know what he would tell Michelle. But she had to know that if she wanted to be evasive and unavailable, he could be, too. But sincerely speaking, it wasn't solely about her being unavailable; it was that he was more fond of her than he'd ever let on.

Tim rummaged around in the cluttered nightstand for his peeling phone book. It was falling apart and had numbers stuffed in every compartment. It wasn't black. He found Sharon's number on a torn-off piece of green paper that was folded into an origami swan. He hadn't even entered it into his book. She had done all of the calling from the beginning, and now, here he was, calling, of all people, her. Of course, he expected her, as always, to be sitting home with nothing to do but suggest takeout and rush right over on a whim, but instead her machine did its thing and picked up on the third ring. He asked her machine if she could stop by tonight about seven. He knew that she would be there with bells on. Some things he could count on, and Sharon was one.

Hanging out with leggy women and his broke friends had to come second. He didn't want to be one of those brothers standing on the corner by the local bodega, leaning on an ice machine until midnight talking about how he was gonna make movies one day. He didn't want to get stuck in the "would have's" and "could have's" of life. So, he smothered himself in protagonist, emotion, character, conflict, resolution, and a clear premise. He had every schoolbook he owned piled shoulder-high around him. He was trying to incorporate all the themes of good writing into his assignment. Dialogue was his strong suit, but it wasn't flowing this morning. His characters were just staring blankly, waiting for each other to make the first move.

Tim released himself, made a sandwich, poured a tall glass of V-8 Splash, rubbed his hand slowly across his head, and tried not to think of Michelle. He promised that the next time she called and wanted to drop by on the spur of the moment, he would say he was busy. Most men would think that it wasn't really so bad being Michelle's sex toy. She came like a thief in the night, but they would welcome her again and again. Tim wasn't up for that emotional drain, or even a dull game of mind tag. He didn't want to be manipulated, and he surely didn't want to lose control. He wondered if she thought she had him exactly where he thought he had Sharon.

He sat at the window and watched the cars go by, paying close attention to a man in a flannel shirt unpacking groceries with an older woman who could have easily been his mother. Whenever he saw someone with food stuffed in paper shopping bags, he always had a vision of the bag bursting and oranges rolling down the street. They didn't. From his second-floor window, Tim observed a lot. He saw car accidents and could determine who was at fault. He saw kids hopping out of cabs and sprinting down the block, trying to beat the fare. He saw the cabdrivers in hot pursuit.

Tim thought a nap would certainly help. His mind was wandering. He'd lost his focus. So, he'd try to doze off for a few. He fluffed up his pillow and bunched it up under his head; her scent was still on it. He inhaled deeply, savoring her sweetness, and made a mental note that he needed to change the sheets. His assignment was again incomplete, so he figured that he'd use tomorrow to develop an idea that would at least leave him with a B. He laid there unsoothed, listening to blaring car horns and people yelling, "You can't drive." "Idiot." "Moron." He tossed and squirmed to get comfortable under the sheets, which weren't necessarily comforting him, thinking of anything he could be doing other than fighting with his mind. A Marsalis tune fluttered in the background. Which Marsalis it was escaped him.

When the phone woke him, the sun had set on the shoulders of the building across the street and the wind was refreshing. It was Sharon. She was whispering and said she couldn't make it tonight, but that she'd try to stop by sometime tomorrow. He knew that things were getting bad, almost pathetic, when he couldn't even get the woman that he wanted to see the least to come by the most. He called his boy Justin.

"What's up, man?"

"Nothing, just hanging. The fellas may shoot by here, you know."

"Cool. I may pass that way."

"You okay, man?"

"I'm straight," Tim said convincingly.

"Later."

The post office was on the way to Justin's. Surely he must have some avoidance issues, Tim thought. There was no other explanation that would satisfy why it was so hard for him to send off his work and become famous once and for all. Peeping in the post office window, he saw that, amazingly enough, there were only three people in line and four teller windows open, motioning next. It was like an undeserved opportunity. Tim slid into the line, reached in his knapsack, and prepared to have them weigh his envelopes and affix the proper postage.

It was like a surrendering. Divulging government confidentials. It was like telling your secrets to the wind. He held on to the envelopes, almost snatching them back.

"You have to pull down the window."

He pulled down the window as the teller eyed the return label.

"How do you want to send these?"

"Priority."

"Twelve seventy-five," she said, generating the label as he finally had his manuscripts postmarked, and sent on their way to either change the world or be rejected and stamped RETURN TO SENDER.

Tim just wanted to sit back and kick it with his boy Justin. He hadn't expected more than a night reminiscing about when Tim had been voted most likely to change Hollywood, and a chance to get his mind off of things. Maybe they had all been dreaming back then, or drunk. Maybe the film industry would laugh him off the lot. They'd think his ideas were the saga of a rambling brother. Maybe he needed to rethink his whole plan. Maybe he just assumed that his ideas could sell dreams and change lives. Maybe his friends were egging him on because deep down they were afraid to say, "Man, hang it up." For a confident brother, he wondered why he was so insecure when it came to his work.

Six forty-five P.M. He made his way up the stairs. He heard loud echoing music trailing down the stairwell and vibrating off the hallway walls. Surely Justin was trippin', because his neighbors were nagging, whiny people, and it was a weeknight. He knew that the cops would have no problems barging in and being all up in a brother's face. The door to Justin's apartment was ajar. Tim walked in, peeping around at what drama was certain to unfold. Charlie and Darius were spread out on the sofa, with some woman in between them who was drinking something red in a glass and smiling the whole time, like she could take on either one of them.

They just nodded at Tim as if to say, *look what we got here*. There were girls dancing offbeat to music that was too fast, too loud. The mingling scents of too many people in a room were overwhelming. A night of wild roughhousing was not what Tim had expected or desired, but he was in no mood to be alone in his apartment, staring at his assignment sheet and fast-forwarding to what he'd considering writing tomorrow to polish his grade.

"I thought the party was on Friday?"

Justin backed into the bathroom to hear Tim speak. He was passing Tim something to drink.

"I know, man," Justin said, laughing. "Today is the day, bro. Today is my birthday." He was intoxicated.

"Why didn't you tell me?"

"Not a problem, man, you know, Charlie and Dee just showed up here with some girls, man. They had this planned. I never had a party before."

"Who are all these people?"

"I know the girl with Charlie and Dee. The rest of them, who knows?" Justin stuttered.

"You okay, man?" Tim asked, sipping on something that was tart, void of flavor, and initially burned going down.

"I'm straight," Justin said, barely convincing.

"What is this stuff, man?" Tim asked, holding up the cup and making a yuck face.

"Shhhh," Justin said, placing his finger up to his lips, nodding, and taking his time looking around to see who was listening to what he was about to say. "It's the secret recipe." He chuckled. "The party drink, you know?"

"Yeah, I know."

"Tim, let me break it to you this way," Justin said. "Women don't deserve us. We are some good brothers who take care of business," he slurred. "Why they treat us like that? Why they take their time deciding to call us back, man?"

"Jay, speak for yourself." Tim laughed.

"Oh, so now you're the mack daddy, huh?"

"Relax, man," Tim said, taking his cup away. "No more for you."

"What you mean? It's my birthday."

"Yeah, I want you to live to see another one," Tim said, gulping down the red mixture in the cup and dragging Justin outside to get some night air.

Tim took his time, walking slowly, trying to steady Justin. He could hear the thumping of the music all the way down the stairs. He felt the vibrations as his hand rested on the wall, taking steps to keep Justin from falling flat on his torn-up face. They didn't go way back, only as far as high school, and that was far enough.

"Jay, what are the neighbors gonna say? Your music is too loud."

"They don't work. Besides, I invited them to the party. They all said they was busy."

"They gonna call the police."

"Nah, nah, nah, they cool. I just want to enjoy my day, that's all. Hey, how's Sharon, Michelle?"

"Don't know, man, I'm not sweatin' that. What about you, Jay? You working tonight?"

"Nah, called in sick. My birthday, you know."

"Yeah, don't overdo it," Tim said, tiring of the whole situation.

Tim stood with Justin leaning on the building door as they both watched cars file up and down the busy street, and Tim thought to himself, *There's got to be a better way*.

Tim looked behind him.

"What's up, man?" Darius said, extending his hand.

Tim looked him over as they greeted each other in the usual homeboy fashion. Charlie wasn't far behind, that girl from the sofa in one arm and a plastic bottle of that red stuff in the other. Charlie started passing out cups.

"We gotta toast our boy Justin, y'all."

Charlie filled each cup, and they waited until everyone had a cup. They all raised them high, and Charlie toasted, "Justin, you my boy, we go way back, may you have many more and find a girl as slammin' as this one." He shook the girl from the sofa in his arms, making her butt jiggle.

Darius said, "Here, here," Justin nodded, and Tim swallowed the contents of the cup, making up his mind to head back to his crib and sleep it all off.

"So, what's the plan, man?" Darius asked.

Tim was feeling nice and mellow. They all piled into his car. The girl from the sofa squeezed into the backseat between two men who wanted her to get drunk enough to strip down. Everyone shouted where they preferred to go.

"I'm heading back to my crib."

"C'mon, Tim, man. This is Justin's birthday. We gotta hang a little. Go cruising, you know?"

"Yeah."

Tim wasn't feeling it, but they all agreed to go for a drive. Justin was like a brother, and a little scenic rendezvous never hurt anybody. They were joyriding down the Westside Highway, passing cars and waving to strangers, having a real bang-up time. Darius started it all by rolling down the windows and throwing his cup out. Charlie grabbed Tim's head. "Where you been, man?" Tim swerved to avoid almost hitting another car.

"Cut it out, I'm driving, you idiot."

"Oh, I forgot, he's too 'West Coast' for us now, y'all," Charlie said, pushing Tim in the head.

Justin fiddled with the radio, blasting some tune Tim had never heard before, but it had a hummable beat.

They were all yelling and trying to talk over each other.

"Excuse me," the girl said. "Excuse me, I have to go."

"Go where?" Justin asked.

"Can we find a bathroom, please?" she whined.

"Why didn't you go before you left?" Justin laughed.

Tim sped up, trying to figure out where the closest restaurant was. Had to get this girl to a toilet before she peed in his car. Not that it was a Mercedes, but it had four wheels, and he wanted to cruise in aromaless comfort. Tim passed several cars on the highway as he sped down the center lane and swerved. A red flashing light zipped out of nowhere, reflecting the blinding light in his rearview mirror. The muffled sound of "pull over" had everybody in the car mumbling obscenities and questioning whether or not Tim had his license and registration.

Tim was almost to the next exit. He got off the highway and pulled over with the police riding his tail. He put the car in park, turned down the radio, and slid his hand inside his pockets for his wallet. His wallet was worn and had the imprint of whatever was in there bulging through. He knew the credentials were in there somewhere. The police car was right behind them with flashing lights, making its presence known. The light circulated color through Tim's dark vehicle. A big brawny cop pushing maximum density bounced up, weighted down by his belt, and shined his oversize flashlight into the back of the car, blinding everyone who'd turned around to watch him approach through the rear window.

"Good evening, officer," Tim said, sounding coherent.

"License and registration." The officer shone the light onto the driver's license and then in Tim's face.

"Step out of the car please. You been drinking?"

"Not really," Tim confessed.

"How much you had to drink?" He shone the light into the backseat, where the girl who still had to go to the bathroom was holding the plastic container with the red liquid. "Is that an alcoholic beverage?" the officer asked, pointing the nose of his flashlight at the container.

The silence was deafening.

"Uh, okay. Everybody out of the car."

The girl squealed, "Oh, no, oh, no, oh, no . . ."

She got out of the car and ran around to the trunk side, crouched down in the corner behind the car, and relieved herself.

DWI, that's what they called it. It didn't get Tim into an accident, although it could have, but it did get him locked up overnight, a hefty fine, and two and a half months of community service. Tim stood in his best suit, hands clasped in front of him, legs slightly apart. Head down lower than dirt.

"You need to be very careful, Mr. Richardson. Driving while intoxicated or impaired is a very dangerous situation. Community service should give you some time to think about what could have happened out there," the judge offered, slamming his gavel.

Tim envisioned his momma sitting in the back of the courtroom with his father, crying and, in the same breath, praising God that they didn't lock up her only son and throw away the rusty key.

24

In the wee hours, when the crickets mated, Troi picked up the car keys and rummaged through the kitchen junk drawer for a pen. She scribbled a note that read, *Take a taxi to work.* She taped it on the bathroom mirror for Vaughn to read as soon as he woke up. She had him timed. He'd get ready and leave at seven-thirty. She'd figured she'd be back by eight. She turned off the lights in the bathroom and the kitchen, and remembered to close the door on her way out. She headed uptown to Shangrila and thought that she didn't want apologies. She wanted someone to tell her that this was all a sick joke.

She wanted everyone to jump out of closets and from behind furniture, laugh, and say, "We gotcha!" but it was real. She knew it was, because she felt scared. For the first time in her life she was afraid. She had put her every morsel of trust she had into their relationship. It was like hot love in cold hands; it had melted. But every time Vaughn said something even vaguely similar to "I'm sorry," the sound of his voice and the words she imagined that he spoke when giving pleasure to someone else helped her place one more piece of his clothing into his suitcase, until finally he'd be out the door. Troi's instinct to pray had eluded her.

What women needed was a man whose word was as faithful as God and gift-wrapped in gold foil like a Godiva chocolate. Her life was a testimony, for sure. She had gone through enough changes to last for endless seasons. *Lord, you must have the ultimate man for me, after going through all this. I mean, he must want to rub my feet, kiss my neck. Lord, you know I'm delicate. I need love. I refuse to pretend. I need a man. I'm being realistic, Jesus. I want my own man though. I'm not trying to be run out of somebody's house at two* A.M. *butt naked,* she thought.

When Vaughn woke up, he'd notice that Troi was gone. He'd read the note and do what he was supposed to do: leave. She wanted him to, she thought as she approached the shop. She unlocked the gate. At five A.M., people who said that they couldn't find jobs were already up and out doing nothing in particular. Troi pulled the gate open and then closed it behind her. She plopped down in the pink salon chair, looking around at all she had left besides her daughter: a shop where women came to dish the dirt. She sat in the chair, spinning around, looking at herself in the mirror. There wasn't anything wrong with her, but she didn't have a clue as to what she would do next. Vaughn had discarded her like a store-bought fruitcake. If she hadn't had a baby to care for, she'd go off to Mexico, learn a new language, and create a new identity, which included possibly being a tour guide and making pottery. She was tired of crying. Tears never washed away the pain.

Troi got out of the chair, dusted off the CD player, opened a case, pressed the CD into the slot, and pushed Play, allowing herself to reminisce about when she was a young girl in high school and every boy in school was crazy about her. Men were predictable then. They'd borrow money and pool it together just to take her out. She'd giggle like a princess in some restaurant that a kid their age shouldn't even have been able to afford. The food had been awful. Mostly because they'd wanted to relish the experience, but could have easily made do with a burger and some fries.

She'd come home after these most inspiring dates and carefully select which boys she'd kiss on the front steps. It wasn't always the cutest ones, mostly the ones who made her laugh though. Her sister had always left the light on for her. She remembered how she would come inside after teasing the boy all night and sit up, sharing the stories of her dates with Nina.

Nina wasn't what she'd consider homely back then. She just hadn't taken the time to make herself feminine. Boys liked femininity. Troi would always take time with her hair, hours sometimes, making sure every braid or strand was in place and her socks matched. She'd wanted Nina to do that, too, but she wouldn't. She'd only complain about how she never fit in, and alternate between the desire to belong and the comfort of the fact that she didn't. Troi thought about how she'd make the boys swoon and spend the money from their paper routes and allowances on her. They'd been so fickle then. Troi shook her head. Right now was what mattered, and right now she couldn't ever be feminine enough for Vaughn. He didn't want what she was offering, or at least he no longer did. And she wondered about when they were together, how many times in his mind he'd been thinking that he was making love to someone else.

Troi didn't want any man to think she was anything remotely similar to a doormat. But now here she was sitting, fumbling with a baby toy, thinking about how a man had put a spell on her husband, capturing his mind and possibly his heart. She knew what the bible said: It was a sin. He knew that, too, but the understanding of something that someone wanted to deny was always justified.

She thought about how this was the last thing she'd ever expected. Troi had never been in love so badly that it hurt to breathe, until now. Mother would have a heart attack and stop drinking for at least a day if she found out; Daddy would maybe stir with the urge to get even, and the Hallelujah Girls would have an official celebration and deem it a national holiday. Love always came with sacrifices.

Troi was protecting her sanity by reminiscing about how Vaughn would kiss her eyelashes, trace her brows with his tongue, and massage her back, press his lips into her shoulders and tell her that that was what husbands were for. She'd felt the earth move under her feet then. She wanted her husband in a way that left her fiending and her mouth wide open, unable to articulate what she was feeling as he did what he did to her. She wasn't just on a quest for a warm body to take the chill off of her feet. If that were the case, she could buy an electric blanket. They said what didn't kill you made you stronger. *Try telling that to my shattered mind,* she thought.

But she definitely wasn't about to mope around in sweats and refuse to comb her hair. She would have liked to think that the situation was torturing him, too, but she didn't know. He had comfort now, even if it was a narcissistic abdomen fixation. But she had no one. She felt like a victim of friendly fire. She thought about stories she'd heard about how psychics could give you potions and rituals to perform to make a man love you. Candles from the Botanica. Flowers, perfume, candles, incense, and herbs. The sign was red and noticeable. She walked by it every day on the way to her shop. But this was not the time to be thinking about things like that. She wanted him back. No egg in a paper towel or crystal to rub could make that happen. It wasn't about tapping into second-rate power; she had to get his attention the old-fashioned way: earn it and pray.

Troi thought of dyeing her hair a shade of blond. Honey. She was content with her weight, but figured she could wear clothing that was a little more feminine, flattering. Ruffles, lace, some cleavage. Three-inch heels, too. Vaughn loved heels. At least he said he did. It was disappointing that she had been faithful, but still found her world crumbling around her when her picture-perfect marriage-before-sex union found her husband succumbing to his repressed homosexuality. She assumed it was repressed; she hadn't seen any signs, and he hadn't said otherwise.

If she couldn't get him back, she alone would have to endure the torment and shame of their marital sham by numbing herself with something, anything that would take her mind off of the fact that her husband was no longer attracted to her. She was struggling with the desire to relinquish her violated marriage, and would have to muster up the courage to face friends and family, who would be overly critical. Trust. Such a tricky word. What did it mean, after all, if not what it implied?

Every time Troi was hurt, gossiped about, or offended, Nina was there to comfort her like a mother. She was sure now would be no exception. She couldn't tell her though. That would nullify everything that she had told Nina. *Men liked femininity and men liked honesty.* What would it say that, with her feminine wiles, she wasn't able to keep her husband attracted for more than three meager years? Some things you had to keep to yourself. Troi always emphasized that Nina should wait for a man who would love her enough to marry her. What testimony would her marriage be to her sister?

Troi piled her braids on top of her head and pinned them up. Her reflection was telling her that she was still young enough to find someone who was all man. But what she yearned for was the man that she knew was in Vaughn.

When the lights in the bodega across the street from the salon went on, she knew it was seven o'clock. If she headed uptown at a moderate pace, Vaughn would be gone when she got there. She'd stop off at the supermarket and pick up some flour, sugar, pie crust, and several cans of peaches. She had promised Sam cobbler. Of all the things she wasn't lately, true to her word was what she was.

Troi was initially agitated by the fact that she didn't have one soul she could tell that her husband was gay and that life as she had known it was splintering before her. Family picnics and New Year's Eve services. It was all gone. She thought of Dakoda, who wouldn't have any idea of all the havoc that would erupt around her. Her father would be one of those men who showed up at functions with someone everyone else thought was an old high-school friend or cousin. And when Dakoda grew up, her father would be living the life of one of the characters in those "I have two daddies" books that everyone was trying to ban from schools.

When she walked into the apartment, Troi could smell Vaughn's cologne. It lingered in the hall and especially the bathroom. She smelled it on the towels. She pressed the terry cloth to her nose, imagining him walking past her, tilting his head back, tying his tie, and asking her to pour him a cup of coffee. The toilet seat was down, and he had hung his robe up on the back of the door. She looked around and observed that he had made the bed, prepared coffee, and removed her note that said, *take a taxi to work,* from the mirror.

She walked into the kitchen and poured a big piping mug of coffee. It was eight-fifteen. She sat in the chair and avoided the sun that was coming through the window. She wasn't in the mood for sunshine in her face.

She'd been up and out before dawn and in bed last night before Vaughn had had the chance or urge to apologize again. "He needs to figure out where he's going to live, since 'here' is out of the question," she said out loud. She couldn't be forced to do this. She didn't like this approach. His face every morning would be a reminder of his betrayal. The denial phase had worn off. She couldn't pretend that Vaughn was merely curious. It was all becoming too real for her. Fleshly.

Troi pulled out the big mixing bowl and began sorting and measuring the ingredients, which would have the whole apartment filled with the aroma of a full-fledged bakery by noon. Flour, baking soda, yeast. She liked to keep her word, and she knew that Sam would appreciate the time she spent making his favorite dessert. It was Vaughn's favorite, too, but she wasn't making it for him. It was for someone else. In some small way she felt she was getting back at him.

She remembered how Vaughn had thought that she was more delicious than amaretto cheesecake. It had been all over her toes as he'd tasted each one slowly tickling her near death. It was times like those that she'd been convinced that he thoroughly enjoyed her. She shouldn't be feeling this pain because she desired her husband. Why was she being punished?

Troi picked up the phone with her flour-covered hands and dialed the shop. Carmen answered, "Shangrila." She told her, "If anyone calls, tell them I'm not feeling well."

"Are you okay? It's been two days, is there something that I can . . ."

"Yes, I'll be fine, thanks, Carmen," she said, not ready for the inquisition.

The pain to which she had been mentally numbing herself was resurfacing. She went into the bathroom, turned on the faucet, washed the flour off her hands, and splashed cold water on her face, drying her hands in the same towel Vaughn had used earlier. His scent was all over her now.

She opened the medicine cabinet and surveyed the shelves for something that would calm her down and ease the dull throbbing of her head. There was nothing but gauze, Mercurochrome, baby aspirin, birth control pills, liquid vitamins, and ear-wax remover. She sat in the bathroom on the fuzzy blue toilet-seat cover, and tears found their way down her face. She convinced herself that tears were not a sign of weakness and began sobbing hysterically. He'd better sleep with one eye open, she thought.

Her hands were trembling as she dialed the first three digits to Nina's and thought against it. She dialed Mother, but before she dialed the last digit, she imagined her own flesh and blood mocking and blowing smoke at the fact that she'd told her not to marry him anyway. She dialed a number that came to the forefront of her mind suddenly, not instantly realizing whose it was. The phone rang three times. On the third ring, the party picked up. The voice was familiar. Troi cleared her nose and her throat. "Hello . . . Carla?"

"Hey, CeCe, girl, what's wrong?"

25

Vaughn entered through the enormous glass doors of the bank. Everything was visually the same. Buffed brass, fourteen tellers, and impatient customers lined up evenly behind thick velvet ropes. It was only his life that had changed. No one could tell. He still had his tailored suit, crisp shirt, and flashy tie. His wing tips could use polishing, but he was trying to maintain his demeanor of manliness.

His mother had reassured him that couples fought and that things would be all right between him and Troi. He didn't believe it then or now. Moma didn't know the details. She had only acquired partial information. Details changed everything.

Vaughn knew that things would never be the same. His marriage had been stalled at a fork in the road. Something as simple as a desire had stunted the growth of a relationship with someone he'd vowed to cherish, and in the process, it had annihilated everything that they had built together. He could have lied, but what would he have gained by that? More time? Another month or two? A single "I love you"?

"How are you feeling, Vaughn?" his boss asked and kept walking.

"Better, thanks," he said, sitting at his desk, staring at the telephone, and pressing numbers into the keypad.

Vaughn fought not to call Tracie. Surely Tracie wanted to know what was going on. But he couldn't give into the temptation, especially not at work. He wrestled with the desire to blame someone else for what he had uncovered and exposed by telling the truth. Maybe he should have lied. He had laid the foundation of his marriage with honesty, trust, and efforts to curb the roaming eye that most women thought men had, and now this.

He thought about Troi; her smile, her lips, and her tears. There was something that he had to say to her, something that he desperately wanted her to know. He'd married her because he'd wanted to be with her and make her happy; a lot of consolation that was now. He hadn't married her because he'd thought it would change him. She wasn't a mask he wore. He loved the way she had about her. He had always been taken aback at how, when she entered a well-lit room, the men looked in her direction and caught her gaze until she smiled and acknowledged them, and then looked over to her husband as if to say, *I'm his*.

He didn't remember the moment that his forbidden feelings sent a live wire through him. He knew it was most recently with Tracie, and he also knew that there was no way he could get hold of himself without burning everyone in his path. He had never been able to love or care without destroying someone or something. That had been the story of his life. If he stayed with his wife, he'd have to end it with Tracie; feelings would be hurt. "I'm falling for you," Tracie had said. Vaughn was surprised by his forwardness. He didn't know what he would do, if anything.

Maybe he and Troi could go for counseling. Maybe he would leave for a while. He'd stay with Sam to avoid fueling the fire and utter disgust that homosexuality usually fostered. He'd do whatever he had to do. He wanted to try. He had made the bed this morning, dropped off Dakoda at his momma's, and hoped that Troi wouldn't be asleep when he came in so they could talk. They needed to talk. Not yell, not bicker and throw insults—talk rationally like two well-meaning adults.

This whole situation made Vaughn rethink everything he had been taught about equality. He smoothed out his tie, brushed off his jacket, and realized that the "don't ask, don't tell" policy could now apply to him. He wasn't sure he wanted to change. Part of him felt that he had a right to his feelings, as they were his. His entire life he had felt incomplete, like the first seven volumes of those supermarket encyclopedias that his momma used to buy, never returning to complete the set.

He shook his head, thinking that it wasn't his fault that he was turned on by the physique of a man as athletic as he was. Skin so radiant that you swore it was coated with a sugary glaze, and had to touch it just to make sure. Vaughn invited conversation that was about nothing in particular but always sounded meaningful, deep and baritone. He enjoyed skin that was as inviting as perfection in a pair of faded blue jeans and a form-fitting tee. He needed more than just marital bliss. That alone had gotten him through three years; he needed something to help him with the remainder of his life.

Vaughn's supervisor, Jill, came by his desk with folders that she needed Vaughn to review. She was an anorexic-looking woman with a flat chest and slightly protruding hips.

"You've got a lot of catching up to do."

"Yes, I understand."

"Process this paperwork and let me give it the once-over when you're done."

"Okay, I will."

"How are you feeling?"

"I'm better," he said, anxious to get through the morning and sure that she had asked that question once before.

He sat at his computer, making countless entries. Plucking away at keys and reviewing everything he did for mistakes. He added, subtracted, and transferred money that he secretly pretended was his. He'd surely run off and discover himself deep down to the core if it was. He tapped his fingers, knowing that there was nothing worse than having to do repetitive work when your mind was somewhere else.

It was almost noon. His mind was scrambled. He delivered the files to Jill's desk. She looked up at him suspiciously.

"That was quick . . ."

Vaughn gave her statement one of those fake smiles that meant *get off my back.*

"I'm going out to lunch. I need some fresh air. You want anything?" he asked.

"No, thank you for asking." Vaughn walked to his office space, flipped on his voice mail, pushed in his chair, and reached in his pocket to pull out some cash.

He put on his shades, disguising himself enough to be alone with his thoughts. He clumsily bumped into a patron on the way out, only to look up and see Tracie's smiling face beaming back at him.

"Hey, what are you doing here?"

"I'm here to cheer you up," he said, grabbing hold of Vaughn and shaking his shoulders. "Lunch, Vaughn, let's go."

They didn't hug, only smiled. Tracie had shown up at the bank in a pale suit, professionally dressed. His hands were delicate, nails neatly trimmed.

"I only have forty-five minutes," Tracie said. "Let's find something quick."

They found an overcrowded luncheonette and squeezed into a booth. The waitress hurried over and began wiping down the table with a filthy rag that left the stench of sour milk.

"You know you deserve to be happy," Tracie said.

"I know, but it's not that simple," Vaughn said, agitated at being constantly interrupted by the waitress's presence. "You don't have prying eyes trying to figure out what's going on. I haven't been to church in almost a month. You know, everybody notices that something is different. I'm just not my normal self. And Troi flew off the handle. I told her."

"You mean that *now* you are your normal self, and before you weren't, right?"

Vaughn just stared blankly. His gaze caught on a woman pulling a tea bag out of the inside pocket of her coat, unwrapping it from a napkin, and dunking it in a cup of hot water repeatedly.

"What did CeCe say?"

"You want coffee?"

"Yes." Tracie nodded.

"Two coffees." Vaughn motioned. He cleared his throat. "Troi. Only I call her CeCe."

"I'm sorry."

"It's okay."

"So, how did she take it?"

"The silent treatment."

"So, why don't you talk to her?"

"She's in bed before I get home and she's up and out in the morning before I wake up."

"How's the baby?"

"My baby girl is fine. I love her so much. I just don't know if I'm making the right decision. I don't know if maybe I should go back to life as it was. It was less stressful then."

"Don't make any rash decisions. Take your time." Tracie paused. "Besides, you can't close Pandora's box."

"Far be it from me to try." Vaughn grimaced.

"Vaughn, I don't mean to change the subject, but I miss you," Tracie whispered. "I hadn't heard from you in a couple of days. I didn't know what to think. I know you were going through drama with your family but . . . come by my place tonight, please," Tracie pleaded. "I'll pick you up in Jersey and we can go out and unwind. I have something for you."

"What?"

"A little surprise. Don't spoil it." Tracie grinned.

"Okay," Vaughn said, knowing he really needed to get out.

They ordered quickly to avoid having to rush back. Tracie ordered a tuna melt with fries. Vaughn was famished; he ordered the same thing.

They sat eating and, with their body language, saying that they were happy to be together again. There was always someone watching. This was all so new to Vaughn. He didn't have the energy to fight discrimination. He wanted to know how Tracie dealt with it. He wondered about what God thought of him now. But he didn't like to dwell on heavenly thoughts. The thing was that you could hardly tell Tracie was gay. If you looked at him, the most you would think was that he was a ladies' man or a gigolo, and Vaughn looked like he had a happy family somewhere, which should have been true, but he no longer did.

They ate quietly, embraced in the nonverbal conversation that had them reminiscing about the day when they'd met at the main branch. They'd had lunch together then, too. Secrets had told themselves and doors to places hidden for generations had opened over fast food that day. Vaughn hadn't known any more about this lifestyle than he knew about ice sculptures. Tracie had convinced him that experience was an excellent teacher.

"Stop worrying, Vaughn. Everything will be fine," Tracie assured him.

They got up from the table, motioning for the busy waitress, who tore a guest check from her pad. Tracie handed the waitress money and they walked out the door, closer than two people in the same section of a revolving door. They gave each other the see-you-later eyes and extended their hands. Tracie clasped both hands around Vaughn's.

"Call me when you get to Jersey."

"I will."

"See you soon." Tracie smiled, walking off into the crowd of people who cluttered the streets with their cell phones, briefcases, and *Wall Street Journals*.

Vaughn wanted to call Troi to let her know that he would probably be home late. He walked back into the office, turned off his voice mail, pulled out his chair, sat down, and dialed the shop.

"Hello, Shangrila."

"Hi, Carmen, is my wife in?"

"She's not here. Home, I think."

"Okay, thank you."

He dialed home and Troi picked up on the second ring. She didn't say anything at first, then sounded like she was asleep.

"Were you sleeping?"

"No," she said unconvincingly. He paused.

"I'm going out this evening," he said. "I'll probably be home late. I don't want you to worry."

"Vaughn, I've been thinking."

"About?" Vaughn said with slight hopefulness.

"About this situation of ours. We need to make alternate plans. This isn't working out for me."

"What are you saying, CeCe?"

Troi was straightforward. "I need the car."

"That's not a problem, CeCe, you know that. Is there something else?"

"Yes, don't come home," she said.

26

It had been a whole walking-on-eggshells month and some days before Nina realized that Derek was getting on her nerves. This was hardly the way she'd planned on spending her summer. Derek was a loner and had maybe one friend who she had actually met briefly. It should have logically triggered that something was wrong with this picture, but it hadn't, not initially.

The men in her life had a way of disappearing or overstaying their welcome. She had chalked up the reality that Derek didn't have many associates to the fact that he was a strong black man and people were usually intimated by that. That was always his reasoning. She believed him for a while because it explained the weird answers he'd give to the questions that she'd ask him. He was always evasive. It was a game for him from day one. She was done playing.

Derek said that he adored her, her dimples and the way she nervously bit her bottom lip. Flattery had gotten him everywhere. After two weeks of borderline dating, she'd allowed him to pack up his meager belongings from his one-room furnished apartment and move them into her brownstone. Yes, she got negative feedback from Troi, who said that she should know better than to be shackin'. People always had something to say. She politely told her sister that it was her life, and that she didn't tell her what to do with her husband. Martha thought Derek was manipulative. "He doesn't deserve you, Nina." All either of them could do for her now was comfort her with their silence.

She felt the way the women who sat alongside her in the counselor's waiting area looked. She had caught herself thinking lately that it was possibly the biggest mistake she had ever made. She should have never let this strange man move into her apartment.

She was always so willing. So helpful. Dragging any stray into what she had already established. She would have told her therapist about him, but she had gone from thinking that no one came perfect to feeling that the fat girl had to take what she could get. But now she knew she was in hell. There were moments when she had come close to something reminiscent of passion with Derek, and she'd had to remind him that she wasn't ready for that. He claimed to understand, although his patience had grown short with her on several occasions.

"You aren't seeing somebody else, are you?" he'd asked.

"Now, why would you ask me something like that?"

"I'm just asking. I mean, I'm not going anywhere, so I don't see why we can't . . ."

"Can't what?"

"What I'm saying is that we live together, for God's sake."

"Goodness sake."

"Oh, so you're holy now?"

"Never mind, Derek."

It was a constant debate about her beliefs and his lack thereof.

"Well, why am I here if you are so holy?"

He had a way of manipulating words, and often chastised her like she was the child and he was the adult.

Of course, Nina's mother didn't approve of them living together either. "It's unbiblical," she said. She could have only found out that they were living together from Troi, because Troi could never manage to keep her mouth shut, especially when she was upset. Mother had already started on her tirade. She loved dogging someone else; it made herself look better in her own eyes. She must have forgotten that she was an alcoholic and an absentee mother. Nina knew her life alone was evidence of that fact.

Nina knew the truth. She didn't need outside input. Life with Derek was far from perfect. She saw that. There were roses and fragrant floral arrangements, but there were also shouting matches, temper tantrums, his disappearing acts, and mail addressed to her that was opened before she had gotten a chance to read it. There were disagreements in every relationship, she persuaded herself.

Airing the dirty laundry between her and Derek would only prove to her mother that she was right and that, as always, Nina was wrong. She would never give her mother the satisfaction of knowing that. So, she tried to be patient when Derek came home, thinking all he needed was for her to be a better listener. She figured that she could take anything, if she had lived with her mother for eighteen years of her life, being belittled and underappreciated. The last thing she wanted was to send Derek packing and six months later overhear how happy he was making someone else.

So, Nina had put the tattered magazines back into the old yellowing shoe box. She'd carefully pulled out the step stool, reaching up and pushing the box as far back on the top shelf of the closet in the guest room as it would go. He'd never look there. It was too bothersome and out of the way to get him started. He thought all that women's empowerment stuff was hogwash. That meant the black women's magazines had to go.

"I can't stand him, Nina," Troi said, every chance she got. She had met him finally, and was trashing men like she didn't have one at home. "Can't you see what he's doing to you, girl? Where did you meet him again?" Troi didn't understand. She couldn't. Her picture-perfect life was framed, and if it got a little off-kilter, she tilted it a little to the left and it was back on track. Nina was cooking and ignoring Troi, who hadn't been spending as much time at the shop as she usually did.

Nina ate from the rich peach filling in the pot, licking the spoon, thinking that if Derek saw her reaching for the knife to cut a chunk of cobbler once it was done, he'd be sure to tell her that with all the weight she was gaining she couldn't afford to eat another blessed thing. She wasn't in the mood for his criticism tonight or ever.

Lately he was always angry about something. She had conveniently fallen for everything he was and a few things that he wasn't, she thought, employed, for one. The stable thing was a seasonal gig. "Be nice to me, Derek," she often found herself telling him.

"I am nice, girl, just remember I'm all you have." He'd grin like a bully who had stolen her lunch money. It was true; he was all she had. Men weren't lining up outside her window serenading her. No one ever even called lately. Her friends went on with their sordid lives, although Shelby still called occasionally. She didn't have anyone to whom she could talk about what was going on except Martha, and she had serious problems of her own.

Martha had been trying to tell Gerald it was over for a whole week, and he was making her life a spectacle. He'd show up early in the morning, three A.M., yelling out the window and ringing her doorbell so much that she had called the police on him twice. Sure,

Nina was fed up, but she was afraid. She was deadened. She was afraid that if Derek left, she'd quickly mutate back to the frumpy, sweatpants-wearing, TV-dinner-eating sister who could eat six bean burritos while watching ER and polish off a whole Louisiana crunch cake for dessert.

Nina wondered how different her life would be if she looked like the beautiful women in the magazines, who came in all shades of copper and bronze, neatly packaged into a size ten or a single digit. These women gave her courage, hope. Women with the sexy pouty way they closed their eyes and posed against anything; they were beautiful with short hair when men told them only shoulder-length would do.

She longed to be a woman who exuded a balance of strength and inner beauty, which sort of spilled over onto the outside if it were possible, and oozed from the core of who she was. Flawless. She wished she could be strong like that. Strong women would never let a man rule them, she said, but then again you never knew. Nina was strong once, too.

For sure she was inspired by sensual women who didn't need to unbutton their blouses down to their navels and crawl around on all fours in music videos to prove it. They were stunning. She wished she had their freedom and their confidence. Right now, just about anybody's freedom would do. She'd take a get-out-of-jail-free card. She really couldn't ask Derek to leave. How would she tell him that this wasn't working? He'd try to persuade her that things were fine, but she knew. They weren't. Everybody was right about him. If she confessed to anyone how disappointed she was feeling, it would show that she was a poor judge of character. She knew that loneliness had a way of making you tolerate things you normally never would.

The thought of being with Derek forever honestly made her want to go out and shoplift some triple-digit item at a department store just to get arrested. She found the idea of sleeping on a smelly cot and being fed a thick slice of bologna on day-old bread through slats in a jail cell down at central booking more appealing than getting the brunt of all that was wrong in Derek's life. That brother had issues, and she wasn't about to get trapped in the abyss of his screaming isms.

They began fighting about his possessiveness all the time. The final word was always his. It was her television, her stereo system, and her telephone, but he always got the final say. She had given him the last word oftentimes out of sheer exhaustion. He lived for a debate. Her rationale regarding him was subtly clouded, like a room with a window partially open that didn't allow you to see that the room was filling up with smoke. She honestly didn't know how much more she could take.

When all of Nina's girlfriends were dating in college, she'd had thoughts about what it would be like to be in love, and never once had this picture of the life she had with Derek come to mind. She'd thought of wine and cheese at exquisite restaurants where they'd linger until they were the only couple left dining and the waiter turned the chairs upside down on the surrounding tables and tidied up the floor. She'd imagined that the couple at the next table would tell them how good she and her date looked together. She'd thought of being blindfolded in a candlelit room as he fed her buttered croissants and shrimp toast with pâté.

She'd fantasized that she'd catch glimpses of the candlelight flickering through the blindfold while jazz instrumentals crooned in the foyer. She'd thought that someone special would sit with her in the park at dawn and read her poetry by Sanchez and feed her frozen grapes until they both bubbled over with laughter and made the pigeons fly away. She'd dreamed of finding out where he was most ticklish and what his favorite color was by just observing, never asking. She'd thought her ideals were quite far-fetched, and so she had dismissed them. But now she wanted her dreams again. There had to be a way to undo the grave mistake she had made with Derek. Just like anything else of less importance, she just had to find out how to work around it, tie it up, and ship it out with the morning trash.

27

He surely wasn't looking forward to doing his community service stint this weekend. Tim had better things to do with his Fridays and Saturdays. Writing, for one. Enjoying the summer weather, for another. Rochelle had been keeping tabs on Tim since the DWI thing. She was too sisterly, in fact. He had to be allowed to make his own dreadful mistakes. Even cats were allowed the chance to land on their feet. But instead of allowing him room to grow, Rochelle and Carl had come over to lecture Tim on life and how he shouldn't waste it. He'd nodded and yet they had gone on and on. They needed some kids to lecture to.

Right after they'd released Tim from lockdown, Rochelle and Carl had bored him with their melodrama all the way home. Tim had been famished, and Rochelle and Carl had dragged out this soliloquy of theirs like a passion play centuries old. His living room wasn't their pulpit, he scoffed. The police had held him in a cell and released him what had seemed like one hundred hours later. They loved to throw a brother in jail. Got a kick out of handcuffing him, too. Weeks later, Tim was still bitter about that. He couldn't understand how people voluntarily gave away their freedom. And though it must have looked to everybody on the outside that he had done just that, he couldn't conceive of it.

Community service. Ten weekends in a row. And all because a bunch of overcelebratory knuckleheads had wanted to go for a drive. If Tim had only followed his mind, he'd be using his weekend trying to do something productive and creative, and could have borrowed the money Rochelle had put up for bail to pay a bill or two and buy some real meat.

Rochelle, in all of her sisterly charm, couldn't have picked a better time to tell Tim that he'd better be in church, front row, on Sunday, and that he was lucky to be alive. Her face was twisted up just like his momma's used to be when she wanted you to know that she was dead serious. He had been to church for the past three Sundays and he was sure that this Sunday would find him there, being fed, as Rochelle liked to say. He didn't see what difference it made.

You sat, you warmed a pew, and you went home to watch TV and listen to lustful music and undo everything you'd heard the preacher yelling at you. Although he kind of liked this pastor. He wasn't the old hearty type, and besides, he was stylish. Tim knew that the man drove the women in his congregation crazy. He could see the sisters tripping over each other trying to give the pastor a glass of water. "Yes, Pastor, no, Pastor." Lusting right there in the church. "They all gonna burn in hell." He laughed.

Tim sat at his dining table, flipping through the most recent copy of *Backstage* magazine, secretly wishing Michelle would call just to see how he was doing. He wanted the chance to tell her that he was fine without her. That would teach her to presuppose that he was always available.

He was having one of those dry spells and still couldn't write. It had nothing to do with Michelle though. Nothing but scribble-scrabble covered the pages in his spiral notebook. The music repeated itself over and over again in his mind, reminding him that he had danced this dance before. He knew that the kids were coming home from school now, because he could hear them climbing the stairs and playing in the hall, making noise that reminded him of his own rambunctious childhood. He had a class at six P.M. He was totally unprepared again.

Tim had broken the news to Sharon that she needed a new port in which to dock her boat. Surprisingly, she hadn't been emotional. "Whatever," she'd kept saying, as if she wasn't phased by the fact that he wanted her out of his life.

"Seriously, Sharon, I'm trying to be honest here. You deserve somebody who can give you time and be everything that you think they should be."

"And are you saying you can't be that?"

"No, that's not what I'm saying. Right now I'm just not ready to be that. I can't. It distracts me. You distract me."

"Okay, whatever you say. You know we belong together, right?"

"Okay, well, if we do then it'll be inevitable, right?" he'd said, silently praying for her to leave without making a scene.

She hadn't called him in two weeks, which was okay. Corners of his mind wondered if she was still alive and what she had for dinner, but he didn't want to talk her up. It didn't please him to think he had that type of power over women. It was sad, in fact. Especially when a woman like Sharon was a chameleon and was willing to become whatever a man wanted her to be just to have a twenty-four-karat relationship. He knew some brothers who pushed the buttons of women like that just for fun. Made women pay car notes, buy clothes, groceries and then even come over and cook. The novelty had worn off for him.

Tim wasn't surprised that he hadn't heard from Michelle. Like laughter, she always turned up. He put on some tunes that were conducive to writing, tapped his pen against his temple, and tried to put himself in the place of his characters. The music was drowning them out. He was losing his focus. He just found himself daydreaming about the premiere of his first film. Blinding lights and cameras blocking New York City streets. Cab drivers content that the meters would keep ticking until they got their passengers to their destinations.

Tim envisioned that he'd be wearing some smooth ensemble and women would scream that they knew him. But it wasn't about the prestige. His characters would change the lives of people everywhere. He tried not to focus too much on the outcome. He had enough to worry about. His plate was full with the harsh reality of utility disconnection notices.

For his entire life, Tim had been told to aspire to be anything. Something great. "You are here for a purpose, son, seek God for your purpose," his dad had instructed in a throaty grumble. Lately Tim had been going to church faithfully yet reluctantly and giving what little he had. Rochelle said, "I don't care if it's ten percent of a dime, give it, Tim. God will bless your finances. Believe he can do it and he will." He was starting to absorb a little bit of it. He tried not to get distracted by the women in church who went out of their way to notice him. He didn't want anybody spilling themselves at his feet. He wasn't a god, he chuckled.

Tim knew that he could eventually get beyond the falsetto solos, the preacher's fancy suits and costly ties. Especially if he put the beliefs he supposedly had to work. "Faith of a mustard seed was all it took, God does the rest," Rochelle said. He had heard a message last Sunday that informed the congregation that they were about to give birth. Even the men understood that the man didn't mean having a baby. They'd stood in agreement. "If you sow this seed . . . you will be blessed . . . God has promised us riches and glory . . . are you ready to receive it?" The static in the mic and sweat forming under the armpits of the preacher's shirt didn't deter a single member from standing on the Word.

He thought about how he could have been feeding the trees six feet under right now. He was glad to be alive. Breathing. If cinema was his purpose and his calling, then he had to seek it with a vengeance. He needed to be able to make a difference. Enough games and no more goofing off. Rochelle was married now. He was the only Richardson who had the ability to keep the family line going and make something of himself. His children would become a product of what he was. He needed to make his parents proud. His name in lights. Something like that.

28

The thing is that, in the midst of all of this, I have been stupid enough to think I love you. Am I an idiot? I must be. I know you say you're sorry and expect me to be a freshly washed chalkboard, with no residue of the past, but I'm not, I can't.

Troi wrote. She scratched the words out. The pen was running out of ink. It tore the paper. She looked around the waiting area and thought that she just wanted to say what she had to say to his face. She balled up the paper in her fist, took aim, and made her three-point shot into the trash can on the opposite side of the room.

She wanted to take bright red lipstick that wasn't her shade and write obscenities on his car for the world to see. She wanted everyone to know what he was. She wanted to tell him that he no longer turned her on either, so there! But it was a lie. The thought of him, the smell of him was inspiring. She wore his robe every night and wrapped herself in his scent and remembered when they'd shower together. Everybody wanted a love like theirs. Only thing was, she didn't even have it anymore, and she really didn't even know why.

"Ms. Aimes will see you now, Ms. Singleton."

"Mrs." Troi glared.

She walked into the pale room, decorated with framed posters of couples embracing and certificates of merit that weren't from any colleges Troi knew. As she entered the therapist's office, Vaughn sat staring blankly at Troi like a stranger. It had been three and some odd weeks since their last scheduled session. Last week she'd found out in therapy that Vaughn had made plans to go to his family reunion without her.

His aunts were a clan of stuck-up women who didn't realize that they weren't queens and that their feet still touched the ground like everyone else's. He was looking thinner. She forced bad thoughts out of her mind. She wasn't going to yell or scream. His hair was growing back. She wished he'd shave it again. She liked him bald. He was wearing a tight black nylon shirt and had started wearing silver jewelry. Had on an ID bracelet with something etched on it. She couldn't make out what it said. It made him look flashy. He didn't smile, only nodded, as if his presence was a mere obligation. She laughed to herself. He hated that. It was her only weapon.

After Vaughn had picked up his personal belongings and taken them over to his brother's, she'd been contemplating lots of things. Ridding herself of this boring shade of hair color, for one. Every black man's dream was to have a beautiful black woman who made him feel desired. She couldn't understand how she'd gotten stuck with the only man on earth who thought that he'd repress his feelings and let them out to run rampant once she was wading deep in their marriage. Maybe blond would change that.

Troi remembered that Vaughn hadn't necessarily wanted to leave their apartment. They had fought about it all evening long, but she'd told him that if he didn't go, she and Dakoda would. She needed time. Revelations like this weren't easily overcome. Looking at Vaughn every morning and not talking about what was going on in his head was torture. She couldn't live like that. Carla was the only one who knew now. Carla had rested her hand on Troi's shoulder and said, "He'll come around." She'd said not to make too much out of it. She was the only person in whom Troi could confide. That was before Vaughn had asked her not to discuss their dilemma with anyone. But she didn't care. She needed the comfort. After all he had done to her, who was he to deny her that?

Troi had been hurt enough in her life. She should have been indestructible by now. She didn't see the point of counseling either, really. If he was going to sit there and act like he had better things to do than try to fix something it seemed she wanted more than he did, she could be off doing other things as well. She loved her daughter and wanted her to have a father, but she couldn't deal with the man she loved telling her that he was in love with another man and that her body just didn't do it for him.

"So, where were we last week? Vaughn, would you like to

begin?" the therapist asked, reading the chart and sounding free of such issues.

Vaughn was gazing out the window at what was going on in the streets, and Troi crossed her legs, folded her arms, and sighed. It was obvious he was elsewhere. He ignored the therapist, he was ignoring Troi, and it was evident that sitting here in an office trying to resolve their issues was the last thing he wanted to be doing.

"Vaughn? She's talking to you."

Vaughn looked in Troi's direction. His eyes were unfamiliar, his gaze penetrating. She had had enough. His attitude and mannerisms offended her. She didn't know how she couldn't see it before she'd married him. She picked up her bag and headed for the door.

"Mrs. Singleton?"

"Ms. Madison, thank you!" Troi snarled.

"Where are you going? Do you want to reschedule?"

Troi's gaze pierced Vaughn. "You're pathetic!" she spat, then slammed the door on her way out.

"I still have to bill you . . ." the therapist's voice trailed off after her.

Troi always called Carla the minute she got back from therapy. She picked up the phone to dial as she allowed her purse strap to slide off her shoulder and the keys to fall from her fingers. Carla always asked the usual questions.

"How did the session go?"

"It was fine. Can you help me dye my hair?"

"Dye your hair for what?"

"I want a new look, something brighter."

"You want him to notice you, that's what you want."

"No, that's not it at all."

"Girl, please, since when are you insecure? And why are you changing the subject?"

"Because I don't want to talk about it or him."

"Maybe it's a phase, you know," Carla said.

"Phase? Does moving out look like a phase?"

"It's part of the transition, Troi."

"Well, I don't want him sleeping with anybody but me. I don't want to think that his hot, sweaty naked body is twisted in the arms of someone else, making sexual pleasure for them commonplace."

"What? Ladies don't talk like that, CeCe," Carla teased.

"I don't care. Who wants to be a lady? I want to be loved."

The telephone beeped. Troi clicked over to the other line.

"Hey, baby."

"Daddy?"

"What's going on, baby girl?"

"Nothing much."

"I'm calling because I thought it would be a good idea for you, Nina, and I to have lunch if you can work it into your schedule. I know you've been trying to get together. I just had so many jobs lined up."

"Sounds good, Daddy, when?"

"You busy tomorrow?"

"No, not at all, what time?"

"Three o'clock is good."

"Okay, Daddy. Is everything okay?"

"Everything is good. Do I need a reason to see my girls?"

"No, Daddy."

"Good."

"So, business is picking up?"

"Yes, doing very well. Don't mean to rush you, baby girl, but I have an errand to run. We'll talk, baby."

"Daddy? Lunch where?"

"Emily's."

"Mmmmm, my favorite."

"I know." She could hear her daddy parting his lips to smile. "See you tomorrow."

Daddy had called Troi, and that almost never happened. Daddy usually called Nina and Mother called Troi. That was the way it had been forever. He'd asked if he could meet them both for lunch tomorrow. Tuesdays and Fridays were busy in the shop but it was okay. It had to be important, or Daddy wouldn't ask. She'd agreed to lunch for her and Nina both. Troi figured that she needed to do something to get her mind off the fact that nothing was helping her marriage. Not even hundred-dollar-an-hour therapy sessions.

Troi knew that people would carelessly whisper that she wasn't enough woman for her husband so he had found another body identical to his to satisfy his needs. Maybe she was being too hard on him. She'd never tried to understand what he must be feeling emotionally or spiritually. She had only looked at her own pain. It was an excruciating, indescribable mass. Maybe they needed to talk about it. Pray about it. They didn't need to argue. They'd done that already. It hadn't helped.

Troi remembered Carla on the other line and quickly pressed the flash button.

"Carla?"

"Yes?"

"Can I call you back?"

"What's wrong?"

"Nothing, I need to make a call."

Troi dialed the number to the bank. She never called Vaughn's office unless it was an emergency. She wanted to know if he could pick up the baby and take her to his mother's so she'd be free to have lunch tomorrow without deadlines and playing beat the clock.

"Vaughn Singleton, please."

"He's gone for the day, can I help you with anything?"

"Uh. No, I'll call back, thanks."

Vaughn always went to therapy sessions on his lunch hour. He did the same with regular doctor's appointments. Of course, her thoughts raced to where he was or with whom he might be. She wasn't going to sit and guess how his arms were possibly comforting Tracie while she sat here still unsure of what she was going to do with the rest of her life. He had never taken a day off to spend time and do something special with her. Fair was fair. Maybe he had taken a little time off for her, but that had been only in the beginning, when their love was new and unrehearsed. Now it appeared that his partner warranted what his wife didn't. Troi wasn't sure if she wanted to know what Vaughn was doing, although something in her desperately wanted a face to go with the name Tracie.

"Hey, Carla."

"Oh, you actually called me right back? The sky is cracking."

"Be serious, please."

"What's wrong?"

"Nothing, I just need a favor."

"Girl, you know I'll do anything for you. You're my sis."

"Thanks, can you baby-sit tonight? Please?" Troi asked, giving her full attention to the light that had come on in her head.

"For what?"

"I have an errand to run."

"What kind of errand?"

"Carla!"

"Okay, okay. I get off in half, I'll be there in forty-five minutes."

Troi was happy to have a friend whom she could count on when she was in a jam, pickle, or some other sort of dilemma. It was situations like these that revealed your friends. Friends weren't the ones you hung out and got silly with. Friends were dependable, flexible, and always on time. That was Carla. Troi changed her shirt and her shoes. She put on a little lipstick and scented her body with something that she liked for a change. She imagined that she would eventually get through this, too, just like other situations that she'd thought would break her.

Sooner than not the doorbell rang. Troi reached for her bag and opened the door.

"You can dye my hair when I come back."

"It'll be too late."

"No, it won't, I promise. I'll be an hour or two at the most."

She kissed the baby, hugged Carla, left feeding instructions, and repeated that she'd be back in an hour or two.

"So, where did you say you're going?" Carla inquired.

"I didn't." Troi grinned.

She trotted downstairs, got in the car, and headed for the busy bridge that always gave Vaughn grief.

Troi looked at herself in the rearview mirror and thought that she was turning into the kind of woman that she'd said she would never become. Needy, sneaky, conniving, and so desperate she had to spy on her husband from behind a tree. She almost forgot the way, but the signs would tell her where Teaneck was. She began thinking back to today's session. A total waste of a new pair of stockings. But it was fine. She was feeling like December 31st, and was determined to go out with a bang.

Traffic wasn't all that bad, she thought as she pulled up under a tree down the street from where Sam lived. She knew that she'd sit and wait, contemplating whether or not she should ring the bell and sit down and finally talk this through with Vaughn. He was Dakoda's father and her husband. They didn't need to be paying some therapist who was learning as she went along to fix something that God had control over anyway. That fact that she loved him and he mouthed the words *I love you* would never change.

She drummed her fingers on the dashboard as she listened to an instrumental CD twice and sat for a little over an hour waiting. She was feeling lethargic and decided to turn off the distracting music, march into that house, and fight tooth and nail for her marriage.

Troi was momentarily blinded by the headlights of a black shiny late-model car that pulled up directly in front of the door to Sam's house. The car was facing hers without being close enough for either driver to recognize the other. A tall slender man with an eye for perfection got out and put something in the trunk. She had never seen his face or his car before. The front door opened, as she held her breath expecting to observe Sam emerging to greet his friend, who may have been an old buddy from school. But instead Vaughn came out of the house, peered around the street and closed the door behind him. He had changed from what he'd been wearing at the therapist's office this afternoon. She examined him head to toe as he looked back at Sam's heavily draped windows cautiously.

Vaughn was grinning like a smitten schoolboy as he walked around the front of the car to the passenger side. He got in and hugged the man, who she figured was a little more than friendly. She could see them reach over to each other with emotion. Instantly she knew it was him. Tracie. There was a momentary pause and the driver made a U-turn, heading to what she figured was some secret location. His car was almost out of sight as she sat there in shock that Vaughn would have the audacity. She forbade tears, pulled herself together, knocked the chip off her shoulder, and started the engine. She was determined to confront this situation head-on, she thought, hitting the gas pedal and leaning back in her seat, on her way to follow them and rain on their parade.

29

Vaughn stood still and afraid while a bronzed man with an oil sheen, wearing a thong and brandishing proportioned muscles, strutted across the bar, slightly missing kicking over several colorful drinks with umbrellas. The dancer stopped and bent over, making eye contact with Tracie in the dimly lit room, where some were moving about and most were just observing. Tracie was excited and dared Vaughn to add a buck to the already well-endowed G-string of the dancing guy.

Vaughn stood, looking amazed as this guy performed for them, wiggling, squirming, and bending over, showing more than he legally needed to see. Some clapped, chanting, "Take it off, take it off," and Vaughn watched as facial expressions in the room mimicked delicious. Tracie took a twenty-dollar bill, folded it horizontally, and invited the dancer. He then put the bill in Vaughn's hand and the performance was on. The entertainer danced in Vaughn's face, coaxing him to release the bill into his well and, with the snap of the elastic, make a wish. The crowd egged him on. Vaughn was more embarrassed than hesitant. Probably more so from what he thought people would say than actually being afraid of the dancer with the shimmery G-string, who was dying for Vaughn to touch him.

Tracie had slid down to the other end of the bar, finding pleasure in the cowboy entertainer who had a pony skin flap hanging in front of him as he marched around with a his snakeskin boots and big black cowboy hat. Tracie used his finger to call the rodeo boy over in a come-hither fashion. Nervousness swept over Vaughn. He felt instantly betrayed. His breath quickened. He thought that he and Tracie were going out to have an evening of relaxation. Time alone. Or time to talk about what was going on in Vaughn's life that was confusing him to the bone. A meat market was never his thing. Not even to pick up women.

This evening Vaughn had seen Tracie in a different light. He wished he'd known that this was the kind of flamboyant lifestyle he led before he had even contemplated getting involved with him. Granted, he hadn't known Tracie for that long, but this was where he drew the line.

Vaughn just hoped that Tracie didn't think that he was going to fit him into this seedy equation. He wasn't about to be an addition to anyone's collection. And although Vaughn had his feelings properly placed about his homosexuality, he knew that this was the last place he ever thought he would find himself. He was bothered by the fact that this was the stereotypical concept of homosexuals anyway. He didn't want to openly feed into the misconceptions.

Vaughn backed away from the whole situation, making himself as comfortable as he could be, considering. He sat at a small circular table in the corner and instantly felt eyes peeling him and stripping him down to his underthings.

"Are you okay?" Tracie asked, sliding in next to Vaughn.

"No, actually, I'm not. What's this all about?"

"What? We're just having a little fun, lighten up."

Vaughn's lips twitched.

"So, this is how you're living?"

"When in Rome," Tracie replied, waving his arms in tune with the music.

"You know, this isn't even how I pictured you, man." Vaughn stood to leave.

"Vaughn, come on. Wait. I'll go with you. Give me a minute."

The music was extremely loud and Vaughn could barely make out anything the men walking by flirting with him were saying. He just smiled to keep the peace, or else they would be calling him Ms. Honey and think he was giving them fever.

Vaughn surveyed the room for the closest exit when a familiar scolding made him shudder.

"So, this is how you spend your time when you're supposed to be trying to work on us, huh?"

"CeCe?"

"CeCe?" Troi mocked. "Yeah, it's me."

"What are . . ."

"What am I doing here? What am I doing here?"

Vaughn stared blankly.

"I thought you said that you'd be staying in Jersey with Sam?"

"I am . . . I mean . . ."

"You said it wasn't permanent, that it was a temporary situation."

"You asked me to move out, CeCe."

"Yes, and I meant for it to give us time to reevaluate our situation, not for you to do male bonding here."

"Look, CeCe . . ."

"You know, I don't even know why I'm here." She pointed. "But, I mean, we were doing fine until you decided you wanted to discover your feminine side." She waved her arms, directing her comment to everybody in the room.

Her statement fell on deaf ears as extravagance had its way throughout the club.

Vaughn's chest rose as he took a deep breath.

"Well, you wouldn't know where I was going if you weren't sneaking around following me."

"Oh, so I'm sneaking around following you?"

"Well, what do you call it?"

"Okay, well, it's what you don't know about a person that can damage you," she said, storming off.

A big-faced woman stepped in front of Troi on her way to the exit, smelling of the cheap rose perfume that great-grandmothers wore. She was dressed in something silvery and long.

"How you doing, baby?"

"I'm fine, if you move." Troi stood with her hand on her hip.

"Come on, mammie, don't be like that."

"Look, honey, I don't get down like that," Troi spat, shoving the culprit into a wall, making a spectacle and her escape.

Troi wondered if she was a magnet. All she seemed to attract were people who thought she was a wonderful listener.

Vaughn stood, wringing his hands. He looked behind him and turned to follow Troi out of the nightclub, only to be accosted by Tracie.

"Where are you going?" He grabbed Vaughn's elbow.

"I need to make sure Troi is okay."

"She'll be fine," Tracie dismissed.

"I need to make sure, man. Just because I feel what I feel doesn't mean that I don't care about my wife." He frowned and pulled away.

"If you cared about your wife, why do you feel what you feel?" Tracie yelled after Vaughn.

30

Nina craved a café with green or red canopies in Tribeca where they served mozzarella garlic bread, fettuccini Alfredo, or chicken and waffles. She couldn't wait to have lunch with her father and sister while sipping Irish mocha. They'd meet at Emily's and enjoy the afternoon, playing slow down and catch-up. It had been so long since they'd been out together as a family. Schedules were tight, but they were learning to make room for each other. She didn't know if her mother would be there, but she hoped not.

She thought that it was such a shame that she couldn't be cordial with her mother around. If her mother would give an inch, they'd be beyond all the childhood nonsense by now. Nina didn't have time or energy to debate with a woman who still wanted to treat her adult children like they were seven years old. She'd had her chance to raise them and had dishonorably forfeited. Nina wasn't about to take any of her mother's war-torn advice on life now.

Nina distracted herself with the thought that she wanted something in the renaissance style to hang on the wall in her foyer. Maybe she'd go window-shopping later, after lunch. Maybe she'd call Shelby. In the back of her dawdling daydreams she couldn't help but think that Derek had walked through the door of her brownstone with a greasy workbag full of tools, a suitcase full of clothes, a small radio that didn't record, and a hooded parka. He hadn't come with furniture, antiques, or artwork to add to hers. He'd come walking up to claim everything that she owned, including herself. Although she didn't own herself, she was bought with a price. Troi said it was the blood.

Nina sat with Martha, looking out the window to where kids ran for the bus with mobile-home bookbags strapped to their backs. "Lemme borrow your bus pass," one kid asked. "Nah, you crazy?" Kids laughed, used profanity, and wore headsets so loud that you thought they were portable hi-fis. Junior was out and about, wearing latex gloves and soldier-marching with an exaggerated gait down the street, determined to get somewhere in a hurry, brushing crumbs from his mouth and exchanging curious glances with passersby.

"What's his problem, girl?"

"I don't know, you know Junior, he's high, or worse."

They observed people in a frenzied hurry to get to work, and as always Nina was thankful for a day off, free from deadlines, copy machines, and counting numbers in her head. By the weekend, Derek and all the baggage that came along with him would be history.

Maybe she'd go to Zion with Troi more often. Her ears always savored the choir's singing, and she could genuinely get beyond the stares. She just needed to take those baby steps. She knew that God would do the rest. Every man she crossed paths with was a walking mishap. She had enough drama in her life to bottle it and sell it. Troi's life was evidence of what she lived. Nina wanted that assurance, the simple abundance. She knew that she might be able to get Martha to grace the halls of a church with her at least once, but couldn't manage Shelby kicking and screaming. That was a humorous thought.

Nina arrived at Emily's first. "Can I have a Diet Coke?"

She took a seat in the restaurant, which was almost empty, but quickly filling up.

"Are you alone?" the waitress asked.

"No, I'm waiting for three more." Nina motioned to the empty chairs.

She was hungry. Her stomach was growling and telling her that she'd better not be on another one of those diets. She ordered seasoned fries that she'd pick at until they arrived. She prayed they would tide her over.

Nina observed a group of four middle-aged men at an adjoining table who were having a conversation that would have been more interesting if they were. The waitresses were short and perky, thin and petite, almost anorexic-looking for sisters. They were dressed in all black with swaying hair attachments. But then again, the hair could have been real. She tried not to knock a sister. Salons like Shangrila had been working magic on hair for years now.

Across the restaurant, past the sheer white nylon curtains that shaded the sun, an older couple in the corner by the window gazed off in thought as if undiscovered by each other. They were merely going through the formalities of dining together. He was consumed with the paper's sports section and she was eyeing every man who walked through the door, checking them out from haircut to shoes.

Everyone glanced over at Nina occasionally, assuming she shouldn't be dining solo. They were staring with eyes that showed utter concern, as if she should have some big hairy man coming to join her, offering shabby conversation and then picking up the tab. But she didn't care what they thought. She sat realizing that she didn't have to beg, perform, or persuade a man to shower her with affection. She refused to do that, and she was mentally holding herself to that promise. Men came in her life to assume the role of a brick that would eventually create a wall. Derek had served his purpose. Momentary entertainment. Now it was time for him to go.

The waitress brought her hot fries. She reached in, then blew her fingers and realized that she was hungrier than she'd thought. She wondered what the urgency of lunch was all about. And she wondered why Daddy hadn't called her instead of Troi. It was funny how you got used to things being a certain way, and then something happened to upset the whole caddy. Nina looked up just in time to see her daddy arriving. He was a little heavier, but still had that presence that let you know when he walked into a room. Troi had that same presence.

"Hey, baby."

"Hi, Daddy. You look good," she said, kissing his freshly shaven cheek.

"Thank you."

"You okay?"

"Yes, I'm good," he said, hanging his red-and-black flannel-lined jacket on the back of the chair.

"It's too hot for that coat, Daddy."

"It's okay, I'm fine."

The tiny little waitress, who was a cheeseburger away from starving to death, came over to the table. "Good afternoon, can I get you anything?"

The waitress held out a menu as Troi came tripping into the

restaurant with high heels, chopped-off honey blond hair, and wide-rim shades, looking like a cheap knockoff version of Mary J. Blige. She motioned to the table where Nina and her father were sitting.

"Hey, sorry I'm late." She breathed loudly. "I had to drop the baby off at her grandmother's."

"What did you do, Troi?" Nina asked with her eyes raised and her mouth partially opened.

"Hi, Daddy . . ."

"Troi, your sister is talking to you."

"Nina, please, I needed a change." Troi waved her hand. Daddy stood up and hugged Troi.

"I'll have some chicken and waffles," Troi said to the waitress, who was standing, twiddling the pen, itching to write something on the pad.

"Nothing for me," Daddy said pensively.

They observed his unease. "Daddy, is everything all right?" Troi asked.

Troi glared at Nina, Nina scrutinized Troi's hair, and they both turned their attention to their father.

"You know I always wanted what was best for you girls."

Troi couldn't take another confession, not even if it would save her. He paused and reached for a french fry.

"Daddy?" Nina said.

"Yes, Daddy, please just spit it out," Troi asked.

He looked at the worried expressions on his daughters' faces and confessed, "I'm leaving your mother."

"What? Daddy, you can't leave Mother, what is she going to do without you there?" Troi wailed, drawing attention to their table.

"I don't know, but I can't live there anymore. You know we stayed together mostly for you girls. I wanted to make sure you had everything you needed and mostly anything you wanted."

"But how you just gonna get up and leave Mother?"

"Please, Troi, don't you remember everything we went through living there? Did you forget so soon?" Nina asked, intent on finishing off her order of fries.

"I know, but what's she gonna do, Nina? She's an alcoholic. She's sick."

"Troi, baby, I know you don't understand," Daddy consoled.

"No, I don't understand, my whole life is falling apart!"

"What whole life, Troi? You have a happy life."

"Happy?"

"Yes, happy," Nina spat. "You've got Vaughn while I find myself struggling with a man that I don't even know how I got involved with in the first place. But I'll remedy that, because today is Tuesday, and by the weekend, Derek is history." Nina shoved fries in her mouth, chewing voraciously.

"Oh, well, I'm glad you finally saw the light where Derek is concerned, because he's controlling, manipulative, and downright ungodly." Troi counted on her fingers. "But let me tell you about my perfect little life, Nina. My husband, the perfect provider, the good catch that all the woman are dying for a piece of . . . he's gay! So chalk that up with your idea of my perfect life."

Daddy's expression was erased. Nina was gnawing her bottom lip. That explained the brandywine toenails and that hideous shade of blond, Nina thought.

After lunch with Daddy and Troi, who refused to be consoled, Nina came home to find a message from Shelby. She and a few friends from college wanted to stop by for dinner and a video. Nina fixed a little something and straightened up the living room so they wouldn't think she was a complete novice when it came to housekeeping. She put a few CDs in the changer and went about doing her daily house-adjusting. A call from her office interrupted. Her boss was on the line, and he was telling her that they wanted to set up a conference call.

"Now?"

"Immediately."

"Hold please." She adjusted herself in the chair and put on her headset as they connected several calls and everyone who was to be present confirmed that they were.

"I'm ready."

"Good afternoon all," her boss continued.

She wanted him to cut the small talk. Get to the point.

"The accounting department has informed us that there has been a decrease in productivity that has left the company in a financial deficit. Ms. Madison, as the manager you must inform the employees working from the downtown office that they will be required to take a two-week leave of absence without pay until we rectify this financial situation. I hate to do it like this, but if we don't have revenue, we go out of business."

"Surely there's another alternative."

"Yes. Of course there is. Find the weakest link by tomorrow and terminate them."

Knowing most of the employees lived from one paycheck to the next, Nina knew that two weeks would have almost all of them behind in rent and other bills. It was easy for the higher-ups to figure that termination was an admirable solution. But she would be the one who'd have to single out one or make them all suffer. Her boss hardly ever bothered her with the little details of running the office. It was as if she didn't even exist. Now here he was with a burden that he gladly rested at her feet. And she would handle it just as she had managed to find a peaceful place for all the other bothersome things in her life.

Nina's college friends arrived to find that she was not in her usual good mood. She served them, smiling but all the while awaiting Derek's impending return. Shelby was brandishing a ring that she labeled *engagement,* although the ring was clearly saying, *You're not worth a diamond, so I'll give you this blue stone and call it love.*

"I have never been so attached in all my life."

"What are you two now, Siamese?"

"What's your problem, Nina? You've been in a foul mood since we got here. If you weren't feeling up to it, you should have said something before now."

"It's fine, Shelby." Nina yawned.

"So, why are you standing here insulting me and my ring? I hope you're not jealous, because you know I wish the same for you."

"I'm not jealous, Shelby," Nina confessed. "I just don't think that you have to go around like everyone wants to hear each tender morsel of your love life all day long."

"So, now I offend you?"

"Listen, I'm not saying that." Although Shelby's ravings had always offended her.

"Well, it sure sounded like it to me."

"Take it how you want it," Nina defended, as the two other women looked on, disbelieving.

"I think I should go." Shelby frowned.

"Maybe." Nina crossed her arms.

"You two staying?" Shelby eyed them over her shoulder.

"Bye, Nina, let's do this again really soon," they added.

Nina felt lower than the heel on a run-down shoe. Misdirected anger. She was always taking her ill feelings out on someone else.

Shelby hadn't done anything except be her usual obnoxious self. Today, however, Nina had reached her limit. She had finally filled her daily quota and woe unto they who crossed her now.

Shortly after eleven, when the news came on, Derek returned home after working late again to find what he elected to call his house consumed with the residue of people whom he cared little to know and lingering laughter that was not invited. He smirked, self-assured as Nina glanced hesitantly at him with her head low. He paced the floor and started in that he didn't like people in his house, eating up his food when he was at work.

"Excuse me?" Nina started in. "Shelby brought Chinese." She gave him the benefit of the doubt.

"I don't care who brought what!"

Nina contemplated her words. She paused only momentarily.

"You know what? I've had just about enough of you. You came here with a tool belt. You didn't bring a chair or a tablecloth, and now you want to call this yours? It's mine, I paid for it. Still am paying, but all you do is complain when the fact is that you should be happy because I'm keeping you. It's because of me that you eat and have someplace to sleep. And furthermore, it was never a head-over-heels love thing anyway, so you can pack your little knapsack and be gone."

She always remembered what her mother said about her, and indeed, she was determined to finish what she'd started. Derek was up close in her face trying to intimidate her now. He grimaced and spoke deliberately. "You think I'm going to hit you, don't you?" He walked away, confident that he had the power to flip a switch and turn her into a terrified idiot who would do whatever he said. He started in with the name-calling. Fat, black, ugly. She was humming a song that Toni Braxton sang, in her head, as she always did when she got tired of hearing all that stuff he said about her. It was a defense mechanism. He raised his hand as if he was about to do something that he'd regret for the rest of his life. She licked her lips and grinned slightly.

"If you hit me, I'll kill you." She spoke calmly. It was over.

Derek paused, tempting fate, then walked out the front door. She walked into the bedroom and started tossing his things into the hall. She flung his radio, CDs, clothing, and other odds and ends with which he'd landed on her doorstep. His things were in disarray by the door, and if he wasn't back first thing in the morning for them, they'd go out with the trash.

Nina skimmed the Yellow Pages and called a locksmith, and they told her that they would send someone over in the morning at nine A.M. to change the locks. So she put on the bolt, said a little prayer, then called her sister.

"I'm sorry, Nina. And about earlier, I didn't mean to be so juvenile."

"Okay, no problem, but why didn't you tell me about Vaughn? I'm your sister."

"I couldn't. How could I tell you?"

"Well, good riddance and sayonara to Derek, he's officially done!" Nina motioned to her head in an official salute.

"Good riddance to Vaughn, too."

"Really?"

"Yes, I'm not going to live my life looking at every move he makes, I can't live like that."

"That's true." Nina nodded.

"What are you doing Friday night?" Troi asked.

"Nothing, why?"

"I have something that we can do that will make us both feel a lot better."

"Like what?"

"Like helping those less fortunate."

31

Tim got a C on his project. A measly C for which he was kicking himself. That was because he had put little or no effort into his schoolwork. He had been juggling women and committing at least three of the seven deadly sins: Lust, greed, and sloth. Lust because his thoughts were anything but pure; greed because he didn't want one, but many; and sloth because after he was finished with the lust and greed, he didn't have the energy to hula hoop.

His professor had said he was surprised at him. He'd told Tim that if he aced the final project, he stood a good chance of bringing his grade up to a solid B and possibly salvaging his dwindling GPA. He hoped so, because the answering machine hadn't managed to lure him with messages from Sharon or Michelle, and despite all of his giving to the church, he was still broke. He needed a job like yesterday. He had an interview this morning with a small company and knew that if he didn't get the job, he would be homeless and selling peeled fruit at intersections by the end of the month.

It hadn't taken him long to feel the pinch of no Sharon and no Michelle, which meant no money. Tim didn't want to think about that now. It wasn't like he was morally corrupt or robbing people. For a season he had honestly believed that someone owed him something. A consolation of sorts. And Sharon and Michelle were willing participants, who just fed his need to have and acquire things without having to give. He desperately wished that his hierarachy of needs stopped at food. But he had occasionally found pleasure in phone sex, of all things. Surely that wouldn't be the way he got through the rest of his life.

Tim didn't want to play games with women. He honestly wanted one day to consummate a relationship where he would wake up deeper in love with a woman than when he'd gone to sleep. A woman with whom he didn't mind sharing his socks and dress shirts. Someone who would finally extinguish the torch he was carrying for lost loves. He looked forward to that, although right now he couldn't conceive of a love that profound. He did anticipate not having to pretend to be busy just to stop women from being too clingy. He anticipated not having to make excuses or give them the runaround.

The weatherman said partly cloudy, chance of thundershowers, though they were always just guessing. Tim put on a tie, brushed his suede shoes, and smoothed down his goatee. He needed a little cologne to make himself smell employable. All he had left was something in a green bottle that Sharon had given him. He filled the palms of his hands and slapped it on. He double-checked his résumé, then placed it in his portfolio. The phone was ringing, but he didn't want to be late. He let the machine do its job.

Tim's car had mist on the windshield, and although he sat inside, pleading, it wouldn't start, no matter how many times he cranked it. The morning chill was dissipating, the mid June heat was trying to kick in. Tim didn't know what to make of the weather lately, but he was determined that the job was his. If he had to scale walls and climb fences, he'd get there on time. He removed the key and inserted it several times. The car still wouldn't start. All it managed was a hesitant hum. In a fit of anger, Tim punched the steering wheel and rested on the horn. He had five bucks, and debated whether or not he should take a cab to the west side and take the train downtown, or just walk and save the few dollars he had left for dinner. Tim walked quickly, passing up the urge for a cup of coffee and a newspaper. His eyes bulged like he was being chased. His breath quickened and he began to sweat; he loosened his tie.

Sitting on the train being jerked downtown, Tim thought that he couldn't rely on jobs and working for other people forever. It wasn't satisfying. Not to mention that it hindered him from what he believed was his true calling. Soon, he thought. Soon. Tim grinned and bobbed his head to an imaginary rhythm, and always managed to notice people wherever he went. He was sitting now, noticing how strangers avoided his gaze. He eyed the man sitting directly across from him. Black pin-striped suit. Conservative shoes. He was probably forty and had a job doing something he didn't necessarily care for. His socks didn't match. One black, one blue. Tim could sympathize. It had happened to him several times too many.

Making his way out of the subway car at his stop, Tim wrestled with people who were trying to get on the train before the doors closed. Tim peered ahead. He vaguely made out Sharon in the distance. She was making her way toward the far end of the platform to the uptown side. His first instinct was to run. His second was to be curious as an average-looking brother turned, leaned in, and kissed her on the lips. His third instinct was jealousy, and his fourth response was unexplained anger as he fought his way through baby-strollers, knapsacks, and briefcases to the exit sign and made his way to the street level.

Tim stood in the lobby of the building where his interview would be held, waiting for the elevator. He said a silent prayer to himself, willing the thought of Sharon out of his mind. On the sixth floor he stepped off into the small cluttered office space, managing a smile. He stepped up to the desk and fiddled his fingers around his portfolio. There was a bulletin board directly to his right that was overflowing with notices of rooms for rent and flyers with torn-off tabs. Flyers for final-week performances on hot pink paper were more distracting than eye-catching where they lined the wall on the left. The phone ran incessantly.

"One moment please. Big Deal Films. One moment please. He'll be in after noon. Yes. Thank you, sir." The woman sighed.

"Big Deal Films. Hold please." Tim grinned at the receptionist.

"Can I help you, sir?" she said, looking up at Tim with gray eyes that made her look blind instead of helpful.

"I'm here for the receptionist position."

"Great." She sighed. "I'll be right back."

"Thank you." Tim smiled.

He surveyed the area. Relatively new carpeting and a coffeepot. Three telephone lines continued ringing. The calls lit up the phone, which already had two callers blinking on hold. Tim looked around the office at movie posters for low-budget films that he hadn't heard of, and wondered what he could possibly learn here, and also if they let employees pitch ideas. The receptionist stuck her head out of the back office.

"Can you get that phone, please?"

"Sure," he said, smiling, nodding, and mentally thanking God for the job. He walked behind the receptionist station and placed his portfolio on the desk. "Big Deal Films. Hold, please." Tim smiled. "Big Deal Films. One moment, please. Big Deal Films. Yes, can you bring it up? Thanks."

A short white man a little on the pudgy side with an expertly cut goatee walked off the elevator. He nodded his head.

"So, you're the new receptionist."

Tim couldn't even get the words out that he was just helping out.

"Glad to have you aboard." He extended his hand, shaking Tim's firmly.

The pudgy man walked to the back of the office, passing the receptionist on the way.

"He's good, nice look," he said to her.

"Uh, line one wants to know about the presummer release. They didn't receive press information. Line two wants Al? And line three was the delivery guy, he's bringing up breakfast."

"Thank you. You're a lifesaver. My name is Abby. That was Al," she said, pointing to the back office. "It seems he likes your look."

"Great." Tim smiled.

"You have a résumé?"

"Yes," he said, handing her the crisp ecru sheet of paper. She scrutinized every entry.

"Tim?"

"Yes?"

"You've never worked in film before?"

"Not actually, but I am a film major and would love to get the experience."

"Well, the job is yours; this is just a formality. Fill out this application. You can start next week."

"Really?"

"Uh-huh."

"Thank you, Abby." He almost hugged her.

"Are you still in school?"

"Yes, but I can work my classes around the job."

"Glad to hear it. The salary is not much, but it will get you along. My husband and I are just starting out. We've only been in this office for two years. I've been the receptionist-slash-everything else. Business is growing and we need the help. Where did you hear about the position?"

"In *Backstage.*"

He sat and filled out the application and thought of something entertaining he could do with the rest of his day.

Tim spent his afternoon in a dank downtown theater, watched a double feature of cinematic waste, and munched on movie garbage. He was trying to uncover why movies made no sense. He hadn't seen a good film in about five years, and that had been on video. When movies started to be carbon copies of each other and only managed to rotate the cast and paste on an adjective as a title, it was time to go back to puppet shows for entertainment, or it was time for his films. Tim smiled at the thought that Big Deal could possibly be his big break. That was, if his pushy sister didn't break him first.

Rochelle had been trying to get Tim to build up his church attendance to include Friday-night worship. He didn't know if he could swing that. She was pushing it. He needed to get used to going every Sunday first. After he'd had it down for about six months to a year, he'd add prayer or bible study. He didn't want to rush it. He didn't want to end up like someone so high on the fact that the local gym had a sauna and a Jacuzzi that they plunked down one thousand dollars, only to manage to make it there two and a half weeks out of the first month before they just quit going altogether and then the membership expired.

He'd told Rochelle that he had to get up extremely early in the morning to go to the soup kitchen. He kidded and called it his part-time job. If he was late, they'd add on another week. He was thankful to God though. "Faith is the evidence of things not seen." That was what Hebrews 11 said. He had memorized that from his childhood.

He had walked into Big Deal, saying and believing that that job was his, and it was. Now he'd have his own money. And although he didn't know what he would do in regards to the spring semester, he still couldn't wait to tell Rochelle how blessed he felt, and that God really was good all the time.

32

Troi's days were quiet and uneventful. She knew she needed to gear up and get her life back in full swing. The dedication and zeal that once had her doing things because they mattered, not because she needed to, was but a periodic flicker now. Her shop was going to pot. Her plants were dried up and dying on the shelves. Hair supplies still in boxes were piled up by the display case, and invoices were in disarray. It had to be symbolic. Everyone was asking about her, knowing she hadn't been her old self. She was grateful for the concern, but needed divine intervention, not sympathy.

She thought on her way to the shop that she needed to boost clientele and reconstruct her image, too, while she was at it. The last thing she wanted was for her shop to be another dingy old hair place that had everyone coming out with a pageboy. Maybe she would print up some discount coupons and mail them to customers or let someone stand downtown and distribute them. Maybe she'd dye her hair a darker shade of blond. Something that didn't frighten her every time she looked in the mirror. She needed to reclaim herself. She refused to give Vaughn the power to change her mood. She wouldn't let him destroy her life's dream either.

The shop wasn't usually crowded on Friday mornings. But that didn't stop Carmen from being the only one in the shop doing five heads. No sign of Sofie, but Vaughn had been calling the house and the shop since that fiasco at the club. She had repeatedly hung up on him or erased his annoyingly apologetic messages. He was using Dakoda as an excuse to keep the lines of communication open, but

Troi honestly didn't have anything for him. She'd once thought she would always be his, but today she wasn't sure. Tomorrow either.

She had so much fire and anger inside of her right now that she couldn't even promise herself sanity. They were both supposed to try to repair their marriage. They were both supposedly trying to be attentive enough to know that it wouldn't work if they didn't find out what the root cause was. When she'd thought he'd been trying, Vaughn had been loving it up in the clubs. Troi couldn't pretend, like some women did, that she just needed a new pack of batteries and would be as good as new eventually. She also couldn't deny the fact that in spite of her faithfulness he had defiled their bed.

Troi was trying to distract herself mentally. She was waiting for a woman to come at eleven and another one at noon. She just wanted to know what they knew about hair. If they could wrap, crimp, and relax without burning scalps, whether or not they had a following, they would be hired. She needed reliability. If either of the women even remotely resembled a hair stylist, Troi would finally fire Sofie. But they had to know hair. Absolutely. No beauty-school dropouts. Her shop had an image to maintain.

The first woman arrived at eleven-twenty. They had discussed the booth fee on the phone. She was late, but readily prepared with a book full of photographs with hairstyles that only her imagination could have created.

"So, where are you working now?"

"I work out of my home. I can't afford the rent for the shop, you know?" the woman explained in broken English.

Carmen just watched, tending hair, not saying a word.

"This is very good," Troi said, raising her voice slightly, forgetting the woman wasn't hard of hearing, only semibilingual.

"You be ready Monday?" Troi asked.

"Yes, Monday is good for me."

"Okay, I will see you on Monday. Thank you," Troi said, shaking the woman's hand.

Troi began unpacking the boxes that were piling up, and neatly lined the shelves with conditioner, relaxer, and a fresh batch of towels. No one was as talkative as they usually were. She hadn't even had to change the radio station when she'd come in this morning. The music was soothing and instrumental.

She had choir rehearsal this evening. She didn't know why they'd moved it from Wednesday. She didn't feel like singing, but remembered someone saying that when you pressed on, you got a breakthrough.

A tall thin black girl walked through the door, the bell jingled, and she looked around, admiring the shop.

"I have an appointment at twelve, but I'm early."

"Hey, I'm Troi, come in."

Troi extended her arm and they walked to the side of the shop where the chairs faced the display cabinets. The girl's attire was distracting to say the least. She had cleavage showing, her waistline exposed, and she looked a few days shy of seventeen.

"How old are you?"

"I'm nineteen."

"How long have you been doing hair?" Troi asked, admiring her neatly styled coif.

"Since I was about thirteen, fourteen."

"Have you been to school?"

"No, more like self-taught."

"I don't know about that. I'm looking for someone who has expert technique. Someone who knows the dangers and how to test the hair and evaluate what it needs."

"I can do that." She popped her gum.

"What type of styles are you familiar with?"

"I can do any style, and I can do it better than anybody," she boasted.

Troi giggled. She reminded Troi of herself as a teen. "Okay. Leave me your number and I'll give you a call next week."

"That'll be fine."

"So, what's the best time to reach you?" Troi asked, noticing Sofie strolling in at what the clock said was twenty-five past twelve, and heading straight for the shop's telephone.

"Mornings before noon are best, but you can leave a message and I'll call you back right away. The machine notifies my pager."

"Okay, that'll work," Troi said. "Thanks for coming, and I'll give you a call."

"Thank you," the girl said, tugging her blouse and giving the shop another once-over.

"Sophie, I need to speak with you." Troi motioned.

"Oh, okay, sure, Troi." Sofie pressed her ear to the phone and smiled, then whispered something that Troi was sure was delighting the person on the other end of the line, but wasn't pleasing her the least little bit. Sofie's lack of dedication to Shangrila was annoying, and so was her lackadaisical attitude. Nothing mattered to this woman except her needs outside of work. Everything Sofie did affected everyone else. Her absence and lateness put undue strain on Troi and Carmen.

Troi wanted options. She had been toying with the idea of taking a few night classes if she could find someone to baby-sit Dakoda. She didn't know what she wanted to study. Maybe general business. Maybe something like how to be an image consultant. Or even just marketing. Maybe she could franchise Shangrila. One in every city. She could establish a future for herself and her daughter. She'd think it over this week, pick up some paperwork at the city college, and then she'd approach Carmen with the idea of managing the shop. But she had absolutely had it with Sofie.

Troi pulled Sofie to the side, away from the prying eyes. Sofie's eyes were red, her hair looked like she should be in the chair instead of behind it, and her breath was saying, *This morning I woke up and didn't even bother.*

"I have to let you go, Sofie."

"You have to let me go?"

"Yes. Because you are unreliable."

"I'm unreliable?" she said, buying time by repeating everything that Troi was saying.

"I need someone who can work with me and the shop. On busy days I need someone here besides Carmen. I need revenue. This shop is my life," she said, explaining, although she knew she didn't have to.

Sofie sucked her teeth and mumbled something in Spanish that made Carmen raise her eyebrows. She stomped out of Shangrila, disgruntled, and stood in front of the shop, begging a passerby for a light. Carmen and the five patrons watched her trail off, attitude hipside. There was nothing sexy about cigarette smoking, not even the butt naked after sex, Troi thought, watching Sofie drag long on the cigarette and blow the chemicals into the wind.

The phone rang and Troi flip-flopped to the phone, removed her earring, and pressed her ear to the receiver.

"CeCe?"

"Yes, Vaughn, what is it?"

"I need to talk with you."

"About?"

"Us."

"We can't do that now."

"Later?"

"I don't know."

"Why?"

"Because . . ."

"Okay, well, I just need you to know that I'm not seeing Tracie anymore."

"Oh, really now?"

"I don't want you to think I'm doing this for us. I mean, I am doing it for us, it's just that I wanted you to know that."

"Vaughn, can we do this later?"

"Tonight?"

"I have rehearsal until ninish."

"So, after that?"

Troi sighed. "Meet me at the church."

"Nine-thirty?"

"Maybe ten."

"Okay," he said, like a child who was given permission. "See you soon."

"Bye, Vaughn."

Sofie came inside after her smoke and began putting everything that had a label with her name on it in a plastic bag. She wasn't friendly about it, but Troi was the one to handle it. The curler, the bottles of conditioner, and the blowdryer. Troi didn't care. This was her dream. She wasn't gonna let anybody defile it. Carmen watched, never once asking a question. Customers under dryers peered from under the hoods, aware of the way Sofie was tossing things around. Troi had always been so nice that people normally walked all over her. Sofie's time was up.

Troi had more serious issues than to be disturbed by a chick who didn't have her priorities straight. Troi told Carmen she'd be back.

"You want anything?"

"No, thanks."

Troi wondered why people thought that divorcée was such an exquisite word. That word just didn't do it for her. She wasn't trying to figure Vaughn. He could be struck with panic, yet his brow remained unmoved. That's exactly how she'd be. Unmoved. She knew women who chased after men. She hadn't done that to get him and she surely denied that she'd do it to keep him. Women did it. It was habit. She wasn't about to follow suit.

Troi sat in the car and remembered when they last made love in the shower. There was nothing in that moment that could have prepared her for what was happening now. There wasn't an inkling of revelation. Not his hands gliding down her hips or his moist lips pecking her gently. Not even the words that he whispered as the water ran down their faces and into their mouths.

She had heard preaching on the topic. None went in depth. It was as if fear wouldn't allow them to. But people needed to hear it. The truth most times did offend. But for the most part they said that homosexuality had nothing to do with male and female, and it had nothing to do with humanity. It had to do with God's order. When one's desires changed God's natural order of things, there was bound to be drama.

Troi's daddy had wanted to talk to her about it ever since they'd had lunch at Emily's, but she didn't want to. It made her feel like the bad judge of character it seemed every Madison was. "Don't tell Mother," she'd told him and Nina at lunch. He'd said it was fine. Nina had nodded. Troi had experienced lots of things growing up. And for the most part, before God her life had felt unfulfilling. But today was another day. She wondered if he wanted to come back to her. If not, she knew that she would get through this moment. If it killed her, she'd get through it, she thought, leaning forward and hugging the steering wheel as passersby wished she'd stop leaning on the horn.

33

Vaughn was pleased that Troi had agreed to see him. He knew that the shortest distance between two points was a straight line, so he got to the point. He needed to move back in. He wasn't necessarily going to say that all was back to normal or that his desires didn't have a life of their own, but the mere fact that he and Troi had been through so much and lived to tell about it was grounds enough to try. He just didn't want to work through the issues that they had if he was living outside of the home. What would the point be then?

Tracie hadn't taken the news of "it's over" well. Vaughn wasn't particularly concerned with that. "You know you can't go back to your old life, Vaughn," he'd taunted. "You'll be miserable," Tracie had offered with a flip of his hand. That was some reverse psychology that he was using to keep him tied to this lifestyle. Tied to him. But Vaughn wasn't going to be undermined by a man who couldn't even fathom what it was like to love a woman, to touch a woman, to smell the fragrance of a woman. So Vaughn put his voice mail on and tried to get through another day where the eyes around him were trying to discern.

Vaughn hadn't honestly been receptive to counseling. He didn't even know if he wanted to change. And poor Troi was struggling with blame and reevaluating everything she was because she was sure it was something that she was or wasn't that had turned Vaughn cold. Blame. Everyone around him would say the feelings he had were wrong. But if he had managed to bed everyone in the female populace they'd label him something flattering, like a player.

Vaughn missed his daughter. The words she tried to speak and the grin that was the spitting image of his. Her hands that were tiny, gentle, and always managed to find their way into his mouth. He had spent the past week searching for some reasoning as to why he couldn't just do the normal go-to-college, get-a-job, find-a-wife thing. Why did things have to be so tough? Why didn't life offer any consolations aside from the fact that it was unpredictable?

Vaughn sat outside on a nearby bench in the cool aromatic summer sun, eating a tuna sandwich and squinting his eyes, watching the sparse foliage blooming and proving that if he wasn't alive, at least the earth was. People with quickened paces and midday errands to run made their way across streets that were congested and sidewalks filled with tanning, tattooing, gourmet, real estate, café, bagels, cigars, pizza, pharmacy, videos, coffee, heroes, home furnishings, one-hour photos, and a slew of other options.

Vaughn knew who he was, who his feelings told him he was, but at times he felt lined with a filth that the world said he needed to peel off. They told him that his desires were like auctioning off his future or narrowing down his options to the usefulness of a petty thief. If you were hungry, would the world say stealing was wrong then? Would your death by malnourishment please the masses and their laws of hypocrisy?

Troi. He knew he loved her, but love was a word that he'd have to validate and justify. He couldn't do that now. He just knew that he loved his baby more than himself. His purpose was to create something that was a part of him, and he wasn't going to allow anything to deny him the joys of fatherhood. Vaughn sat and figured that he would try to be honest and see what the two of them could work out. But he couldn't offer much more, he imagined, as the heat from the summer sun beat down on his back like an additional burden.

When Vaughn returned from lunch, his voice mail was blinking. He undid it and pressed Play, leaned back, and made himself comfortable in the chair, fiddling with writing instruments in the cup holder. Jill approached his desk, fingers first, with a floral arrangement, and he mentally searched for evidence as to whether or not it was his birthday. He turned down the volume on the machine.

"These are for you, Vaughn."

"Thank you." He smiled.

"Don't thank me. I didn't send them," she said coldly.

He searched the bouquet for a card. The tape on the card was lifted, and it was evident that Jill had read it. *Sorry about the other night, let me make it up to you, Tracie.* Vaughn tore the card in half, pressed Erase on the voice mail and made up in his mind to scurry through the rest of the day and meet Troi this evening.

Vaughn's momma was always happy to see her boy.

"Hey, Pop." His dad just nodded, pensive.

Vaughn's childhood images of his father hadn't changed much over the years.

"You hungry, baby?"

"No, I'm fine, Momma. How's the baby?"

"She's fine. She's sleeping now. How's Troi?"

"She's good, Momma."

"You sure?"

"Yes, why?"

"Just asking."

"Well, yes . . . we're fine."

"You would tell me if you weren't, right? 'Cause you know I only want the best for you."

"Yes, Momma, I know."

"Okay, so why is it that you didn't tell me that you've been staying with Sam, baby?"

Vaughn's face heated as the lie strolled across his brow, caught. His momma looked away.

"Momma, we just need a little time. I didn't want to worry you with that, that's all."

"Can't hide things from your momma. It all comes out in the wash. Here, baby, have some pie."

"I'm not hungry, Momma. I just stopped by to see the baby."

"She's in your room." His momma smiled proud.

Vaughn embraced her shoulders tightly.

"Momma, you forgive me?"

"For lying? Of course I do. But you know you don't have to lie to your momma."

"Does Daddy know?"

"No, he doesn't. Do you want that I should tell him?"

"I don't think my life interests him much anyway."

"That's not true. You know your daddy loves both of you."

"Yes, it is, Momma. It's true, but you know that he couldn't care less."

Vaughn walked into the masculine room where old pinup photos of Sheila E and Patrice Rushen reminded him of sports, dates, and feelings he couldn't label or locate. He kissed his baby girl on the head and brushed her hair back. His momma was behind him, leaning over, gushing without worry.

"I'm going out to Jersey, Momma, but I'll be back later, around eleven-thirty. Is that too late?" he whispered, not wanting to wake the baby.

"No, baby, it's fine. You know you can leave the baby here if you want to. Not a problem for me at all."

On the way out, Vaughn grinned like a six-year-old.

"Momma, can I borrow the car? And take that piece of pie to go?"

She hugged him. "You my baby and I love you."

"I love you, too, Momma."

"You know, some marriages go through a lot of pushing and pulling. Sometimes you get tempted to water someone else's grass, and all the while your grass is dry and dying."

"I know, Momma, but that's not it. I'm not watering grass. I'm not . . . watering grass."

Vaughn's momma wrapped his hands around the slice of pie. He reached for the keys, kissed his momma, and headed out the door for Jersey. He wanted to sit down and talk with his brother. They weren't extremely close growing up, but they were close enough now. He didn't want his brother's image of him to change. Of course, Vaughn could say that he didn't care what people thought, but the fact was that he cared. Way too much.

Traffic was always at a standstill no matter what time of day Vaughn managed to venture anywhere. Everybody was in a hurry to get anywhere except home. Vaughn turned on the radio, turned off the AC, cracked the window a bit, and tried to relax. He wanted to be in a good mood when he saw Troi later in the evening. He wanted her to feel how hard he was trying. He would try hard to promote understanding, patience, and compromise. He wanted her to know that it wasn't her, he was willing to try, and yes, he still cared.

When Vaughn got to his brother's house, Sam was in the extra room working out. The music was so loud that after a few seconds, Vaughn could feel a slight headache trying to creep in and ruin the mood he was trying to preserve. Vaughn stuck his head in the room.

"What's up?"

"Nothin' much, just want to get a shower and go back over to the church and try and talk to Troi."

"What?" Sam frowned.

Vaughn walked into the room and turned down the music.

"Someone named Tracie called twice and left messages. Said it was important, urgent, and the last time he just said to tell you he called."

Vaughn frowned now. "Okay, man, thanks."

"What's up?"

"Nothing, just somebody I know through work." Vaughn tried to end any insinuations.

Sam didn't necessarily look convinced. Vaughn couldn't disclose to his ex-quarterback, prowoman brother anything about the situation. He'd be better off hurrying off, showering, changing, and trying to salvage what was left of his nuptials.

The church was still bright and neatly decorated with plants and stained-glass windows. Vaughn walked up the center aisle until he reached the middle pews. He always sat in the middle, third row. If you sat in the front, you couldn't see who was in the back, and if you sat in the back, well, the same thing. He was greeted with nods and a few brothers shook his hands. He knew that there was where he belonged, but he no longer seemed to fit. He felt like all eyes were on him. Like he was about to make a speech, an announcement.

Hello, brothers and sisters of Zion Missionary. As you know, I am Brother Vaughn Singleton. I'm married, and have a baby girl. My wife trusts me with all her heart, but I'm gay. I'm gay. Did you hear me? I'm gay! Vaughn shuddered at the thought.

Troi acknowledged Vaughn from the front of the church. She walked to where her bag was and slung it over her shoulder. The Hallelujah Girls whispered to each other. The one who always wore the brightest shade of pink lipstick ever made went over to where Vaughn was sitting.

"Hey, brother, where you been? We missed you around here." She dawdled.

"I've been busy with work and family," Vaughn lied.

"Well, don't forget about us here. God first, then family, and church third." She smiled coyly.

"I know," he said, dismissing the thought of her.

Troi walked over to Vaughn and stood, prompting him that it was okay to kiss her. He leaned into her cheek. She didn't pull away. He put his arm around her and ushered her out of the church. Rochelle turned and waved good-bye and Carla wasn't even visible. They crawled into their car and entertained the silence that surrounded them. Troi looked out of the window and Vaughn headed as far away from the church as fast as he could.

As always, Troi broke the silence.

"We don't have to wait to talk. We can talk now."

"Okay, fine," Vaughn said. "Troi, I know that you probably feel that I haven't really been trying or working to make our situation better. It's just that it's extremely confusing for me. But I do want to try. I needed you to know that."

"Well, that's bright of you, Vaughn. At least our future and the future of our child mean something to you."

"Yes. Very much so. Our future is important to me. I miss Dakoda."

Troi sat still, unable to conjure a comeback.

"Troi?" he said, drumming his fingers on the dashboard. "I don't like being away from my baby, or you," he added.

"Well, what do you want me to do about that?" Troi asked.

"We need to work something out."

He knew deep down where it mattered he loved Troi, but *love* was a word that was too needy for him right now.

"I've been trying, Vaughn, you haven't."

"I'm willing to try now, Troi. I'm willing to do it for us."

Troi was silent again, looking out the window and trying to make out faces as they whizzed by.

"You matter to me, Troi. I'll do whatever you want, if . . ."

"If what?" Troi shrugged.

"If you'll let me come home."

34

Nina could spot a player a mile away, so when she peripherally observed a brother who was intent on getting her attention wheedling his way onto her line, she found it necessary to purposely avoid his gaze. He stood in the front of her line after he had squeezed in between two men who were rather anxious to eat. He was most appropriate for schoolyard conversation or idle chit-chat at the most, she could tell. He appeared to be the type of man who would trap you into a conversation and go on and on as if it were his job to convince you that the world was flat or revolved around him.

Tattered orange-and-brown Thanksgiving decorations hung from the ceiling and doorways, giving a false impression of festivity. These people weren't in any holiday spirit. More like broken spirit. They were homeless and hungry. Lumpy potatoes did a pathetic job of imitating yams and the processed aroma of gravy wafted throughout the soup kitchen, and it wasn't even November.

"Nina," the stranger said, reading her name tag. "I'm Tim," he said, pointing to his own tag.

"I can read," she mumbled under her breath.

"I volunteer here, too," he said with a wide grin.

Troi elbowed her sister. Nina looked at her and sighed. "Yes, I'm volunteering, and you?" she said, trying to sound as cheerful as Troi wanted her to. Troi would only tell her to be nice. So, she tried.

"I'm sort of volunteering," he said, looking up at her with his pretty eyes and long lashes that made her want to sympathize.

"Volunteering or community service, Tim?" She smirked, knowing full well that this was punishment.

Most of the help was here because they had to be, not because they wanted to be. He smoothed down the hair on his face.

"Okay, you got me." He nodded. "I'm working off a little community service, but I'm a film student, really." He widened his eyes.

"Is that the truth now?"

"Only a few weeks left to go. Honest." He raised his right hand.

Nina found it odd that she'd meet a film student at a soup kitchen in New York City.

"Where you from?" Nina asked.

Troi bumped her. With Nina's eyes fixed on Tim, Troi whispered in her ear something too fast for Nina to understand.

"Belize," he answered.

"Yep, so that would explain the eyes, the complexion, that look?"

"I guess," he said. "Where you from?"

"New York." Nina grinned, almost laughing.

"Well, nice meeting you, Tim." Troi waved with her clear plastic serving gloves.

"Okay, I'll let you both get back to work, I see your line is getting long." He backed out of the line, like he was something special.

Troi eyed Nina.

"Don't even start, girl, I'm not getting into that mess again," Nina defended.

"Girl, you need to free yourself from emotional bondage. Allow yourself to be happy."

"Maybe I'm just having a bad week."

"Nope, you're just really grumpy. And please do something with your hair."

"You sound like Mother."

"Sorry, I'm just happy when you're happy, Nina."

"You don't even know what he's in here for."

"Listen, they put murderers in jail, they don't give them community service."

"Whatever. I didn't cut back my hours at work to spend them here warding off advances from underprivileged men."

"Girl, he's cute."

"So?" Nina frowned, sucking her teeth.

"Shhh, he's coming back," Troi squealed.

He cleared his throat. "Nina?" He rubbed his hands together.

"Yes?" Nina said, taking a deep breath and making physical attempts to remain calm and not so grumpy.

"I wondered if you'd consider having coffee with me tonight after you're done here."

Nina enjoyed that she could take her time deciding. Troi kicked Nina's leg behind the buffet. Nina frowned at her and corrected it quickly with a smile in Tim's direction.

"Well, Tim, I came with my sister, so I have to go back with her, you know," she said, letting herself off the hook.

"Oh, well, I can drop you off anywhere you need to go, it's not a problem, really. I mean, if you want to go out, that is."

Nina eyed Troi. Troi grinned and kept piling the potatoes on, then placed the packaged slice of bread on the tray next to the paper plate.

"Okay, that's fine, if you're sure it's no trouble," Nina said.

"I'll be done by eight. Is that good for you?"

"Yes, it's fine." She smiled as he walked away, admiring her and feeling accomplished.

"He's not ready for this," Nina said, shaking her head.

"Girl, you know he was born ready," Troi kidded.

Nina went against her initial decision not to go with Tim for coffee. But then, it was only coffee, brown stuff in a cup, not a date. DWI. He had shown her the paperwork and made feeble attempts to explain that it wasn't really even his fault. She batted her lashes. She was feeling flirtatious. His invitation for coffee reminded her that she was capable of receiving second glances. After dealing with Derek, anything was a picnic. But she was determined that there was no way she would allow Derek to convince her that she could no longer enjoy a man.

Nina would chat, give, receive, and enjoy this evening. She was hesitant, although it leaned more on the side of caution. Tim was a womanizer, there were no two ways about it. She could tell by the slight curl of his lips and the blush that bade her to turn away and enjoy it. She would definitely lay the ground rules. Men needed rules, which showed them where the boundaries were. She'd put him on notice, she would not be victim thirty- or forty-whatever. She mentally chastised herself. She was not on the rebound.

After Tim dropped Troi off at home, he and Nina headed to a French café near Columbus Avenue. In a matter of minutes she wasn't nervous. She didn't know this man, and had no idea what he really did for a living or where he lived, but she propped herself up on her elbows, tilted her head to the side, and grinned. The neighborhood near the café was quiet and theatrical-looking, and although it seemed that they had rushed to get there, now he was being smooth and taking his time.

Tim opened the passenger-side door, making a mediocre first impression, and pointed across the street to a curio shop that he said was built in 1898. She was fascinated only by a portrait hanging in window. She noted the store hours. Ten A.M. until six P.M. He held the door open as they walked into the café. Courtesy was seemingly second nature with him. The aromatic coffees greeted them and hugged each nostril, each scent overwhelming the other in rich complementing blends. Nina adored the café with its convenient lighting that made conversations just sort of flow and the tables that were shaky but small enough for you both to lean on and be face-to-face with each other without smothering.

"What's your pleasure, Nina? The hazelnut is really happenin'."

"Sure, that'll be fine." She eyed Tim as he walked away, tall and confident.

He came back and sat with his offering, two grandes, and made everything messy with too many napkins. Nina looked around at the people who were doing that late-night let's-chat-and-then-we-can-go-back-to-your-place thing. She refused to do that. It was almost nine-thirty, quarter to ten, and she was wide awake for a change. The atmosphere was young and tangible. She could feel his presence across the table. He was open and loving every minute of it. The mood was subtle and playful. She swirled the coffee in her cup and savored it by the mouthful.

"So, Nina . . ."

She knew she could handle this man. He was messing with the wrong one if he thought this would be a hit-and-run or some other casualty.

"How long have you been volunteering at the mission?"

"For a few years, sometimes in the summer but mostly around the holidays," she said.

"That's cool, I mean, caring for others and everything," he said, sipping his latte at regular intervals, eyeing her face and shoulders, and glancing down at her hips.

"Yes. Caring is sometimes my biggest fault."

The statement went over his head.

"So, Tim," she said, warming her hands on the cup, "if I may be so bold, tell me the truth, how exactly did you get into this whole DWI stint?"

He laughed. It was a natural laugh that caught her by surprise. Men wanted you to be impressed by the idiotic rambling of insecure wanna-bes who babbled about how they were gonna rule the world one day.

"Partying with a few friends, you know. I should have known better but . . ."

"Really? You gotta be careful, honey." The term of endearment caught them both off guard, and she quickly added, "They can revoke your license for that."

Tim was telling Nina about his latest film project and how he wanted the men and women in his scripts to celebrate each other. He seemed genuinely creative, and he kept telling her that she should act.

"You have that look," he said.

"That's okay," she told him.

"Why? Are you shy?"

"No, I'm not shy, I'm just not an actress, and I'm hardly skin and bones either," she said, covering up her insecurity with laughter.

"You look fine."

"Do you act?" she asked.

"No, but I might, never know what you'd do," he said.

"Are you acting now?" she slipped.

"Acting? Why would I be acting?"

"You know, a girl, a guy."

"Yeah, and?"

He didn't get it. "Never mind."

"No, come on, I wanna know."

"It's okay, really, Tim. I'm just . . ."

"Just what?"

"I just got out of a relationship."

"Right, okay."

"Yes, so, you know, I'm taking it slow and just seeing what transpires."

"Sounds cool, I can dig that." Tim smirked. "Nina? You know, one bold statement deserves another."

She agreed and smiled wide, trying to anticipate what he would say.

"When do we get to do the real thing?" he said.

"Real thing?" Nina frowned.

"Yeah, a full-fledged date," Tim said, hugging his cup.

"This is the real thing," she said seriously.

"Well, I just thought that you were the type of woman that I could take to a nice dinner in an intimate restaurant."

She observed him obviously stumbling, regretting using *intimate* to describe his idea of their date.

He must not have wanted her to get the wrong impression. But she had.

"Here's my number," he said, scribbling something almost illegible on a napkin. "I'd like to stay in touch." He nodded. "I like your look. Besides, skin and bones is overrated."

She nodded, too, and hoped that this part of the evening wasn't over. She had glided safely through it, but was dumb about how to handle the I-had-fun-and-don't-want-it-to-end-because-it's-still-early-but-I'm-not-going-back-to-your-place part.

"We can do that, dinner sounds fine, Tim," Nina said convincingly.

She figured that as an actor, filmmaker, and womanizer he could show her a good time. She just didn't know how to handle what would inevitably come next.

35

It was no surprise that Tim had enjoyed the several hours that he and Nina had spent vibing about nothing in particular. Those were the best kinds of conversations. He loved a woman who allowed her hips to be evidence that she was well fed and wasn't cutting off her circulation with something that obviously looked better on a hanger. He was glad that the conversation lacked the usual are-you-dating, who-are-you-dating and how-long-were-you-dating questions and had allowed him to feel comfortable instead of scrutinized. They'd had coffee and two refills. She was pleasant company.

The whole coffeehouse date lasted about three hours, his normal toleration limit for most people. She was witty, attractive, and cautious. He didn't mind driving to Brooklyn, then back uptown. He was just pleased that she wasn't trying to play a game to get him to stay. He didn't like games. He wasn't that complex, but it was surprising, the lengths women went to to get a man's attention.

His boy Justin often said that Tim must resent women because of the death of his mother. Tim didn't think that was true. He tried not to think about it much at all for that matter. He guessed he did use women for whatever he deemed plausible, and he figured that Nina would be entertaining also. She was friendly and they had fun, but he wasn't looking for the "dearly beloved" part. She wasn't a stick, so that was a plus. He loved a woman with some curves. But he wasn't trying to get more distracted than he already was.

Tim just wanted to do his gentleman thing. He was old-fashioned; she was hesitant. He had observed that when he'd reached for the check and his hand had brushed against hers reaching for her coffee cup. She'd shied away as if she'd thought he wanted something from her. More than she was willing to give. All he wanted was a good time with a woman who knew how to enjoy herself.

When it came to women, Tim didn't know what his style was. Was he intrigued by a woman who could throw on a jersey and a pair of kicks simultaneously and maintain her femininity? Or did she have to be the constantly well-manicured showpiece? What he did know was that he wanted to be the one to ask for more. He didn't want some woman hemming him up in a corner, trying to convince him that she was the total package.

Tim had, however, made a date with this coy woman for early next week. He hadn't heard anymore from Sharon or Michelle, and thought that Rochelle had always warned him that what went around came around. Now he was the one sitting by the phone waiting for it to ring. But it was no biggie. He was putting on a neatly pressed shirt and one of his designer ties. He was thanking God all weekend for the job at Big Deal Films. Everything was falling into place. He would work on his final project, which was due in about four weeks, and enjoy himself with what his boys would call his newfound flavor.

The church service had been energetic that morning. Tim laid on the sofa now, reflecting on the thunderous applause that had settled on the room with faces that welcomed God's peace and joy. Rochelle had been noticeably proud of her brother, who was getting the feel of what preceded eternal life. He'd been singing, clapping, and fumbling with the pages in his bible, trying to highlight the important stuff. He'd been greeted warmly by both the men and the women in the congregation. It had been that way since the whole DWI thing.

That morning the preacher had been sweating and teaching about expectation, and how we ought to expect God to do the miraculous in our lives. That had to do with relationships, jobs, and family. Nothing was impossible. People had leapt up and down, excited at the possibilities of what God could do. Nothing was outside the reach of God. "Amen" had resounded throughout the church, and the congregation had became a moving force that progressed in the belief that God had a message for every single one of them today. "There is nothing that we can conceive that is considered a hard case. God spoke the world into existence, so rearranging a few things in our lives is hardly an effort at all," the preacher had said.

The sermon had made Tim think about how he knew he had no

business drinking or womanizing. But these thoughts always manifested themselves in his mind, and he was too weak to resist them. He had made an effort lately to think about something other than sex, but a nice thick pair of legs would come walking up, demanding that he delight in them. He thought about Nina. She was warm, with the fullest pair of lips he had ever seen. *There it goes again,* Tim thought.

Tim closed his eyes for a second, and an idea for his final project danced in his mind. He took up the pen and tangoed with a few words on paper that would initially make sense to no one but him. Didn't matter. He was used to dancing the dance alone. A group of women had approached Tim after church, snickering and smiling up the aisle, each telling the other, "You go ahead." He'd known they were up to no good, or something in that vicinity.

"Good morning, brother." The brave one had spoken, as the others surrounded him so he wouldn't get away. Tim had glanced at his watch and grinned.

"Afternoon, ladies."

"That was a powerful service, wasn't it?"

"Yes, extremely enjoyable. Uplifting."

They'd all hesitated. "You're Rochelle's brother, right?"

"Yes, that's my big sister."

"I told you," one had elbowed the other.

"Tim," he'd introduced, extending his hand.

Rochelle had walked up and hugged her brother. "Ladies." Rochelle had glimpsed over at them, then nodded. She was always polite.

They'd looked around at each other. "Okay, so, you have a blessed day, Tim." They'd backed away with foiled plans.

"They call them the Hallelujah Girls, Tim."

"Why?"

"I don't know. Use your imagination," she'd teased.

Tim had thought of women with red-and-blue ruffled dresses stomping and shouting barefoot, smacking a tambourine. Carl had approached them and extended his hand, embracing Tim.

"Come by the house, man."

"Nah, I've got work to do."

"Rochelle cooked your favorite," Carl had teased, knowing Tim well enough to know that he never ever turned down a meal.

"Roast beef?"

"No."

"Chopped barbeque?"

"Oh, you picky now?" Rochelle had interjected.

Tim had laughed. "No. You know I'm coming. I always need a meal."

At Rochelle's house it had been just the three of them. Cozy as always. Tim had been surprised. He'd expected an eligible woman to come dashing out of a back room once Rochelle had given the signal. Instead they'd lounged around and talked about how Tim had gotten the job at Big Deal, and how faith was important.

"Without faith it is . . ."

"Yes, I know, impossible to please Him." Rochelle was impressed with her brother.

Tim thought that it had been only a few weeks since he'd seen Justin last. It had been his party. Justin had apologized over and over again, though he didn't remember much. Tim had assured him that there was no need for that. "I had no business drinking anyway."

"You right," Justin had said. Tim hadn't heard from Charlie or Darius. They had made him the scapegoat, but it was all good, because he wasn't trying to live in New York forever.

Tim had been half listening to the conversation that the three of them were engaged in around the table as the ideas for what he was working on were flowing like two people who were really digging each other. He'd made attempts to interject an "uh-huh," pretending to listen. When Rochelle had offered cake and Tim had said, "That's okay," she and Carl had slapped their legs and broken out into hysterical laughter. Her brother was on another planet for sure. There was no way he'd turn down food or dessert. She had seen him eat half a pecan pie while he was nursing the flu and trying to ward off a temperature of one hundred and four. He loved a baking woman. Lord knew that was what he'd end up with.

After two servings of German chocolate cake and evidence still on his face, Tim had made his good-byes to hurry home and spill his head on paper. There was no way that he would allow a C to make a permanent appearance on his record, marring what was probably the most expensive education in the city.

Rochelle had wrapped up something in foil as usual, and slipped folded bills into his hand. Tim had hugged his sister and his brother-in-law, then headed out the door.

He missed his momma and his dad more than ever now. They hadn't know Tim as the man who had consciously given his life to Christ with a little nudging from his sister. He was trying to take control and cut himself off from those tired circle of morons. Justin excluded. At dinner he had thought about the woman he had shared coffee with the other night, and wondered how soon was too soon to begin thinking about someone twice a day. *It all depends,* he convinced himself. There was not one rule that applied to everyone or every single situation.

Now here Tim was, home, lounging on his sofa, trying to sort out a premise in his head. He wasn't in the mood to be sidetracked, not even when the phone rang, demanding attention. He snatched up the phone and mumbled, "Hello."

"Tim?"

"Yeah, who's this?"

"It's Estella." He paused and refused to offer another word.

"Are you there?"

"I'm here." He surveyed the room for something that would give him an escape.

"I know you don't want to hear from me. I'm probably the last person you want to hear from, but I need to tell you something. Can I come over, please?"

"No, Estella. It's over. Whatever you need to tell me, tell me now."

"I can't."

"How did you get my number anyway?"

"I saw your friend Justin and . . ."

"You what?" he said, cutting her off and feeling his old self rising.

"Tim, this is very personal. I'd rather not on the phone."

"Estella, I can't do this with you. I thought we established that a long time ago."

"Can you just spare an hour to let me come by? I promise it won't take more than that. I just want to say this face-to-face. You owe me at least that."

"Owe you? Estella, I have deadlines and I can't meet with you. If you won't tell me now, maybe it should wait. I can give you a call next week. I'll see what I can do then, but I don't owe you a thing."

"It can't wait that long, Tim."

"Okay, well, what is it?" Tim sighed loudly. "Tell me now or I have to go."

"Okay, okay," she pleaded. "I was in the hospital. I had an accident. Well, really, I mean, I had been taking too much medication and couldn't see. My vision got blurry. I passed out in the street.

They thought I was high, but I wasn't, not really. I mean, I had been drinking, but not that afternoon. Earlier in the day maybe, but . . ."

"Estella, can you please get to the point?"

"Okay, Tim, but don't be mad. You know I still love you, right? Uh, sorry, I didn't mean to say that. It's just . . ."

"The point, Estella." Tim clenched his teeth.

"I think you need to see a doctor."

"A doctor for what?"

"When I was in the hospital they took blood. I'm not sure how accurate they are, but they said I tested positive for herpes."

36

Troi and Vaughn agreed to try intensive reparative counseling before moving back in together. That meant digging deep and uncovering the layers. His burden had her bound, and she was tired of the struggle to keep her marriage together all by herself. Some people figured that she shouldn't complain, because her marriage hadn't been a struggle until now. But she wanted her marriage to work; like a clock, always on time. She dared not let it dwindle down to what her mother had. She was trusting God with all of her heart for this reunion. God alone could do it. She didn't need luck, luck was for the unsure. If she had to compromise her beliefs to keep her husband, then he was never hers. Ignorance of the Word was forty percent of the world's problem, and nonapplication was the remainder.

So, with bells on, Troi confirmed in her mind that she'd march into the office at the scheduled time as her therapist's Banana Republic, Ann Taylor, preppie chic dictated to her that her marriage was in jeopardy. *Enlighten me, will you?* she'd say. Troi was lethal with words, so she had to be careful. Her tongue was capable of damage that defiled. She had wrapped her tongue around Vaughn and told him where he could go. It suited her fine at the moment. She'd been fuming mad, and she often didn't care about the damage until she had to sift through it days later. But she was trying.

Carla had been making attempts to show genuine concern by asking what the status of the marriage was. Troi didn't want to elaborate. After Troi had come from the meat market of a club and sobbed in Carla's arms, seeking comfort from the things that had raped her eyes, she'd vowed she wouldn't talk about it. Ever. She preferred to be a doer. She needed to find a solution and implement it. This was something that she and God had to handle. She wasn't gonna let the devil torture her. She wasn't going to say, "Okay, you win." She wasn't crazy. Just convinced that amazing things happened when you prayed.

Troi had a child and a life to live. She had a beauty shop for which she needed to make calls now. She wanted to leave all remnants of her childhood behind: the poverty, the anger, the alcohol, and the madness.

She needed to set up a photography session for the shop and take photographs of hairstyles so she could submit them to a few hair magazines. The more outrageous, the better. Wild and disastrous, it sold magazines, but people never went anywhere with their hair half crimped and twisted blue like that. And if they did, it just didn't make sense.

Troi tried to clear her thoughts. It was hard living, not knowing. She thought out loud how she'd surely die before she lived how her parents did. Daddy working all the time so he wouldn't have to come home and look in Mother's face, and Mother a smelly and sorrowful drunk because she wanted a man but never kids. Troi had prayed until prayer seemed to pray for her.

She yearned to call Sam. It was only a passing thought. She wondered if he knew. Vaughn's momma hadn't said anything either. Not even hinted. She was probably elated that she had found somebody naive enough to take on her sexually-crippled-to-the-opposite-sex son. But she had to be kind and give at least the benefit of the doubt. Maybe his momma didn't know. Other than Carla, Nina, and her daddy, it seemed that no one really knew what was going on with her and Vaughn. Outsiders and church members must have thought that they had had a lovers' spat, and that was fine. They could think that.

But Troi didn't know what to think of Vaughn, really. She loved the person she thought he was. The man who kept fit and had to-die-for abs and a bald, perfectly shaped head. He had lips that were supple, and when he put them on her, she knew she was being kissed. And his strong masculine hands left her knowing for certain that she had been touched. But with the turn of events, Troi wasn't sure how far she should trust her feelings. They had deceived her in regards to Vaughn's sexuality, and they could just as well continue to lie.

Troi hadn't necessarily been looking for anyone in her life when she'd met Vaughn. She'd been content doing odds and ends around the church, singing in the choir, and trying to negotiate the space where her shop was now servicing hair. There were no guarantees.

There also wasn't anything she'd ever put past that husband of hers. Vaughn had surprised even Troi by making an appearance in church Sunday. He'd sat in the middle as he always did, and read from the Word, pretending not to feel the pressure of the eyes on him. After service, he'd waited for Troi until she'd gathered up Dakoda's things. He'd whispered in her ear on the way out that he wanted them to just get through the summer and be together for Christmas. But they still had a long way to go. Troi couldn't agree to that. They both compromised because Troi knew that, if nothing else, she loved him. But she understood that he had now become willing mostly to save face. Vaughn had kissed Troi in front of the church because he always had, and she'd be embarrassed if he didn't, and Troi had kissed him back because nobody needed to know her husband thought he was gay.

They'd walked to the car, and Vaughn had reiterated that he had stopped seeing Tracie.

"I broke it off, CeCe."

And Troi had smiled because she was happy, and because Vaughn breaking it off was a major step in saving their marriage.

"I want to come home, CeCe."

"Vaughn, you know we can't do that yet."

They had driven the rest of the way to Jersey in silence. She'd dropped Vaughn off at his brother's, and hoped Sam didn't try to convince her to stay. Troi didn't have time to act like things were perfect. Sam could hardly think that Vaughn was staying with him because they were blissfully happy. *Au contraire.* But that was fine by Troi. She didn't want everybody in their marriage. She and Vaughn were the only two who'd taken those vows, so nobody should interfere except them and God.

Troi had told them both that she needed to head home, and promised Vaughn that they'd talk. Vaughn had hugged and kissed his baby girl. Troi had reluctantly gotten back in the car and driven slowly and carefully, thinking momentarily that she should give him a hard time. Play games. Make the chase exciting. But she'd thought against it. The last thing she needed was the enemy continuing to rear his ugly head in her marriage because she had opened the door and invited him in by implementing tricks and playing mind games.

She was patient, and at times even kind. That's what love was supposed to be. Troi had driven home with Dakoda cooing in the backseat as she thought about how she was never as agitated in traffic as Vaughn was. When she'd crossed the bridge into the city, she'd realized that she had driven the entire way without music playing. She hadn't realized how distracted she was, but she'd promised herself that she wasn't about to start doing foolish things now.

Troi had parked the car and made her way into the apartment. She'd rested her bags on the kitchen table and relished the familiarity of her kitchen, living-room sofa, and bedroom. She'd sat Dakoda down on the bed and looked at her own weary reflection in the mirror. Her reflection had told her to take it easy. Her hair was neater now. It was a darker shade of blond that actually complemented her complexion.

She had bought a couple of bright tops and a berry shade of lipstick. She'd worn the new lipstick to Vaughn's momma's, to the cleaners, to the supermarket, to the shop, and to church.

"Oooh, girl, that looks good," Carla had said on Sunday.

"Thanks. I needed something to brighten up my face."

"That's a good plan. Vaughn better watch out," she'd kidded, not knowing that was exactly what Troi had intended. She'd been wearing it when they'd kissed, but he hadn't noticed.

Morning came quickly as the sun beaming directly on her bedroom mirror confirmed that it was almost nine A.M. Troi brushed her teeth with the water running softly enough to overhear Dakoda playing with her cereal. She made a mental note to call the therapist this morning and schedule a session. She'd leave the appointment date on Vaughn's voice mail. He had been more than eager lately, so she was sure he'd oblige. Troi was trying to mentally dress Dakoda cool enough for the weather that had been fluctuating from sweltering to brisk. Stuffing the baby into a long-sleeved tee made Dakoda agitated more than anything else. She reminded Troi so much of Vaughn.

The cool morning weather made Troi think about Christmas, which was months away. Five to be exact. Things were so out of touch for both of them, she'd be happy if they could just sit and watch television together, eating hard candy out of a red mesh Christmas stocking, or flavored popcorn out of a sectioned decorative tin and sipping on sparkling cider. Troi remembered enjoying the Rockefeller Center Christmas tree lighting with Vaughn every holiday season until it reached what was now considered a star-studded spectacle. Used to be a time when people who lived in New York could enjoy something that was just for them. But the Christmas tree-lighting ceremony had become as commercialized as the ball dropping in

Times Square. There were costumes, bright lights, singers, dancers, and television cameras blinding everyone in a ten-block radius.

Troi parted her lips and put on her lipstick as she pressed her lips together, puckered, and admired what she saw in the mirror. She appreciated herself, even when Vaughn didn't. She wanted to ask somebody to look at her and tell her what was wrong, but this situation was too delicate. She knew the church secretary, and she had a way of overhearing and telling just one friend in confidence, and then, before you knew it, the entire church wasn't whispering your business, but outright telling it.

Troi was a praying woman, and she knew that even though some people scoffed at that, she was seriously a calloused-kneed sister. She had prayed her shop into existence with zip credit, and she had also prayed a man into her life, whom she now had to pray deliverance for, if he wanted it. It all boiled down to if he wanted it. She couldn't make him be something that he didn't really want to be or no longer did. She wasn't about to beg, persuade, or try to desperately convince him that he should love a woman because that's what the bible said. Love given freely was a gift. Forcing someone into a corner was charity.

Yes, Troi was hurt and felt defiled, but she knew that her happiness didn't come from Vaughn, although it had its moments. God had made her happy. She couldn't deny that. She had to confess that everything she wanted wasn't good for her. She remembered as a child overdosing on Oreo cookies and milk. She could hardly stand the site of those nasty little cookies still. She'd eat the cream out of the middle and throw away the black part. Never made sense, but she did it. She wondered if wanting Vaughn to love her still made sense either.

Looking down at her little girl, she could see that Dakoda was growing increasingly agitated, fidgeting and signaling that she was long past ready to go. Dakoda was like her momma in that respect. She liked the wind in her face and the freedom of the outdoors. Troi put the baby's jacket on. She turned off the lights and double-checked the coffeepot. Troi picked up the baby's bag and another tote that she had to take to the shop and slung them on her shoulder. She picked up the baby, feeling weighted down and almost unable to manage when the phone decided that it desperately needed to ring.

Troi pressed her ear to the receiver. The voice was unfamiliar, but the words it spoke told her exactly who it was.

"CeCe, listen, honey, you need to let go."

"Who is this?"

"Your marriage is over. He don't love you, so you need to stop stressing him and trying to run that guilt trip. You think you can hold on to him just because you have a baby? Who you trying to fool?"

"Look, don't call my house without identifying yourself."

"You know who I am. I'm the one."

"Yeah, you were the one, honey," she spat, using that Madison tongue.

She wasn't trippin'. She could handle it like a woman. She would be calm and not let him have an inkling of satisfaction that he was getting to her. And she would definitely handle it without going crying to Vaughn to fight her battles.

She didn't want any messages on her phone when she came in telling her what she was or wasn't to Vaughn, so she rested the receiver next to the base of the phone and could still hear the voice on the other end trying to get a rise out of her as she walked out the door and it shut behind her.

No devil in hell was gonna stress her. And ending her marriage would be the choice of either her or Vaughn, not this infamous Tracie, who was dead-set on ruining someone else's life just because he didn't know what he wanted to do with his.

For Vaughn's love for Troi to be gone would mean that it had never existed. And she knew that wasn't true. He would never intentionally use, manipulate, or hurt her. And the baby wasn't a mistake either. He'd planned it. Her marriage was rooted in love for sure. She knew it. She felt it. She welcomed it. She believed in it. She prayed for it, she savored it, she needed it. And no one's devilish tongue could change that.

37

Vaughn knew that he wanted Troi to take him seriously. Church was a beginning. He needed to go for himself, but for now he had too many issues. He didn't want people staring, prying, and deriving pleasure from his plight. "Lord, that was too much to bear," he found himself saying, sounding all too much like his momma. The storms brewing at work didn't help either. He knew it was more than just his imagination. There was no idle chit-chat, and when Monday mornings in an office didn't offer the usual dose of "how was your weekend?" he knew he was in trouble.

His boss, Jill, was more to the point than normal lately. With her curt manner of speech, she dropped off folders and came back an hour later to retrieve them, like a preprogrammed robot. She didn't even hint at concern, although she'd always been rather stiff. But all he could do was grin and bear it. Far be it from him to start mimicking his father's they're-out-to-get-the-black-man soliloquy. He had a job to do, and he would just do it so he could collect his pay.

Coworkers periodically passed by Vaughn's desk, smirking. They used paperwork to conceal their concern, trying not to catch his gaze. He was tired of fleeing. He debated whether or not to answer his voice mail, which was always blinking now. But it was time to face whatever he was so set on running from. He leaned forward in his chair, reduced the volume, and pressed Play. Several clients and a message from Troi confirming an appointment with the therapist for next Tuesday.

He didn't fall in love with Troi to satisfy Christianity. He didn't fall in love with her to satisfy anyone else, he tried to tell himself. He had remembered how Troi loved to keep up appearances. At their wedding she'd tried to convince him that her mother had just had a bit too much to drink, when in fact it had been ten A.M., they'd been at the church, and cocktails hadn't even been served yet. Had he been doing the same thing with Troi? Keeping up appearances? He felt for her, he just no longer felt the urgent need always to be there.

The last thing Vaughn desired was to embarrass anybody. He wanted to be the kind of husband who would go shopping with his wife and doze off in between her trying on several pairs of shoes. He wanted to be fair. That was always his main concern.

Vaughn didn't care if people believed how he lived or what he felt sexually. They told him he couldn't have always felt these things. But he knew he had. Didn't mean it was right, but he had. The sad thing was that there were so many issues in the church left unresolved, and people were still so busy pointing the finger. It always amazed him how people who served the same God could have varying views. Views on divorce and homosexuality and then opposing views on issues as simple as whether or not Christian singles should kiss.

He knew he was in no position to talk, but he figured the devil was having a picnic right about now. He justified that when people who lived sinful lives didn't get caught in their sin, they were always the first ones picking up a rock, ready to cast the first stone and banish their brothers and sisters to hell. There had to be a problem. And when people with real issues couldn't get help because the congregations and denominations were so busy measuring hemlines and scrutinizing hairstyles, the end was truly near.

Lord, that was not what it was all about. It was never what it was about. There had to be more. Troi always said, "There has to be a fullness of joy that overflows." He had heard people talk about joy that overflowed, but he never did feel it. The only thing he ever felt was the stripping exposure of conviction. There was always something he was feeling that was under scrutiny. He was a man, and it seemed the world wanted him to prove it by flexing muscles and talking loudly. No one ever took the time to think that he wasn't that kind of man.

Vaughn pondered that if any of his so-called friends had found out that he was harboring lustful feelings for another man, any man, they would probably relocate him telepathically to the South or change their area and zip codes. Granted, he had some friends who were game for anything, but nothing in which Vaughn would be interested. Life was so complicated as it was, and his situation just exacerbated the problem. He drummed his fingers on his desk, then impulsively pressed the button repeatedly to erase all of the messages on his voice mail. He penciled in Tuesday the 26th at noon on his desk blotter calendar and packed up for his journey home.

Vaughn's long arduous train ride to Jersey was boring and silent. Even the voices in his head weren't talking to him. He was pleased that he and Troi were talking, but it was hardly a consolation. They weren't officially back together. The music that he was hearing from another passenger's headset radio was dull and bluesy. Boring. He wished he could change the station, but all that came to mind was how he would always try to switch the station in the car, but Troi had only programmed in Christian radio and CD 101.9. At least she was in his head again. He loosened his tie and inhaled deeply, as the air conditioning had gone out fifteen stations ago. Just two more stops. He flipped through a discarded newspaper quickly, then left it behind as he exited, too.

Vaughn walked quickly from the station. It was sticky. His warm breath stung his cheeks like he was smoking a cigarette. He only wanted to get home, take a cool shower, and unwind with some tea and the television news. The streets were cluttered with kids who always seemed to multiply each year. They'd play this summer, go inside for the winter, and come out with a little baby brother or sister next summer. Vaughn quickened his pace. He brushed past a woman with a big straw hat. She smiled as if she knew him. He stepped up to the front door and pulled the mail out of the box. He dug deep in his pocket for the key, opened the door, and walked in, searching the rooms for Sam, whom he knew was always bench-pressing at least one-fifty. He was trying to stay in shape for nobody in particular, he always said.

"What's up, man?"

"Nothing, bro, just gonna shower and change. You have company coming?"

"I don't know. Maybe. Why?"

"I just thought we could talk," Vaughn said, always slightly fearful of rebuke.

"What you wanna talk about?"

"Nothing, something, everything, you know, just old times, new times or whatever." He shrugged.

"That's cool."

No sooner than Vaughn had rested his scratched-up briefcase against the doorway, the doorbell changed their plans. Vaughn's immediate thought was that Sam hadn't showered, so Vaughn would have to entertain his brother's date, or whoever was at the door, when all he wanted to do was be left alone and watch television or do something nonverbal.

Sam drifted toward the door with his towel around his neck, resting on his shoulders and absorbing the sweat off his brow.

"Hey. Come in," Sam said, putting the voice on the phone with the unfamiliar face. "Have a seat in the living room." Sam extended his hand. "Vaughn. You have company," he called.

Vaughn shook his head. He couldn't comprehend why it was so hard for him to get his way tonight.

Vaughn stood at attention in the doorway, glaring at the nerve of Tracie. Cold glances were exchanged back and forth. Vaughn didn't have the mind to play tag tonight, he thought, as Sam left the room, sensing there was a problem.

"What do you want,Tracie?"

"I just wanted to see how you were getting along."

"Fine. I'm fine."

"Funny, Vaughn."

"I'm not being funny. I just want to rest, I'm very tired."

"But we need to talk."

"About what?" Vaughn was hardly in the mood to tap-dance around issues.

"You know what, Vaughn. So, what are you going to do?"

"About what?"

"About CeCe . . . uhh, Troi, I mean."

"We are seeing a counselor and we will be fine."

"And what about me?"

"What about you?"

"You can't just come into someone's life and leave."

"You think I can't. I didn't ask to be put in this situation, man," Vaughn confessed.

"Neither did I, but I'm still here. What about us?"

"I can't do this with you, man, and there is no us," Vaughn tried to whisper. "You know I love Troi. You know I want to make things work."

"So, you are willing to live a lie?"

"How do you know that what I'm living is a lie? Maybe what I feel for you is a lie."

"Does it feel like a lie?"

Vaughn hesitated. "Sometimes."

"Really now?"

"Can we talk tomorrow? I mean, I'm really out of sorts tonight."

"So, you want me to call you?"

"Yes, call."

"Will you be taking my calls, Mr. Singleton?"

"Of course. Why wouldn't I?"

"Because voice mail comes in much more handy," he scoffed.

"You just don't know what it's like. There's just too much pressure for me to do the right thing. I can't think straight. People at work are losing their minds. There's just weird stuff going on, you know?"

"Oh, I know," Tracie said, making his way for the door. And I tell you this, you can't do it alone."

Sam reappeared and stood leaning in the doorway, lurking as he waited for his brother to walk his guest to the door. He watched Vaughn pause and make eye contact with this man. In his observation, there was a little too much friendliness going on, a little too much chemistry. He didn't want to understand the message that was being conveyed by this guy's presence. Sam looked away and Vaughn locked the door, turning to begin finally his process of unwinding.

"Bro. What's that all about?" Sam asked, motioning at the doorway where Tracie stood moments ago.

"You mean Tracie? Ah, that's nothing, man."

"I don't believe that. I heard your conversation. It's sick, man. What's the deal with you two?" Sam frowned and squinted his eyes at his brother. "Is that why you're here? You know, you really shouldn't do that to your wife, man. If Brenda were like Troi, I'd still be married now. I don't understand how you can go around trying out stuff."

Vaughn stood, staring blankly, waiting for Sam to finish his ranting so he would feel that he had done his good deed for the day and go play somewhere.

"Do you hear me?"

"Yeah, I hear you." Vaughn nodded, wearing a look of total exhaustion.

"Does momma know?" Vaughn was silent. Sam's voice got louder. "Well, does she?"

"No, only Troi." He sighed.

"So, you leaving her, man?"

"I don't know what's going to happen. I can't predict the future."

"You taking this lightly, man." Sam was up in Vaughn's face now.

"Too nonchalant. Your wife is a good woman. You should cherish her. She loves you, man."

"Listen, my marriage is my business. If you were so insightful you would have seen what your own wife was doing."

"That's brilliant," Sam said. "When you feel wounded, attack, but you know what I can't do?" Sam offered. "I can't condone this."

"Look, man, it's my life."

"I know it's your life, but if this is what you choose as a lifestyle, then you can't stay here. Practice that stuff somewhere else. I should have known something was up." Sam shook his head, disappointed.

"So, what? Are you putting me out?"

"What do you think?" Sam stormed off.

38

Nina was bored stiff sitting in the middle of her cold floor spraying Reddi-wip in her mouth for entertainment. She could think of several other uses for it, but she wasn't up for the frustration that daydreaming about sex would conjure. She wasn't really bothered by the fact that Tim was a few years younger than she. Women reached their peak at forty, and a younger man could "hang," so to speak. It sounded like something Shelby would utter, so Nina laughed. She deserved to be a little frivolous. She assumed that most people no longer thought it was a negative to date a younger man. It was what she felt inside that mattered anyway. The way Tim's hand had brushed against hers made her think that she was a fool to try and let herself fall again. Lord only knew what she'd do if he came with fries.

He was a filmmaker. Basically a workaholic, translated. She could see it. He would wine her and woo her with nice intimate encounters and then shelve her. Making excuses about deadlines and how he needed her to understand would inevitably come next. The more you understood for a man the more they wanted you understand. She wasn't about to go from one extreme to the other. She didn't know why in her mind she was already pairing her and Tim up together. She was always doing that. But not pairing them up in her mind didn't mean that she couldn't enjoy the thought of him.

Nina wrestled to keep what Derek had done separate from the other possibilities in her life. She knew that Tim probably worked more overtime than ten men. She smiled, because she liked a man who was tall and well versed. She frowned, because she thought that he would have made a move the other night. His place, her place. Not that she would have gone with the notion, but she liked to turn them down. It sent the message that she knew she was worth waiting for and she wanted him to know that up front.

Tim didn't seem particularly disturbed by the fact that she hadn't pressed him for personal information. She didn't need to know if he was single. He was there the other night enjoying her. It was all that mattered. Nina had enjoyed the evening as he'd kept the conversation flowing.

"So, where in Belize are you from?"

"Well, not me, my mother."

"Really?"

"Yes."

"So, you speak another language?"

"No, I barely speak English," he'd kidded. "Wanna go?"

"To Belize?"

"Yeah." He smiled.

"I thought you'd never ask."

"Actually, I am bilingual," Tim had added.

"Really?"

"Yeah."

"You read and write?"

"Read, mostly."

"What language?"

"Body language." They'd gotten a chuckle's worth out of that.

So, Nina wasn't surprised that she had awoken the past few days thinking about Tim. He was unrehearsed. She reminisced about how she'd thought that Derek would do, too, and look where it had gotten her.

"So, Nina, you have plans next Friday?" Tim had asked, as if it was no real effort at all.

"What am I doing next Friday?"

"Do you always answer a question with a question?"

"Sometimes." She'd grinned.

"You know why I asked." He'd smiled.

"Seriously, I don't." She'd stared at him with her warm brown eyes and feathered lashes, attempting to draw the truth out of him. She'd known; she'd wanted to hear him say it. *Ask me,* she'd said to herself.

"I was wondering if we could do dinner and a movie or something remotely similar."

"Remotely similar? Oh, I see," she'd toyed. "I don't know, I'll have to let you know by Wednesday, if that's okay. I have a fund-raising event to attend and . . ." She'd paused.

Men didn't always need to get what they wanted. They didn't always need details either. She wanted someone who wasn't trying to be the proverbial Romeo. She needed someone who knew the art of patience. She desired someone who'd be ear and eye candy at the same time. She could work with Tim.

But today was Tuesday. Although she'd told him she'd call Wednesday, she felt the need to call him. She just hoped that her call didn't reveal her eagerness. She'd call, but not first thing in the morning. Make him wait at least until the evening. She had never loved until it hurt. She had liked until it embarrassed, but never love, never hurt. She didn't want to be one of those women who fell for every guy they ever met, claiming each one as her one true love. She refrained from using that *L* word, but it was like an undeniable pain that throbbed and took her heart and made a liar out of it. Nina didn't know if she was ready to go there. Especially not after one date. Women were so eager, or so men thought, but coupling up or pairing was a well thought-out concept in women's minds.

Love was like the pressure of holding your breath under water until you felt you no longer struggled to hold your breath. If you ran from it long enough, it would disguise itself as something that you willingly accepted and it would catch you. It would make you deny it, only to tell it the truth. It would make you hide the truth, only to confess. That was how love was. She smiled.

Nina examined herself in the mirror. After struggling for years with the freshman ten that had actually turned out to be more like thirty, Nina had become comfortable with herself, knowing that she couldn't get hooked on a dress size. Derek had opened up old wounds by criticizing her frequently. But he was gone now. She had to remind herself of that over and over again. He was gone. She couldn't lay helpless, waiting to be rescued. She had to rescue herself and move on. She used to diet and strive to lose weight and make futile attempts to get back to her pre-high school weight of one-twenty. After college, she'd begun to focus on other things, and left her weight and midnight cravings in God's hands. They were still in his hands, and she was still the chubby girl, but she was determined to hold her own.

It had also become apparent to Nina that Derek had been what Troi would call a trick of the enemy. The residue of him still lingered.

He'd littered her phone bill with long-distance calls to Arizona, Georgia, and Syracuse. She didn't even want to know who lived there. He had since left messages and notes taped to her door, begging her to take him back, but she didn't feel the need or the urge to explain. For years she had been caged so effectively by other people's opinions. It was enough that Derek had done so much to her already, but after Derek, she was afraid of how the next man would have to prove himself.

Nina didn't want to carry that fear into her interaction with Tim. She felt free with him. Coffee and polite conversation were a plus, especially since he didn't know the awkward girl whose thighs rubbed together. He didn't know the girl with the slight lisp who hadn't dared to wear a bikini since she was seven. She didn't want that person to be known. That person was hidden. It wasn't really her. It was who she had become under the influence of other people. She needed someone with whom she could be who she really was. She needed another chance. Just one more.

Nina called to check on her sister. She felt that if anyone deserved perfection, it was Troi. Her little sister had been so faithful and dedicated to God and her faith that she should have been floating through life on a cloud. Nina thought that she'd eventually take Troi's advice that her church attendance needed to improve. She didn't want to end up in the same situation with Tim as she had found herself in with Derek. And when God wasn't in the center of your relationships, then you really had nothing at all, Troi always said.

On the phone, Troi confessed to be holding up well. She said that Vaughn wanted to move back in, but she felt they needed more therapy. She didn't want a roommate, she wanted a husband. A man who was there because he desired her to the core, like an apple, with teeth marks. She said she didn't want people talking about her or about her husband's infidelity with a man. Nina agreed, not just because she loved her sister, but because she was right, and wise. But you could hardly stop other people's tongues from having a mind all their own.

"On a lighter note, how was coffee the other night?" Troi asked.

"It was good."

"I'm happy for you, Nina, he seems nice."

"Well, they all do, so time will tell."

"The choir is in concert Sunday. You coming?"

"I don't know," Nina said hesitantly. "I might."

"Girl, turn that doubt into a positive. You need to be there."

"Okay, okay. I'll really try."

"You hear from Mother?"

"No. You hear from Daddy?"

"Not at all. What's up with them?"

"I don't know, but I've got my own issues."

"What's up?"

"Derek leaving notes telling me I'm his and blah, blah, blah."

"Well, you know you had no business living with that man. Now he thinks you're his wife."

"No lectures please. I've got enough problems trying to pay off this paper trail he left behind. People think I'm made of money. But at least he's stopped calling."

"Well, praise God, and if he knows what's good for him he won't."

"What's up with Vaughn?"

"He's still at his brother's. He said it's over between him and that guy, but I don't know."

"Sis, you are good. I don't know if I'd honestly have the strength to fight for a marriage that seems . . ."

"Nina, I don't worry about that, because I know what God promised me."

"I know, but I mean . . ."

"I can't doubt. If I doubt, it means I don't believe God. And I believe Him. Yes, I was upset; I wouldn't be human if I wasn't. But, I have to get beyond that. I can do all things through Christ that strengthens me."

"I understand what you're saying, sis. And I respect that. But you're human. You deserve love and faithfulness."

"Yes, and I will have that," Troi said, convinced.

"Okay, sis, we'll talk."

"Keep me posted." Nina knew she meant about Tim.

"Will do."

Nina had read for several hours. Tried giving herself a pedicure. She was dying to go down on Atlantic Avenue to see what new treasures had come into her favorite shop. She'd wait until her toes dried before she'd throw on something colorful and take her time browsing at a snail's pace. She liked to take her time with things. Never liked to rush. You missed the good stuff that way. And she wasn't about to miss anything that life had to offer just because she was a little impatient.

Once on the strip decked out in a sarong skirt and cute little patent leather sandals, Nina didn't feel that usual urge to buy, but she was looking for something she could hang in her office. Her mind went back to the curio shop across the street from that café she and Tim had gone to the other night. She tried to avoid second-guessing what he felt, but her mind took her there anyway. *What does he think of me? Et cetera.* Her therapist always asked her why she put so much importance on other people. She still hadn't answered the question. But she did return home with a lamp that could surely be refurbished once she got past the tarnish. Nina figured she'd add a little of the moss green moleskin fabric, tack on a little fringe, and she'd have a matching set.

Nina had been preparing herself not to sound overly interested in Tim. She had fought calling him all afternoon. She was sitting next to the phone now, looking at it. She wondered, if she thought long and hard enough, if it would ring. She knew it wouldn't. She took a deep breath, and when she dialed the number that Tim had scribbled on the napkin the other night, the machine picked up on the third ring.

"Tim, it's Nina, I . . . my schedule is clear, and you were saying something about going out this week. Let me know what day this week is good for you. Give me a call or leave me a message. I really enjoyed myself the other night and I'm looking forward to getting together again." Nina rattled off her number to the machine and placed the receiver in its cradle, then smacked herself in the forehead, feeling she had given up too much information.

39

"Tim, it's Nina, I . . . my schedule is clear, and you were saying something about going out this week. Let me know what day this week is good for you. Give me a call or leave me a message. I really enjoyed myself the other night and I'm looking forward to getting together again . . ."

There was a pause before she hung up, and he figured she was just another unsure female. He didn't know if he could continue doing this. Things were better when he was alone. He had less to explain. Less compromising to do. Women just complicated things. Especially now.

Women all said the same thing: "I understand if your schedule is hectic, and I just don't want to stop you from doing what you're doing." But they meant the exact opposite. They meant "give me a play-by-play so I can be assured you're not with someone else."

Work had been keeping Tim busy, but not having much money or a real job meant not having insurance, and not having insurance meant that he would have to go and get tested down at one of those free neighborhood centers. Chances were he would see someone he knew, and the rumors would begin. He wasn't down for that. He was more apprehensive now than he had been at his parents' funeral. His feet felt heavy and, more than that, he was fearing the fact that Rochelle would worry.

He couldn't believe that his life the way it was now could be over. Ladies' man no more. He wasn't an angel, and being Tim Richardson was hardly bliss, but if all he could possibly look forward to was women not wanting to take a chance on him and never having the ability to be intimate again . . . He had heard all the talk before about being careful, and safe sex, but it hadn't applied to him. It wasn't of any interest. Until now. Tim didn't want to fathom that it was possible that he would no longer be known as an aspiring filmmaker. He'd be a statistic, another black man who had an STD. Tim's brows wrinkled. His anger was evident.

Tim couldn't help but think that if it hadn't been for Estella, he would never have found himself in this situation. He wouldn't be contemplating and rationalizing. But she was somewhat attractive, it had been one of his low points, and he'd been doing his thing, and had needed someone with whom to do it. It wasn't anything to write home about. But she had been there for Tim. Calling, coming by, and eventually making his life a living hell. There were no words to describe what he would do if he saw Estella face-to-face. Or rather, there were words, but he dared not utter them.

His judgment, however, couldn't be blameless. He had purposely decided to sleep with her. She hadn't coaxed him. He'd thought he was the one getting over. He'd been filling his need. And, more than that, if it hadn't been Estella, at the rate that he was going, it could have been any one of the dozen women who had come before or after her.

In the brief conversations that Tim had had with Rochelle since that Sunday night he'd left her place, he was sure she had figured that something was up.

"Are you okay?" she asked over and over again.

"Yes, I'm fine," he lied.

He had always practiced keeping harm from his sister. At times the harsh realities of the world eluded him, too. Rochelle wasn't excluded from feeling disappointment. But Tim felt it was his job to make sure that his sister had the kind of life that their parents aspired for them both to have. He couldn't help but chuckle sarcastically at the fact that what his future might hold was nothing that his mother or father would expect. They'd be supportive, yes, but disappointed that he didn't know better than to think that appearances were enough to judge whether or not someone was sexually safe.

In the interim, Tim had managed to distract himself with his final project for editing class. His assignment was nothing elaborate. It was the common scenario that consisted of woman meets man, falls in love with man, man is in denial, he loses woman, and they reunite at the end. A few location changes and obscure details to throw his professor off of the fact that his story was the same overdone premise.

Tim was stalling, and he knew it. Anything not to have to think about going to a clinic and making a list of all of his sexual partners. He couldn't remember all the faces, let alone names. He hadn't thought about sex much since the DWI thing, which was a start. He had been trying to change his way of living, and shook his head, thinking to himself that exactly when he'd decided to save himself, along came something to throw a wrench in it. There had been about eight partners in total. Wait, nine.

There were that few only because he was selective. That wasn't much, but it was enough to have the whole city fearful of a good-looking brother with some herpetic virus running through his veins. Tim didn't want some lab-coated volunteer asking, "What are your plans?" And he definitely didn't want to sit in some chair mulling over his life. He didn't look like he had herpes. *There go those deceiving assumptions again*, he thought.

The phone interrupted his thoughts, as it always did. There was so much weighing down on him now. The pause and harmonious hum before she spoke into the receiver on her end told him exactly who it was. Tim wasn't pleased.

"Long time," she said.

Pleasure had resurfaced temporarily to the forefront of his mind. But Tim had waited several weeks to tell her this.

"Hey. Busy tonight?" She paused.

"Why?"

"I need to see you."

"No. I can't see you, Michelle."

"Why?"

"Do I need a reason?"

"Well, no, but I'd like one," she said, almost demanding.

"Okay," Tim obliged. "You only have time when you want to see me. Other than that, I don't hear from you. I have no idea where you are, and I'm not here to entertain you."

"I see."

"You see? Or are you just trying to see how far you can go without getting caught?"

"Tim, since when are you, as you put it, 'all tangled up' in me or any woman? You know I need freedom, and I thought you did, too. I can't be stuck," she said in her coy voice.

He wasn't buying it. "Michelle, I don't have time for your games. I'm sure there are other guys you've acquainted yourself with on your weekly flights in and out of town that you could be trying to seduce right now instead of me."

"Yes, but it's who I choose, not who chooses me."

Finally, the truth, Tim thought.

"I've gotta go," he said, shoving the phone forcefully into its cradle.

Tim turned on the TV and put it on mute. He switched on the radio. ANR. Kelly's single was playing, and Tim was thinking out loud, "This ain't even funny." He lowered the volume and reached for the Yellow Pages. He flipped the flimsy pages, looking for something under *clinics*. Reluctantly his eye was caught by something that said *free screening*. He got a sharp pain in his chest, so tight that he could hardly breathe. He imagined that this was what preceded death.

Tim methodically dialed the number and cleared his throat, then deepened his voice, asking the person on the other end of the line if he needed an appointment to be tested.

"Tested for what?"

"What you think?" Tim spat defensively.

"Well, sir, we test for gonorrhea, syphilis, hepatitis, HIV, and a host of other STDs. Pregnancy, too," he added.

"Umm, herpes," he said, lowering his voice a bit so that the neighbors couldn't hear.

"Yes, we can schedule you for tomorrow, sir."

"Anything in the evening?" Tim inquired. "Six P.M.-ish?"

"Last name?"

"Richardson."

"Do you have our address, sir?"

"Yes."

"You need to come in at least thirty minutes before and register at the receptionist desk."

"Okay, thank you."

Tim switched off the TV and changed the radio to something instrumental and jazzy. He turned off all the lights and could see the red glow of the stereo as he went into the bathroom, reflecting. He undressed and stood, examining his body in the mirror. It didn't look different. Not even with the possibilities of what it could contain. He closed his eyes and prayed silently, asking for a chance to do right. To be right. To be true. For once. He looked at his face and wondered why women loved him. He wasn't anything special. He was just as unsure of what he felt as they were. But they came. And even the ones he even remotely cared about might now have something more than just a breakup for which to despise Tim. He turned on the shower and stepped in, searching for the soap and reaching for his loofah. Fate had him believing that if he scrubbed hard enough, it might come off, eventually.

A restless night and dreams of gnarled tree branches that choked him as he tried to progress through life haunted Tim. He was always able to tell the difference between a dream and reality, but that night the ability to distinguish between the two eluded him. He woke up in a sweat that had his whole body damp. He wiped his face in the pillow and flipped it to the other side. He felt like he was being suffocated. He inhaled deeply, savoring his breath, and glanced at the clock. It was in the vicinity of three A.M. Tim wandered to the refrigerator and made a sandwich that would tide him over until sunrise. He didn't know how he would make it through work, but he'd manage. He went back to bed. Now he was dreaming again.

Estella was chasing him through rooms in a big house, and his sister's voice was echoing through the corridors, telling him to pray. He was looking for a room. A room where he could finally find rest. Each door revealed a woman from his past. There were Sharon, Michelle, and women whose faces he recognized, but whose names escaped him. He wasn't trying to remember. He had to forget. There had to be more.

He walked down a lonely corridor, where enchanting music was coming out of a room. He pressed his ear against several doors until he found the room from which the sultry sounds emanated. Cautiously he turned the doorknob, preparing his legs to run in the opposite direction. The music was calming, soothing. Luring him. He opened the door. The room was dark and held the fragrance of flowers. He squinted and could make out a chair by the window. The curtains were slightly parted. A figure in the chair crossed its legs and rested both hands on its knees, than began looking up slowly.

The alarm clock went off, flashing six o'clock, waking Tim from uncertainty. He dressed quickly, guzzling a glass of orange juice. He grabbed a tie and some loose change on his way out and headed for his temperamental car. Damp mist in the air made him breathe deeply, wishing he was still in bed with a toasted bagel. This morning the car started with no trouble. He was grateful for some goodness.

Something that went his way for a change. He hoped this wasn't where the favor of God ended. He sat, mentally recollecting the address to the place he had to be at six P.M. Twelve helpless hours. Rochelle was extremely verbal in her love of God. She always said, "When you don't know what to do, pray." So that's just what Tim did.

40

Troi had dozens of tiny flashbulbs going off in her shop. It was nine in the morning, and the click and flash of the bulbs were annoying and blinding her, not to mention the scissoring of the lens shutters. Photographers were shooting heads that the girls had been up all night creating.

"Turn to the left."

"Look up."

"More attitude."

"Hold it."

"Right there."

Crimps, waves, and weaves that buried imagination and gave birth to ridiculous. There was a gold canvas backdrop with Egyptian pillars in front of which they were photographing a few styles. Troi was sure these shots alone would win her favor and at least a four-page spread in any hair magazine she chose. She was excited, semi-content, and energized, but she still needed to have everybody out of there by noon. She had a therapy appointment. She was anxious to be done working on this project to get back to the long overdue process of working on her marriage.

The shop was busy, and everyone seemed to be more excited at the fact that passersby were peeking in the windows trying to find out what was going on than the fact that there was a possibility that in a few months Shangrila could be big-time. She didn't care about money. She just wanted to see her dream reach the next level. She wanted Dakoda to go to college, no student loans and no work-study headaches. She hadn't had the heart to further her education.

She had always wanted her own little something on which to depend. She never wanted to be a woman who depended on a man, or a woman who was financially helpless because he decided that he wanted to leave.

Troi thought about how Vaughn had been verbally convincing lately, but her heart didn't buy it all. She tried to think back to when he had her full trust. She couldn't pretend that he still did. There was a part of her that would always be guessing. The feminine part that would wonder if the UPS man was only delivering packages, and if the mailman was truly only dropping off mail.

She didn't want to spend the rest of her life making coffee, tying his tie, and secretly harboring resentment for something that he claimed he couldn't help. Of all the tests and trials in life, why had she been given this one? Love was the only thing she couldn't compromise. Love put scales on your eyes. Her upbringing had proved that. If her finances were shot, she could cope with that. If she had to make do on bread alone, maybe she could muddle through that. But her husband? She tried not to be, but emotionally she was bordering on destruction.

She wasn't a total wreck. Her hair had been freshly washed and pinned. One of the new girls had offered to do her toes last week. They were still looking vacation fresh. She smiled to herself, thinking that if she were her old high-school self, she wouldn't have a problem trying to entertain herself emotionally. She'd call up some gentleman and coax him into doing exactly what she wanted when she wanted and for as long as she wanted it. It had been awhile. She had packed that part of herself away. Never thought she would need her again. Now she didn't know.

Carmen, who was always close enough to answer the phone when it rang, spoke loudly over the hum of hair dryers, "Yes, she's here." Troi's eyes squinted suspiciously.

"Troi, telephone."

Her curiosity had her frowning when Sam said, "So, I'm assuming you two are working it out."

"What do you mean?"

"I mean his situation. I didn't know, Troi, honestly, and I'm sorry. You deserve more than that."

"I'll be fine, Sam." Troi twisted her lips. "I don't want anyone feeling sorry for me."

"I told him that what he does is his business, but I'm not condoning this. Not under my roof, that's all I'm saying."

"You put him out?"

"Sis, you know under any other circumstances I would be there, but I can't deal or swing with that theory. It's too much. He might as well be asking for blood if he's asking me to understand something like that. I can't."

"So, where did he go?"

"I thought he was with you."

"He's not with me!" Troi lowered her voice so the patrons wouldn't overhear.

"His friend was here last night . . ."

"Friend?"

"Some pretty boy. I overheard the conversation. I just assumed that . . ."

"Listen, Sam, I've gotta go." She rested the telephone receiver in the base and felt a peculiar anxiety dance through her body as she thought of Vaughn with Tracie after he'd sworn up and down this city it was over for good.

The bell on her shop door jingled and, adding fuel to her already heated morning, her father walked into the shop with a determined look draped on his face and headed in her direction.

"Daddy? What are you doing here?"

"Are you okay, baby?"

"I'm fine, Daddy, but what are you doing here?"

"I need to talk to you."

Troi thanked herself three times; the new girls were a big help in the shop. Troi motioned for one of them to do whoever's head was next.

"You wanna get coffee?" Troi wiped her hands on a nearby towel.

He shook his head no. "I finished moving some things out of the house."

Troi couldn't pretend to look pleased. "How's Mother?"

"She's fine. Seems to be taking it well." He paused. "Of course, you know she's still drinking."

"I know," Troi said, not realizing that she was holding her head low, as she had when she was being scolded as a child.

"So, what is it, Daddy?"

"I'm coming to you, Troi, because your sister wouldn't understand. She's so mad at Sadie that although she says she's glad I left, she wouldn't understand this."

"Understand what, Daddy?"

"Well, baby girl, for the last few months I've been seeing someone else. I've been spending a lot of time over there and she makes me happy."

"So, you mean when we all thought we were still a family, we weren't?"

"We will always be a family, Troi. You know that. Anything you need, you let me know, hear? This woman is special to me. I know it's too soon, and you may not be ready now, but I want you to meet her."

"What about Nina?"

"Don't tell your sister. She won't understand. I mean, I know you all didn't have the most royal upbringing, but I tried. Guess I'm just not a good judge of character."

"Neither am I, Daddy," Troi sulked, as her father embraced her for the first time in she couldn't remember how long.

Troi kissed her father and hugged him as she had when she was a little girl and could reach no higher than his knees. She was holding on tight. Maybe he could help her with the pain and the aching that had her contemplating all sorts of attention-getting scenarios.

"When are we gonna have lunch again?"

"Soon, baby girl," he said, walking outside to the old Chevy that always broke down a few blocks from their high school. She couldn't believe that the car had outlasted her parent's marriage.

Troi batted her eyes to obscure her vision, but her eyes were telling the truth: There was a woman sitting in her father's car. She sat up front, passenger side. She was confident-looking, like she belonged. The woman watched her daddy walk around to the driver's side of the car. He smiled at the woman, leaning over with lips that belonged to her mother, and kissed her. The woman threw her head back, laughing like something was funny. They were too comfortable together for Troi's taste. But she had promised her daddy that she wouldn't tell anybody. Unless, of course, they asked directly. She couldn't lie. Not even for her father.

When Troi got back into the shop, the photographers were wrapping up their camera equipment and packing everything neatly into red velvet-lined boxes. The girls were putting the props back on the shelves and the phone was ringing off the hook. The head models cleared out, things quieted down, and Troi got the nerve to call Vaughn's office. She needed to know where to go from here, and it all would be determined by where Vaughn had spent last night. Troi thought, *Now he knows he could have called me and asked to sleep on the couch, even the bathtub, but to go back to this vile man who's harassing and violating my household?* That she absolutely could not believe.

"Vaughn Singleton, please."

"Loan Department, Singleton."

"Vaughn?"

"Hey, CeCe, what's up?"

"Where did you sleep last night?"

"What do you mean, where did I . . ."

"Where did you sleep last night?"

"What's with all the questions?"

"What's with not answering?"

"Troi, listen, I'm at work. If you want I can come by after work and we can talk about it later."

"No! Where did you sleep last night?"

"Okay, okay . . . Troi, I know you probably won't believe this, but . . ."

"But what?" Troi smiled.

"If you give me a minute, I'll tell you what." He spoke sternly into the phone. "Sam and I got into this big altercation and he decided that I needed to be somewhere else. Anywhere else."

"And?"

"And I went by a friend's."

"Why didn't you call me if you needed someplace to go?"

"I asked you, CeCe. I told you how much I wanted to come back so we can work on this, and what did you tell me?"

"I don't know."

"You don't know?"

"Don't turn this around on me. Who's the friend, Vaughn?"

"Come on, Troi, let's not get into that. It's not important. It didn't mean anything."

"So, can I take your evasiveness to mean that you hooked up with Tracie? Is that what you're telling me?"

"I'm not telling you anything, seriously."

"Vaughn, you have hurt and disrespected me for the last time," Troi yelled, not caring who overheard.

"CeCe, you know, despite everything, I love you. And I don't care if you believe me or not. I know the truth."

"Love me? This is love? It feels like a filthy garment to me."

"Don't say that," he whispered.

"Listen, Mr. Singleton, you can see the therapist all by yourself, because I won't be there. I've had enough. This is dead."

The minute she laid the phone down it rang again. She lifted it off the hook, rested it down again, and headed for the door.

"Whoever it is, tell them I'm not here." She frowned. "I'm going home."

Troi spent the next few days on her knees, asking God, "Why?" Why her? Why did she have to be the victim of someone's star-crossed sexual desires?

Troi had had a nasty childhood. Many men had offered to take care of her and buy her cars and shoes and take her places that were far away from New York's hot, sticky cement streets and homeless situation. She would have gone, too, if she had been sure. If she had not taken the road less traveled. If she had not wanted to secure her future. If she had not heard that sermon fifteen years ago that changed her life forever.

Troi dismissed dismal thoughts, dragged herself off the couch, and threw on something for choir practice. A little frumpy, she turned, looked in the mirror, and told herself that her attire was still no reason for her husband to go wandering. She had to go to Zion. At least if she was in the building she would feel better. Maybe someone would have a word for her. She hoped that Carla was there. She needed somebody to talk to. She was sick and tired of being used, abused, neglected, and lied to. She'd had all she could take for a good while.

Before heading to the church, Troi made a quick stop at Virginia's to pick up Dakoda. She had no time for chit-chat, and hoped that Vaughn's mother wouldn't try to serve her dinner or some other snack. In five light minutes she was there front and center to collect her daughter and her belongings. Troi absolutely didn't want to talk about Vaughn either.

"How's everything?" Vaughn's momma asked, fishing.

"Everything is fine." Troi smiled, reaching for Dakoda's jacket and hurrying to make it on time without standing still long enough for a slice of pie. "I wish I could stay," Troi said, stuffing Dakoda's arm into her jacket, "but I have practice."

"Oh, baby, I understand. Tell that boy of mine to call his momma."

"Yes, I will, Mrs. Singleton."

Troi reached the church in record time. The choir was still warming up and waiting for a few more members to show. They stood around, talking about how the cameraman had cut off their heads in the video of the last concert.

Troi set the baby down in the play area and prayed that rehearsal wouldn't take all night. She wanted to go home and crawl up into bed and lose herself in memories of something other than her husband. Something reminiscent of the smile she left on a brother's face that let her know that if she gave him her phone number, he'd be calling before she even got home.

Troi smoothed the wrinkles out of her blouse with her hand. She wanted to kick herself for being so hasty and shabbily dressed. All the Hallelujah Girls stood in the corner off to the side of the church by the drums, whispering and shaking tambourines. One of the girls eyed Troi while talking and smiling at the same time. The others just listened and responded in her ear.

"Get ready, y'all," the choir director instructed, clapping her hands to begin prayer first.

The youngest-looking Hallelujah Girl in the group walked over to Troi.

"Praise the Lord."

"Praise Him," Troi replied in anticipation of something she would have to say to defend whatever this girl was about to say about somebody else or their momma.

"Can I say something to you, Sister Singleton?" she whispered.

"Sure, what is it?"

Troi wondered if she was going to inquire about gossip or spread it. The girl rested her hand on Troi's shoulder and said, "I heard about Vaughn, and I wanted to say that I'm sorry. None of us knew that about him."

"What?" Troi swallowed hard. She thought that surely this girl couldn't be talking about Vaughn's sex life.

"I know it seems like there's so much division in here, but I wanted you to know that I never wanted any harm to come to your marriage."

Troi touched her own cheek and could feel her face lose color. She knew that if the Hallelujah Girls knew about Vaughn, then the whole church did.

"I appreciate your concern," was all that Troi could manage.

She was terrified of what Vaughn's homosexuality made her. Not knowing what to say or not say to anybody, she winced as the embarrassment of it all clothed her. As the prayer was almost done, Troi gathered her baby, held her pride up like a shield that conquered all, and headed for the church doors, which would free her, once she was on the other side, from feeling like she was on horrible display.

She held her baby as if she were the only shred of reality she had left in life and glanced back only to see all three of the Hallelujah Girls looking up at her hurrying off to outrun the shame.

41

Vaughn was trying to show Troi he meant business. He called his momma for a smidgen of sympathy, and she went on and on about how it was hard being a single parent, so Troi needed all the help she could get. His momma said that they both needed to get over their petty bickering and realize that the baby was the one who would really suffer in all of this.

"Each day you're separated is a day closer to the end," his momma said. Vaughn agreed to go over and sit down with his momma and talk.

Her pearls of wisdom might help once she knew the full monty. He didn't know what he would tell her, but he'd tell her something, because she was totally deluded about the whole situation.

His momma was thinking that they had merely had a disagreement about him leaving the toilet seat up or leaving a teaspoon full of orange juice in the carton, but it was deeper than that. He didn't know how his mother would take the news. He hoped she didn't react as Sam had. The nerve of him, putting his own flesh and blood on the street. He had so many bedrooms, they could go weeks in that house without seeing each other if that was their desire. He had expected more compassion from his own brother.

Vaughn was at the end of his rope. Desperation enveloped him. He had hesitantly asked a buddy at work if he had a spare room where he could crash for a day or two, someplace he could lay his head to prevent being deemed totally homeless.

"I'm sorry, Vaughn, but I'm not like that," he'd responded, looking around suspiciously as if their conversation were top secret.

"Not like what?"

"I'm not gay, I mean." The man's coffee cup had trembled in his hand.

"What do you mean, you're not gay? What does that have to do with anything?"

"Oh, hey, I'm sorry." His coworker's raised hands had defended. "I just heard that . . . well, you know that under other circumstances that I would . . ."

Now Vaughn understood why everyone at work was leery and backing away from him, Jill in particular. Vaughn tried to rationalize that it could have been the flowers that Tracie had sent, the couple of appearances Tracie had made for lunch dates, or the times that Tracie had picked him up from work in the evening, even after Vaughn had asked him not to. But for the most part, they could have just been assuming. He tried to be angry at the fact that his job was full of people who were jumping the gun, but in the end he knew they were absolutely right.

It was excruciating getting through eight hours at work with no one to offer stimulating conversation. Zillions of thoughts raced through Vaughn's mind. He could relocate to a different branch. But then he thought that that was what had started the whole thing. That was how he'd met Tracie. He thought that even if he did relocate, rumors traveled. They associated gay with disease, and they discriminated and ignored you. Vaughn didn't mind being ignored as much as being discriminated against. It just took a lot of getting used to.

After work, Vaughn ventured to his mom's. The familiarity of the aromas reminded him how to smile. His momma's house always smelled like real home cooking. You could smell the sausage for the stuffing and the greens simmering with the delectable hint of smoked turkey. There was always something going on up in there. He could smell cinnamon now, but didn't know whether his momma was making sweet potato pie or baked apples again. Didn't matter which. He felt seven. In his mind he flashed back to when he'd dodge around the kitchen with his brother, sneaking behind his momma's back, licking batter out of the mixing bowl. They'd always knock something down, and she would threaten no dessert, but he always knew better. The more he ate, the more pleased his momma was. And he liked to keep his momma happy.

His momma was wearing a loose-fitting denim dress, and he hugged her for longer than he normally did and waved at his father, the dark figure glaring at the television. Her frown told Vaughn that she thought her son was feeling something that she couldn't reach. She gave him a stack of mail that had still been coming to the house for him since he'd moved out.

"Momma, can we talk?" Vaughn asked, sitting in the kitchen chair closest to the stove, the way he always had since he'd been able to reach the table and pour milk into a cereal bowl.

"Sure, baby, let's talk," she said, sliding him a hot shriveled apple with cinnamon sauce running down the sides. "You want ice cream?"

"I'm fine, Momma." He inhaled the tart warmth of the apples.

His momma went to the freezer and came back with a scoop full of Breyers that melted and ran down the sides of the apple, mingling and making a carmel-colored liquid that prompted him to eat up.

Vaughn had been raised to stand on his own. It was for that reason alone he hated to ask for favors. Even from his momma. She had raised him until he was eighteen. It was his job henceforth to take care of himself.

"Hey, Momma, you think I can borrow the car again? I just have some errands to run."

"Well, I don't see why not."

"Car? Where you taking my car?" his father asked, leaning forward in his chair and looking at his son over glasses that were round and too small for his face.

"I'll be back by eleven. Is that too late?"

"It's fine, baby," his mother said, patting him gently on his shoulder.

Vaughn looked at his mother's happy round face and thought that her biggest worry was not getting her yeast to rise. She had no other real issues. Pop did all the dirty work: bills, finances, and the like. Vaughn just wished that he didn't have to destroy what seemed like a time of peace in her life, where all she should have to worry about was what her grandchild would eat for dessert. She was getting along fine, and here he was putting burdens at her feet and giving her something that she'd dwell on all night. He told himself no. He said he wouldn't tell her. But there was a part of him that wanted everybody to know. He wanted people to embrace him, not what they thought he was or what he might eventually become.

His mother had helped herself to a serving of apple. She sat across from her son, pulled up her skirt a little, dragged the chair forward, and asked, "So, how you like it?"

"It's delicious, Momma, as always." Vaughn nodded. She blushed, and he took a deep breath.

"Momma, I have to tell you something. I don't know how you are going to take this," Vaughn said, eyeing his father, who was bent over in front of the television, slapping it on its side.

"Take what?"

"Momma, are you listening?"

"Yes, baby, Momma hears you."

Panic set in for Vaughn as his dad pried himself away from the chair and the television on the premise of heading toward the aroma of cinnamon.

"What's going on in here now?"

"Vaughn has something to tell us."

Vaughn winced. He didn't know when "Momma, I need to talk to you" had become plural.

Quickly he retorted, "Troi and I are having problems. I don't think they're getting any better. We're going to counseling, but it's not helping. There are just too many issues, and I'm tired."

"Tired of what, baby?" His momma hugged his shoulders.

"Tired of trying, tired of working at it. Tired of being told that it's something I'm doing or not doing that keeps us in this place where we're not going forward or back, just standing still."

"In my day you didn't need no counseling," his dad said. "They need to let you handle your business is what they need to do."

"I am handling it." Vaughn sighed.

"Son, take control of your house. Let your mother tell you. We are where we are because I had the final say. I had to take matters into my own hands. Your mother knows, ask her."

"Dad, please, it's not about that. I don't want to take control. I just want it to work. I care about Troi."

"I care about your momma, too, son. I love her."

"Dad, I just want everything to be the way it was before."

"Before what?"

Vaughn's heart palpitated, his lips twitched. "Before I found out . . ."

"Found out what?"

"Before I had these feelings . . ."

"Boy, what are you trying to say?" his father snapped.

"Momma, I think I'm gay." Vaughn stared at them both, then the floor.

"Gay?" His dad stood frozen, like ice had settled on his cheeks. He made an about-face, backing into the safety of his reclining chair. Now his dad wasn't watching television, it was watching him, and he was staring right past it into the hidden plot to destroy his son's life.

Vaughn's momma reached out her arms and couldn't help but cry all over him.

"Oh, baby, no. It can't be. Don't let the devil tell you that. You're not gay. Why are you claiming that, baby?"

"Momma, I don't want to claim it. It's what I feel. I never asked for it. I don't want it. But it's what I feel." He fell limp in his momma's arms. She rubbed the back of his head and caressed his back as he sobbed.

He shook his head, knowing that he was disappointing people. He hated having people looking up to him and then disappointing them. His mother walked away momentarily and came back. She put the car keys on the table. His father's face, even from a distance, conveyed to Vaughn that, as always, he was displeased. Sam was always the more athletic one, although he wasn't into all of that problack stuff like their dad was.

Vaughn needed someplace to stay. He dared not spend the night under his father's viligant eye. He'd size him up and pick him apart headfirst, because his father always wondered what went on in people's heads. He knew that if he mentioned staying, his momma would insist, almost demand. His room was almost the same as it was when he'd left for college. Momma slipped another baked apple right under his nose and slid a few more pieces of mail into his hand. He didn't even have the strength now to say, "No, thank you."

Vaughn lifted his head long enough to sift through the mail before he left. He looked at something that resembled an invitation. He opened the ivory-and-gold envelope that he already knew was a wedding invitation. He thought back to his wedding briefly, with the cake and the gifts from well-wishers who assumed that Vaughn's marriage to Troi would last longer than most. He missed her warmth, her smile. She was, after all, still his wife. Vaughn didn't know if the idea he was kicking around in his head was too far-fetched. He thought of the invite as the perfect opportunity for him and Troi to show up as a couple. He wanted Troi to know that he seriously loved her, and he didn't want the words to be something that he said behind closed doors to smooth things over. He wanted other people to know that he still loved her as well.

Vaughn wondered if Troi would dare be seen in public with him, knowing that he had spent the other night at Tracie's. There had to be a long lost friend with whom Vaughn could have crashed, he scolded himself. He had taken the familiar route, and now he might have done damage that was irreversible. He found the strength and shook his head. He wished all it was was sexual experimentation. He knew it was more than that. He just needed to figure out how to undo it. When he got home, he would reschedule the appointment with the therapist, that was the first thing. Home. He and CeCe were a family. He'd be honest this time, just like she wanted him to be. He'd tell her the truth: "I've got nowhere else to go."

42

Nina dressed swiftly, clothed in something a little shorter than she should have normally worn to church. It was navy, hardly her favorite color, but everything she owned was either at the cleaners or totally more inappropriate. Cleavage was a no-no. If you came to church showing too much flesh, they'd slap a cloth on your lap and mess up your whole coordination thing. She tried not to complain. She hated sounding like Shelby, to whom she hadn't spoken since that whole pre-Derek breakup thing. But at least Nina was there, center pew. Her heels made the skirt shorter than it was before she'd put on the heels, and she had contemplated wearing flats, but thought against it.

She hated her thighs. They were huge. As she sat, she could see her skirt rising. She'd tug it down and it would rise again. Men loved women with big legs. Troi always told her that, but Nina couldn't understand why, and she surely didn't think that meant hers. Of all places to have dimples, her thighs weren't supposed to be one of them. But she tried not to tear herself down today, so when she arrived she made her way up the stairs and sat in the middle section of the church, looking on as the worship leaders led the members in prayer. She recognized Carla from behind by her colorful scarf, and she knew Troi had to be near. Nina lowered her head as everyone said, "Thank you, Jesus."

Nina peeked up and saw her sister looking around while everybody else had their heads bowed praying. Her sister was peeking just like they had always done since they were little. She smiled at her sister, and Troi sort of grinned. She didn't look much like laughter today. Everybody had a cross to bear. Daddy had Mother, now Troi had Vaughn, and Nina figured she was her own burden.

Getting past things. Nina didn't know how forgiving she was supposed to be. Troi seemed to let people walk all over her. Nina confessed that she wasn't that kind of woman. She thought of all the people in her life who made an impact, mostly negative. Derek was at the top of the list. Credit-card charges and long-distance calls. That whole experience had cost her $3,079.52. What a price for a lesson. A bought lesson. Heck, it was better than none.

She wasn't asking for glass slippers. She was asking for a fragment of the love that God was. No one could equal Him, but she needed arms, someone who wouldn't hang her out to dry, but instead water her. Her mother used to nag her compulsively about some guy she used to date. "You know, you should have married him. He asked you even though you knew nobody else would." But even back then, Nina wasn't about to be tied to a man she loathed in the spirit and the natural.

Nina closed her eyes in church and thought of how the birds sat in their trees, perched on the leaf-covered branches, telling each other stories of places they'd traveled, while we humans paced the concrete jungles of this life, smiling with our eyes and telling each other lies. Nina wanted to change her life, but she didn't know how. Criticism was all she knew. Her mother had planted that in her. She was a nervous breakdown waiting to happen. And as far as men went, the minute she got close to a man, she knew he could smell her desperation like a dog smelled fear. The scent of it was all over her. She walked into their life with *save me* written all over her. Everywhere she went she looked like a sale-priced item with shrink-wrap. She tried to shake the thought of feeling unworthy, but it wouldn't budge.

After over ten years, it was funny how church always made her think about her mother. Her mother was a puzzle Nina would die trying to figure. She could clean up so well for show. Everybody mattered more than her kids. The choir was singing a song now, and Nina opened her eyes and glimpsed around the church, looking for familiar faces. The choir was about all she recognized. And then she only knew half of them. Mother needed to be there, Nina thought. She hadn't been to a service in much too long to remember. Television wasn't the same. Her mother had two legs and needed to get up and walk in there. Nina lowered her head as if she were scolding herself.

Nina tried to be positive. She tried to think of twenty-five things she loved about herself. It was harder than she imagined. Okay, okay. She loved the way her voice sounded, but only at night and only if she was talking to a man. She loved her lips. They were full, and her bottom lip was slightly larger, making it always appear that she was ready for a kiss. She loved her creativity and the way she could decorate a room that would have people thinking that a professional had done it. She loved the way she walked, but only when she was wearing something nice. She loved her intelligence. She wasn't just in the college dorm having a perpetual book experience for eight tiresome years, she had actually acquired some knowledge.

She loved her taste in clothes and, despite their unwillingness to comply, she loved men. She loved her hands and the things she knew how to do with them. She loved her hair. After years of frying and trying the latest styles, she was content even if it was pulled back in a bun and had oriental stickpins pushed in the back. She loved the fact that she was a good listener, although she wasn't a good judge of character. She loved her short fat toes that didn't have corns or bunions. She loved the way she kissed. She loved the fact that if she wanted to go on a vacation, she could do it right now without saving or borrowing. And she loved the fact that although her legs were out of control, her waist was still inviting enough for a brother to get a thrill wrapping his arms around it.

Nina was missing the message. But she continued even more quietly in her mind, because it was making her feel better. She loved her stubbornness, because it came in handy sometimes. She loved the way that everyone came to her for advice although they never took it. She loved her hips, but not the way they led to her thighs. She loved the way she was willing to take risks, especially for love.

Nina loved her generosity and her kindness to animals, although she didn't own any pets. She loved her ability to encourage everyone around her. She loved her appreciation for nature and the love in her that prompted her to give second chances and sometimes thirds. She loved the fact that there were things about her to love, and she totally loved the fact that she could say that she was the most sincere woman that most men ever met.

She fidgeted and tried to flip the pages in her bible to appear as if she was paying attention. Her mind was elsewhere, and she would have been better off staying home, making a big breakfast, and listening to some music. Nina tugged at her skirt again. The woman next to her looked down at Nina's skirt as if to say, "If it wasn't so short, you wouldn't have to keep pulling it down." Nina eyed her back and grinned.

From the pulpit, Pastor was saying that some lives would be changed this morning. He said, "You will not leave the same way you came." Nina nodded, as if she knew for sure.

"You see, when we come with an expectancy, it pleases God. Expectancy is like faith."

Nina nodded.

"Y'all don't hear me in here. I said, expectancy is like faith!"

The applause of agreement moved thunderously through the church. Belief was there, and so God dwelt therein.

"When you praise God, the power and the glory comes down. Come on now, can somebody praise Him this morning?"

A sister in the pews on the left jumped up and threw her head back while she was waving her handkerchief.

"Hallelujah is the highest praise. Praise Him. He's kept you all week, we've come a mighty long way. The mere fact that you are here right now in this building gives you something to praise him for. Come on, somebody."

Nina fanned herself with the floppy cardboard funeral advertisement.

"You," the voice echoed from the pulpit. "You in the navy . . ." Nina looked around, then looked down, pointing at herself.

"Yes," he said, with a firm grip on the microphone. "God is calling you to a new level. God is saying, love, love yourself. Not selfishness, He's saying there are things in you that you need to forgive. They are not your fault. He said that you will also travel and relocate soon, for there is nothing for you here, but you are afraid to move forward and always live in the past. He said if you seek Him, He will deliver you."

Nina's hands went up in agreement, and she closed her eyes, and the tears began to flow impulsively from the corner of her eyes and down her cheeks onto her jacket. Her face was hot, and she couldn't control what she was feeling. Nina had only experienced His presence once before. She was nineteen then. She smiled, and all she could think to herself was that she almost hadn't come to church this morning.

"Rejoice for this sister, God has freed her." The woman sitting next to her embraced her tightly. She whispered in Nina's ear, saying, "God is good."

Nina couldn't even say, "All the time." But God knew she appreciated Him.

"God's gonna change some lives up in here today. I'm telling you." Pastor reminded them that without faith, it was impossible to please Him. "Man will fail you," he said. "But God, He will keep you in perfect peace, whose mind is stayed on thee." Nina felt the depth of what he was saying, and she knew that it wouldn't be long before old wounds closed up and began to heal for good.

The bass guitar vibrated through the church and the presence of God was evident. Prophecy excited the people. The Word concerning Nina's life was confusing to say the least, but she received it. From the front pew, Troi was smiling wide at her sister, like someone had given her a gift.

Nina loved her brownstone. She wouldn't easily part with the antique shops of Atlantic Avenue either. But he was right in saying that there was nothing for her here. She felt dried up, like a crack in the desert. There was no life here. She always felt like there had to be more, but she couldn't find it. Like a game of hot peas and butter, she was always warm and sometimes even near enough to be hot, but she never found what she was looking for.

An overwhelming urge came upon Nina. She couldn't explain it, but she wanted to see her mother. She needed to find out if she was coping. She hadn't seen her mother since the whole Daddy leaving thing. But that was because her mother always acted like she didn't need anybody. Nina wanted to take her mother some fruit and flowers, brighten up her space.

The service was energetic, and Nina had really gotten into it. She was clapping her hands and stomping her feet, and felt as if a weight had been lifted off of her. Something that was telling her that she wasn't alone, even though when she looked around in her situation there was no one with tissues to dry her tears or arms to hug her. God knew. God knew her heart, her needs, and just how much she could take. After the offering and a few announcements, the congregation was dismissed. Troi ran over and hugged her sister, and Carla was shotgun, smiling and touching Nina's hair.

"Are you okay?"

"I'm fine."

"Hide that Word in your heart, God wouldn't lie to you."

"I will. I'm going to see Mother, you wanna go?"

"You are?"

"Yes."

"No, I can't."

"Hey, sisteren," Rochelle called as she approached.

"Hey," Troi said.

"Rochelle, this is my sister, Nina."

"Yes, I remember, long time no see."

"Well, I have to take it one day at a time, you know."

"That's all you can do," Rochelle said.

Troi leaned over and whispered to her sister through clenched teeth, "Look who's here."

"Who?" Nina turned discreetly, facing the doors.

Tim was standing tall, dark and finer than he should legally have been allowed.

"Tim?"

"Hey, Nina, right?"

"Yes, that's me." She smirked.

"You two know each other?" Rochelle questioned.

"We've met." Tim nodded.

"My little brother, don't know what I'd do without him." Rochelle grinned.

Tim faced Nina. "Listen, about last week . . ."

"No need to explain, it's fine."

"It's just that I got caught up and then when I realized that I had missed out and had you waiting, I wasn't feeling too valiant. So, I didn't call."

Now he knows he's lying, Nina thought.

"You still volunteering?" he asked.

"Yes, on the weekends, on and off whenever I have the time."

He smiled, inquiring as to when she was available and if they could possibly do something soon. She wanted to lie initially just so he'd think she wasn't sitting around willing the phone to ring. He asked if Friday would be good for her.

"We can get a bite to eat. You like jazz? I know a nice little place in SoHo."

43

Tim thought about Nina briefly, but longer than he needed to. He had made a date with this unsuspecting woman whom he knew he wouldn't keep. And right in church, no doubt. He had another twenty-four-hour day to contemplate what his test results would be, and the months it would take for him to readjust his lifestyle were beyond comprehension. He was already living his life like he was branded and diagnosed incurable. He deserved it. The last thing he wanted to do was try to grin and entertain some woman at a jazz club over veal parmesan. He could have ignored her and pretended not to recognize her, but that would have been rude. He just didn't want her to think that he was heartless. He wasn't. Just not in the mood for distractions at this point in his life.

Nina was nice-looking and well spoken, but he wasn't mentally up to the strain it would cause to continue to be interested in her. Tim met women all the time. Lately their presence hadn't done much for him. He had been on his knees pleading for a reprieve. Tim made a lot of promises. He had never been so serious ever. He had let go of Sharon, Michelle, and those knuckleheads that Rochelle was always going on and on about. "They're dragging you down, Tim," she'd say. For the most part, his womanizing ways never brought him anything but trouble or women who didn't know how to let go. Although there was still some freak left in him, he knew he could keep that under wraps or rid himself of it totally if he chose.

Tim thought about where his mind would have been two months ago. He knew that he would have been the old him, who met women in and out of the church and thought it would be entertaining to watch them profess faith and willingly give into sex, repeatedly. Anything for a "hello." They'd declare, "Jesus is Lord," and then a minute later they were in between his sheets yelling, "Oh, my God!" for another reason altogether while pulling their own hair out. He tried not to judge, even back then. He was a benefit-of-the-doubt brother. He always gave it. Maybe they were just hopeful. Some women, all you had to do was promise them a ring, they'd consummate the relationship on the kitchen floor. Wasn't their fault really. It was all those fairy tales. They lied. Made women think that men actually threw their coats down over puddles.

Nevertheless, he could see the changes in his life. He allowed other people's feelings to matter. Not just his own. Rochelle had wanted him to come over after church again. She wanted to fatten him up for the kill, plump him up for marriage. He'd convinced his sister that he was hardly starving. She'd asked briefly how he knew Nina, and inquired as to how old she was. "That's not important," he'd tried to smooth past her. He didn't feel up to the company or the third degree about Nina. He'd gotten in his car after church and had been driving around Manhattan all afternoon. He ended up at the same little French coffee shop on Columbus Avenue to which he had taken Nina when they met. He was eager about her then. He relived it all in his mind. She was so standoffish at first and hopeful, but now? He was on a road to an unknown destination. Who would have ever thought he'd be alone?

Tim walked through the doors of the café and the aroma arrested him as it had done before. He paused to catch his breath. He had thought back briefly to how everyone had been talking barely above a hush and how Nina had sat and listened attentively to every word he'd said. She had moved her hand away from his when he'd reached for the check. He remembered her voice and her eyes saying she understood what motivated him as an artistically inclined brother. He remembered her saying that caring was her biggest fault.

Negative or positive, he figured he'd be out of luck. Nina wouldn't dare entertain the thought of him after he stood her up twice. Sharon might, but Nina wouldn't. He tried to relish the thought of a third chance, but Nina was different. He knew she was cultured enough to get any man. She was confident and educated. He liked the modestly educated woman who read lots of books but didn't go around quoting Shakespeare or Freud. Yes, he had issues. That was a given. She was desirable, funny, poised, and her body said, *Wait a minute, can you handle this?* But he was backing off. He wasn't intimidated, just trying to be cautious, just as she had been. Caution didn't mean fear.

His current dilemma had given him motive to search himself and his actions for the past eight or nine years. All he could think was that now he'd get what many women said he deserved, no children left to carry his name. His life was being rewound before him like an old black-and-white movie that he'd only seen once. It was all too real for him. He wished his momma was here to sit him down and ask him what was wrong. He'd tell her. He always did. He couldn't lie to her big brown comforting eyes, and although he needed to be closer to his sister, he couldn't be. She was planning a family and had a husband who loved her more than gold. He didn't want to be a burden to what she and her husband had built.

Tim couldn't lie. He had never been able to. And he definitely couldn't fabricate the fact that he did get undue pleasure out of watching women obsessed with doing and saying the right thing to keep him. He smoothed down his goatee out of habit and thought to himself that soon he wouldn't have to worry about love, attraction, and settling down. Women were better off without him. He could never give any of them what they wanted anyway. It was too hard not being in control. Control was something he had learned to master from day one. Never fully feeling good enough to date the really talented and smart girls. Never having quite enough to give.

Tim remembered telling a woman once, "Men want sex. They all want sex. If women would just understand that, we wouldn't have to play the games and distract you so you'd think we want more." She'd pretended to be devastated, and after she'd left he'd still been physically satisfied. She'd thought she'd change his mind. Persuade him. Sex never made a man love a woman.

"If we were friends before sex, we're still going to be friends after sex, you understand?"

"Yes," she'd said, looking as if she wasn't sure if she wanted to crawl back in bed with him or dash out the front door.

Tim wasn't mean; women just thought they could mold him. He wasn't clay. He was what a woman once called "a bronzed ready-to-be-sampled brother who tempted you to take a sip like a cup of coffee with two sugars and three capfuls of cream." He was ripe for the pickin'.

Tim was thinking now about what traits his ideal woman would have to possess. He toyed with the word *ideal* and came to realization that there was no such thing. But any woman who wanted his heart would have to be a lot like his momma. No one could break him but her. She had the subtlety of a pot of crabs that didn't know they were being cooked until they were red in the shell. Women gave up too easily. And they were all a bit too presumptuous for his taste. They judged him by his associates.

He had seen his friends hit women, bad-mouth women, use women as sex objects, cooks, maids, and he had seen his friends make women they were genuinely interested in jump through hoops to see if they had staying power. Tim had done that, and in the end all he'd ended up with were the crazies who fell for anything. Secretly he wanted a woman who would tell him where to go and how to get there. He didn't want a woman who would do anything to get a man.

He wanted a woman who was so sure of herself that it made him doubt himself. A woman who assumed nothing and took everything for granted. And although his actions were sometimes contrary, he felt that there was absolutely no reason for a man to be able to talk the panties off a woman on the first date, the second either. Once the respect was gone there was no relationship, only lust. And lust was like a vivacious fire that was given permission to do what it pleased until it consumed itself and died.

But lust was all he had to offer thus far. It was all he was willing to contribute. "Can I confide in you?" the legs walking through his life would proposition. As if he didn't have enough secrets. Baggage. He didn't want women to pry and struggle to know the most intimate parts of him, like how he was so devastated emotionally as a result of his parents' deaths. Baggage. He was also barely able to supply his own needs, much less entertain a woman every weekend. Baggage. He knew he wasn't where he was supposed to be financially. He had zero savings except for a few stocks in minor companies that his father had willed to him. Still, baggage. He had recently come to grips with his anger at God, though he hadn't realized that's what it was until after the fact. Baggage. And now his pending herpes status, which would have made a weaker man contemplate giving up women for good, had him rethinking his whole existence. Baggage. It was for these reasons alone that Tim couldn't promise a woman anything.

When men promised women anything and failed to deliver, women girded themselves and transformed into something from one of those horror movies. He didn't have the patience for yelling, screaming, and bickering. He just wanted someone who could accept him and would grow into whatever they desired to be together. No qualms, no broken promises, and no lies.

Tim eyed the colorful coffee mugs and the sticky danish behind the display in the dimly lit coffee shop. Everyone around him was on a caffeine high. He saw women sitting alone, reading fashion magazines and sipping coffee. One woman sat surrounded by four empty coffee cups and was on her fifth. Music played softly. He nodded his head and the words of Patti Labelle entangled him. He mentally turned down the volume.

An older man caught his gaze and nodded.

"You alone?" He motioned with his chin.

"I'm cool."

"I didn't ask if you were cool, I asked if you were alone."

Tim looked around, always ready to humor even himself. "Yes. I'm alone."

"How old are you?"

Tim grinned. "I'm twenty-eight."

"Yeah?"

"Yes," Tim replied.

"So, where's your woman?"

"I don't need a woman," Tim said confidently.

"I ain't ask you if you needed a woman . . . I asked you . . ."

Tim got the point. "I don't have one."

"Don't have one?" The man chuckled with his tattered hat and exaggerated manner of speech.

"I loved a girl once," he said, with a serious face. "Married her, too. She was the prettiest thing I ever seen. Dimples like craters and delicate shoulders, soft like a baby's bottom." He laughed to himself. "I was fifteen, you know. The other fellas were sweet on her, too. Heck, we all were, so I had to do a whole lot of convincing." He twirled his cup and fiddled with the wrapper on a package of saltines.

"What happened to her?" Tim asked, taking a sip of his coffee but still keeping his distance.

"We was happy back South. I was working hard fixing things here and there, and she was ironing and cleaning, until she got pregnant."

Tim nodded.

"We was happy, you see, it was our first baby. But things wasn't quite right," he drifted. "Our families were causing strife and she kept saying, 'Let's leave from here, Junior, let's leave from here.' But I wanted to work a few more months. Save and get a nicer place up North, a extra room for the baby . . ." he reminisced. "I remember it like a national event. They came running over out of breath and dusty one afternoon right before lunchtime you see, yelling at me to come quick 'cause she was in labor and the baby was coming. I ran swifter than I ever did in my whole life. I was there holding her hand the whole while and the doctor, well, he was on his way, too, but he wasn't there yet. Next thing I knew, she started getting what they called them seizure things, and I couldn't do nothing to help her. The doc finally came and tried holding her down . . ." The old man paused. "God knows I love her still, but there was nothing I could do. Her fingers were holding my hand and squeezing real tight. I could feel the blood 'bout to burst forth. Then her hand went limp and cold. Lost my baby and my wife that day," he said, staring off past Tim into the streets.

"I'm sorry, man."

"It's been twenty-three years. They say I'm crazy, but not really. This is how I cope. Yeah, I walk the streets, but who's to say what normal is? I hear what they say about me. They say I'm dirty. They say that I need a job, but you know, I ain't never been the same since she gone. She took half of me with her. Only thing is she don't know it. The other half is still here. I'm waiting for her to come get the rest of me. I don't belong here. Or at least that's what they say. How about you, brother? You got somebody you sweet on?"

"I'm not lonely; matter of fact, I'm quite content." What colorful lies, Tim thought, shaking his head at the mockery he was making of this man's true love. He could have bit his tongue in midsentence.

"Content? Yeah. I was content. Love is contentment. That's the way it was supposed to be."

"So, you ever think you'll fall in love again?" Tim asked.

"Once you in love, you in love for good. Ain't no turning back. You can't love then not love. I love once. She's the only woman ever touched me down deep. She the only woman who ever will."

He took his hat off and shook it. Onlookers shied away from his not-so-sterile appearance. "Let me tell you something, son. You don't know me from nobody. But if you ever love a woman, tell her. If you don't, it'll haunt you for the rest of your life. Believe me. It'll haunt you for the rest of your life."

On the drive home, Tim kept replaying the man's story in his head. His mind kept coming back to intimate thoughts. The things he enjoyed about women had a lot to do with his mother. But he couldn't make promises. He knew that. In the natural he was just looking at women as the opposite sex, but in his mind he was seeking certain traits that were appealing. His mother was nurturing and a good listener. He could use that right now.

He hoped down deep that he didn't run into Nina at the mission. Another week or two and he'd be done with his community service stint. He was hardly up for the freeze-frame that would be replayed from other relationships he'd had.

Acquaintances, associates, friends. That's all they were. Nothing more. Old man was right. Tim knew he was far from content. Not quite lonely though. More like confused. He headed home in preparation for a long day tomorrow. The sun couldn't rise quickly enough for him. Fate held him in the palms of both hands, and he just had to know exactly what the outcome would be.

44

Vaughn's plea was convincing. Here he was now with his face too close to Troi's. His lashes brushed against her face as he blinked. She closed her eyes and sat motionless. He kept trying to convince her that he wanted to spend time with her and wanted their marriage to work. She didn't know if it was him or his imagination talking. Sometimes after midnight people said anything. Troi tried to play it safe. She smiled a lot at the reception and she tried not to exchange glances with men who were available and some who were too familiar for comfort. Those were his school associates, not hers. But he wanted to show her off.

"We had fun, didn't we?"

"Yes, it was fabulous. We should do this again," he said, trying to be calm and unthreatened by the atmosphere.

I am my beloved's and my beloved is mine, Troi thought, shifting in her seat. Her skirt rose, exposing her thigh, and she pretended not to notice, just as she had pretended that she didn't catch Vaughn stealing glances at her cleavage. He was attracted to her still, although his revelation had already put a damper on things. Perhaps if they were alone, she thought, but then chances were he would feel cornered and clam up.

He hated being put on the spot. She had had enough of him getting tongue-tied and not being able to express what should have come naturally, and she was tired of holding back to appease him. She wanted to tell him that she was enjoying this, but she dared not for fear of appearing foolish. *He already told you what he preferred,* her mind kept telling her, but he was here breathing his tantalizing breath all over her, and that in itself was saying something totally different.

Troi remembered earlier on in their relationship when they were deep in love, they had stood on the darkened street on many a night about one-thirty in the morning. There were never any cars coming, the streets would be bare, every light in every apartment would be off except for the yellowish shadow of someone through a window blind who fumbled around because he couldn't sleep. They'd stand there baiting each other, pretending that they each needed to leave, knowing full well neither really wanted to. She'd play hard to get and he'd extend his arms, hugging her tightly. That's how she'd known he was the one. His touch had confirmed what reason didn't.

Tonight they were coming from Queens and he was dropping her off in his momma's car, just as he had done that New Year's Eve almost four years ago after she'd agreed to go with him to drop off some pies for his brother.

Troi wanted Vaughn to stay. Stay with her the whole night and wake up making love as the sun rose behind the dusky brick buildings. Her spirit cried, thought it was probably her heart. She was feeling hot; the presence of something other than herself hovered around her neck like a scarf that was too tight.

He broke the silence first.

"My momma said that I could use my spare room. So, if it's too much for you to deal with all of this now, I can, you know, go over there," he said, looking away.

She wanted to say that it was okay that he come back home. Something wouldn't let her. Her tongue was heavy, and he was waiting and had paused for her to interject something, anything. She was perspiring and doing something with her hands that stopped her from putting them in her face. She was sure her eyeliner was running. She refrained from rubbing the corners of her eyes. He was doing this on purpose, she thought. He wanted to make her beg.

She wanted to scream, but feared ruining the moment. *Take me back, please take me back,* she yelled through her chest. But it sounded like she was murmuring instead. He turned to her and they made eye contact. She wanted to hold his head in her arms and plant lipstick kisses on his glistening head as he hugged her waist. But she wouldn't beg; she was like her mother in that respect. She wasn't good at begging.

His friend's wedding wasn't something that she had initially looked forward to. She had almost said no. She wasn't in the mood for anything other than the truth, and Vaughn hadn't given her a definitive answer about their relationship yet. She had things to do. The shop and the promotions . . . business was trying to creep into her head. She closed the doors of her mind. Maybe he wanted to keep up appearances, she thought. Was that all this was? Her feelings, his gentleness? Was it a ploy to make things appear kosher? She wanted him. He tapped his fingers on the dashboard. She turned and smiled, wishing that he'd allow an opening in his heart big enough for her to squeeze inside and take up residence.

Troi refused to spend the rest of her life looking for a spasm of hope. She wasn't about to put her feelings in a wicker chest under his bed until he decided that he could put aside his cravings and get back to his one true love, her. She wanted him to tell her that Tracie meant nothing to him. She wanted him to say anything.

But Troi knew she had enough femininity to help him rethink his sexual confusion. Hair color, curled lashes, pastel nails, smooth feet, and showing a little more leg. There had to be something to stir his interest, like tonight. She was hoping that she'd be able to divert his attention back to the fact that he already had everything he needed in her. It wasn't hard for him to do, but the question was, would he take the bait?

She tried not to rationalize their relationship. She prayed and knew that heaven had heard her. She focused instead on the night. She loved herself in navy. Chiffon was a particularly friendly fabric. Her hair was curly and a few short curls purposely hung down near her face but didn't really block her vision. Vaughn leaned over, moved her hair, and admired her face.

Why is he doing this? He must want to see where my head is. He knows that gets to me, she thought. She tried to fight pouncing on him with everything she had. Like that amaretto cheesecake he liked so much, she could devour him without leaving a crumb.

This would be one of those memorable nights. Something that young girls wrote about in their pink diaries. She knew it. And she would envelop every detail, commit it to memory, and etch it in her frontal lobe. Permanence. Troi wanted everything about this day to last, linger. The moon shone and Vaughn squinted, something she knew him to do mostly out of nervousness. He didn't wear glasses. He turned away from her and fiddled with the radio, pushed a few buttons and slipped in a tape. The lush horns surrounded them and she was amazed at the impossibility of it all.

She tugged at her dress and his eyes followed her hands as they made their way around her curves and she tried to conceal what she desperately wanted to reveal to him. She wondered if another child would change things between them. She tried to remind herself not to worry or frown.

He leaned over to the glove compartment and rustled around for another tape that she could have just as easily passed to him. She wondered if he could smell her. The scent of her on him. She closed her eyes only momentarily when he placed his hands on her thigh. She was elated that she had put on the silky stockings. He liked those. She kept her eyes closed and head back as she relished the warmth of his hand.

Both of his hands were resting on her now. She fought it, pretending she didn't notice. He wanted something. Innocently she gazed at him as he lost himself deeply in her eyes. The words spilled out of her before she knew what she was revealing.

"You know I love you, Vaughn," and the gentleness in her voice made him feel as if things were progressing.

He wasn't sure if it was the high of the whole evening, the tuxedo, or Troi's skimpy dress that had him going. She didn't know what to make of the whole evening, but she made up in her mind that she'd stop fighting it. Enjoyment had her name on it. Enjoyment was wearing a tuxedo. Enjoyment had lips that said, *Come and get me and let me be thine.* Enjoyment was Vaughn.

He was the most precise and tender man she knew. So few words, so much promise, she thought as the beads of early morning mist swelled on the windowpane. It was the quickened breath of anticipation that bade her to forget the initial revelation that had almost destroyed her life. She knew it had been a mistake to take him so seriously.

He was still in his prime, and the familiarity that surrounded them at this moment was enough to make her want to marry Vaughn all over again. He desired her, always would.

Vaughn undid the buttons on his jacket, opened his door, quickly walked around to the passenger side, and opened the car door for his wife. He loved the thought that she was his. She was entranced as he held her hand and simultaneously pushed the door shut behind her. The streets were cool and the glare from the streetlight made the insects visible. He held her hand still. He was trying to convey faithfulness. She welcomed him with her eyes, giving him permission to proceed. She moved closer to the warmth of his breath and nudged him with her lips. Everyone wanted her to hate him and never forgive him. He pressed her against the car and three words escaped her lips that conveyed everything she was feeling.

"Vaughn, please stay."

45

Nina couldn't believe that Tim had stood her up for the second time. Not that she couldn't think of several brothers off the top of her head who had more class than he could muster on a good day, but she didn't want mustered class, she wanted to enjoy another evening with him to see where his head was and what he was about. She could pretend that she didn't want him, but the truth had to prevail.

Men she had known wanted to attach themselves so quickly. He wasn't like that. She admired that in him. Before you could make up the bed after an impromptu romp, most men had their mail forwarded, sandwich meat and nachos in your fridge, and tube socks in the top drawer. She knew it was about the chase. *The chase is what gets us all out of breath and yearning, and then when we're caught we lie helpless like a rabbit in a trap, waiting to be skinned for our lucky feet.*

Nina didn't mind spending the weekend doing nothing, just not all the time. There was only so much reading that she could get done, and she knew all the songs she loved by heart. She had forgone the mission on the weekend mostly out of respect for Tim. She couldn't be gentle with words. Never could. And if she had seen him there at the mission, he'd be wearing some chipped beef instead of her serving it.

She promised herself that she wouldn't think about him and his lack of courtesy to even call to cancel, reschedule, or whatever. A filmmaker. That hardly gave him carte blanche. But she knew they'd cross paths eventually, and when they did, it would be easier to get frostbite in hell than it would be for her to agree to go out with him again.

Sadly enough, Nina thought about her mother all the time now. After church last week, she had gone by, and Mother had been sitting at the same kitchen table with the peeling Con-Tact paper, dragging on the same brand of cigarette, and drinking the same overproof vodka on ice.

"What you want?" Mother had snapped.

"I just came by to see how you were doing."

"I don't need nobody feeling sorry for me," she'd said, shuffling to the trash can to empty a mound of cigarette butts and ashes.

Seemed as if she was back to more than a pack a day.

"I don't," Nina had lied. "I feel like talking."

"About what?"

"Anything."

"Anything, huh?" her mother had said, refilling her glass, unaware that it was nearing the rim. "Well." She'd inhaled. "How's that man of yours?" Her mother had grinned as if she knew.

"He's gone."

"Gone, huh?" She'd blown smoke purposely in her daughter's face. "They never stay, do they? Just like your father. Gone. Well, who needs 'em? I can do bad all by myself," she'd said.

And Nina had nodded, because she was doing bad.

"Mother, do you need anything? I can pick up a few things for you if you need something, just let me know, groceries or whatever."

"I'm fine. Why you being so helpful? What you up to?"

"I'm not up to anything. I just want to make sure things are okay."

"Your father send you over here? Tell him to go on with his new woman. I don't need him, I'll be fine. Been fine. Ain't gonna start not being fine now."

"What woman, Mother?" Nina had smirked. Her mother was always ready to blame anybody but herself. "You need to get out of the house, Mother."

"Get out and go where?"

"Church for one, or a walk. You need some fresh air."

"I don't need nobody's church, and what good is fresh air gonna do me now?" she'd said, lowering her head and dragging on the cigarette again. She was as miserable as a tapeworm in an anorexic.

But Nina's mother had reluctantly agreed to have lunch with her. It was a strange proposition, and it had to be God and the anointing up in church on Sunday, because Nina wouldn't have bothered with her mother otherwise. She didn't have time to sit and be verbally abused, or have every effort she put forth shot down by her mother and her evil ways.

Nina had promised she'd go back by the house near eleven so they could grab a quick bite around twelve o'clock, and then she'd run the rest of her errands with the remainder of the day.

Shelby had finally resurfaced. She had no doubt pried herself away from her latest victim and wanted to come over to dish the dirt on him. "I'm coming over tonight," she'd said. Nina had reluctantly agreed.

Nina was determined that she would not entertain nonsense. That was a little promise she knew she didn't have to wait until New Year's to make. That included Shelby. Nina was sitting on her cool floor now, flipping through a magazine and killing time. She had dog-eared some pages, and wanted to do some shopping soon. She desperately needed a vacation or a getaway. She had never been on one with a man. Before she could propose the idea, fully conjure the thought, or get him to convey his undying affection before the trip, their affair had always fizzled.

Maybe her mother was right: They always left. Gone. No explanation and no warning. It was like a hurricane almost. Left damage in the wake of its trail, and there was no one left to clean up or rebuild but her. Nina didn't like the things that she learned from her mother. They were unprofitable and vain. She learned to criticize everybody and everything. Nothing was perfect. And if it seemed too perfect, Mother said all you had to do was dig a little to uncover the nasty secrets. If you heard something enough, you'd believe it, adopt it, practice it. She wished somebody would tell her how to unlearn some things.

"Why don't you do something with your hair?"

"Mother, it's my hair, please stop telling me what to do with it." Nina said, driving around the block twice, trying to find a parking spot closer to the restaurant.

"Where are we going, anyway?"

"To eat, Mother. Are you hungry?"

"Not really."

"Well, you have to eat something. What are you in the mood for?"

"Sleep."

"Sleep? You sleep all day. What do you want to eat?"

"I don't know. I don't have much money on me."

"Mother, I'm taking you to lunch. Can you understand that?"

"Yes, but I don't want nobody doing me no favors. You know how people say, 'I did this and that for you, you owe me.' I don't wanna owe nobody nothin'."

"Get to the point, Mother. What is all this about?"

"Nothing, I'm just saying." Her mother paused, lighting up a cigarette that left Nina with the taste of it in her mouth. "Aww, never mind, you getting an attitude." She exhaled smoke.

"I'm not getting an attitude."

"Yes, you are."

Nina fought the urge to say, "Forget it!" She inhaled deeply.

"Let me see if I can fit in here." Nina maneuvered the car into a tight spot. The sooner they ate, the sooner she could get her mother back home and out of her hair.

The restaurant was empty except for an overweight man in the corner who ordered for four.

"Smoking or nonsmoking?" the waitress asked. Nina said, "Non."

"Smoking," her mother corrected.

"Smoking is fine," Nina said calmly.

The waitress walked them over to a table, placed down two menus, and came back with a couple of glasses of lukewarm water. Mother put out her cigarette in the glass of water and asked for another, with ice.

"So, how are you really doing, Mother?"

"Mother is fine, not to worry. And I don't need you and Troi fussing over me. I'm not helpless."

Nina ordered and ate mostly in silence as Mother went on about how her comrades still cheated at cards and how everything around the house needed fixing.

"Maybe I can find somebody who'd do little odds and ends for a fair price. What you think?" Nina asked.

"Whatever you want to do, you know I . . ."

"Yes, I know that you don't want nobody saying they did this and that for you."

"You making fun of me?"

"No, Mother, I'm not making fun."

Nina had so many questions for her mother, but there was one in particular that was just dying to get out. Her tongue swelled up in her mouth in expectation of asking. Her face mouthed the words with the expectation of thirty years.

"Mother, do you like kids?" Nina stuffed her mouth full of food so she could chew while deciding how to rebut her mother's comment.

"What you mean, do I like kids? I have two. What's wrong with you, asking a silly question like that?"

Nina chewed her food and dared not continue; she didn't want to fight. It had been a struggle getting her mother out of the house for lunch, and verbal wrestling was not how she wanted to remember their first outing in years. She looked at her mother. Her eyes looked as if she had done hard time in a dark jail cell, hardly seeing sunlight. They didn't show hope, promise, love, or concern.

The pause was purposeless. Her mother was a generic type of woman. She did exactly what you expected her to do: nothing.

"We going out next week, or is this a one-time thing?" Mother mumbled.

"We can. Would you like that?"

"Doesn't matter to me. Just don't tell me we're gonna do it then cancel at the last minute. How's the baby? Do you know?"

"She's fine, from what I can tell."

"Well, nobody can pick up the phone to see how I'm doing. I don't know what's wrong with this family."

"But, Mother, you just said . . ."

"I know, I said I don't need nobody, and I don't," her mother interjected.

Why'd her mother have to say *cancel?* It only made her think about a brother who was too stuck-up to pick up the phone and say, "Nina, I know I said we were going out, but I've got a deadline," anything. Troi always wanted Nina to meet somebody. Who knew why? People let you down. It was best not to expect anything. Nina had lived a life of disappointment; she wasn't about to spend her adulthood doing the same thing.

But it's cool, Nina thought. *I can buy my own coffee.* And the cheesy company, please . . . she could get that anywhere.

"You gonna answer me?"

"What?"

"Never mind, just take me home."

"Mother, I didn't hear you. Why are you being so difficult?" Nina whispered.

The waitress reappeared.

"Dessert?"

"No, that's okay," Nina said, answering for her and her screwy mother. Nina shoved the tip under the water glass and headed to the car.

The ride was stifled, and her mother didn't utter so much as a good-bye leaving the car.

"Bye, Mother."

"Uh-huh," she grunted.

Nina wasn't gonna let her mother dog her mood. She honestly didn't know how Troi put up with it. She didn't see what difference lunch or anything made anymore. Her mother wasn't about to change, she thought before she pulled off.

Nina figured that while she was out she'd swing by Shangrila. She didn't want to get deep into Troi's business, but she could at least see how her sister was doing. They used to have lunch together regularly until Daddy started calling Troi and everything just got all offtrack.

Nina walked into the shop, which wasn't really crowded, but was looking snazzier than she remembered. Carmen was always the first to greet anybody who walked through the door.

"Hey, Nina, how you doing?"

"I'm fine, tired, what's going on?"

"Oooh, Nina, look, look, look. You've gotta see this," Troi said, running from behind the display cabinet waving a magazine.

Nina looked at the pages, showing women posing with hairstyles that looked more like basket weaving. Looking to the left and right, there were women with too much makeup and captions underneath that read SHANGRILA SALON, NEW YORK CITY.

"Girl, I'm blowing up." Troi danced around.

"Awww, I'm proud of you, Troi."

"Yeah, I did it." Troi grinned.

"You need to make copies of the article to distribute."

"Yes, I know, I'm already on that." Troi nodded.

"Where you coming from anyway?" Troi looked suspicious.

"Lunch."

"Oooh. With who?"

Nina shook her head no. "I had lunch with Mother."

"Really?" Troi stiffened her neck and twisted her face.

"Yes."

"How did it go?"

"Girl, don't ask." Nina chuckled. "How's Vaughn?"

"What? He's mine, that's what he is," Troi said, convinced it was the God's honest truth. "Have you heard from that guy?"

"What guy?"

"Tim. From the mission and from church, you know."

"No, I haven't heard anything," Nina said, afraid to tell her sister that he stood her up twice.

"He'll call, don't worry. I got the feeling that he really likes you."

"Likes me, huh?"

"Yes, I could tell."

"And how are you so sure? Because, as idiotic as it sounds, men usually play hard to get for women they really like."

46

A long, drawn-out, phone-ringing, delivery-bringing, question-asking, looking, finding, ordering, opening, closing, packing, padding, editing, filing, writing, reviewing, researching day ended, and Tim had little or no energy left. He wanted to go home, strip down to his boxers, and sit in the shower to cool off. This weather was unpredictable. Tim had managed two bites of a burger and had tossed fries around in ketchup, but hadn't eaten enough to sustain himself. The phone interrupted his thoughts all day and he didn't have a second to focus on his appointment this evening, which might have been a good thing.

Tim knew he hadn't been the best man in the world. He didn't have the most radiant personality or the warmest pickup line. He had led women on and hurt them. They had given to him and he had taken. He had made his bed and, as the cynics would say, now he had to lie in it. There had to be a gentler way he could think of for getting what he deserved.

"You can leave now, get a head start on tomorrow," Tim's boss urged.

"Thanks, Abby."

She was kind and more helpful to him than he imagined he had been to her. But all he could think of was how he would be treated if people knew. Tim had already made up in his mind that he wouldn't tell Rochelle a thing. Not a word. She would worry and spend every second praying for him when it was evident that he had brought all of this down on himself.

Tim snatched up his portfolio and made it out of the office

quickly before the phone had an inkling of an idea to ring again. He was on the elevator and counted each floor down. He brushed past the people who were trying to get on as he was getting off. He stepped onto the curb and looked down the block, noticing people rushing past, in a hurry, always in a hurry to get someplace. They could be rushing to their own death, he thought.

Tim sat in his car and felt the heat. It made him uncomfortable. A bird tagged his windshield, and Tim flipped on the wipers to clean the glass. He bent his head and nodded to the swoosh of the wipers going back and forth. He mumbled a few words of encouragement to himself.

"Whatever it is, I'll deal with it."

He flipped down the visor and looked at his solemn face, pasted a smile on it, turned the key in the ignition, and headed to his destination. Traffic wasn't too bad considering. He thought about his boys and the night he got arrested. If someone had said that the chick sitting on the sofa was high-risk, he would have believed it. But Estella hadn't looked that bad when they were dating. And if he had managed to infect Michelle, well, she didn't look bad by a long shot either. He didn't know how he would break it to Sharon or Michelle.

It just went to show that nails, hair, and eye color played no part in STD status. Women went crazy over Tim, and he had his share of obsessions, he thought as he pulled into the available spot, thanked God for a space so close to the center, and wondered if that was where God's grace would end. A parking spot. Tim needed a lot more than that now. He was feeling things that sorry couldn't blanket or convey.

Tim took the elevator up to his doctor's appointment, checked in at the reception desk, and picked up a pamphlet. He tried not to look around the room. He was angry that he had forgotten his shades. He took a seat across from a couple of white men who appeared to be in their early twenties. They were chatty, as if their reason for being there was purely routine. He glanced momentarily at a black woman who looked good for her age, but he could tell she was near forty and was used to the finer things in life. She was wearing a brown blouse and brown slacks and had a pale blue sweater tied over her shoulders. She was separating her newspaper and putting it back together again.

"Eli Constantine. Constantine, Eli?"

The two white men looked at each other, and one rose to his feet as the other clasped his hand and patted it. It was as if he believed that his friend was going off to war and might never be seen again. Panic crept through Tim. He rehearsed how he would respond to his name being called in front of these people who were all here for the same thing and just pretended they weren't. He would pause and then, looking straight ahead, he would walk until he was behind closed doors. He didn't know why he had met Estella. Women for him had been a curse from day one. His looks were more trouble than they were worth. If he had the chance to do it over, man, he would just work, work, work. No women, no sex, and no unprotected encounters.

Perspiration had begun to soak the armpits of Tim's white dress shirt. He loosened the tie and unbuttoned his collar. He didn't make eye contact. People kept stepping off the elevator and checking in at the reception desk. It was obvious the late-night appointments were to disguise the fact of what they were all here for. There were posters hanging on the wall that had people smiling with captions about various sexually transmitted diseases. He squirmed in his seat, but tried to look confident, as if it were just a formality, and Estella had never called ranting about how he needed to go to the doctor.

He thought back to nights with Michelle, and how he'd gotten off on the enjoyment of it all, but failed to see the pleasure in any of it now. He failed to see the humor in how his knucklehead friends treated women.

There was a couple sitting on the far side of the clinic, almost as if they didn't want to be in the vicinity of everyone else. The whimpering cries of the woman could be heard across the waiting area. Everyone pretended not to hear. She wept softly at first, and then she got uncontrollable. The receptionist looked in their direction, but only momentarily.

"Agnes Pile. Pile, Agnes. Pile?"

The forty-something black woman folded up the remaining papers and fumbled with them until they all slid from her hands onto the floor. The white man seated near her bent down to assist her.

"I don't need your help!" She scowled.

He raised both hands, surrendering. She scooped the papers together and carried them to the trash. She stood there at the trash can, trying to stuff the papers into it without touching the sticky flip door. She marched over to the reception desk.

"Where do I go?"

The receptionist handed her a slip of paper and pointed down the hall. It was five after six. The clock on the wall was ticking slowly and making every minute that Tim was undiagnosed an excruciating pain.

It was thirty more minutes before he heard them call.

"Tim Richardson. Richardson, Tim."

When they called "Richardson," Tim paused and wanted to just continue sitting as if it weren't him they were calling; then whatever the results were, he could pretend they didn't exist. There was too much at stake here. There were Michelle and Sharon he'd have to face. He'd be labeled at least twenty undesirable references. But he tried to be brave. He retrieved the paper from the receptionist. There was a long sterile hallway with five doors on each side. He passed a young black woman no older than twenty-one in the hall, who made eye contact only for a moment. He knew her, he thought.

Tim went into the room marked *10* and had a seat in the chair facing the desk. There was a poster that depicted the parts of the human skeletal body. There were boxes of condoms piled up on the filing cabinets next to the window. Dozens of pamphlets and brochures explaining everything from herpes and other STDs to a diagram of how to put on a condom.

A tall slender female in a lab coat walked into the room, around the desk, and pulled in her seat. Tim looked up, surprised, catching her gaze.

"Mr. Richardson? Would you be more comfortable with a man?" she inquired with a slight smile.

Tim cleared his throat. "I'm fine."

"Okay, hello, I'm . . ." the worker said.

Could have been a social worker, but Tim wasn't listening. He was listening for key words. Just like a pregnancy test: positive or negative. He just wanted to cut to the chase. Enough with the greetings and social exchange, he just wanted to know the results, sign a release, and be up out of there.

"Now, Mr. Richardson, you know that statistically speaking . . . and we want to assure you that no matter what the outcome . . . we also have counseling for the stress involved in dealing with . . . and family members can also sit in on the sessions with your permission."

Tim was panting like a dog who had run miles in the sun and desperately needed a drink.

"Are you okay?"

"Uh, yeah, I'm fine."

"Okay."

Tim readjusted himself in the chair.

"The bloodwork you took on . . . testing you for the presence of the herpes virus . . . we just need you to sign here giving us permission to release the results."

Tim took the pen out of his inside pocket instead of the one that was extended and signed his name, glanced at the calendar on the wall behind him, and scribbled the date.

"Mr. Richardson, the results of your test to detect the presence of the herpes virus in your system are *negative.*"

Tim's head fell to his chest, exhausted from worry, wanting to cry. He rejoiced in his head. *Negative* was all he'd needed to hear. Tears welled up in the corners of his eyes, his heart settled back in his chest, his shoulders relaxed, and his breathing slowly went back to normal. He felt reborn in the sense that his life wasn't over; it was, in fact, just beginning.

All the tension that had built up in his head, neck, and back was slowly released like the ocean's tide washing away sorrows. God had spared him, granting what he had asked, and it was time he did some thanking. The counselor went on and on about condoms, safe sex, and how it was important to protect himself.

"This is a copy for your records, Mr. Richardson." Tim folded up the paper in four and put it down in his pocket.

Tim made his way home quickly with a pocketful of condoms. He dodged through the light traffic. He just wanted to get home and pour himself a nice cool drink, turn on some music, and thank God.

"He will never leave thee, nor forsake thee." Tim chuckled uncontrollably.

That's what Rochelle was always trying to get Tim to remember. He knew it, but it was a lot easier to believe when you had a testimony to tell. Testimonies amazed people.

"I was broke, now I have a job. I thought that a woman gave me herpes, and now I have evidence that I'm clean."

Tim had so much to be thankful for.

Tim walked into his building and checked his mailbox. It was stuffed full, mostly because he had begun receiving rejection slips from the submissions he'd sent in. He reached in and pulled out a bundle of folded mail. On the way up he opened an envelope. This one company was telling him that they only considered agented submissions. He balled up the paper.

His final grades were in. They had come in a manila envelope stamped NYU TISCH SCHOOL OF THE ARTS. He tore open the envelope, more excited at the fact that he had completed another semester than wondering what his grade was. His latest idea flowed. Made him contemplate chivalry. A well-balanced man could handle a job, a relationship, and other outside interests. If he couldn't, then he had a whole other set of issues, Tim believed.

Tim walked into his apartment and pulled off his shirt and tie. He poured a glass of orange juice while dialing Rochelle's simultaneously.

"Hey, baby boy. What's up?"

"Nothing much, working, that's all."

"You need to meet somebody. All work and no play . . ."

"I don't need to meet nobody. Let me do things my way."

"Sure, whatever you say. Just find somebody your own age. Not like Troi's sister. She's too old for you."

"What are you saying? Isn't Carl older than you are?"

"Yes, but he's a man, it's different."

She didn't know what she was talking about. The more Rochelle said that, the more it made him want to call Nina and leave a message.

"You need a nice, petite girl. Someone a little more fitness-conscious."

"You're tiring, Rochelle . . ."

"Well, I'm sorry."

"Yeah. Listen, I just called you to find out when bible study is."

"Bible study? Tomorrow night at seven. You going?"

"Yes, that's why I'm asking." He chuckled at his sister's unreserved attempt to pry into his spiritual life.

"Can you swing by and pick me up?"

"Maybe."

"Why maybe?"

"Because I'm not sure where I'll be coming from."

"Okay, well, can you call me and let me know?"

"I sure will."

"Bible study. That's a thought, brother dear. You'll meet some sisters that are serious about the Lord in bible study."

"I'm not going to bible study to meet women, I'm going there to study the bible."

"Don't be so touchy. God doesn't want us to be so deep we can't have relationships. Relax."

"I am relaxed. Talk to you later, Rochelle."

Tim tried to whip himself up something tasty. He was tired of his sister thinking that single wasn't happy. He was content, he lied again. But seriously, he had been contemplating changing his life into something more meaningful after the whole DWI-STD thing. Tim had subscribed to *Gourmet* and *Saveur* magazines and watched *Emeril Live* on TV now almost everyday. He always did want to learn how to cook those exotic dishes and make swiggly lines with sauces and decorate the plate with the ruffled parsley that no one ever ate.

Tim envisioned having someone to cook for. But that would go along with Rochelle's theory. He didn't know. Maybe he could find someone and they could label it friendship until it was deemed otherwise. But then the next thing he knew, they would be exclusive in her mind, and she'd be planning weekend getaways in which he never displayed interest. He wondered what Nina was really all about. Without all the fluff and babble. He wondered if caring really was her biggest fault. He didn't have time for all the tap-dancing. He'd find out. There'd be other times. He'd call her tomorrow or whenever he good and well felt like it.

47

Troi woke up earlier than she usually did. She had found it extremely difficult to sleep last night. It wasn't humid or damp, she just kept waking up throughout the night, even though she still had hours left to indulge. She sat at the breakfast nook, replaying her vivid dreams in her mind. But they were more like flashbacks from the other night with Vaughn. She'd been having a lot of those lately. Her mind was on spin cycle, and her heart, well, it followed. She was making a list of things she had to do. Lately it seemed that she was beginning to really feel what it was like to run a business. She felt useful, intelligent, and sexy again. But she didn't want to be hurt.

She had made flyers with coupons, giving students a discount on Wednesdays, and a wash-and-set special for eighteen dollars on Mondays. And with her shop given kudos in *Hype Hair,* she figured that her salon would be just like Sylvia's. People would come way up to Harlem simply because of the prestige of it all, just to say that they had been.

Troi flipped over the worship tape and browsed through the course catalog from the city college. She had almost mustered enough nerve to register. She was really thinking of doing this. It wasn't like she wanted a career and briefcase and all that, she just wanted something that let people know that she knew her stuff. Marketing. That would be appropriate for her business. Maybe an art class or something like that. She could take a midday course. She was sure that the girls in the shop would be more than eager to cover for her in her absence.

Morning had held her captive in her thoughts. The coffee was dripping and she couldn't wait. She wasn't fully awake until she had a cup. She knew the delectable aroma woke the whole building each day. It was a morning ritual that she figured they were used to by now. She only had enough ground for a cup and a half of coffee, but she added extra water and would have to play innocent when Vaughn wondered why the coffee was weaker than usual.

Troi was reading Ephesians 5:25 and trying to spread her butter evenly on her toast. She then pulled the laundry bag from the hall closet and put a load of white clothes into the machine. It was like everything Dakoda owned was soiled long before the end of the week. Troi toyed with the thought of having another child. Silently she forgave herself for even contemplating using a child as a pawn to get Vaughn back. Looking back now, she hadn't even needed that. As she sat by the window looking out at the graying skies, she wondered if it would rain before or after she got to work.

Today was Wednesday, and though the shop's clientele was steadily increasing almost to overwhelm Shangrila, she'd go in, do some heads, check on her merchandise, and make it her business to be at bible study tonight. She had a few questions, and furthermore, she couldn't wait to put their little rumorfest about Vaughn to rest by walking in there with him, arm in arm. She hoped that Vaughn would go with her. He had said he loved her the other night, and his presence back in the apartment again agreed with that. Her heart agreed with that. Her mind, well, it always had some doubts.

She had sat by the window early this morning around three and just wondered where they would be a year from now. If they only had one year to love each other, how would they do it, why would they do it? Where would they go and what would they experience? She just wanted them to blend, mesh, melt together. A family. That's all she wanted to be. Hearing the key in the door around seven P.M. and knowing it was her husband, and that they could unwind and enjoy the evening together, reading the paper, watching a movie, or balancing the checkbook, that was all she ever wanted.

She had known brothers who put more importance on a pair of brand-name sneakers than a woman. There were men who'd knowingly prefer to make the women in their lives second-class citizens. Far be it from them to see a movie or be entertained at a Broadway theater with their girl. Nina did it alone; Troi never was the alone type. She didn't feel women had to go there. But that was just her opinion. All she wanted to do was hatch a man who possessed a driving curiosity of what affection was. A man who wasn't afraid to cook for her. A man just like Vaughn.

Troi found that there were also men who would polish and spit-shine their car up to an egg-white finish, vacuum their carpets inside out, and buff their tires religiously. But these same men didn't have a spare moment to pull their lady aside and say, "Hey, I like how we are," or drop them a card with an acronym for love scribbled under the poetic verse. She couldn't deal with that. Troi had chosen Vaughn because he was different. Nothing like those scrubs or whatever the hip-hoppers were calling each other nowadays. True, all men had their individual issues, but she couldn't deal with cheap. She was high maintenance, time-wise. All the Madison women were. Men usually had to find that out the hard way. Then either they put *H*s on their chests and handled it, or they had to cry uncle.

Troi remembered, growing up, the men who said that women came a dime a dozen themselves came cheaper than dirt. She'd passed these brothers who sat out of the side of their cars all day, propositioning every woman with a pair of legs to come over and talk. Then there were the ones who circled you on bicycles. Why they did that she never knew. They needed some umph, some get-up-and-go. The desperation was sickening. And when they did manage to snag a sister who was about something, they fumbled.

Troi poured Vaughn the remainder of the coffee as he mumbled something to her and shuffled from the bedroom into the bathroom. He walked back into the kitchen with his toothbrush poking out of his mouth, opening and closing cabinets.

"What do you need?"

"We have any baking soda?" he asked, holding his head back trying not to dribble.

She handed him the carton and he nodded.

"Can you dress Dakoda?" Troi managed, over her worship music.

Troi heard the shower running and thought back to that morning not far removed from her memory. He had given her a token of him to take with her to work that day. He had lathered her and made her feel more desirable than she had been feeling in a good while. *He is a man and he loves me,* Troi convinced herself. She took a swallow of her coffee, which was lukewarm now, rolled up the course catalog, and put it down in her bag for work.

The shower shut off and Vaughn emerged, drying his glistening head and wearing the towel around his shoulders. Troi's eyes were drawn to his chest.

"What's wrong?" he said, breaking her concentration.

"Nothing at all." She smirked.

He snatched the towel off of his shoulders, held it at both ends, spun it around, and let it pop.

"Stop, Vaughn. It's too early to play."

"Stop, it's too early to play," he mocked, reaching for his cup and taking a swallow. "Why this coffee taste like this?"

"Taste like what?" Troi asked, almost giggling.

Vaughn was wearing a crisp white shirt with one of the ties Troi loved from Bachrach. Dakoda was drinking her juice and saying words now. "Ma-ma," and "Da-da," but that was it. They were running late this morning. Troi usually liked to be by the shop at eight o'clock, but Vaughn wanted the car today, and after he dropped off the baby, then he'd drop off Troi. It was almost nine. Traffic was blocking most intersections, and she could hear the usual sirens in the distance. Vaughn double-parked and made it in and out of his momma's house in record time. She had managed to wrap him up a muffin, and he was squashing up a paper cup that probably held juice. The rain fell softly.

"What's wrong?" Vaughn asked, looking at Troi's displeased face.

"The streets are just so congested."

"Let's go through the cross streets then," Vaughn said, sensing the traffic was getting heavier.

At the light he tapped his finger on the dashboard and fiddled with the radio.

"Pass me a tape." He smirked, with his hand extended.

He shoved it in, adjusted the volume, and tried to relax, but the instrumental didn't manage to calm him a bit. The fire engines clanged down the street, closer and closer, blanging their horns and police cars raced by in twos.

"Make room or you'll get a ticket," the officer announced on the horn.

The light changed and they pulled the car over to the side, pausing only for the fire trucks to pass.

"Let me off at the corner up there," Troi said impatiently.

"You sure?"

"Yeah, I'll be fine." She blinked repeatedly as a hint of smoke got in her eyes.

"I'll see you later," Troi said as she leaned over and kissed her husband good-bye, just as she had always done when they had first started dating. "Bible study tonight. You going?"

He nodded. Vaughn pulled off, beeping the horn good-bye, and Troi walked, silently counting her blessings. She was up to three. She had thanked God for her baby girl, her husband, and a nice apartment. This wasn't it. There was more to come; she just knew it.

Life was full of surprises. Troi was thinking to herself that a little bump in the road wasn't such a bad thing. When she turned the corner, she could feel the pressure of the heat. It was like opening an oven and almost getting your eyebrows singed off. If she had been walking a little faster, the heat would have lifted her off of her feet.

A fire marshall shoved her back away from the glass that shattered just as she stumbled backward.

"You can't walk here. Block off this side, now!" the fire marshall ordered someone in a blue uniform and motioned Troi to the other side of the street.

The water gushed forcefully into the air from the fire engine's hose. Troi backed away and crossed the street, startled. On the other side of the street, a woman shrieked, "Oh, my God!" As Troi paused and looked up into the thick gray smoke clouds, she was confused and disoriented for a moment. She blinked as the smoke burned her eyes. She tried to focus. Her mouth hung open as she recognized that leaping and lunging from her blessed Shangrila were rabid flames, which now totally engulfed the adjoining shops in the building and threatened to send the whole structure tumbling down onto the street.

It wasn't just the awnings on fire, it was a literal inferno eating everything in the shop like the jaws of a hungry lion who had meat between his teeth, but still surveyed the fields for more.

Troi's hands trembled and she stood with her mouth quivering with disbelief.

"Oh, Jesus, no!"

Troi sank to her knees on the wet splintered concrete. She held her distorted face in her hands, shaking and asking over and over and over again, "Why?" The crowd of onlookers grew as people stood looking down at her, confused as to why she was in so much pain and taking a mishap so personally.

Carmen ran over from the crowd, pushing past the lookers, and reached out, knelt, and held Troi in her arms, brushing her dampened hair away from her face, rocking and reassuring her that everything would be okay.

"You have insurance, right?" Carmen whispered.

"Yes, but . . ."

"Don't worry, God will fix it. He will fix it. Isn't that what you always say?" Carmen consoled.

The rain came down slowly, not impeding the flames much. People stood by, watching for a remnant of what still stood, waiting for it to crumble or fall. Troi could hear the ripping sound of the walls and the hiss of the water sizzling.

"Oh, that's a shame," someone said.

And it was. It really was. There were no news cameras or flashbulbs now. Cameras had no need to come to this part of town. Troi's hopes and future were in every tile and on every shelf in that shop. Pain had always seemed to find her. No matter where she was, pain lurked, waiting for its moment to come and devastate her. At this point she stood numb, emotionless, with her face washed by the rain, which was making a useless attempt to aid in extinguishing the fire, and wondering if this was all that life was offering her.

She didn't know what she would do next. She felt isolated.

"I'll be okay, Carmen," Troi said, and all she could think now was that she'd forgotten to take the clothes out of the washing machine.

48

Vaughn knew the source of his mood, but he knew that he had no choice but to go with Troi to the church. It was the husbandly thing to do. He knew the eyes would burn holes in him, wondering all sorts of things about him. Most of all about his sexuality. Troi had told him what that woman had said. He figured people knew; they would know eventually, and he couldn't help that and he didn't care. He had to live. So he had begun preparing himself for their holier-than-thou condolences since he, too, had received the call at work.

Troi's beloved Shangrila had been diminished to sooty cinders and the job of comforting her had been foisted onto him. Troi had initially thought they were holding bible-study classes, but they had organized an emergency prayer for Sister Singleton instead.

"When one of our own is in need, we have to be there to pick up the pieces," the pastor's wife said.

Vaughn's momma was there, looking as plump as ever. His father had a brotherhood meeting. Vaughn furrowed his brow at how his momma always covered for his father. It was sickening how gullible she was. Vaughn could see right through them all.

Sam had heard about the shop from momma, no doubt, and he came all the way from Jersey to grace them with his presence. Sam was embracing Troi and saying something about how she would get through all of this. Vaughn knew he was making reference to him in his "all of this" statement. But let them talk until their tongues fell out of their mouths.

Carla, Nina, and a bunch of friends and girls from the shop

showed up. They all gathered together, crying and blubbering as if somebody had died. Rochelle was there with her six-figure husband and her unemployed brother. She still had her nose up in the air, like she was trying not to drown in the filth that the common people muddled through. She was still as happy as a clam, doing and giving. There was no way Rochelle would give up ties to all that money her husband made. And the Unemployed Mack must have been who her brother thought he was, strolling into church after all this time.

The drama of it all was enough for two Academy Awards. Best Actress in a Tragedy would go to Troi's mother, who hadn't set foot in a church in almost a decade, but instantly felt the spirit of something moving through her uncontrollably the minute she crossed the threshold. She was obviously drunk, and was feeling nothing more than Jack Daniels making his daily rounds.

Best Supporting Actress at an Emergency Prayer Meeting would have to be a three-way tie: the Hallelujah Girls. They made empathy an art form, complete with tears on cue, so they'd get a handclap for that, too. Incredible. People didn't amaze him, just caught him off guard sometimes.

Vaughn didn't want to be here. It should have been evident. His face could have given that away for free if anyone stopped to take a peek. Troi's tragedy was just forcing him to stay in a place where he no longer felt drawn. No longer felt comfortable. No longer felt needed. But he couldn't leave now. Troi's dream was burnt to a crisp, and as the husband, he knew they expected him to pick up all the pieces and put them back together again like Humpty Dumpty or some other nursery rhyme. They didn't know how the fire started, but they were investigating. *I hope the investigation doesn't take months,* Vaughn whispered to himself. Vaughn knew that if he left Troi now, then he might as well have struck the match.

Vaughn sat off to the side, flipping through a bible while everyone hugged Troi and kept reassuring her that God would never leave nor forsake her. He wondered if that was true. He also wondered if you could love someone yet not want to be with them. Love was confusing. Love was like a cottony cloud in a vivid blue sky, taking shape. It looked different to everybody.

He wanted to tell Troi the truth. He wanted to tell her everything. He wanted to say, "I can't love you like I should. The other night was the other night. It just sort of happened. I can't promise that forever." But instead, he had grinned in the moonlight and she'd felt that she had a place that welcomed her—his arms and his heart.

"There's your friend Tim," Troi told Nina, with total disregard for her own current situation.

Nina was smirking as the Mack approached and offered what Vaughn knew was a superficial apology. He could see his hands trying to be tender, gentle. Brothers like him were always trying to be a player. But Nina was smiling, so it seemed that he had accomplished what he'd set out to do. Made her victim number whatever. Nina had always been the silly one, and Vaughn had had enough of this whole scene. He wanted to get some fresh air. The stench of people being overly polite was stifling.

"Vaughn? Vaughn, where are you going?" Troi approached her husband's defensiveness.

"I need to get some air."

"But the service is going to start any minute. He's just going to say a few words, it really shouldn't take long at all."

"Listen, I need air . . ."

"C'mon, Vaughn, can you just do it for me?" She tried to convince him. Vaughn wasn't impressed by the appearance of it all. "This is too much for me," he mumbled under his breath, making his way back into the pew and sitting attentively next to his wife.

He looked around and took in the rich hues of the burgundy and gold that lined the chairs and the sections of the pulpit. This place was decorated for royalty. It was too fancy to be a movie theater. *Yeah, a sanctuary,* Vaughn thought. He tried to distract himself to no avail.

The organ played and Pastor stood solemnly, but not discouraged. He embraced the microphone like a banana about to be peeled and spoke directly, with purpose.

"Members, family and friends. We are here today because there is a need."

"Amen," somebody was hollering already.

"We never know what life will bring us. Each day is a mystery, and our only consolation is that if we live in God's will, God will see fit to bless us accordingly."

Vaughn heard footsteps, thick and hard from the back of the church, and turned to observe Troi's father entering the church with a woman who was dressed a little less conservatively than was appropriate for present company. Vaughn pretended not to notice. Others weren't so kind.

"We need the Singleton family to know that God's hand is on

their situation, and that he will not suffer the righteous to be moved."

"Amen!"

"We need them to know that no matter what the day brings, God is faithful. Can we stand? I'd just like us to say a little prayer for them."

"Glory." The organ accompanied.

"Brother and Sister Singleton, please stand," Pastor instructed with his hand extended.

Troi stood, smoothing down her blouse. She looked down at Vaughn still sitting and pulled on him to stand beside her as he had done on their wedding day all those years ago. He pulled away from her.

"C'mon now, don't pull on my clothes, you know I don't like that," he whispered harshly.

Troi smirked and tried to appear unscathed. Vaughn brushed off his jacket to smooth the wrinkles. He got to his feet on his own accord, but couldn't look his pastor in the eye, so he handed Troi the keys to the car and excused himself, brushing past his wife, past the judgmental faces, the high shine of the pews and down the aisle and out the door.

He was positive that Troi had never been so embarrassed in all her life.

"Brother Singleton, God is with you still," Pastor said down the aisle after Vaughn. "God is faithful."

Vaughn didn't want to hear about miracles or a situation that would make it difficult if not impossible for him to leave now. He couldn't leave his wife and child hungry. No food and no means of support?

He stood in front of the church, sure that Troi wasn't the kind of woman who would come running out after him. They were singing a song now, something about the walls of Jericho. Vaughn surveyed the streets for a pay phone. The only one across the street was occupied, with another person standing off to the side waiting to use it.

He couldn't believe his day. Not only had Troi's world fallen apart, today they had given him notice that they were transferring him out of the office. Just kicking him out. It didn't matter that customers knew him by name. Jill had verbally delivered the news herself, along with a sealed envelope containing a letter that was cc'd to the main branch.

"I'm not one to gossip, but some of your coworkers have concerns about, let's just say 'your preference,'" she'd said. "A coworker, who I will allow to be nameless, mentioned the fact that you propositioned him for 'a place to sleep,' may have been how you put it, I'm not sure. I understand that this is a delicate situation for you, but we have to do what's best for the team as a whole," she'd babbled on.

Vaughn hadn't had the presence of mind to nod.

"So, you realize, in a situation like this," she'd begun, flinging her overprocessed blond hair away from her lying lips, "it really would not be wise of you to think of filing a discrimination or harassment suit, or any other type of legal action, as you, too, could very well be brought up on charges of harassment or soliciting." He'd shaken his head in disbelief, nauseated by the hint of satisfaction than she had regarding the situation. Vaughn was silently defeated.

His whole life was a challenge. He knew that wherever you went, your reputation went with you. They didn't care that you worked hard. If your coworkers couldn't get along with you, workloads suffered. So, he knew that he needed to spend the next week faxing résumés so that he could leave this company on the best terms that he could and still use it for a reference. Vaughn's stomach was making audible noises. He was hungry and his stomach was in knots, but he couldn't eat. He was angered more at the fact that this type of thing still went on than that it had happened to him.

People discriminated all the time. There were still areas where housing was predominantly white. It was like lockdown. You would not get in unless they said so. They kept it that way. Maybe his father was right.

Vaughn thought about how every eye in the office would be on him when he went to gather his things, just as they had been on him as he'd exited the church. He would be the target for ungodly remarks and condescending thoughts. Maybe he'd just have them mail his things in a box. He didn't dare go back there. Vaughn mentally fought the taste that the thought brought to his lips. The bitterness of an ice-cold beer.

He was dangerous enough without alcohol in his system. The last thing he needed was to get filthy drunk and act out with no remembrance of a solitary action the next morning. He would use every ounce of strength he could muster to get through today and then tomorrow and then the next day. One day at a time. It was all he could do at this point. It was all he could ever do, he thought, rubbing his head, then shaking it in disbelief.

He couldn't pretend that he was empowered by the fact that his desires separated him from his wife. He couldn't be thankful of desires that defiled his bed and his wedding vows. It wasn't as easy as the outspoken ones made it seem. The thoughts of one day being normal and untempted lingered.

Vaughn crossed the street and dug deep down in his pocket for some change. He stood behind the man yelling, "Whadayamean?" into the receiver.

"Can you tell her to come to the phone? I just want to ask her a question," the man pleaded, before rage had him slamming the receiver over and over again onto the cradle. Sanity then returned and allowed him to turn and see Vaughn waiting behind him, almost patiently.

Vaughn jingled the change in his hand.

"Sorry, man."

"It's cool," Vaughn said.

Vaughn stepped into the half booth as the man walked away talking to himself. He dialed the numbers that he knew he shouldn't have memorized, but he had. On the third ring, in response to "hello," he asked, "Are you busy?"

He paused. "I'm in the city. I can meet you at 86th and Third Avenue," he said, making it sound more like a question. "I know it's short notice, but it's kinda important." He paused again. "Can we talk about that when you get there?"

Vaughn placed the receiver down, closed his eyes, and rested his head momentarily on the phone booth. He opened his eyes, looking around curiously. His eyes followed someone up the church steps. He took a deep cleansing breath and headed over to Third Avenue to get a bite to eat and meet Tracie.

49

Nina had done something with her hair finally. Big deal. They called them *twists* and had used tiny little butterfly clips for which the woman at the shop where she got her hair done had convinced her she wasn't too old.

"It's summer. You must look festive, bright, radiant," she'd said.

Nina had done her hair not because her mother had always commented snidely about it, but because she had a date and wanted to be different, new. She never felt the need to doll herself up. She didn't know why. All she knew was that if this man who practically begged her to give him a third chance didn't show up, then she would not only give him a piece of her mind, but she'd . . . "Never mind," she said out loud, shaking her head. She didn't want to think violent thoughts.

Nina figured she would definitely tell Troi about the date, but she didn't dare tell Troi that she'd had her hair done. If she did, Troi would not only be upset because Shangrila was now ash and soot, but because she had been fiending to do something with Nina's hair for the past six years. She wouldn't understand why her sister hadn't given her that pleasure. She didn't know how to tell Troi that she needed to make her own decisions, and that her hair was something that she'd keep to herself like a personal preference.

Nina was wearing a pink tube-top dress with thin straps, and the woman in the salon had given her a tiny compact full of glitter that she said Nina should brush sparingly across her shoulders. Her dress wasn't too short and her heels, well, they were almost four inches high. She could walk comfortably and sit with her legs crossed without exposing too much thigh. Thigh. That was her test. It didn't matter what the dress looked like while she was standing up; it was sitting down that counted most. She smoothed out her dress and admired her pastel nails, which were subtle enough to make more of a statement of patience than flamboyance.

But despite common sense telling her not to be a fool three times, it was almost eight P.M. and she was still on her first cup of coffee, thinking about how she could feign interest. She was almost at the point where whether they went out or not really didn't matter anymore. She was excited to a degree only because she hadn't been out in a while. Going out with Derek never counted. She might not have been thin and model-like with sucked-in cheeks and a tight belly, but she had a little something going on. That much she knew.

Nina's only major problem now was trying to restrain herself from being inconspicuously drawn to the creamy chocolate-drizzled danish in the display case that sat between what looked like a cheese danish and an apple turnover. She sat convincing herself that she didn't need it, when he walked into the room like music, bearing flowers that could have been orchids, but were slightly wilted, so she couldn't really tell. She stood up and tilted her head a little as he leaned over to peck her cheek.

"Hey," he said.

His breath was fresh and she nodded at the two points she'd give him for that gesture.

"Have you been waiting long?"

"No, I'm still on my first cup," she said, looking at him as if to say, *so far so good.*

In her mind she was strong. In her thoughts she would not allow him to conquer her or dominate the conversation. But the minute she opened her mouth, she knew it would render her into submission.

"So, how have you been?" he asked, pulling up a chair.

"I'm fine, you know, trying to be there for my sister. What about you?"

He nodded in exchange for the words *I'm fine, too.* She knew that already, because he was fine. But she'd never tell him. He was well versed, and unlike most men she had dated, after fifteen minutes into the conversation he was still making sense.

She fought the urge to respond to him in a way that might have reassured him that he was in control. There were men in Nina's life who had been dismissed for less than what Tim had put her through. But she'd allowed him another chance, so he'd better make it worth her while.

Tim was nothing like Derek. Derek was someone who didn't compliment her, but instead dismissed her Ph.D. as nothing more than a piece of paper that any idiot who could read a book could obtain. He was a derelict working at a country club to schmooze unsuspecting women into thinking that he had some actual financial connection there. The whole thing was Shelby's fault. If it weren't for her, Nina knew that she'd never ever have found herself at the country club trying to fit in to begin with.

But she closed her eyes and shook her head; she wouldn't dampen this evening with thoughts of Derek. That was a closed chapter, and she didn't backtrack.

"So, how are your studies coming along?" Nina asked.

"Oh, great. I've really been inspired lately. So, I'm just going with the flow, you know. I'm working at a company where the owners are teaching me the film business inside out. It maybe be a vehicle to help me launch my own one day."

"Is that what you want? Your own movie company?"

"Perhaps," he said, grinning.

"How about the mission? Is your service time up there, or are you still doing your weekly stint?" Nina questioned, trying not to giggle.

"I'm still there." He smiled. "Got a week to go. But I'm hanging in there. I tell you one thing, it's teaching me two lessons."

"Ohh, what's that?" Nina teased.

"One, to work hard so I'm never put in a situation where I'm homeless and hungry, and secondly . . ."

"Don't drink and drive," they both said in unison, laughing loudly.

"Would you like a refill?" he asked, noticing her cup and the cold, thin white film that had formed on top of it.

Nina was elated that Tim was stylish enough to know that polka-dot shirts were out of fashion, and individual enough not to think that wearing a sweatervest in the summertime was a cool way to show off his muscles. They talked music, mostly jazz. They had that in common.

"Ever been to the Blue Note?"

"Once, I think," she said. "Years ago."

She started to tell him that she didn't go out much, but she didn't want him to think that she was boring or, worse yet, antisocial.

Like any gentleman would, he asked what she'd like to do this evening. Dozens of thoughts raced through her head.

"Dinner is fine," she said. "You have any place in mind?"

He named two restaurants, and she picked the one that was easiest to pronounce. She stood up and tried to smooth out her dress the best she could and manage her flowers at the same time.

"I'll get those for you." Nina handed him the bundle of wilting flowers.

"They're not wilted," he said, reading her mind. "They're supposed to hang low like that."

"Oh, really now?"

"Seriously." He nodded.

Over a colorful dinner in a Mexican restaurant, they both talked about their families and his desire to one day own a dog. In between the distraction of the red flashing chili pepper–shaped lights, he was saying how he never thought that he'd lose his parents in a car accident. Nina offered her condolences.

"It was tragic." He nodded. "Took me years to get over it. I'm not even sure I'm over it now."

He said that he knew people died. It was part of life, but he just never thought that it would affect him the way it had.

"How long ago was that?"

"Not long enough," was his response.

As the giant parrot piñata dangled overhead, Nina was saying how her family was hardly ideal, and that her father had left her mother two months ago, and how it was more traumatic for her little sister than her, but it didn't seem to change the family structure much at all.

"My mother still drinks, and my father, he's still hardly ever around, even now," she said, trying not to sound like she was competing for empathy.

The conversation lightened up as Tim told Nina about how his sister, Rochelle, was always trying to fix him up on blind dates.

"Yeah? My girlfriend, too. Her name is Shelby. She's always trying to drag me somewhere, like I must have somebody. I choose who I date."

"I'm with you on that one. I can pick my own. I don't want somebody else's ideal."

He smiled and she bit her bottom lip, feeling a little like she had started ranting.

She wasn't sure which, but one of them tossed the idea of a movie around. It was refreshing that Tim didn't have a problem seeing an African-American film that didn't have a euphemism for sex as the title, or an independent film either, for that matter. It said a lot about him really being into this film thing and being able to appreciate the industry as a whole, so she gave him an extra point. He was up to three now, and she was taking in the scenery, but mostly him.

Through the movie, he didn't constantly try to upstage the filmmaker's ideas, but instead enjoyed her company, interrupting only long enough to place popcorn in her mouth. *He's pulling out all the stops,* she thought every time his fingers neared her mouth.

The movie wasn't all it was cracked up to be, more appropriate for video rental, but it was his choice, and she dared not complain unless he wasn't enjoying himself either.

"Have you ever been on the Staten Island Ferry?" he whispered.

"Oh, goodness. Yes. When I was ten. It was a school trip with my class."

On the Staten Island Ferry they discussed how horrible the movie really was like two critics, pulling apart each scene and the dialogue, of which there was hardly any.

"How does a Siamese twin fall in love with a prostitute?" Tim asked.

"I don't know, but I think that when they allow men to be more human in movies, it draws you into it deeper and quicker. I mean, we expect men to be tough, so a man with such harsh dialogue is not exactly ingenious."

"Yes, I get you."

"Right, because, I mean, if a man is tender, generous, the women will fall for him every time."

"Say that again."

"What?"

"What you just said."

"The women will fall for him every time?"

"You really should act. I think you'd be good."

"Act? Please." Nina blushed, covering her face.

"No, serious. You have that voice and that presence," he said.

"You keep saying that. I'm not one for the spotlight though."

"Well, it's just like you're saying, those who want the spotlight would be better not to have it and vice versa." She thought she knew what he was getting at.

Nina was remembering one guy she'd dated. He'd thought she would love him forever just because he had soft feet. Occasionally he'd shared a kind word, and been under the impression he could talk her into anything. He'd always talk about what he had, what he did, or things that he had accomplished so long ago that they didn't even bear repeating. And Nina, throughout the whole relationship, had been determined that she could make him over into a caring, loving man who would eventually marry her, or be good for someone else, if not her. *How wrong our concepts of people can be,* she thought.

Nina felt at ease with Tim. He had a way of allowing her to unravel herself in the conversation without feeling vulnerable. He was generous in the compliment department.

"I like your shoes," he said, as they watched the water spray on deck and the moon dance over the tepid water, which made her feel more relaxed as she watched the skyline in the distance.

"My shoes? Really?"

"Yeah."

On deck they faced each other.

"I'm sorry about the other two attempts," Tim apologized finally. "You are very nice, and I'd definitely like to see you again."

"Sounds like a plan. Let's just see how it goes," she said, surprising herself.

Departing the bright orange boat after several trips back and forth in a melodic rhapsody, they strolled back to Nina's car, and he allowed her to walk a few paces ahead of him, so he could watch her from behind, she imagined. She stopped at her car and turned to face him.

"I had a lovely evening, Tim."

"Cool," he said.

"Me, too. Pick another word."

"Exceptional?"

"Another."

"Charming?"

"Yeah, I like that. I had a charming evening, too."

She closed her eyes, totally swept up in the moment, and leaned forward, taking the liberty of kissing him first. His response made her initially shy away. She felt embarrassment color her face.

"I'm sorry," she started.

She wasn't really the aggressive type. She didn't understand what about the moment had her feeling the need to press her lips to his. But it was almost evident from his response alone that he didn't much care for the aggressive type, and that she'd end up a footnote in the story of his life. Just then he reached for her hand and stroked the back of it gently with his finger, and she held her breath, as he assumed his place as the man and showed her how it was done.

Tim was a brother with lips so ripe, they were lingering on hers, and their rhythm was in sync with the sighs that escaped her. Tim was up to nine points now, because this kiss was worth at least six. She was thinking that it might even be enough to forgive him for his past transgressions. But she wasn't trying to go there with Tim. She enjoyed herself, and she just wanted him to know that. After all, she wasn't about to arm wrestle all three Hallelujah Girls for one of the only two available men in church. That just wasn't her style.

50

Tim had a compulsive need to control every facet of his life. He didn't want women to think he was playing games. Don't call too much, hold back on the interest, water down the concern. That had been his way of life forever. People whom he couldn't control, he had no need for. Looking back on his life, he knew it was true. Michelle. He wasn't bragging, because he knew it would eventually become a major issue with Nina. She was the same type of woman Michelle was, only a little more accessible. He didn't want to be detached from people about whom he cared. He knew if his momma were here, she'd sit him down and give him a stern talking to. He'd learn his lesson then for sure.

His momma would tell him to be real, be honest with people. Holding back was like being fraudulent and putting people on hold, and, well, that was just downright rude. He knew certain things about him didn't comply to society's norm, but he was wounded still. There were things that he just couldn't fathom in his life right now. Love, being tied down, was one. He had fun, but he just didn't want Nina getting too serious on him. Women always fell first. And when they started talking about future and commitment, it was mainly because they wanted it more than he did. He had his whole career ahead of him, and there was no telling where he'd end up.

Tim had been awakened by the sun at 6:17 this morning. It had torn through his curtains and opened his eyes. First his left, then his right. He was feeling exuberant. Ideas and mind-altering revelations fluttered around him as he thought back to last night with Nina. He didn't necessarily care for pink. But he loved heels. High heels, and big legs. And he was enjoying the fact that she was more entertaining than she had initially let on. He didn't usually plan a movie for the first date either. He normally saved that sit-down type of atmosphere for the third or fourth date so that there could be more verbal exchange and getting to know each other initially before holding hands and silently watching the silver screen became an option. But it had been her idea, and he'd been making a conscious effort not to monopolize or struggle for control.

Tim sat bright and cheerful at his table, nursing a glass of orange juice with his bible opened to Hosea 6. The last thing he wanted to do was displease God. He hadn't forgotten. That close call was something he'd remember eternally. He glanced at the pile of *Backstage* magazines that had been tossed carelessly in the spare chair and vowed that Monday after work he would come straight home, go through them one by one, and begin gathering information to send out more submissions. He knew he couldn't afford next semester's tuition; that was a given. He just didn't want all of his studies to be for nought. He needed to be in the field he was studying. Either you had it to make it in film or you didn't.

Tim pulled out a pair of freshly pressed black slacks and a silk short-sleeved heather polo shirt for church. It was almost eight o'clock when the phone rang.

"Hello, Rochelle," Tim mocked.

"How did you know it was . . . never mind. Dinner tonight. I'm asking in advance, because I need to prepare enough."

"Dinner is fine. Can I bring a guest?"

"Let me guess, Troi's sister?"

"Yes, Nina."

"Tim, I just don't see why . . ."

"Why what, Rochelle? I don't see why we are having this discussion."

"She's so much older than you. There are plenty of young . . ."

"Rochelle?"

"Okay, you win. It's too early to argue."

"Who's arguing?"

"Later, brother dear."

Tim had convinced Nina to let him pick her up for church this morning.

"I'm perfectly capable of driving." She'd smirked beneath silvery glitter before reluctantly agreeing.

Tim couldn't swallow his pride long enough to allow her to see that it was the pleasure of taking her home that he was after. Tim spent twenty-five minutes outside in the sun trying to vacuum the carpets and wipe down the vinyl, and fifteen minutes trying to start his temperamental car. He hoped it didn't stall on the highway. He climbed inside, popped in a tape, and told himself not to be too eager. He knew her. She was a woman. He knew what women wanted. They wanted husbands. They knew from day one if they'd marry you, what color the flowers would be, and where you'd be vacationing afterward. He wondered what Nina thought of him. She was open and expressive, but life had taught him early on not to underestimate people, or overestimate them either. He had heard such shocking things about the quiet ones.

Tim was glad about the fact that Nina wasn't one of those all-men-are-dogs type of women. They drove him up one side of the wall and down the other. They slithered around like rattlesnakes ready to strike, and then they wanted you to sit calmly while they coiled themselves around you and rendered you impotent. That wasn't about to happen. Nina wasn't a pushover, and he really dug that about her. Those carbon-copy types got boring quickly. Besides, a woman who could keep him talking did wonders for his ego.

But there were just so many hurdles and obstacles that Tim had to overcome. Not needing anyone was the first hurdle. He had made that point clear to many women, rendering them useless, and they'd eventually given up trying to convince him otherwise. He wasn't trying to complicate anybody's life. It would take more than just the I-work-I-have-a-car-a-fancy-apartment-and-over-fifty-thousand-frequent-flyer-miles types. He wanted a woman who made him look at life like the apple of temptation and coaxed him into taking a bite.

The light flow of traffic had brought Tim back to square one. Brooklyn. He hadn't been in front of her house since their first date, he thought. He rang the bell and admired the flowers that surrounded the window and the bees pollinating and hovering nervously over the fragrant flowerpots. Tim bent down, picking up the newspaper that had fractured a few buds.

"Hey, you're early."

"And this is yours." He handed her the newspaper.

"Thank you, come in." She walked through the house in a vibrant red dress, trying to fasten her earring.

"I just made a fresh pot, would you like a cup?"

"I'm fine," he said, eyeing her vast collection of books from afar. *This candle is huge,* he thought, taking a whiff to see if it was scented before sitting down.

"I love this chair," he said, rubbing the arms. "It's big and comfortable."

"It's my favorite." She smiled.

He looked around the apartment, impressed with her nonintimidating decor, which still made his place appear meager and shabby. He cased the bookcase while flipping through several books he assumed she'd purposely laid out on the coffee table. Colorful covers, catchy titles. He loved a woman who read.

"What was your major?" he asked.

"Psychology."

He smoothed down his goatee and nodded slowly. "A headshrinker."

"No, I don't shrink anything, I help people. Well, I used to, at least parttime."

He was extremely tired of the type of woman who only did what she thought that a man wanted her to do. Tim wanted a woman to have a mind of her own. *Like sports because you like them, not because you think it will make me fall deeper in love with you.* He didn't want a piece of clay to mold, he wanted someone with a little backbone but still feminine enough that her presence said *woman.* His radar was pointing in Nina's direction.

"I'm done," she announced, stepping out of what he imagined was her bedroom with her arms extended.

He allowed his eyes to tell her that she looked wonderful. His lips said it, too.

"You look beautiful, Nina."

"Why thank you, Tim."

He nodded to himself, thinking that he couldn't help the fact that he was a born flirt. It offended most women he dated, but it was a part of him with which he wasn't ready to part soon. It made the recipient of his flirtation think he was smooth.

Their drive back to the city was stimulating. They talked about everything from why white people got suntans yet fought tooth and nail to preserve their whiteness, to how a man could father children with four different women, and why those women let them. She was strikingly beautiful, her eyes like laughter even in their defensive state. She was logical, educated, independent, and appeared to be the type who would tell you when she was done, not vice versa.

"Is that too much air on you?" Tim asked, anticipating a yes and raising the windows a little.

"I'm fine," she said, reaching for the button and lowering the window again.

She was independent for sure. Last night she had convinced him to let her drive home alone.

"You don't have to take me home, really. My car is right over there." She'd pointed to a dark vehicle under one of the only trees in the neighborhood.

"Are you sure?" he'd said, not wanting to reveal too much about what was in his head.

"I'm sure."

They'd stood on the corner. He'd wanted her to get home safely. In one sweet piece. Their lips had exchanged good-byes again, making their own music in front of the Juilliard School on 66th Street. He'd been impressed that long after she was gone, he remembered her lips. He'd fought with himself not to enjoy it. He had held her, not wanting to let her go. He couldn't look like he was desperate. He wasn't.

She had jokes about men in general and their philandering ways. He was flirting and trying to tell Nina about his legs. He loved telling people he had nice legs. Not because he was showing off, but because he did. He had kept the conversation light and open-ended with Nina last night because he wasn't trying to be the deepest brother on the block. He was laughing to himself thinking about Trattoria Spaghetto and Bel Viggagio. She'd chosen Trattoria because it was easier to say.

"What's so funny?"

"Nothing." He grinned, thinking how novel her honesty had been last night.

With all the double-parked cars in Manhattan, mercy had found him a spot closer to the hydrant than he would have liked, but the service had already started, and he really couldn't be choosy. Walking into the church now, he and Nina appeared arm in arm as careless whispers made their way back to his ears. Nobody owned him. He could date whomever he liked, walk down the street with whomever he liked, and talk until midnight and beyond with whomever he good and well pleased. After all, it was he who said, "If you're not married, you're single." He had to live up to his own creed. He never liked the way women claimed men. Women whom he wasn't even dating took too much interest in him. They wanted too much. Women wanted everything, and it was anything but everything that Tim was willing to give.

Tim had been impressed with the fact that wherever he had taken Nina, she fit in. The coffee shop, the movies, church. She blended well on the canvas of life. He didn't care who said what. He was his own man. He'd decide when, where, and who. And that went for Rochelle, those Hallelujah Girls, and the whole lot of them. He caught himself thinking and frowning, and he turned to Nina and whispered, "Would you like to have dinner at my sister's house after church?"

She nodded a gleeful yes.

Back at the apartment, while Nina was trying to help Rochelle in the kitchen by taking the bread out of the oven, Tim pulled Carl aside. He needed a seasoned man's opinion. Not Justin, who didn't even have a woman.

"How much do you think age plays in relationships, man?" Tim asked quickly. Carl rubbed his chin, contemplating.

"It does have an impact. I just don't think it's deserving of all the scrutiny."

"So, it really doesn't matter then?"

"I didn't say that."

"Well, what then?"

"It depends on the individuals."

Tim thought back to what that old guy in the coffee shop had said about loving only one and his wife taking a part of him when she died. He had a point, Tim thought as they all sat around the table about to bless the food. He surely didn't want to fall in love over and over again.

Tim noticed that Rochelle was more quiet than usual. He wasn't up for a debate of any kind. He was old enough to make his own decisions.

"You okay, Rochelle?"

"I'm fine," she said. "You want sweet potatoes?" she asked, passing the bowl to Carl to serve Tim.

"Are you sure you're okay?" Tim teased.

Rochelle gave Tim one of those momma looks. He hoped he wasn't jumping the gun with Nina. He was a passionate man, and he liked to take his time with everything he did. He always did get a little annoyed when people rushed him or tried to make up his mind for him.

"Pass the greens, Tim." Rochelle spoke through slightly parted lips.

Tim was about to heat things up. Rochelle was obviously bothered by Nina and what her presence with Tim symbolized, but it was no biggie. He leaned over. "Are you okay, Nina?"

"Yes, I'm fine."

"I know this isn't really private, and I'd really like to go out with you again."

"It's fine, really."

"Do you have to go straight home after this?"

"Not really, why?"

"I have to make a stop. Will you come with me?"

"What's all that whispering about?" Carl chuckled.

Tim glanced at his sister. He didn't know why Rochelle was stressing it. It wasn't a love thing.

51

"Girl, I really like him. Is that safe to say?"
"Why shouldn't it be?"
"You know, people and time limits and all that."
"Forget people, do your thing."
"Okay, well, pray for me before I mess it up."
"Why?"
"You know, when something's too good it happens subconsciously. I think deep down I think I don't need anybody."
"Of course you do. We all do. Enjoy it and don't question it too much. He knows even more than you do what you need."
"Let me just tell you that the kiss good night didn't help."
"Hmm, kiss good night? I see."
"Are you ready to order, ladies?"
"Umm, not yet." Troi eyed the nervous waitress. "You, Nina?"
"Let me have an iced tea, and a few more minutes, please." Nina munched on breadsticks. "I'm sorry, Troi," she apologized.
"Sorry about what?"
"About not letting you talk about you. How's it going with the insurance company?" Nina lowered her voice and adjusted herself in the chair.
"You don't want to know," Troi sighed loudly.
"Know what?"
"Arson."
"Arson? You're kidding!"
"Kidding? Hardly.
"Sofie set that fire. Girl must have duped the keys months before.

She gave me back the set I gave her, but she had to have another copy, and she had probably gone in there before she figured that anyone would come in to open up."

"What? How do you know?"

"A couple of people said they saw her."

"But why?"

"Because I fired her. Her jealousy fueled it, but trust me, everything is fine. The reports are back. It wasn't my fault, so the insurance will cover it. God is good. I think they may have lifted some prints from the scene."

"Yeah, but that girl must be crazy."

"Of course she is, right-minded people don't act like that. I mean, hairdressers come a dime a dozen. She could have found a job anywhere along Broadway."

"True."

"Why she burned my place to the ground I'll never know."

"Well, now she'll be doing hair in jail with big Bertha."

"Sure will," Troi confirmed, still haunted by the faint scent of smoldering timber.

"Well, did you at least go by the place and assess the damage?"

"Girl, damage? Total destruction. Everything is gone. Dryer hoods melted and the walls charred beyond recognition. It's gonna take more than some plasterboards and some magazines to fix that place up."

"So, what are you gonna do about the shop, rebuild?"

"I don't know. I don't have the strength. Besides, it's not up to me, it's up to the landlord. But I look at it this way: at least I lived my dream for a little while, better than never living it. I'm waiting. Maybe I'll just get on a bus down to Georgia or someplace else south of here and forget all this ever happened."

"You sure are calm about this."

"Why fret?"

"Yes, girl, don't get your pressure up."

"What pressure? Girl, I ain't claiming that." Troi hated when people said things out of habit.

"Lord have mercy. Let's talk about something else, please."

"Okay, let's." Troi grinned. "What you up to, Miss Sister-Girl?"

"Girl, nothing."

"Nothing? I saw Tim up in church all cozy. That ain't nothing, girl. And you saying you 'really really like him,' that's hardly something to be overlooked."

"Okay, well . . ."

"Okay, well what?" She baited her sister.

"Well, we just go out."

"Go out like what?"

"Like Saturday, Sunday, and Tuesday."

"Today?"

"Yep."

"Where?"

"Gonna hear some jazz, you know, hang out a bit."

"Well, it sounds like something to me. No need to lie, you know I'll find out anyway." Troi smirked, confidently motioning for the waitress.

"I'm not lying. It's just a date. We go out and we both go home separately."

"I see."

"Well, I mean, I'm trying not to show too much concern. I don't want him to think that he's got me, you know, open or something."

"Well, at least he's a praying man."

"That's for sure."

"You heard about his momma?"

"Yeah, and father."

"Sad situation. Raised him in the church. You know he needs some love after that," Troi hinted. "Speaking of raised in church, how was lunch with Mother last week?"

"Lunch was lunch, sis. You know your mother. She's as friendly as they come," Nina said sarcastically. "How's Vaughn?"

"He's fine," Troi lied, not wanting to go into the whole sordid details about how he hadn't been home since the service at church and how she was again left feeling like a fool. His fool. Everybody's fool.

She didn't know why she couldn't just tell him to hit the road. If it had been anybody else, she would have licked him with her tongue by now. But Troi remembered that Mother said, when you fall in love, you lose your nerve. She guessed that was partly it.

It wasn't hard being faithful, Troi thought. If you loved and you allowed nothing else to come before or jeopardize that love you had for your spouse, then you were at least three quarters of the way there. The rest was compatibility, and she and Vaughn complemented each other in the sense that what she wasn't, he was, and vice versa. But realistically speaking, her situation was different. Vaughn's newly discovered desires left her feeling like a rainbow in a colorblind world. No purpose and little or no redeeming value.

"So, you two still going to counseling?"

"No."

"No?"

Troi closed her eyes, frowned a little, and silently prayed for Nina to change the subject. She didn't want to discuss their relationship, passion, or the lack thereof. She refused to think about where Vaughn had spent the past five nights. She refused to think that the reason why Tracie stopped calling and harassing her was because Vaughn had gone back, and this time to stay.

"What's with the new hairstyle? You get it done?"

"A little something," Nina said, hoping Troi didn't ask where or when. "For my date."

"So, what exactly does Tim do?"

"He works in film. I mean, he works at a film company, he's in film school, and he's working on his own films. You know, I mean, at least he has a goal, right?"

"True. More than I can say for the last one."

"Please don't utter his name."

"Why? You dated him."

"I know, but it was sort of like voluntary amnesia. Give me the benefit of the doubt, please."

Troi drifted in and out of awareness of what Nina was saying. She was consumed by the thought that when she needed Vaughn the most, he walked out with no regrets. She just hated having given up everything for her marriage and ending up with nothing in return. At this point, she couldn't even save face. He had stood up and walked out. Not privately but publicly in church. She was giving and compromising.

Troi put two and two together, figuring that the other intimate evening they shared most possibly boiled down to exchanging favors for somewhere to sleep. Troi thought back to the first intelligent thing that Peaches had ever said. "Love is accepting others regardless of their situation and circumstances." That was an understatement.

"Carla." Troi waved, only looking up momentarily and seeing her, with her neck stretched, her colorful chiffon scarf swaying, and trying to locate where the gab session was being held.

"I thought it was just us," Nina whispered to Troi.

"She wanted to come, so I let her." Troi shrugged her shoulders.

"What's up, y'all?" Carla said, plopping down in the empty chair, reaching for Troi's water and gulping more than just a taste.

"Nothing, girl," Troi said, "except that Nina's dating some fine brother up in the church."

"Fine? Who's fine?" Carla crept all up in Nina's business, dabbing the corner of her mouth with an unused napkin.

"Tim Richardson," Troi volunteered.

"Girl. You got him?" Carla smirked.

Nina smiled, not wanting to put it how they did, but it did sound good. He and she together, she having him.

"Listen, we go out, that's all." Nina giggled.

"You go out? That's all? So, you ain't kiss the brother yet?" Carla locked eyes on Nina, waiting for the revelation.

"Waitress!" Nina raised her hand, motioning for service.

"Don't even try it," Carla said, "the waitress can wait, that's her job. Tell us. Did you or didn't you put your lips on that fabulous chocolate-looking brother?"

Nina mumbled something.

"What?" Troi and Carla leaned in.

"I said yes! Goodness, it's not love and all that stuff."

"Not yet, you mean," Carla pointed out. Troi nodded, too.

"Girl, that's what we need. Let's find us some real men," Carla said, nudging Troi.

"What you mean, real men?"

"You know, a brother who can do more than just sit there and look cute. I don't need no man pretending."

"So, what are you saying? Like Vaughn?"

"No, I just meant that, you know . . ."

"No, I don't know, that's why I'm asking."

"Look, Troi, you know that Vaughn and his, you know, problem," Carla whispered, "might not be in the plan for you and your life. I'm just thinking that maybe you'd be better off just letting him go and finding someone who wants you, the total package. Go out and meet some people. That's all."

"Listen, I didn't wait, pray, wait, pray some more, and wait even more just to give up in the end. I refuse to chase another man. I have one," Troi said, turning away, frowning.

"I'm sorry, CeCe. I'm really sorry," Carla pleaded.

"She's sorry, Troi, she didn't mean it. You know we're like sisters," Nina said. "She's just looking out for you. I mean, I know you are strong because we were never raised to be weak, but you have to rest the load. You have too much on you, and you're acting like you can handle it all. It's okay to say that you can't handle it. It's okay to say, 'I need help.' I'm here for you, and so is Carla."

Troi wasn't sure about any of this, but she knew Nina was right. So was Carla. Maybe Vaughn wasn't in the plan for her life. Maybe he wasn't her perfect will, but rather God's permissive will that was allowed because she had fallen so willingly and eagerly. Maybe she'd just put Vaughn there in her life and expected him to fit. She swore to high heaven that she'd die trying to figure.

"Awww, I know, and I love y'all," Troi said. "I'm just a little on edge. Group hug?"

They each extended their arms as they got to their feet. Feeling all eyes on them, they solidified their sisterhood with smiles and a confirming embrace.

"Nina, look!" Troi screeched, looking over Carla's shoulder.

"What?"

"Isn't that Derek?"

"Girl, leave that brother wherever he is, don't even look over there. I don't want him to see me. He stopped calling, let him move on." Nina ignored the urgency in Troi's voice.

"Girl, you better get an order of protection."

"I've seen on the news where people get shot down in broad daylight on the court steps. A piece of paper isn't gonna keep him away," Carla said.

"Well, if he knows what's good for him, he better back off or else."

"Or else what?" Troi twisted her lips.

"Or else I'm gonna give him some of your fried chicken; then he won't come back no more." She and Carla giggled.

"Oh, now my food is nasty? Is that what you sayin'?"

"C'mon, girl. I'm just playing. I know you can throw down; besides, you're the one who talked him up." Nina smiled at the appetizers.

Troi touched her sister and looked her in the eyes. "Well, whatever you do, just be prepared. They have crazy people out here, and he may just be one."

"Well, I'm not going anywhere without a fight."

"Amen to that!" Carla bit into a mozzarella stick.

52

"Listen, Vaughn, I know it makes you feel weak, but I'm working and I can take care of us both."

"So, I'm supposed to sit around the house and do what, make breakfast and bring your slippers when you come home?"

"That would be nice," Tracie kidded.

"That's not funny, man. Not funny at all."

"Stop being so touchy. This is the way it's supposed to be. Why else would all of this have happened?" Tracie asked, waiting at the door for some form of affection.

"Shut up, you're gonna be late," Vaughn snapped.

Tracie turned, mumbling something under his breath to Vaughn, who was too confused to sort out the fact that he didn't want to be a concubine. He didn't want to be kept. He didn't want this life. He didn't want Tracie.

He sat watching television and flipped through the newspaper's want ad section, contemplating something as far away from the bank as he could get. He weighed his life like a before-and-after photo. The measly momentary gratification wasn't worthy of the trail of destruction he had left in its wake. Vaughn felt no one should have anything to say about the way he lived his life but his partner, and that was only long enough for him to crawl out of the used, wrinkled sheets.

Vaughn had mangled the truth. There was no little white lie and there was absolutely no such thing as a fib in this case. Only a bold-faced distortion. There were no Saturday-morning basketball games and there was no Anthony. Troi had been grossly deceived for a while now.

The phone rang, and Vaughn knew that Tracie was always caring enough to apologize. He had never intentionally hurt anybody. Tracie had confessed that he was sort of new to this whole way of life, too, but he wasn't weak. That had been Vaughn's attraction to him at first glance. He was proud of what he was, and he could justify himself out of a noose at a witch hunt.

"Hello, may I speak with Tracie?"

"He left for work, can I take a message?"

"Yes, tell him that I'd appreciate it if he stopped avoiding my calls. I just want to get to the bottom of this whole situation and be rid of him for good, and I can't do that if I can't talk to him."

"I'll tell him."

"Are you his new dish?" the caller taunted.

"Dish? I don't belong to anybody."

"Well, whoever you are, I feel it only fitting to warn you that what he did to me he'll do to you. So, don't get too gleeful and cushy over there. Your days are numbered, too."

"Look, I'm straight to the point, so come at me like that," Vaughn spat.

"I mean that he uses people. He plays games with people's hearts."

"Who is this and what do you really want?"

"Okay, don't believe me."

"I assume you're kidding, right?"

"Ha, ha, do I sound like I'm kidding? Get real. He's a joke."

"Prove it," Vaughn demanded.

"Give me a sit-down session, I'll spill the beans. I don't have a problem with you. You're merely a victim like me. I can't hold that against you."

"Okay, let's talk then."

"When is good for you?"

"Now. If you're on the up-and-up."

"Now?"

"Yes, the address is 1425 . . ."

"I know the address, I've spent more than enough nights wrapped up in his sheets. I'll see you in about forty-five minutes to an hour, depending on traffic."

"Sure."

"What's your name, anyway?"

"Vaughn."

"Oh, so you're Vaughn?"

"What do you mean?"

"We'll discuss it when I get there." The line went dead.

Vaughn showered and changed into some comfortable sweats, thinking back to how vulnerable Troi always was. They'd played the game that he'd wanted to play. He'd compromise when it was appropriate for him and beneficial. He hadn't spoken to his mother, father, or brother since his revelation, and he had turned his back on Troi and walked out on her in the same church in which she'd walked up the aisle as a representation of her commitment to him and their life.

Vaughn rummaged through Tracie's pots and pans and put on a kettle to boil water for tea. He turned to CNN and flipped through the paper, puzzling over who this person was and what information he had under his hat. Maybe he should have met him at a remote spot away from eyes, somewhere less familiar.

But if what this guy was saying was true, then Tracie deserved to have his lies exposed and his apartment left ransacked. Vaughn had no money, no job, nowhere to live, no wife, no sanity, no trust left from anyone he knew, and he missed his Koda sorely. He didn't want advice and theories, all he wanted to know was, what was he to do next? How could he have all the comforts of home without necessarily having to be there?

The doorbell thrust Vaughn forward into the moment. He pulled open the door and hurried to the kitchen to rescue the kettle, which was whistling.

"You want some tea?"

"No, thank you."

"I'll only be a minute," Vaughn said, sounding more comfortable in Tracie's home than he should have been.

"No problem, take your time."

Vaughn prepared his tea and cozied himself on the sofa next to the newspaper, switched off the television, and braced himself for what was next.

"I know you don't know me, but I have nothing to gain by telling you what I'm about to tell you," the casually dressed man, who was probably in his early thirties, said calmly. "But if I was in your shoes, I know that I'd want someone to tell me."

Vaughn tapped his fingers on the base of his mug.

"Tracie is a liar. He ruins people's lives and leaves them grasping for straws. I met him four years ago. They sent me to the main branch, just like you."

"How did you know I was in banking?"

"I'm getting to that."

"Okay."

"From the moment we met, Tracie went on about how he wanted me to be the one. Everything was moving too fast for me and I told him that I wasn't sure about any of it. He took that as a rejection of him as a person. It wasn't that at all, I just wasn't about to leave my wife for him."

"You're married?"

"Was. My wife, she's proceeding with the divorce. I tried to keep my other life separate. I have a home in Hempstead, but I had a studio apartment in the city. So, Tracie and I, we'd meet either there or here. But somehow he got hold of personal information that I hadn't given him. He demanded money not to tell. I refused; he began calling my wife. He was harassing her. She confronted me, and I had no choice but to come clean. I had nowhere else to go. He moved me in here with him. It was all so convenient and I didn't have a clue. It wasn't until after the lawyers were negotiating our belongings that she told my lawyer that he had taunted her about the affair we were having. So, I was paying him to keep quiet about something he had already told."

Vaughn didn't know what to believe anymore. His feelings lied, people lied, and common sense had taken a backseat to rationale.

"Vaughn, I say that to say, Tracie told me all about you. He told me about how you were married and had a little girl. He told me that you were confused, but that he'd help you make up your mind whether you liked it or not. He sent you flowers at work purposely. He wanted to create a situation where you'd have to depend solely on him."

"They practically fired me!" Vaughn yelled.

"That was his plan, don't you see? He leaked it. Probably showed up unannounced, causing suspicion. I know that we aren't the first ones that he's done this to. How else could he afford all of this?" The guy gave the room the once-over. "He doesn't love you. He can't. He's not capable."

"My wife already knows. I've hurt her too bad. And I'm unemployed, so I don't have a dime for him to extort from me. What do I do if I leave here?" Vaughn asked.

"I'd call my wife, patch things up if I were you. Maybe you can salvage a morsel of love that can grow into something to get you through the rest of your lives together."

"But why would someone be so hateful and deliberate? What could he gain?"

"I asked the same thing. I learned the hard way. When we met, he told me that since we were in a committed, monogamous relationship that it would be safe. After several months of unprotected sex, I found out that years ago he tested positive and has been on an emotional crime spree ever since. Last year I tested positive, too."

"He what?" Vaughn trembled with his fingers balled into fists.

"AIDS. The virus . . . you didn't know?"

"C'mon. It can't be. This is wild! You're kidding, right?"

"Like I said, Vaughn. You can believe me or you can believe him. I have nothing to gain by lying to you. I have nothing to gain at all. He has everything to gain. He's a liar; he can't help it. If I were you, I'd get tested. They have all types of drugs that can help us live longer lives."

Vaughn stood up feebly and fell back to sit.

"My reaction exactly. The last thing I ever thought about was being HIV positive. My wife won't even come near me now. Everything we say to each other is on an answering machine or through our lawyers. It's not a flattering label."

Sipping on tepid tea trying to calm himself, all Vaughn could do was close his eyes, tilt his head toward the ceiling, and silently plead, "God, please, I don't want to die alone."

53

Nina hardly spent any time with her sister or at work since Dartmouth had opted to make her position mobile. She had voluntarily cut her hours, and now her position was like drive-thru takeout, sort of. She worked from home, on the go, and needed less time to do what normally took all day for about the same pay.

Instead of cutting her lunch date with her sister short in anticipation of her date with Tim, she just took her time, letting the day do what it needed to do for both her and her sister, Carla, too. They talked more about relationships and how one needed a balance of faith and sensibility.

"When the ring goes on the finger, the brain doesn't evaporate," they agreed.

"But I want that," Carla said, pointing to a pseudo-fine brother paying her no mind, who thought that he had the etiquette of mackin' down to a science.

He sat at the table next to theirs, alone, with an oversize nylon, almost transparent sweater, managing to cause only a minor distraction with the Arts section of the *New York Times* as he tried to be chic.

Nina kind of believed Carla as she went on about how when she got married she would take off from work just to surprise her husband at his office for lunch, trenchcoat style, armed with whipped cream and chocolate-covered something. Carla was like Shelby in some respects. They revered those brothers who claimed that they read Plato and understood it, ate pheasant, and only drank mineral water. Their girlish gushing always managed to amount to a little more than a graphic episode of *Sex and the City.*

Troi managed to interject and confess haphazardly that Vaughn hadn't been home since the emergency prayer he'd walked out on, and although Carla thought they should go and kidnap Vaughn and throw him in the trunk of a car, Nina felt that time would reveal more than just his intentions.

"You have to give them enough rope to hang themselves."

"Yeah, but what if he can't make a knot?" Troi had to interrupt Carla again.

"Listen, you two don't understand. I love my husband. I mean, the only way I can describe it is . . . well, you know the feeling that you get when you are dead tired and people around you keep talking and trying to keep you up but all you want to do is crash? And your sink is full of dishes that you know you need to wash because you had tuna for lunch and in the morning your whole kitchen will be fishy if you don't? And you know how your best friend calls," Troi said, eyeing Carla, "and she has a crisis, so you can't tell her to call back tomorrow? And you know it's been one of those really hot days that made you sting instead of sweat?"

"What's the point?" Carla asked.

"Okay, I'm getting to that . . ." Troi rolled her eyes.

Nina thought the whole description was funny.

"Okay, so you know after all of that, you take the most refreshing hot shower and squeeze sesame oil and a bit of lemon all over you? You drip dry and put on your most luxurious satin pajamas, turn off the phone and the lights, and open the window, which at that very moment permits the coolest breeze you've felt all day? And when you crawl into bed finally and mash your pillow into shape and sprawl out comfortably and giggle to yourself, smiling at the pleasure of finally being able to go to sleep?"

"Yeah," Carla said, exhausted at having to keep up.

"Well, I love Vaughn like that. I love him just like that," Troi said, as they all looked around the table at each other, at a loss for anything that could refute that.

Nina cherished these girls-only moments, the void of which left you detached from reality and consumed in everything uttered by the opposite sex.

Lunch had been a blast, but she had a date, so after they were done they hugged, giggled, and promised each other the same time next week. Nina rushed around, stopped by the luncheonette, got something that she hoped her mother would eat, and took it by her so she wouldn't starve. Nina enjoyed being busy lately, but she had to pick up the pace.

She had to, she thought as she came rushing home to freshen up before Tim would arrive and set her mind in motion. That man had levels. She needed some of that, and he had come with an overabundance. It was six P.M. and Nina had put on a simple brown dress that made her look slimmer than she was and some uncomplicated but matching shoes. She sprayed her fragrance and walked into it. None on the neck or wrist. Only the hem of her garment and her hair.

Opening her windows and peeping through her parted curtains, she could see that her plants needed watering and that Martha, who must have seen her come in, was making her way in the gate with something wrapped and tied up in royal-blue cellophane. Nina didn't want to get into what she and Tim were or weren't. It didn't warrant that type of attention yet. But her mind couldn't help but anticipate enjoying herself tonight.

"You look pretty," Martha said, making her way up the stairs, breathing heavily.

Nina stood by the doorway, quietly observing. "Thanks."

"You really like him, don't you?" she said, barely making it in the door.

"Yes, I guess I do." The long pause prompted her that Martha had something else to say.

"So, you think this is it?"

Nina thought momentarily, making her way inside. "Maybe. I mean, I understand that they're all different. I'm trying to be patient and wait, but I just want to know what it is we both feel before I go opening up. I mean, honestly, I'm not a young girl with tricks and all that."

"Then wait."

"I am waiting, girl, I've been praying so hard Jesus should be sitting right next to me."

"Oh, is that who that is?" Martha laughed.

"What I feel is a whole other level. It's making me vulnerable, and I don't like that."

"I know, you can be a tough nut to crack." Martha smirked.

"I mean, I feel like he's opened me up, but I really don't want to go there again. I mean, it always feels fabulous at first, but then after a while, the bickering and the annoying little habits start. I refuse to let another man play me like a violin."

"But if you don't let someone in, you'll never know truth."

"I know, but if I can get through today's date, I'll be fine. Right?"

"That's right," Martha agreed.

"I need to open up or else I don't know what."

"But if you can't open up, Nina, you know true love will wait until you can, and will understand."

"That's what makes me so tough. I said I'll never allow another person to use me."

"What has he said about the whole thing?"

"Nothing really. I mean, I know there are lots of women after him. Those saintly wonders at church."

"Are you jealous?"

"I'm not jealous. Jealousy gives you wrinkles. I can't afford to be wrinkled."

"So, enjoy it and just don't put too much pressure on him."

"I won't," Nina said, rearranging books on her coffee table. "You want some coffee?"

"Sure. I mean, I'd like to meet him finally. Can I stay?"

"You can stay, you can stay," Nina agreed, rummaging in her music collection and giving Martha a sideways glace. "Just be on your best behavior."

"I will, and this is for you," Martha said, holding out the baked goods wrapped in cellophane, which were silently bidding Nina to break her vow of not eating until she met up with Tim for dinner.

"Oooh, thanks."

"I have to get that stuff out of my house before I eat it all."

"Oh, so you give it to me?"

"Gave Junior one."

"Really? I didn't know he ate food."

"Why you say that?" Martha frowned.

"I don't know. I just see him and figure he just wanders all day. I never thought of him in terms of sitting down and actually having a meal." Nina giggled.

"Well, I'm sure he eats just like the rest of us."

"I guess."

"Girl, I bet he'll clean up just fine," Martha said.

"Girl, I don't know, who wants to go giving that man a bath?" Nina said, filling up her watering pitcher.

"You want me to do that for you?" Martha offered.

"Sure, thanks, I . . ."

"Yes, I know. You wouldn't want to get wet or messy," Martha mocked. "Where's your girl Shelby?"

"I don't know, loving and leaving them probably. The world wouldn't be the same without her."

"Yes, I know." Martha chuckled. "It would be less colorful and a whole lot less dramatic."

"Yes." Nina thought back to Shelby and her orange ensemble and hair that almost matched.

The buzz of the telephone made Martha look at Nina and smile wide.

"Uh-huh, speak of the devil," Martha interjected, as Nina said, "Hello."

Nina paused, covering the phone with the palm of her hand. "It's Shelby."

"You ready?" Shelby asked.

"Ready for what?"

"The opening."

"That's not tonight?" Nina panicked.

"Yes, it is," Shelby sang. "You forgot?"

"Ah . . . no, it's fine. What time?"

"Eightish."

"I won't stay long, but I promise that I will make an appearance."

"That's all I'm asking," Shelby said.

"Shelby, that's my other line, I'll see you there, girlie," Nina said, clicking the flash button with her thumb before Shelby had a chance to respond.

"Hello?"

"Hey."

"Hey, you . . ."

"Listen," Tim said. "A slight change of plans. Can you meet me downtown?"

Nina paused. "Only if you agree to make a stop with me first for an hour or so? It's downtown, too."

"Deal."

Nina smiled and cradled the phone a while before resetting it.

"So, I don't get to meet him, huh?" Martha pouted.

"Not this time, sorry."

"Remember not to be too eager," Martha said. "Breathe and let him make the suggestions."

"I don't need lessons in being passive, I get enough of that from Shelby."

"Well, I'm just trying to help."

"I know, but can someone please just say that they hope I have a good time?" Nina hinted.

Nina and Tim had joined Shelby and her poisoned-pen comrades for an evening of pushing the envelope and rattling on about blotches on canvas that they tried to convince someone's pockets was real art. True art needed no convincing. Faces lingered and contorted, trying to figure out from which angle of the frame they should be scrutinizing the work. Introductions were made all around. The people were colorfully pretentious, and Nina eyed Tim, who was grinning and bearing it.

"This is the curator," Shelby said, tugging on the arm of her next conquest.

"Fabulous to meet you," Nina said, putting on her professional voice.

"So, what exactly do you do?" he asked Nina.

"I'm in marketing," Nina said, cuing Tim that he was next.

"I'm in film," Tim said.

"Film? How quaint. Am I familiar with any of your work?"

"Not exactly. I've finished up two scripts and am in the process of shopping them. But I am assisting at a small company in the city. Big Deal?"

"Oh, yes, independents."

"Yes. Independents."

"Well, Tim, I have friends anywhere and everywhere," the curator boasted, waving his hand as Shelby stood grinning, still within earshot. "Here's my card." He barely held it. "Give me a call. I'm sure I can find someone to help you along. That's the only way, you do realize that?"

Nina watched as Tim took the card, opened his wallet, and filed it with the rest. The curator's back faced them now, and the hors d'oeuvres on the table to their left looked like a four-course meal as they moved in closer.

"Have one," Nina said, prompting Tim to open his mouth and slip in all but a finger as he chewed slowly and winked at her.

"You ready to go?"

"Yes." Tim grimaced, apologizing with his eyes for not being more tolerant.

"I know, and I'm sorry, it's just that Shelby is my friend and I try to support her."

"That's a good thing." Tim nodded.

"Are you hungry?"

"Not really," Nina said, as her body was craving anything short of a breath mint.

"I know a little place. We can have coffee or something. I had a bite earlier but nothing since about three o'clock," Tim said.

After chit-chat, eyeing each other nervously, and a bit too much to eat in a secluded jazz restaurant on Third Avenue, they both agreed to indulge in grande iced cappuccinos to go and another tryst on the Staten Island Ferry. It was a welcome treat from the humidity that dogged the city streets and had both of them clinging a little more to their clothes than either probably wanted to. They rode back and forth in the night air as Nina leaned over the edge of the boat dangerously and mentally craved his arms, but mostly didn't want to end their date. She wondered if she fell over, if he would rescue her, and she wrestled with images of the feminist types who would urge her to rescue herself.

She glared out at the murky water and felt tears making a flamboyant attempt to well up in her eyes. Maybe she had been overwhelmed by the water's symbolic cleansing. No more Derek, for real. Tim was new and unrehearsed. Her hair was damp from the mist that sprayed as the big steel boat maneuvered through the water. She thought, *I really have to be digging a brother to get my hair wet.* She was amazed that even from the first embrace her lips never felt as though she was kissing a stranger. He was familiar, like a puzzle missing a few miscellaneous pieces.

The evening was electric, and they were telling each other more with their bodies than they could say with their lips. His laughter complemented her smile, and they both tried not to read too much into the evening.

Sitting in front of her home in her late-model car a little past two A.M., Tim manned the driver's seat, and Nina couldn't believe that he had offered to drive her back to Brooklyn, then take the train back uptown near the gallery to his car. But here they were, and she couldn't help but feel rescued from the depressing sound of Nina Simone. Tim was showing her his hand and making her feel like a Brian McKnight song. She wasn't afraid to need him and, being a man, he was allowing her to see that fear was something he didn't possess.

"Needing isn't weakness," Tim said, turning down the volume on the car's radio.

"What?"

"Needing someone isn't weakness," he said, distracted by the sultry sounds of instrumentals coming from across the street. "I just wanted to thank you for coming with me after church the other day to see my parents."

"It's nothing, really."

"It's something to me. Most women would have had a problem sitting in the car alone for twenty-five minutes."

"I understand. I'm just glad that I could be there for you like that."

"I hear music," Tim said, changing the subject and looking in the mirror on the sun visor, smoothing down his goatee.

"My neighbor," Nina said, eyeing the window and pointing to the curtains that were waving lightly in the night.

Tim clapsed her hand in his, then examined it.

"He likes to play. I think he's in a band. I listen to him all night sometimes. Mostly when I'm restless."

"This is a busy avenue late at night, huh?"

"Not really," she said, brushing something from his face.

"I dig that piece he's playing." Tim nodded. "It's smooth."

"Like you, huh?" Nina kidded, as she observed Junior next door to her, creeping into Martha's place. At that moment she truly knew the face of desperation. "So, are you going to call the curator?" Nina asked, pretending not to see Junior, Martha welcoming him in, or the television flickering hues of blue through her window, which was a telltale sign that she had been waiting up for him.

"I don't know, maybe," he said with his male braggadocio. "Maybe."

54

On the smelly train ride home, Tim wondered if he was showing too much. Exposing his hand. Giving too much of himself away. Overbidding. He watched as people decked out in silver lamé halter tops, suede shorts, and skirts as skimpy as panties came from parties and other stops people often made near midnight when a tune came on the radio and made you think of who you were with when you'd last heard the song.

He dug Nina, but he didn't want this woman's fragile heart in his hands. Women always got emotional and rational thought normally eluded them after they'd fallen. He didn't know what he was capable of doing. Never stopped to notice even. He wondered if his momma would have liked her. She might have chosen her. It was true. She was independent enough to impress his mother without disappointing his old-fashioned father.

He thought about the curator and the business card with the paintbrush and figured if he couldn't do it on his own, he would definitely give him a call and see who he knew. Connections were always a plus. He wasn't too proud to accept a favor. He wanted to be working on his second film this time next year, not answering phones for Big Deal, he thought, visually locating his car near the gallery. Tim pulled out the key, opened the door, sat, adjusted his mirror, and popped in one of those artsy jazz tapes that he and Nina had in common now, and he drove uptown with the almost silent hum of the tune through what was virtually no traffic.

Tim had confessed to himself finally that he'd been hurt, and it had taken him a long time to accept the fact that love was a part of him that he desired, and that intimacy was important to him. Extremely. Dogs were not born, rather they were created from the direct result of heartbreak or the mutilated affections of others and their reaction to the situation. They had to learn to get off the hamster wheel of bad relationships. Love better; communicate more.

Tim squeezed into a parking spot close enough to his building that he could probably see his car from the window. He flipped his wrist and focused on the dial; it was almost five A.M. He walked in the building and could see the overabundance of mail in the box from the slots. He stood in the lobby, trying to get it all out without ripping an envelope. There were the usual bills, subscription notices, and a plain letter addressed from California with a logo of a film strip. His brow furrowed; then a smile formed on Tim's face as his fingers flipped open the letter without getting a paper cut and read as this company went on to say, *We have reviewed your script. Please give us a call at your earliest convenience.*

Tim stood there leaning against the mailbox, dazzled.

"Yes!" He congratulated himself. "Yes, yes, yes!"

They only wanted to talk to him, but he knew that it meant that his foot was at least in the closing door. He would sell himself with gift-wrapping paper and a gold leaf card, or yodel if he had to. He'd need a new tie, he thought, as he was high on the possibilities of it all. He was elated that an A company was definitely interested in what he had been desperately trying to convey. It was there in black and white. He could pull this off; he patted his chest. The overwhelming bliss came from knowing that he'd gotten in and didn't have any connections. He had done this on his own merit. It was the chance of a lifetime. He'd definitely need a new tie.

Tim thought about Nina all the way to Los Angeles. The ride was plush, but he couldn't help but think that he hadn't even said goodbye. In the clouds he saw her face, felt her touch, and sensed her warmth. She was that kind of woman. She was always close enough in his mind lately for him to feel her presence. He winced momentarily, thinking that maybe commitment had too many sharp edges that might cut him deeply. But he figured that it wasn't all bad. Maybe he just had to find the right one, and then all the fears of her changing into something he couldn't recognize would dissipate. He thought back briefly to Michelle and her games. He had played a few himself. He thought about Sharon, Estella, too, and he shuddered. "Thank the Lord," was all he said, and sighed in response to the load of worrisome burdens being lifted.

Tim thought about Nina as he flew into LAX and as he read and reread a seven-month-old issue of S(c)ript that he had brought along. He figured that if she were here with him now, he would possibly be feeling comfortable enough to talk about taking a trip to someplace that wasn't an overpopular Carribean island. Someplace that would make them feel that they were in their own world. She wasn't pushy, and that was cool. Sand was optional. Somewhere where there were possibly no telephones, and where the natives still wore leaves and grass for clothing. He liked that. He was pushing it; he knew things were changing. He wasn't even sure if he was even over Michelle fully. But he was surely trying.

Tim was thinking about Nina when he was gnawing a rubbery, tasteless piece of Salisbury steak and sipping the tart day-old coffee that the stewardess insisted on serving. He tried to imagine the taste of the coffee they had shared together in that little café downtown. In his mind he saw her delicate hands hugging the cup. Her full lips that gently blew on the coffee amazed him still. He wondered how good a cook she was, and vowed to find out when he returned. There had to be more to a woman he'd even contemplate than just appearances. After the height of emotions and mutual attraction was reached, you needed something more than sex to keep it constant. There was intimacy on various levels, and he wanted to reach them all.

Tim thought about Nina when the icy cold water from the shower refreshed his jet lag and make him more alert, and the thirsty towel hugged his waist, threatening to fall. Now he was attentive enough to read over some of the things he would discuss at the meeting tomorrow with the executives considering his script. They didn't seem bothered by the fact that he didn't have representation, and it pleased him that he hadn't had to lie. He tried to concentrate, he really did, but he was so enthralled by the thought of Nina and how she had just let her silence comfort him at the cemetery that afternoon, and how she was just so caring and gentle that he'd no longer let her count it as a fault. She could be his type. He knew it to be true; besides, the shower had helped in more ways than one. He was glad. He had vowed to wait to be physical with another woman, and he would. There was something about built-up passion that was underestimated. Undefined. Even though all women didn't seem to know it, they were worth the wait.

Tim thought about Nina as he dined alone in the hotel's café. He observed a couple with their necks stretched, kissing each other hungrily and totally oblivious to the waiter, who placed their platters discreetly next to their water glasses. He wondered why people had to be so obvious about their affection. Even to Tim it made no sense that they ordered off the menu when it was obvious that they were dining on each other. Tim, however, couldn't help rewinding his thoughts to Nina as the man reached in his pocket, placed money under a cup, and led his partner away, massaging the back of her neck and lightly skimming her thigh with his hand.

Tim was thinking about Nina when he met with the execs the next morning. It was as if she stood beside him, supportive the whole while. And his thoughts were on her when they said that they wanted to work closely with him on some changes, but that they wouldn't take away from the theme of the script, because they loved the character's personal premise and thought it would sell.

They said that they would generate a contract for him to look over. Negotiation was the stressful part. Tim smiled as they inquired about a wife or children.

"Do you have any objections to relocating?" the VP asked. As his lips said "no," Tim missed her even more.

He thought about Nina when they invited him to a party for the privileged "haves" that he didn't mentally or physically want to attend. His mind thought about her while some overzealous groupie type kept interrupting his thought process by slithering up and down his leg all night, whispering obscenities in his ear and begging him to come back to her place for a fine time. She had slipped her card key in his shirt pocket and patted him on the butt.

Tim thought about Nina when he called back to the East Coast to check his messages. It was late and there was a time difference that he fought to respect. He couldn't escape thoughts of her. "She's everywhere," he mumbled as the slight drizzle wet the tips of his suede shoes and blurred his vision. Sleep was something Tim had avoided this whole trip. He wandered back into the hotel café past the red-embered OPEN sign, and sat as the waiter announced, "We're closing in an hour and a half, and the kitchen closes in twenty minutes."

"I'll just have a cup of coffee," Tim said, reaching for the napkin and dabbing the excess water from his shoes. He overheard the bartender consoling a distraught patron.

"Have you ever been in love, man?"

"Yes," the bartender said.

"Well, if you loved a woman, would you tell her?"

"I have already told her, and showed her."

"What one thing would prevent you from telling her, if you didn't tell her?" The patron nodded.

"Fear."

"Fear of?"

"Rejection."

"Rejection is strong."

"For us men, you mean?"

"Rejection is the same all around the board." A woman approached the bar, pressing her match to her cigarette and tapping her empty glass for a refill.

"It really is," she said, blowing smoke.

"Well, what makes you fall in love with a woman?" the bartender asked.

"The way she carries herself. Or what she wears and if her hands are clean." The man laughed. "Dirty fingernails turn me off."

"Okay, so if a woman is all of these things, is it automatic love?"

"Sometimes."

"What special thing sets her apart?" the woman interjected.

"Conversation. When she is able to talk and express herself by talking, not actions," the patron said, not sounding so drunk after all.

"So, if you loved a woman, would you tell her?" she asked.

"Nope."

"Why?"

"When I was younger I would. It's not the same now."

"Why?"

"It's hard when you really love them, because you feel vulnerable."

"Okay," the woman interrupted, "but wouldn't you fear losing her by not telling her? A woman could be left feeling that you don't love her," she said, taking it a little too personally.

"I never thought about that," he said.

"Hey, you," the woman said, nudging her chin in Tim's direction. "You look lonely enough. How about you?" She drew Tim into a conversation that would reveal more than he ever wanted strangers to know.

"If you love a woman but don't tell her, what would your response be if she said it first?"

"I never told anyone that."

"Never?"

"Never." He sipped his coffee.

"But you wanted to, right?"

"Once."

"Why didn't you?"

Tim rubbed his chin, took another sip of coffee, and thought of at least seven more things he could do to avoid answering the question.

"After I said it, I would've been scared of losing her," he confessed.

"All right, buddy." The guys patted him on the back.

"Having a good woman makes everything okay, right?" the bartender questioned.

"It helps." Tim nodded.

He sensed that he was becoming something other than himself since Nina: giving.

55

"Troi?" Nina spoke between heaving sobs.

"What is it, Nina? You okay?"

"Derek . . ."

"Derek?"

"Yes, he's standing across the street. He called yesterday and first thing this morning . . . and . . ."

"I told you to get an order of protection. Did you call the police?"

"They said that standing on the sidewalk isn't a crime." Nina sobbed.

"Does Daddy know?"

"No, I couldn't . . ."

"We have to go before the judge and have them grant you an order of protection. File a complaint with the local police department. There has to be a stalking law."

"I'm not leaving this house, Troi. You don't understand. He's a nut. He's crazy. I don't know what he's on!"

"Okay, calm down, Is he still there?"

"I dunno." Nina peeped thru the curtains.

"I'll be there in less than an hour. Just keep the door closed, Nina, and don't answer the phone."

Troi dialed several numbers. The landlord for Shangrila told Troi that he didn't necessarily want to rebuild. "After all, you're only renting," he said flippantly.

"But think of the revenues and my clientele."

"Your clientele isn't my problem."

"Well, at least think about it, please?" She prayed silently.

"We'll see."

Troi thanked him and dialed her mother's.

"How are you, Mother?"

"Fine, makes no sense to complain."

"Lunch tomorrow?"

"I told Nina that I don't want you two fussing over me. I told Nina that weeks ago."

"We're not fussing, we're just . . ."

Troi paused for the interjection her mother always placed in the middle of any thought that someone else was trying to convey. There was no interjection.

"Are you okay, Mother?"

"Yes, I'm fine, makes no sense to . . ."

"So, what about lunch?" Troi cut her off.

"Lunch is fine, I guess."

"Okay, Mother, I've got to run, but I will give you a call later."

Her mother grumbled a halfhearted good-bye and Troi proceeded to stuff the baby into her overalls and a light jacket. She grinned to herself. She was strong beyond her years. She hadn't heard a peep out of Vaughn, and she hadn't managed to go crazy just yet. The first night alone was the worst; it was getting better. She still prayed and included him in her list of urgent requests.

When they had met, she'd been moonlighting in that thing called love, which should have been an ice cream flavor, it tasted so good. Now all she had was what was before her: her baby girl and the rubble formerly known as Shangrila. When Daddy had left Mother, Troi had thought her mother would die a literal death. But in Mother's weakness, she saw her strength, and knew that if need be, she could be that strong, too. Troi ran her fingers through her hair. She was forgiving, just not very tolerant.

Troi eyed herself in the mirror. She looked motherly today, not very feminine, and she didn't care. She had no lipstick on and her jeans were wrinkled.

"Let's go, baby," she said to her little girl, only to place her down on the sofa hesitantly and pick up the phone. Her hands itched. She placed the receiver down, only to pick it up again and dial.

"Loan Department."

"Vaughn Singleton, please."

"I'm sorry, Mr. Singleton is no longer with us. Can I help you with something?" the voice inquired, as Troi mashed the button and frantically dialed Sam's number in Jersey.

On the third ring, "I'm sorry, no one's here to take your call at the moment . . ."

Troi forwent the message, grabbed up the keys, and silently willed both jealousy and panic to disappear.

The phone hadn't rung more than once before Troi picked it up and pressed it to her ear.

"This is she . . ."

"You did?"

"Now?"

"I'll be there in less than thirty minutes."

After dropping the baby off, Troi headed for the precinct. She looked around the faded station, trying to get information.

"I'm here to see someone about the Shangrila fire. . . ."

"Yes, you can speak with the officer over there." The desk clerk motioned with a pen. Troi walked back toward the old wooden chair and glanced across the hall at the familiar face. She thought they wanted to give her information about the fire; she hadn't expected to see Sofie anywhere in the vicinity.

"They're all lies. Lies, I'm telling you," Sofie rambled. "She wants everything." She pointed. "Little Miss Popular. She's nothing now. How does it feel for somebody to take what you have?"

Troi turned her back on the commotion and stood her ground. She had no idea what this lunatic was babbling about.

"In ninth grade," Sofie sobbed, "she stole my boyfriend, the only person who ever loved me for real."

"Calm down," the officer instructed her and handed her a paper cup of water.

"How does it feel to lose something that you love so badly, Troi?" she yelled. The officer closed the door to the room, and Troi waited for the officer to reappear and give her whatever they had for her; then she wanted to be out of the dusty place. She didn't even want to breathe the same air as that psycho.

"Her fingerprints are on the gas can."

"I had no doubt." Troi eyed the officer.

"She'll probably get out on bail."

"Just keep her away from me."

"If you have any problems at all, give us a call." He handed her a business card, which she shoved down into her purse as she stood to leave.

"I have another question," Troi said. "How do you go about getting an order of protection?"

"You have to go down to the courthouse, ma'am."

"Okay," Troi nodded.

When Troi pulled into a parking space directly in front of Nina's prized brownie, all she could see were the flowers still in bloom and no one standing across the street now as Nina had said earlier. Her sister always complained to her but never took her advice; it made her crazy, among other things. She had thanked God over and over again that she was more tolerant than her sister. Tolerance was just something you needed more of in this life. It was the only way to survive.

"I see he decided to leave," Troi said, finding her bags a comfortable spot on Nina's floor.

"Yes, I don't know what his problem is, but he needs to back off." Nina sat, wringing her hands and smiling to mask her uncertainty. "I think he was messing around with the locks and broke the mailbox."

"Did you file a complaint?"

"They said I could come down and fill out the complaint form and then use that to get an order of protection."

"I see."

"Look at the note he left on my door." Nina ushered Troi over to where the scribbled paper said, *you are mine, forever.*

"Well, how do you know it was him?" Troi balled up the paper.

"Wait, don't do that. It's evidence. Besides, who else would it be?" Nina said.

"I'm sorry, I'm just asking you what the judge is going to ask you when you go before him."

Troi lowered her head. She couldn't blame Nina this time. She was about to start this.

"Let me ask you something, Nina." Troi shook her head. "Why we don't have nothing? I mean, anything we want is so hard, we ain't got nobody, can't keep nobody, and Lord, if we do get something, we have to basically become a doormat to keep it."

"What's wrong, Troi?"

"Nothing, I'm just saying, Madisons have it hard, harder than most."

"Every family thinks the same thing. We just experience things to get where we need to be, that's all."

"And what is this Derek thing doing for you?"

"It's showing me not to be the dogcatcher. Stop picking up every stray I see along the road of life that needs a little affection. Trying to fix up men just to have one laying beside me in the wintertime."

"Oh, you learned that, did you?"

"Yeah, and you?"

"I learned that a word is not enough, you need a confirmation, a reconfirmation, and, by all means, Lord, confirm it again."

"What are we talking about exactly?" Nina shied away.

"Nothing."

"Vaughn?"

"Perhaps."

Sunday found them all in church, center section, third row. Carla, Troi, and Nina. Troi didn't sing that day. Someone else did. Sang a new song that had her leaning back with her eyes closed, dwelling on each word and allowing the love of God to move a lonely tear from the corner of her eye down the curve of her cheek. Even without Vaughn, she still wouldn't give the Hallelujah Girls the satisfaction. She was, however, determined that she would not be like her father; she would deal with issues head-on. Even as a preteen, Troi had been right about her daddy's other interests.

Across to her right, in the next pew, a new face was giving her the eye. She totally ignored him and moved out of the aisle to pay her tithes. Troi purposely avoided his gaze and his stature, which had to be at least 5'11". Maybe he was just friendly; maybe it was more. Maybe he was eyeing someone behind her. Maybe she wasn't worth a second glance at all. It ceased to matter. There was no pleasure receiving attention from someone she didn't want. She pouted and made her way back into her row. She had always had any man she wanted, gift-wrapped special. Now here she was second-guessing, double-checking, and making an illogical mess of a life about which months before she had been so certain.

After service, Troi wrapped Nina's arms around a tray of peach cobbler and dragged her uptown. Nina reluctantly accepted. They bunched up in the car and headed back to Troi's place, and although Shelby had forgone the service, her arrival at the apartment was announced by an armful of knickknacks and the faint scent of garlic.

"Long time no see, girl."

"You know where I am," Troi kidded.

Shelby always conjured enough finesse for even the most fashionless.

"I'm sorry to hear about your shop. That girl must have been out of her head."

"Totally."

Troi was leaning against the stove and putting a new battery in the kitchen clock; then she would put her sauce on to perk, fry her sausage, and boil loads of pasta. Nina had music going colorfully, and through the denial of it all, Troi truly missed the rock-hard man who used to be hers, leaning over her as she cooked and impatiently tasting dinner out of the pot.

She thought back to this morning. She had been awakened by Dakoda's hungry I-want-cereal cries and rolled over to find a wedding picture of her and Vaughn willing her to envy it from their cluttered dresser. She had stretched, yelled, "I'm coming" to her baby girl, then reached over and tossed her shoe across the room to send the framed photograph smashing to the floor, where it would stay until she came home to pick up the pieces later on tonight.

Vaughn no longer had a job, no longer wanted a wife, and had turned his back on the church that had nurtured him since he was a babe. She wondered what the perky little therapist would have to say about that. His momma hadn't said much or even called either. *Troi Madison will cope,* she thought, thinking again how her father always said, "You have to let a man be a man." That's what she had done. Now what?

Carla was sharing hugs and kisses in the living room. She was always so noisy about it. She walked into the kitchen, smiling and spreading sunshine.

"Hey, girl."

"Hey."

She was standing next to Troi now, washing her hands and preparing to spread minced garlic on French bread.

"You okay, sis?"

"I'm fine," Troi said, as her face moistened the longer she lingered over the steaming pot of pasta. "It's just that . . ."

"What?"

"Never mind."

"C'mon, tell me. You know we keep it real."

"I know, it's just that I don't like complaining. I don't want to be a burden to anyone."

"Now, you know we are there for each other. This friendship isn't one-sided."

"I know."

"So, relax and let us help you. You can lean on me, CeCe."

The phone hadn't stopped ringing yet. It demanded attention again.

"Can you lower the music?" Carla yelled from the kitchen and lifted the receiver from the hook.

"Hello? No, this is Carla. Yes, she's here, hold on . . ."

Carla covered the phone with her palm. "CeCe, it's Vaughn."

Troi shook her head no.

"I know it's none of my business, but whatever's gonna happen, you two need to talk, and that's the bottom line."

"I know, but how? Look at what he's done to me, Carla . . ."

"I know, just see what he wants, CeCe, please?" Carla pushed the phone at her.

Troi held onto the phone, still unsure, and closed her eyes tightly. She pressed her ear to the receiver, swallowed hard, and tried to keep in mind what Carla had just said.

"Hello?" Troi listened silently for his comeback.

"CeCe?"

"Yes?" she hesitated.

"I . . ." he managed, as the grumbles and familiar intermittent pauses on the end of the phone revealed to Troi that Vaughn hadn't called to fight, rub it in, or hurt her; he was crying.

56

Vaughn dialed the number to what he now only loosely referred to as home. It had been about eleven days since he had seen Troi's familiar face pleading with him to let Pastor pray about their situation.

"CeCe?" He sat on his bed with his curtains drawn, the light off, and just listened, unable to hear her voice without feeling remorse or humiliation.

She was what most men wanted, even when they didn't know what they wanted. Loyal. He was unable to move forward or back in his mind. His pride moved the receiver from his mouth; his hand had him now wiping tears from his nose, and his voice cracked, making it all the harder for Troi to understand what he was saying.

"Vaughn? What's wrong? Talk to me."

"CeCe, I need to see you. I need to talk to you."

"For what?"

"I know I'm probably the last person . . . that you want to see . . . hear . . ."

"Where are you?"

"I'm at my mother's. I need to talk, not long, I promise."

"Are you okay? I can come there . . . the apartment here is too crowded . . . I was cooking and the sisters came with me after church, so . . ."

"How long will it take you?"

"Shouldn't take long. But you're right, we really do have to talk. Did you eat?"

"No, not hungry."

"You sure?"

"I'm sorry, CeCe. I'm really sorry."

"We'll talk when I get there, okay, baby?"

"Sure."

"Twenty minutes?"

"Yes."

"Vaughn?"

"Huh?"

"I'll see you soon."

In a fit of rage, Vaughn had taken every remnant of Tracie ever knowing him and put it in his duffel bag. Vaughn had left the silver bracelet that Tracie had given him as a gesture of their newfangled love by the telephone. As soon as Tracie reached for the phone to track Vaughn down and find out where he was, he'd know it was over.

Vaughn couldn't believe that this man had premeditated his attempt to kill him. He didn't look like the type. There were psychotic people out there for real, and it had to be his luck to run up on one who was deliberately seeking to destroy not only his life, but his marriage. Troi had been everything to Vaughn that a husband would need a wife to be. She was patient and had tried over and over again to salvage the remains of what Tracie had left behind. She was forgiving almost to a fault.

"Listen, Vaughn, I know it makes you feel weak, but I'm working and I can take care of us both," Tracie had said that fateful morning. It had seemed charitable enough. Vaughn had had the nerve to joke about fetching slippers, making it all the more humorous. But the Good Samaritan had come along and put a damper on all the laughter as he'd explained, "I have nothing to gain by telling you what I'm about to tell you."

He'd said, "Tracie is a liar."

Vaughn's own voice echoed, "How did you know I was in banking?"

"He ruins people's lives . . . I met him four years ago . . . he sent you flowers at work purposely . . . he wanted to create a situation where you'd have to depend solely on him . . . he doesn't love you . . . he can't . . . he's not capable . . . years ago he tested positive . . . and has been on an emotional crime spree ever since . . . if I were you, I'd get tested."

Too much revelation for one afternoon. Vaughn's mind had struggled to catch up.

Vaughn cupped his hands over his head. The voices were repeating themselves.

Vaughn's momma tapped on the bedroom door.

"Baby? You all right in there? I made your favorite."

"Leave the boy alone," he overheard his father scold. "That boy has enough worries without you trying to feed him all the time."

"I just don't want him to go hungry."

"When he gets hungry enough, he'll eat. Now, in the meantime, just leave him alone."

Vaughn was still thinking back to the afternoon he'd learned all about Tracie.

"I don't have a dime for him to extort from me," Vaughn had explained to the stranger with the life-changing revelation.

"I'd call my wife, patch things up if I were you. Maybe you can salvage a morsel of love that can grown into something to get you through the rest of your lives."

And Vaughn had done what the stranger had suggested. He'd sat in the dismal office, surrounded by fashion-spread faces and magazines that made a morbid effort to conceal his nervousness.

"The doctor will see you now, Mr. Singleton," the receptionist had cued as he'd walked into the office and sat in the wobbly chair across from his family physician.

Vaughn had surveyed the doctor's face, trying to discern the results.

"Mr. Singleton, how are you feeling?"

"I've been better, but I'm alive." He'd hesitated.

"And your wife and baby?"

"They're fine. She's going on three now."

"Good. Okay. Mr. Singleton, now, as far as I can see, the results you are here for are from the test that determines whether or not you have the HIV virus present in your system. Have you ever been tested for this before?"

"No, I haven't."

"Has your wife?"

"Not to my knowledge."

The doctor had written in Vaughn's chart as he spoke to him in ten-second intervals.

"Mr. Singleton, I wish what I had to tell you was good news, but you've tested positive for the HIV virus. Now, that doesn't mean that you have full-blown AIDS, but your wife should come in and be tested also, and your daughter."

"No, my daughter is fine, I haven't had it that long . . . I mean . . ."

"You never can be too sure. But there are a lot of services available for you and your family, and this medication that I am going to prescribe for you will just aid your immune system in helping to keep your body healthy and prevent it from going through any drastic changes in the next few months. Have you been practicing safe sex?"

"With my wife, yes. She doesn't want any more kids right now."

"Do you have any idea where or how you contracted the virus?"

"Probably."

"The best thing to do would be to create a list of partners that you've had unprotected sex with. You need to contact your partners and have them get tested also. Early diagnosis is crucial. I'm going to give you a referral to our in-house counselor and also the nutritionist. How and what you eat are very important. And this bloodwork, you need to have this as soon as possible. It tracks blood cells. Do you understand?"

"Yes." Vaughn had nodded.

"Any questions, Mr. Singleton?"

"Yes, can I go now?"

The knock on Vaughn's bedroom door was intrusive. He ignored it. His mother was always forcing him to eat something.

"Can I come in, Vaughn? Are you asleep?" Troi's voice called to him.

Vaughn opened the door slowly, and his silence welcomed her in. He sat on the bed, trying to examine her face in the absence of light, wondering what she was made of deep down inside. She was love to the core, wrapped in flesh. She had taken every revelation he had given on the chin. She didn't swear or hit, just questioned why.

"Are you okay? Turn on the light. It's so dull in here."

"I'm positive, CeCe . . ." There was no way to cushion the blow.

"You're what?"

"Positive."

"Positive about what?"

"HIV positive."

"What! Who said?" She reached out for him.

Vaughn put his arms around his wife, crying not only because it was him now who needed comfort from her, but more because he knew in his heart that everything they'd ever had had been changed forever.

"How long have you known?" Troi's nose tingled as she began to cry.

"Two days." His voice trembled.

"And you're just now telling me?" she whined. "Why are you just now telling me, Vaughn?"

"I'm sorry . . . I wanted to tell you before but . . ."

Troi heard a tapping and looked up to see Vaughn's momma in the doorway overhearing, holding on, and gently sliding down the wall, sobbing silently. His momma groaned, pounding the floor. The shuffle of his father's footsteps was quick.

"What's going on?" his father yelled, looking down at his wife heaving on the floor.

Vaughn had never seen his father panic. His momma cried, pulling at her clothes and hair.

"Is somebody gonna say something?" His father pounded the wall.

"I'm sorry, CeCe, I really am. I don't know what else to say," Vaughn pleaded.

"Don't say anything. You will live and not die." Troi embraced her husband. She turned to Vaughn's father and paused. "He tested positive for HIV."

57

"Mother, you will not upset me today." Nina turned the flowerpot upside down, patted the bottom, and loosened the roots from the soil. "I don't care what you do or say, my buttons will not be pushed. Every time I leave you, I have a headache. I don't want a headache today," Nina said, trying to straighten up the mess her mother had acquired around the house.

"I'm not trying to push your buttons, I don't feel good."

"Well. Say you don't feel good, Mother. What's wrong, anyway?" Nina emptied mounds of ashes into the sink and rested a row of highball glasses on the counter by twos. "You really should quit. Smoking is not good for you. It's a filthy habit."

"We all gotta die."

"So, you in a rush?"

"I used to be."

"What?"

"Nothing."

"You want to go to lunch, Mother?"

"No."

"Are you hungry?"

"No."

"I thought we agreed that the three of us would go out to lunch?"

Nina looked around the cramped dull kitchen at the greasy dust that had settled all around the peach ruffled curtains. She looked up at the clock, whose second hand was making a futile effort to tick past eight. For an instant her mother sat motionless, then reached for the deck of cards and set them up for solitaire.

"Mother, let me ask you something." Nina hesitated. "Why did you marry Daddy?" she asked, expecting the normal brush-off.

Mother never wanted to talk about anything except other people. She went with the no-blame theory that nothing was her fault, and everything happened because of something or someone else.

"Because he asked me."

"So, you didn't love him?"

"Y'all young ones never understand. Old-timers didn't marry because they were seeing stars. Cupid ain't have nothing to do with it. They married because they needed to belong to something. To be a part of something that wasn't ending, but just continuing."

Mother stared at the cards, placing them down expressionlessly.

"I despised my own father. He was lazy, broke, and he never did respect my mother. And my mother, well, she was no prize, but that was no reason. He'd go out and come back in the wee hours, drunk and angry, talking about 'where's my breakfast?' And she'd get up from whatever she was doing and get busy cooking like a day laborer. He was always telling us that we wasn't nothing special. I guess 'cause he was nothing much himself. But I swore up and down that when I had kids I'd never . . ."

Nina threw a suspicious glance in her mother's direction. "So, you married Daddy to feel special?" Nina overlooked her mother's hesitation.

"He made me love me. He showed me that, child. Not many men are like that. I never liked looking at myself in a mirror until he told me how beautiful I was. Then I'd look and try to see what he saw. After he told me I was beautiful, I started looking at myself all the time. Sometimes I'd ask him, 'Do you think I'm pretty?' just to hear him say it. His words made me want to do good, they made me want to do better. He'd smile and tell me, 'Sadie, you are the most beautiful woman I know.' He said my eyes told stories and that my hands could do anything that my mind could conceive." She flipped the cards over and focused on the game now.

"After you girls, things were different. He didn't tell me nice things much anymore. And I thought, my Lord, now I'll have what my mother had, a shell of a marriage. All I wanted was to hear it again, to feel his gentleness, to keep me going. You'd think I was asking him to raise the dead. I never did see what he saw in me. I never could bear to look in that mirror now . . ."

"But he loved you, Mother. Still does."

"Child, I never went to college. Barely finished sixth grade. I had nothing to offer him. I was just glad he picked me."

At that moment, Nina saw the humanity in her mother.

"You are beautiful, Mother."

"Yeah, but it's not the same thing now, is it? Now he's gone, telling somebody else they're beautiful. And me? Well, I'm just trying to get along the best way I know how."

"Mother, why you so down on yourself? You just need to clean up a little. You have such potential," Nina soothed with words that had a mind of their own but did their job. "Did your daddy drink much?"

"Sometimes too much. Sometimes not enough." Mother continued, "I never liked looking in the mirror until he told me how beautiful I was. I never could bear to look in that mirror now," she repeated, obviously stuck on thoughts of Daddy still. Her mother feeling something for once, that was new to Nina.

Nina thought back to her conversation with her mother this afternoon as they forfeited on lunch and she now relaxed in her room on her crisp bed linens as the ceiling fan cooled her and cleared her mind long enough to realize that her mother's dysfunction was handed down. Nina herself thought about being too much or not being enough. She thought of all the men to whom she'd given noticeable attitude. She had kissed more than enough frogs. It was good and high time that she was delivered from whatever was over her. Most men made her nervous. That made her overcompliant most of the time.

Nina heard the mailman make his way into her gate. She waved to him from the doorway, grinning as if she had donated her good sense. Life was unpredictable, so was the weather. One day it seemed to welcome fall and the next, it was so hot she knew for sure that the devil had come to town on vacation.

Junior wasn't far behind the mailman. He passed in the front, humming. Nina just observed, never said much to him normally. Seemed he had a new profession. Melon man. At least it beat harassing the young girls in the neighborhood.

"Hey, I got one for you now," Junior said. "It's the last one." He squinted, sweaty from the heat and the trickle of perspiration.

"Where you get that thing from, Junior?" Nina questioned, hands on hips.

"C'mon now," he pleaded like a hungry thief.

"Okay, is it cold?"

"No, ma'am, they're room temperature. I guess more like hot."

"I like them cold, Junior," she kidded.

"Why you do me like that?"

"Okay, how much?"

"Five dollars."

Nina ran into the house to grab her purse. She peeled off the bills and counted five.

"Here. Five dollars, right?"

"Much obliged," Junior said, walking up the stairs, balancing the watermelon on his shoulder and delivering it to her doorstep, then tipping his hat and heading off down the street.

"Hey," Nina called, "you fix locks?"

"I don't know, I'd have to take a look at it."

"Can you come by later?"

"Around seven."

"That's fine," Nina said.

She didn't understand what had become of the Junior who marched up and down the block reaching out to touch the young girls on their way to school and made the usual nuisance of himself. Just when he had gotten predictable, he had turned around and surprised her. People changed, she supposed.

Nina rolled the watermelon from her doorway into her living room and grabbed the biggest knife she could find in the kitchen. She sat on her floor, bare feet propped against the oblong fruit, and used both hands to press the sharp point into the middle of the melon. She tried to cut a slice, but crooked was what she got. She picked away a few seeds, licked her lips, and stuck her whole face down into the slice. Watermelon juice ran down her cheeks and chin, dripping onto her shiny floor. She spat excess seeds into her hand. She felt like a little kid again, only this time, living something more like the life she should have had, something to relish.

Nina smiled. She had acquired something that she'd thought was only for those svelte, ginger-skinned girls. The way that they walked down the street with those overrated Ivy League brothers who belonged to those fraternities that people went on and on about. They weren't better than her, only shinier and more appealing on the outside, like an apple covered with wax. She couldn't unleash herself with a brother like that.

Nina's phone rang once, then stopped. It rang twice, then stopped again. On the next series of rings, Nina snatched up the receiver and spoke a harsh "hello."

"Sorry, it's my phone. The reception isn't good. You busy? I'm in the area."

Nina wondered if she would confess. She had to prethink everything she said to Shelby. Nina had been known to knock romance and marriage. She had emphatically disbelieved in the power of love. It had appeared for the most part illusionary. She called it self-deception. Someone had said love was the opiate of the people's mind and unscientific bosh, delusion, or both. Then there was Tim.

Nina sat, impatiently anticipating Shelby for a change, and, she didn't know just when, but the words came tumbling out of her mouth, landing at Shelby's feet.

"I've thought about him every day since we met and I'm saying, is he a maniac? How can you tell before you've fallen? There aren't always signs. Troi said, just stay in prayer, because when God is sending a blessing, the enemy always tries to send a counterfeit."

"Girl, you've already got the man."

"I know, but I want something lasting, and this relationship could be the right fit I've looked for," Nina said, pleased to be the one doing all the talking for a change.

"What does he do, and where did he take you?"

"He's in film, and we went out and had cappuccinos and rode the ferry."

"The Staten Island Ferry?"

"Yes."

"Girl, you need to raise your standards. If you let a man think that he can overlook you, after a while, he won't take you nowhere."

"What?"

"Has he said that he wants you or a commitment? Anything?"

"Not exactly."

"I told you to leave those twenty-year-olds alone. This spiritual maturity you keep talking about and emotional maturity are two different things. I mean, he can't even swallow his pride long enough to tell you that he wants you?"

"Shelby, please. I'm not worried about that."

"Girl, you better get your hair done, buy something nice and slinky and . . ."

"I'm not gaming. This is me. He's seen me. He knows I'm no nineten. He knows I'm no sucked-in Barbie doll."

"Okay," Shelby said, flipping channels.

"Are you listening to me?"

"Yes, I am," Shelby said, pointing the remote control and clicking Power, turning the television off. "Now. You've got my undivided."

"Okay." Nina sighed. "Well, I did a lot of blushing that night. See, it's all so innocent. When our lips met, it was like my first kiss ever."

"See, that's what I'm saying. But what happens after the kiss, that's what I wanna know."

"His lips were so soft, I can't even explain. It's like they were made for mine." Nina giggled, obviously ignoring Shelby's comment.

Nina was getting her life balanced. She was almost ready to throw her therapist a going-away party.

"Well, this is for you, if you can spare a moment to step down off of the cloud you're on," Shelby said, sliding a rectangular object wrapped in brown paper in front of Nina.

Nina raised a brow and tore the paper off, revealing an abstract oil painting similar to the one in that little curio shop across the street from the café she and Tim had visited. She had fallen in love with that piece months before. Nina adjusted and examined it.

"Thank you, Shelby."

"My pleasure. Hang it in the bedroom. Brighten up the place."

"I probably will. I can't hang it in the office I no longer have," Nina joked. "Where'd you get it?"

"My friend." Shelby blushed.

"The starving artist?"

"Yes, I've got about four more at home."

"Why?"

"I like to support him. He's so talented."

"So, you're giving him money now?"

"No, I'm buying his paintings."

"Same thing, Shelby. Nobody needs all that art. You just want to give him money, admit it," Nina teased.

"Well, he falls on hard times periodically. Has had to pawn some of his work, and I hate to see that."

"Yeah, me, too, I guess," Nina added, without a hint of sarcasm.

There was nothing more Nina could do to convince herself that she didn't need to be afraid. Men had taken her mind on joyrides and she'd come back again and again. She fought to rationalize the desire she had to see Tim. The fear and passion she had for Tim that were eating her alive. She wanted her hands to tell the story, just him and her fingers tracing and brushing crumbs from his spoken words. She wanted him to be feeling what she felt, and she wanted the emotion they shared to be a standard by which others measured their feelings.

Nina remembered someone had said that women who say they want to be happy should be able to describe what happy would feel like for them. Many people said, "I want to be happy," as an umbrella phrase that didn't really describe anything. *Happy* and *love* were overused words. The core of the matter wasn't the word, but the feeling. What was the pleasure, what was the ultimate? Nina thought. Her ideas had been simple. Liberating.

Lying in the tickling grass naked, the sunshine stinging the back of her legs and a zephyr cooling her slightly and blowing wildly through her hair, as damp butterflies fluttered and tiptoed on her back, exciting her, making her body stand up and take notice that somebody loved her as much as she loved herself.

That was what happy was. That was how happy would feel for Nina. She loved to be lost in thought; it had been the only place where life was perfect.

Nina ached for someone with whom to interact. The shih tzu with the limp made his daily deposit, and Nina wondered when she'd live her life more effectively. Maybe find someone who'd give her heartstrings a song to play. Someone who'd fulfill her dreams.

In her dreams, damp kisses fluttered around the nape of her neck in a slow and circular fashion. Her shimmery silk nightgown hugged the contours of her body as the wind blew it slightly above her knees. Her hair had lost its curls in the determined breeze, and there were hands that clasped her waist—his. His presence was magical, and she felt sure that the way his lips lingered on hers was enough to start an emotional fire.

She knew that there were no warning signs that came with Tim. She burned to be near him. She throbbed to touch his face and run her finger across his bottom lip. He was deliberate in what he said to her as she imagined that they'd linger on the terrace with almost no traffic hindering the way he spoke of how he wanted her to come away with him in her ear.

"Pick a place," he'd plead. "There has to be somewhere that you've always wanted to go."

"I want to go to the beach," she'd say. She had no one for whom she was responsible. He had to be all, besides a towel, that she would want to take.

He'd give her warm glances that assured them both that the steps they were about to take were right. Nina knew it was true. Tim's presence always made it hard for her to breathe. He'd always allow her to feel him. His warmth would emanate and would take her on this journey that she was sure would lead to a fragrant, overripe vineyard or winding, leafy country road.

"So, Shelby, what's new with you?" Nina smirked, placing a fresh pot of coffee on the table, next to some fancy nineteenth-century china cups she had gotten at one of her favorite antique spots.

"I'm just being me, you know, I . . ."

The phone interrupted what was sure to be Shelby's repressed soliloquy.

"I'm sorry I didn't get a chance to speak with you before I left. I had to go out of town on business. But I'd like to see you. Are you busy tonight?" his husky voice asked her heart. Nina flashed almost all thirty-two; Shelby rolled her eyes.

"No, I'm not really busy." Nina shrugged. "What time?" she asked, rummaging for a pen to jot down the address and pending instructions for dinner at his place.

This man had better know what he was in for. Nina suspected that he had a clue, but it would be just like the new her to reconfirm things.

58

Tim woke early as usual and fiddled with his camera a bit. He hesitated calling his sister, and instead toyed with the lens and wrote some dialogue that he could actually hear coming from Nina's parted lips. The thought of her wouldn't let him sleep. "Great thoughts come from the heart." It was four A.M. and he'd wanted to call Nina the moment he landed in New York, but then he'd seem desperate. He couldn't do that, so he waited. Fearful and unsure of what the next step should be, he was still charmed and impressed at the fact that in this year alone he had matured greatly. Someone once said that "pleasure and love can't exist without pain." They were lying and evading the mere fact that the pain itself came from loving and lying about it. Tim had decided to ignore the media and other biased propaganda and charm her to death.

He had tons of things to do. He had to sit down with his boss, Abby, and give Big Deal at least a week's notice. He hoped that they would understand that opportunities like these hardly ever surfaced for a struggling brother in New York City. He also had to officially withdraw from school, since he didn't know how long this new project of his would last, or if he'd eventually end up right back at square one. He also planned on stopping by Justin's. He didn't want his boy feeling abandoned and kicked to the curb.

It was 8:37 now, and, being unable to restrain his urges any longer, he had called Nina to jar any plans that she had and gone about preparing a special evening of food and music, where he would tell her what he really thought. Fragile as hearts were, he knew that lies would catch up to him eventually. He'd have to come clean. Tell her about everything. There was nothing more special than caring about someone who cared back. And if she did care, he promised himself he'd cherish that, forever. Panic surfaced periodically; he didn't fully grasp whether or not he was ready for this.

Tim spent the day shopping and perused the market for fruit and a salt-free cracker he could serve with dip. At about four-fifteen, while cutting up fruit for salad, Tim called Justin and ran down his whole saga.

"You mean, she has herpes?"

"That's what she said, man."

"And you're positive you don't have it?"

"I'm certain." Tim frowned.

"Yo, that was close, man!"

"You telling me? I know."

"You never know. Ain't that a trip?"

"Yeah, well, I thank God. I told you player is tired; besides, I have my films to look forward to. I don't have time for creepin'."

"Yeah, you big-time now."

"Not actually, but soon."

"What's up with Nina?"

"She cool."

"Cool? That's it?"

"Yeah."

"So, your boy don't get more than that?"

"Okay, I'm cooking her dinner." Tim laughed.

"Dinner?"

"Yeah, you know, the thing on a plate that you eat with a fork?"

"She whipped you, man?" Justin's voice rose an octave.

"See, I can't talk to you. Later, man, you gonna make me burn the broccoli quiche."

Tim had spent all day trying to impress this woman. He'd cleaned up and boxed all his loose magazines and piled them behind his old drum set in the closet. He'd called Rochelle at work, and on her lunch hour she had walked him through the seasoning, egg dipping, and breading the chicken part. He was so out of character that he enjoyed it almost as much as learning a new song. Diana Krall was crooning, most appropriately, "When I Look in Your Eyes" over the aroma of chicken parmesan, garlic, and half-baked French bread.

A persistent rap on the door cued Tim to turn down the volume and light a few candles. He looked at his watch and frowned, because it wasn't time yet, and he wasn't one hundred percent ready.

"One sec." He deepened his voice, only to be thoroughly annoyed by Michelle's impromptu presence and skinny legs posing uninvited at his door.

In all the time he had known her, she never was where she needed to be. Always defying and manipulating. A little too much like himself, he thought.

"What do you want, Michelle? And why didn't you call first?"

"Ahh, I see. We having company?" She leaned in the doorway. "Smells delicious. You never cooked for me." She walked over to the stove and stuck her finger in the sauce.

"I should have, you're starving."

"Very funny, but not funny enough."

"Why are you here, Michelle?"

"Well, I was looking for a blue sweater that I might have left here."

"Here? What makes you think you left it here?"

"Only because this is where I spent most of my time, you know that, Tim."

"Hardly." Tim glared. "Look in the bedroom. If it's not in there, then it's not here."

"Okay." Michelle winked.

"And hurry up, I'm busy here."

"What's the rush? Relax, baby, or have you forgotten how?"

"I know how to relax, I just don't need your help doing it."

"Testy, aren't we?" Michelle pouted.

Tim dried his hands, smacked around the salmon-colored sofa pillows, and then rummaged through the refrigerator and slid three ice trays from the freezer, twisting them upside down into the wine chill.

"Tim, can you help me in here?" Michelle called from the bedroom.

"I can't do that, Michelle." Tim chuckled at her vain attempt to conjure a teaspoon of affection.

Tim eyed his watch and the doorway to the bedroom as the doorbell rang again. It was 6:07 P.M. Tim peeped through the door and answered it reluctantly as Michelle stepped out of the bedroom. Tim observed the infectious smile disappear from Nina's flushed face as her eyes darted around the room, attempting to figure out what was going on, and why Tim had asked her over if someone else was already comfy there.

"Wait a minute, honey." Michelle draped herself across Tim. "Who is that?" She pointed at Nina.

"Stop it, Michelle . . ."

"Tim and I are friends," Nina responded simply, not giving her an inch or the satisfaction.

"Well, isn't she cute? Tim, she's a little on the healthy side, but . . ."

"Knock it off, Michelle!" Tim yelled. "Just leave."

"Leave? You weren't asking me to leave last night."

"Last night? What? Shut up, you delusional little wench."

Michelle giggled and stood with her arms crossed, determined to bust up this little saga that had written her out of the script almost three months ago.

Tim's confusion was visible, and gave Nina the confidence to say what she was about to.

"Listen, Miss Whoever-you-are." Nina grinned. "I, unlike you, was invited here. I understand if you feel desperate enough to show up unannounced to scratch and mark your territory, but the next time you try to claim something, make sure it wants you back. And you, Tim"—Nina pointed—"you need lessons in learning to handle your business. Now, you two just have a fabulous evening. Goodbye." Nina waved her hands, fed up with the sitcom mentality that the situation presented, and slammed the door behind her.

Tim stuck his head out into the hall. "Nina, c'mon. Wait. I can explain . . ." He turned and looked at Michelle behind him. "You, out!" He motioned with his thumb.

"Well, I might as well." Michelle laughed. "It looks like the party has been canceled." She laughed hysterically.

As Tim approached Nina's home, the curtains blew outside of her window to some imaginary rhythm, and there was a tiny glow of a light in one of the rooms near the back of her brownstone. He rang her bell, ignoring and imagining that she was sitting there thinking of him. He wondered if he would have to give up everything he desired for this woman. She wasn't common. She was something that most women only wished they could be. The moon shined forth in its glory, and Tim found himself enveloped, engulfed. Wanting to touch her, smell her. Women should be peeled delicately. They had many layers.

Reluctantly, Nina listened to Tim rendering an apology with her arms folded, sitting in his car nearing midnight, talking slightly above the Quiet Storm, the radio program.

"I won't let you treat me any kind of way." Nina bit her bottom lip. "I don't need a man, I want a man. There's a difference. I am beautiful, inside and out. I own a mirror, Tim."

She had to be a woman who knew she blew his mind, and took her time deciding that she would acknowledge that fact. Planes roared overhead, and they were hardly able to hear themselves in the comfort of each other. But they knew the drill. Tim had tasted the delight that she'd brought into his life, and the smell of her, "My My My," as the song went. When he thought of women who made themselves available, it made him cherish all the more a woman who wasn't desperate to make a man hers. He needed to have her; there was no way around it.

Tim was satisfied. He just needed to hold her face between his fingers and feel the slight curve of her cheekbones. Caress her skin gently. He could blame it on her wiles and quivering kisses. And in his mind, he was rewriting a scene that was insistent on a happy ending. Instantly he craved something besides his cameras and scripts. He didn't care. He just lingered, like an insect drawn by the natural sugar in ripe fruit. He held her, waiting for the perfect moment.

She had to go, so standing on a quiet street in Brooklyn at one A.M., kissing a woman who was so brilliant that their attraction should be illegal, he was now forbidding her to end this moment. He hated women for not being Nina. What a waste of time they had been. Women who were easier to read, easier to direct into a scene. She didn't even know what she was doing to him. She made him think of how he surely appreciated her the way she needed to be. She was free and natural. It left more to the imagination. It made him crave her more, like an overripe peach minus the fuzz.

Tim wasn't thinking. His concentration was replaced by a desire to sit somewhere quaint and listen to her laugh. Giggle. She was something extraordinary. There was no doubt that it wouldn't take years to fall, or months. If there were ever a need, she was it. If there were ever a story, he would rewrite it around her. She was his, or he'd die trying. In life he knew that there were four absolutes. Love was one. Then there was unselfishness, honesty and purity.

There had to be more that she had done to him. He could deny it and revert to his old self, but it would still be the truth. What he felt would still exist like an underlying emotion. She was very efficient in the way that she communicated. They may have seemed incompatible, but when they were face-to-face, there had to be rules broken, there had to be denial, it was the only way he could explain how she defied everything for which he supposedly stood. There was enough of him to consume her and vice versa until they both surrendered, willingly.

Tim didn't notice her hair. He watched as she adjusted it and tried not to get touchy-feely. He held her around her waist and waited until his eyes drank in all there was of her to savor.

"Come here, you need to be in my arms."

He forgot the time he had wasted with women who were purely superficial satisfaction. He wished he had never shared himself with another woman; he wanted to be Nina's gift. He wanted her to be his only level, he wanted to know no depth but her, no pleasure except what she gave. But how could he risk everything he had struggled for? His films. His goals.

"Save something for later," his father had always told him about women. "You don't have to go spilling everything. Take your time. Choose your words carefully." And now Tim was glad he had. He wasn't about to punish himself or struggle and sacrifice Nina's happiness because he needed to drag this craving out long-distance. She had ties to the city. It would never work.

"I don't want to leave, Nina, honestly I don't." He brushed her hair from her face.

Her lips pecked his as he read her thoughts.

"And just where do you think you're going?" She grinned.

59

Vaughn was her husband. Troi didn't care if everyone on earth stood up and told her to leave him. She wouldn't. People sure knew how to talk and give someone else advice, but when they found themselves in a similar situation, they did exactly what they warned her heart not to do—give in. *She forgives him too easily.* She could hear them saying it now. And that was her business. Prayer was the key. She had prayed that her husband come back to her, and he had. She had to be strong. She didn't need to be the weeping woman who let pity become her shadow, especially not now. He needed her. He said that he'd had no idea that Tracie was playing with a loaded gun. That man had changed their lives forever. She knew that even if Vaughn had a total disregard for her, he'd never purposely do that to himself. He was good-looking. Fine. She knew that women would approach him still. They often did. But she had never imagined a man.

It was one-thirty P.M., a brisk barren afternoon. Vaughn asked Troi if she would mind meeting him at the doctor's office. So she did. His insurance was only good for another five months, and the doctor had suggested that Troi get tested. Troi walked into the waiting area and left her name with the receptionist. She turned, and her husband was standing, waiting to hug her.

"Thank you, CeCe." He smiled with the familiar gratitude that she had come to know and love.

They sat in the waiting area. They both sat biding time and concealing their fear. Whether she was positive or negative, she could deal. She was a Madison by blood.

After Vaughn skimmed a magazine, then passed it to Troi to flip through, the receptionist called them both into the doctor's office. Silently Troi sat, closing her eyes, and reached for Vaughn's hand, holding on tight and praying a silent prayer that they hoped God would hear the minute it passed their lips. The doctor entered the office and adjusted himself in his chair.

"Morning, Mrs. Singleton. Mr. Singleton."

"Good morning, Doctor."

The doctor opened their charts to the laboratory section.

"How's the baby?"

"She's fine. Getting bigger every day. She's almost three."

The doctor reached into the cabinet and pulled out several referrals. He flipped through the chart a second time.

"All right. As you know, Mrs. Singleton, your husband's blood sample came back positive for the presence of the HIV virus."

"Yes."

"Now, this doesn't mean he has full-blown AIDS. But he does need to be careful and follow up with me or someone else on a regular basis."

The doctor discussed ways Vaughn could stay strong, and how he needed to eat to keep himself healthy, and added that eating healthy was a wiser way of life anyway.

"However, Mrs. Singleton, you on the other hand, your results for the presence of HIV are negative."

"Negative?" Troi squeezed Vaughn's hand.

"Yes, now, if you and your husband plan on engaging in sexual activities, you need to protect yourself. There are various ways you can do this." The doctor handed her a couple of booklets and samples of women's condoms. "There can be no exchange of bodily fluid. Prevention is the key here."

Troi embraced Vaughn and hugged him tightly.

"I love you," she whispered in his ear.

"You know I never wanted you to be . . ."

"I know." She nodded. "I know."

"Yes, Doctor. Whatever we can do. We have a little girl and . . ."

"Yes, she'll be fine. Just bring her in for a routine blood workup. All I do advise, however, Mrs. Singleton, is that you get retested in a couple of months, and then maybe a year after that."

"Yes, Doctor."

Troi and Vaughn had spent the afternoon discussing in length whether or not they would tell the entire family. His mother and father knew, but Troi's mother and father had no idea.

"We can tell them. I don't have a problem with that," Vaughn said.

"Okay, then." Troi hugged her husband. "We'll be strong together."

Vaughn backed away from the embrace and looked at Troi seriously. "CeCe, I do love you, you know that, right?"

"Yes, Vaughn, I know."

"It's not just because of my condition or Dakoda."

"I know, Vaughn." Troi frowned. "You know I want to take care of you. I love you with all my heart, and when that's not enough, there's more love still."

"I know, that's why I felt so horrible. I don't know what I would have done if you were positive."

"We would have let God's will be done, Vaughn, that's it."

Troi had made a few calls to gather her family together along with his. They both wanted everyone to know what was going on together. She didn't want any whispering behind their backs or rumors that were far from the truth of the matter. If anyone had something to say, they could say it right there in front of both of them.

Troi couldn't wait until Nina arrived, so she had disclosed the facts to her sister on the phone, and Nina had cried so painfully.

"How could this happen to him?"

"Just pray. That's all I'm asking you to do. Please don't feel sorry. He needs prayers, not pity."

"Okay. I know. I'll pray," Nina had promised.

When Troi's father arrived, he only cornered her near the kitchen and asked, "Well, do you love him?"

"Yes."

Troi's mother said, "Once you're in love, there's no turning back." Her mother eyed her father and patted her daughter on the shoulder.

Troi tried distracting herself with anything other than the situation at hand. She sat pensive, thinking that the truth wasn't as flattering as folks made it out to be. It hurt her heart that it took a near tragedy to bring everyone together. There were never as many people present for a birth as there were at a funeral, that much was true.

Vaughn's father had surprisingly done an about-face regarding him and his preference. Homosexuality was one thing, but a pending death was another.

His father asked, "Do you need anything? Just let me know what you need, son."

And as usual, his mother had prepared enough food to feed everyone who showed up. That included pies, just as she had done the night Troi had gone with Vaughn out to Jersey on what was now considered their first date. Sam heard the news secondhand. He hadn't returned any calls, and he still refused to see his brother face-to-face. Troi knew that hurt her husband to death.

"I'll pray for him," was the message that Sam had sent.

In the next few weeks, Troi and Vaughn began taking care of finances together and budgeting his unemployment check, along with what she had saved from the shop. They had secured an account that would be a college fund for Dakoda. And they were currently making sure their insurance policies hadn't lapsed. They were working together, and becoming closer than they had ever been. Normally Vaughn had taken care of the finances. He said that's what his father had done. There were court matters to go through, and another hellacious lawsuit surely pending.

Troi still couldn't fully comprehend that Shangrila was gone. She couldn't imagine Sofie harnessing that much hate. Troi had known Sofie Cardona since high school. From third grade to graduation. Her whole life, Troi had watched Sofie destroy hers with drugs, alcohol, and multiple men. Any man would do. She had always put men first, as if they were saviors, when most came with an ulterior motive not only to eat the cake, but to destroy any evidence that it had ever existed.

When Troi had opened her shop, she had given that silly woman a job out of the kindness that she alone possessed. Nina had always said that Troi was vying for sainthood. Doing for someone who would end up kicking her in the face. And look at what that woman had done to her dream, to her life, Troi thought. Burnt it down to the ground, rendering it nonexistent.

The man who opened the bodega across the street at seven A.M. sharp every morning had seen Sofie hanging around the shop two days before the fire. She hadn't worked there in over a month, had no airtight alibi. The evidence was mounting. She was out on bail, and they were in the process of selecting a panel of jurors. The prosecutor was confident she'd be on board that slow boat up the river, and Troi figured that that was exactly what she deserved.

Vaughn's father persistently urged him to file suit against that Tracie character. Initially, Vaughn wanted to forget the fact that the brother had ever existed.

His father told him, "If you don't do it for yourself, at least do it for your daughter."

Vaughn agreed, although they still received late-night phone calls urging them to forgo the legalities and forgive.

"I never meant to hurt you, Vaughn," Tracie had said.

"You ruined my life. What do you mean, you never meant to hurt me?"

"It's not my fault. Blame society."

"I don't feel sorry for you, Tracie. I have a family. A child. You have nothing, so of course you want my forgiveness."

"C'mon man, you know we had something," Tracie had tried to convince him. "Don't you want that again?"

"Hell, no!"

The doctor had told Vaughn not to put himself through any undue stress, so Troi always urged Vaughn to ignore the calls and let his father handle the legal matters. Sometimes he listened.

It wasn't until the day of the arraignment almost three weeks later that Vaughn and Troi found out just how far some people would go to get revenge, and just how far jealousy and envy imbedded themselves in the hearts of some. Despite his father's protest, Vaughn appeared in court, dressed in his Sunday best, but feeling the overshadowing darkness of a life that hadn't always welcomed him with open arms.

Vaughn needed to be there in court. He wanted visually to observe what malice looked like in action. The last time he had laid eyes on him, Tracie had been leaving the apartment for work and joking about the fact that Vaughn could fetch his slippers and he would keep him like a pleasurable trick. Vaughn hadn't been amused then and wasn't now.

Troi, Nina, Carla, Vaughn, and his father sat on the right side of the courtroom in the last row. The courtroom was full of young energetic males and flower-clad supporters, who could have been models or jilted lovers. Vaughn couldn't tell. There were women dressed in short skirts and skimpy blouses with their shoulders and bellies exposing postpregnancy stretch marks.

"All I want is money for my baby."

"Me, too," another woman agreed.

"How old is yours?"

"My daughter is seven. You?"

"My boy is ten. And it's a shame. He never got to know his father. I had to call my uncle over to have him teach the boy how to tie a tie."

"Well, y'all just stand in line," the man behind them both added. "He owes me in a big way. And I ain't leaving until he pays."

"You get tested?"

"No, you?"

"Look, you need to get over it, honey," a crisply dressed teen scoffed. "You're just mad because you were used."

"Used? Shut up! You don't know nothing. They need to hang him."

"Yeah, and he deserves everything he gets," another woman added.

"Sure does. I hope they give him the chair."

As the court officer ushered Tracie into the room, Vaughn looked in the eyes of the man who had told him repeatedly that he was falling for him. Vaughn's lips twitched. Tracie had lied, just as Vaughn had lied to Troi.

Troi nudged Vaughn and whispered, "Just be calm, Vaughn, okay?"

Vaughn ignored the fact that Tracie smirked past all the people who had involuntarily been his judge and jury before the trial had even begun. The look in his eyes said, *If I had the chance, I'd do it all again.* Vaughn's brow said, *We'll just see about that.*

The defendant's attorney shuffled papers that could never contain enough evidence for the case to be dismissed.

"Mr. Tracie Nunez." The judge read the complaint and appropriate case number. "You are charged with attempted murder. On the count of willfully concealing your medical status of being HIV positive, and knowingly passing it on to other parties without their knowledge or consent, how do you plead?"

The attorney stood as Tracie rested his chin on his hand and directed his gaze forward. The attorney nudged his client and Tracie rose to his feet.

"My client pleads not guilty, your honor."

"He's guilty," two women yelled.

The courtroom doors flung open. Sofie, in all her drunken glamour, stormed in, pointing.

"Shut up!" Sofie spat at the woman who was standing and declaring that Tracie was guilty, with her baby resting delicately on her hip.

"You shut up!" the woman said. "You don't know me. I'll cut you like paper."

"Order in the court! Order in the court!"

The court officers accosted Sofie and pulled her to the back of the courtroom as her eyes rolled around and took in the high ceilings and large windows.

"Let me go!" She kicked.

"I hate you, Troi." She pouted. "Little Miss Madison," Sofie mocked.

"Order!"

"Your husband is dying," Sofie yelled. "I wish him dead. How does it feel? Huh? How does it feel to lose something you love?" Her voice echoed off of the wood paneling.

"Don't stand there. Remove her from this courtroom, now!" The judge smashed his gavel repeatedly.

The court officers dragged Sofie's contorting body out of the courtroom on her heels as they scuffed against the indoor tile. Sofie's voiced trailed off as the judge slammed down the gavel on polished wood frantically. Troi reached for Vaughn's hand. *How does it feel to lose something you love?* Sofie's muffled voice echoed in Vaughn's head. *I wish him dead.*

After court recessed, Carla pulled Vaughn to the back of the courtroom and lit into him almost as drunkenly as Sofie had stormed in the court and performed. Vaughn walked away from Carla, and she pulled on his clothing. A few choice words later, Carla brushed past Troi, Nina, and the crowd of glory seekers.

"What happened?" Troi asked Vaughn.

"Nothing. Everything's fine." Vaughn closed his eyes and nodded.

Nina interrupted Troi. "Vaughn, I need to speak with you."

Vaughn's father was waving Troi over to the conversation he was having with the attorney.

"Sure. Carla let in on me. It's your turn, I suppose."

"I'm sorry, but I just need to get this out, so please just let me say my piece, and you can respond afterwards."

"Okay, fine."

"Now. Because I respect my sister and she loves you, I won't tell you what I really feel about what you did to her. Besides, I think you know that already. But the fact remains that God allowed her to be negative, partly because she had been so dedicated and faithful to you."

"I'm grateful for that . . ."

"I'm not done," Nina said harshly.

Vaughn sighed.

"But, if you decide that you want to come back to her, you need to make sure that the words aren't just on your lips, but in your heart and in your spirit. Because if you hurt her again or cause her to shed another solitary tear, God is my witness, I will not be legally held responsible for what I'll do to you."

60

In her bathroom, Nina discarded her red jacquard silk kimono, believing that there were some things that people didn't know about each other that hindered growth, and that there were things that people futilely denied that never managed to masquerade the fact that love lingered. You couldn't wash it off, pretend it off, or ignore it off. The residue of love lingered, crawling into the nooks and crannies, leaving behind the lasting impression that it was there, alive, breathing, and real. She couldn't believe it was all over. The chase had been invigorating, they had made up, but distance wasn't her thing. She didn't want to have to close her eyes to imagine him, although her heart told her that distance was only a mode of transportation.

If she had mentally been where she was a year ago, she would have taken Tim's good-bye way too personally. She would have cried and eaten until the ten extra pounds she gained would have been the reason for Tim's departure. She knew that she was worth a lot more than other men in her life had let on. Like Daddy had done for her mother, Tim had allowed Nina to see the beauty in herself. He'd shown her that it was okay for her to believe in something, to have an opinion, and to expect that a man would not only be honest, but respect her, no matter what she weighed.

She thought about how she had a fetish for a man in an apron. He didn't necessarily have to be cooking anything, but an apron was something to imagine. She smiled, spraying her fragrance into the air and walking into it, holding her breath. The car honked its horn from downstairs, and she snatched up her trench coat and trotted downstairs with an eagerness that was only overshadowed by having to say farewell. Nina was embarrassed that her breakfast dishes were still sitting in the sink and that her hose were hanging over the shower curtains. Her hair smelled like bacon, and she hoped he didn't notice.

Nina had browsed the card shop all morning and stocked up on cards for any occasion, as she normally did. Birthday cards, thank-you, sympathy, and love. But mostly love. She'd read the inside of one card that said, *Sometimes I feel as if God created love just for us.* She had bought a blank card for Tim's parents. He wanted to see them at the cemetery again before he left. She'd agreed to accompany him. She wasn't believing this. She needed a good cry. How could he be leaving just as subtly as he had entered her life, unaware of what he would stir in her, unaware of the afteraffect? Surely she hadn't waited her whole life for this. Nina belted her trench coat, nibbling on her bottom lip with card in hand, re-entered the waiting cab, and instructed the driver to drop her off uptown. She leaned back in the car as the driver hit the gas. She licked the corner of the envelope and sealed the card with the lasting impression of her lips.

Tim entered the cemetery with the same type of wilted tulips that he had placed on their headstones their last visit. Five delicate flowers for his mother; one for his father. Nina stood hesitantly in the rocky path as he made his way to the spot where his parents' sites were located.

"Come here." Tim waved Nina over.

"It's okay, Tim. I'm fine here." Nina stood hugging herself.

"C'mon, I want you to see something."

Nina stepped over into the section where Tim was pulling away weeds and vines and brushing dirt off of slate. Tim stood, examined Nina, then hugged her. He was ready for introductions now.

"This is my mother and father. Mr. and Mrs. Richardson."

Nina smiled politely.

"Mom, Dad, this is Nina."

Nina bent down and placed the card in between the two headstones, then gave Tim a peck on the cheek and a sympathetic look. She stood, rocking back and forth, and began to weep silently.

"C'mon, girl, don't cry. You okay?" Tim lifted Nina's chin and looked in her face as she nodded. They stood for just a moment and then turned, arm in arm, and headed back to his car.

Tim's hands hugged Nina's shoulder as he leaned over and kissed her on her cheek. She was bashfully holding her gaze fixed on anything but him. *Cowardly* was not a word she would ever use to describe herself, but she found herself fearing what his touch meant and what that look in his eyes did to her. Mornings would have normally found her waiting for his call; she knew that. The call that always confirmed their plans.

"I'll be back in a few months to finalize some things, Nina."

"I understand."

They drove back into the city, making small talk and plans that they hoped they could keep. She was suppressing the fear that was trying to surface. She couldn't allow uncertainty to sway what she knew was fact.

Tim parked his car in front of his building, opened Nina's fingers, and placed the keys in her hand.

"Give these to my sister on Sunday, okay?"

"Yes, I will."

"You okay?" Tim placed his hand delicately against Nina's back.

"I'm good. Really."

Tim extended his arm to flag down a yellow taxi, which would take them to the airport for a flat fee.

She didn't want to see him off. She didn't want to be anywhere near good-bye. Common sense told her that good things never lasted and that when someone seemed to be too good to be true, it was either a dream or a myth. They slid into the backseat of the taxi together.

"What's wrong?" Tim asked.

"Nothing, I'm just thinking. I'll be okay." She smiled, pressing her lips gently against his, and grinned, pleased to leave her scent.

Tim had spent a portion of the previous day convincing Rochelle and Carl that he knew what he was doing and would be okay.

"California isn't that far," he'd told Rochelle.

Carl had reviewed the contract the VP had given him in LA, and said it seemed fair. Valid. They were a reputable company that had been in business for at least six years, and had no complaints against them thus far. They had produced nine films that did relatively well for their genre. Only three had taken a severe loss.

Rochelle seemed proud of her brother, who, a few years ago, she'd thought would end up overdosing, stalked, or bound and gagged somewhere, being held hostage for a measly ransom.

His sister, Rochelle, was a woman married to a good man. Pretty soon they'd have a house full of little feet leaving a legacy. Rochelle had cried and cleaved to her brother's strong shoulders more tightly than she had at the funeral.

"I'm gonna miss you, Boogie."

"Stop, Rochelle. You're gonna make me cry and I'm a man. Besides, you know only Momma called me that."

"I know . . ."

"Leaving is killing me, you know."

"Why they call you Boogeyman?" Carl had asked.

"Not Boogeyman, Boogie."

"Because he'd never keep still." Rochelle had lowered her eyes. "Still can't keep still." She sniffled.

Tim had refused to let his sister see him off at the airport, and Carl had sided with him for a change.

Women were weepy, and he didn't want his sister hollering and carrying on in a crowded airport which, for most, was as common as a bus station. His sister had mothered him to the altar of salvation, and now it was time for her to let go. He understood her fear. She must have thought that he was still so young and new to the responsibilities of life. But he was going to make a go of this whole film thing. He had to. He wanted his momma and dad smiling down from heaven, proud.

He had sat down with Justin and discussed plans and his fear of leaving a woman for whom he had obviously fallen.

"Maybe she'll go with you, you never know."

"Nah, I can't ask her to do that. She has a life here."

"So, you don't think she feels the same as you do?"

"Yeah, I think she does. I want to believe she does. But I can't, I don't know."

"Whatever you do, I'm behind you. Okay?"

"Cool." Tim had embraced his friend. "Keep an eye on my stuff. No wild parties," Tim had said, handing Justin his extra key.

"C'mon, man. You think I would do that?"

"Yes."

"Okay, okay. But do you think that . . ."

"No wild parties."

"I gotcha." Justin had chuckled.

Right now, everything Tim was familiar with was changing.

Tim wished his momma could really see what he was doing with his life. He sulked as the trees blew and Nina leaned into his shirt, breathing in his scent, content with the slight musk that was masculine. Nina wasn't aware of the curious onlookers in passing cars or the cab driver, who eyed them from the rearview mirror.

The weather was cooperative, and Nina offered that she enjoyed every moment of it. She was looking for an opening in his heart where he'd allow her to fulfill all that he desired, free him from his cave, where memories both true and false attempted to dictate what his future would be.

His very presence was chivalrous. She, like he, seemed exhausted by the games that one played with one's mind, trying to convince themselves of things that would please and rationalize their lives for other people, never themselves. She had been hurt by past relationships, and so had he, but they had no intention of allowing the past to wreck their future.

Nina thought of every inch of Tim that she adored. His lips. She loved his lips. They had a purpose. To please her. She motioned for him to come closer, enjoying their verbal freedom. He spoke deliberately in her ear.

"Nina . . ."

She shuddered as if she were wearing something as flimsy as silk. The thought of him made her feel like cooking.

His plane took to the sky, bruising her soul. They spoke occasionally, pretending that three twenty-minute calls a week were enough. Each of them lingered, nursing a dial tone at three A.M. Each too sleepy to master a logical thought and too smitten to relinquish the other.

"I'm sorry about before I left and that whole Michelle thing," he'd apologized when last they spoke.

He was adjusting to life away from everyone he cared about; he just didn't like it much. He was more than making do now in an airy studio apartment with an enormous backyard about an hour's drive from the beach. A clear day in LA and Nina on his arm would definitely be something to grin about.

All that the women Tim ever met appreciated was what a man could finance. Nina's kindness was addictive. Any thought he could muster had been said and any gesture, overdone.

Freshly shaped-up goatee, manicured hands, he paused, relinquishing the memory of her to the here and now; then he dialed her number. Four. He'd let it ring four times, and though he missed the sound of her, he absolutely would not romance her answering machine.

"Hey, you."

"Hey . . . you find a church yet?"

"No. I've visited some that were kind of small but intimate."

"You find coffee?" She giggled.

"A vast selection, but nothing as quaint as our place."

Nina smiled, basking in the pleasure that all things weren't easily replaced. They had both gotten into the habit of calling each other's name just so it would linger in the air, then pausing, allowing the other to fulfill the thought. The telephone was all they had.

"Tim . . ." She didn't know what to say. "Your sister doesn't like me." She hesitated, not wanting to use their brief conversation for such weighty matters.

"I like you, that's all that matters."

"Yes, honey, I like you, too."

"Do you?"

"Yes, and I miss you."

"You miss me?"

"Yeah."

"Pick another word."

"I adore you?"

"Another."

"I require you."

"I love that."

"Yes, and I love . . ." Nina paused, almost biting her tongue. "I mean, I am really looking forward to seeing you. When are you coming back?" She camouflaged.

"Me, too," he confessed, leaving her unsure of which statement he was responding to. "I'll call you soon."

"Tim?"

"Yes?"

"Be safe."

Nina hung up the phone and placed her hands against the glass on her window. Her fingers grew numb. It was cool, reflecting the temperature outside rather than the warmth of the room. She was pleased that he satisfied her basic needs. Not many men could do that.

Was there anything so sensuous that it could become profane? Was there any love so ripe that, if it burst, dripping its essence, it would affect the world and how we treated each other, becoming contagious, semifatal? Would love ever reach the point where it was no longer harnessed, but instead had no limit, like a sweet-toothed child who gnawed tangerines, oblivious to the rind? He loved Nina, though his flesh would only allow him to think it, ponder it in his mind, but never say it. It was there, no longer extinguished by fear, now only by distance.

I was like a kitten with a warm bowl of milk, I was surviving on this now, Nina jotted in her journal. *There had to be at least six women off the top of my head that could seduce Tim with their eyes and taut bellies, but I couldn't afford toying with that notion. He had taught me to fight for my needs. I had been as deprived as a parched desert and he watered me. My thirst was mounting and I was absorbed in finding out about him. He was naturally smooth and had characteristics of a good man without appearing weak or vulnerable, even if he did almost cry at the cemetery. He was for the most part sincere with me. He was prompt and he was dedicated to completing his education and pursuing his goals. If he let me love him, I would touch him like . . .*

"Like damp butterflies," she spoke aloud. *Like damp butterflies,* she wrote. Here she was, pondering the marital bliss that she adamantly convinced herself didn't exist. Tim miles away and needs unfed. Tuesdays would never be the same.

A week later, tapping a pack of Marlboros on his fist and observing Nina peeping through the curtains, he was approached by two uniformed officers before he could think of a reason to be standing across the street, obviously spying.

"Are you Derek Conway?"

"Yes, I'm . . ."

"Can you come with us sir?"

"What is this about?"

He had never had a reason to stutter before; now he had several.

"You're under arrest, harassment."

"Who did I harass?"

"The telephone is considered a weapon, and you're supposed to be at least two hundred feet away from Ms. Madison and her home. Come with us, sir."

"I'm not going anywhere." Derek struggled. "Nina!" he called, as if he believed that she would actually come and rescue him.

The uniformed officers held his wrists down and then behind his back as he squirmed to get free. Free, as Nina had craved to be from the mere thought of him. She glimpsed through the curtains as they cuffed him, led him to the car, and shoved his shabbily dressed frame in the back of the patrol car and slammed the door shut.

All Nina could think was that she was free. Her thoughts raced from Tim to her mother, who only marginally acknowledged the fact that she needed anybody. Nina thought that it was about time she did something nice, not only for herself, but for someone else. She wanted to give her mother a makeover. Hair, nails, everything. Help her become beautiful enough on the outside that she could see it and allow it to influence the inside. No man should hold such power. She wanted her mother to see her own beauty and be able to summon it at will.

Nina needed changes and she couldn't wait for a man to come make her life worth living; she had to take matters into her own hands, press them to her bosom so her situation could hear what her heart was saying. Tim's leaving made Nina think about her own life. Her mobile job wasn't satisfying in the least, but she'd continue to do it for now. She was thinking of something extra. Horticulture. She'd look into it. Nina thought back to high school, and back to not so long ago with Derek. For once in her life, it seemed as if she was being dealt the good cards and was getting the last laugh.

61

The last time Tim had spoken with Nina, Michelle had arrived to pick up the check that Tim had rationally convinced himself he would write to reimburse her for all the tuition she had given willingly. He had mailed Sharon's, and would have done the same with Michelle's if he had known where to send it. In between her many stopovers in LA, Tim had caught up with one of her messages. In her mind, Michelle was probably certain that Tim's gesture was more a ploy to get her back than anything. She was sadly mistaken.

"People aren't objects to be used. They aren't furniture," his momma's voice echoed in his head, resounding through his being. He was sure that Nina had jumped to conclusions, but although he couldn't logically explain to Nina why Michelle—with whom he claimed it was over—was two thousand, five hundred miles away from New York, being heard in the background of his telephone conversation with Nina, he wished he could.

Nevertheless, his thoughts couldn't help but saunter back to midday traffic in the back of a yellow taxi as his kisses licked Nina's soul. His arrival at LAX that day was depressing to say the least. The fondness he had for Nina hadn't waned. Distance had never managed to do that for him.

He had been purged of the past. "But I'm too old to be this easily smitten," he told himself. "You're a tenderheart," his momma would have said. "That means that you have goodness inside of you that you aren't afraid to feel." He closed his eyes and imagined that if he had her in his arms right now, there were so many things that he would ask her. "Why do you put up with me?" would be the first question. He had purposely pushed people away all his life. Women were needy. Now here he was, needing the scent of her. He would finish his line of questioning with, "Can you tolerate me forever?" He knew it was high time that he stopped battling against something that he wanted so desperately. No one else was fooled.

Tim picked up the phone and dialed. On the second ring, Rochelle answered.

"Hey, little brother."

"I'm not little, I'm big," he said, sounding seven years old.

"Well, you're always little brother to me."

"What time is it there?"

"Almost eight, why?"

"Nothing. Let me ask you something, Rochelle."

"Sure."

"When you fell in love with Carl, did you know instantly?"

"I felt his eyes from across the room. He came over and introduced himself. I ignored him and gave him a hard time, but mostly, I enjoyed him." She giggled. "Why, you think you love her?"

"Love who?"

"Don't play games with me, boy."

"Nina?"

"You know who."

"Why you say that?"

"Why you say that?" she mocked. "I say that because you never let another woman close enough to invite her over for dinner with your sister. She's the first one that's got you asking all these questions. Making you want to give up all the rest? It has to be real. Besides, once you get your head on straight, God blesses you with the desires of your heart; before that, you're not ready."

"So,what do you think? She doesn't think you like her."

"No, it's not that, please tell her it's not. I'm your big sis, I want you to have the best, and you have to know what you're getting into, that's all."

"Yeah, and?"

"She's older, I didn't initially think that you two had anything in common."

"We both like jazz."

"And what else?"

"Jesus."

"And what else?" Rochelle kidded.

"Art, theater, and film."

"Sounds positive. I'm surprised, Tim, I thought you were going to go through life looking for a reason not to love. I'm glad to see you opened your heart. If you don't clear it out and allow God to renew your mind, it leaves no room for you to grow, you know?"

"Thanks, sis. You know I love you, right?"

"Yeah, in your own sick way, I guess you do. Call us soon."

"I will."

"Love ya."

With that, Tim put down his shield and sword. All this time he hadn't been protecting himself from anybody but himself. He hated fighting against what was so natural. But it was easier for a man to go down a mountain than up it. He picked up the phone again and dialed the numbers that would change his life forever. When the phone picked up and he was sure it was her and not the machine, he said, "No more games, I want to be honest. I really dig you, Nina."

62

Saturday morning the doorbell rang nonstop. Peaches, Martha, Shelby, the Hallelujah girls, Carla, Carmen, and Rochelle, who had orchestrated the whole Hair Fest, arrived successively.

"What's this about?"

Troi winced, barely dressed and clutching at the fabric of her robe. Vaughn sat in a chair facing the television, looking over the want ads. How he mirrored his father tickled Troi to death. She giggled loudly as Rochelle approached to make her announcement.

"Girl, there is no way that we are going to let your dream die. There is no way on God's earth that's gonna happen. When He gives you something, it cannot be erased. Maybe it will get blurry, out of view, or temporarily disconnected, but here we are."

"Well, what y'all want?" Troi laughed.

"We want our hair done!" their voices chimed.

Rochelle hugged Troi tight and whispered, "My brother loves your sister, so I guess we family now," in her ear.

Troi widened her eyes and nodded.

"Anyway, back to doing hair," Rochelle announced.

"You think this will work?" Troi asked, hand on hip.

"Sure it will," Rochelle said. "Besides, there's no overhead!"

Peaches picked up where Rochelle left off, explaining how her hair just wasn't the same without Troi doing it. Nina slipped in unnoticed, grinning as if heaven had opened up, serving her a hefty slice of forever.

"Hello, hello, hello. I need my hair done, too." Nina pouted.

"Hey, Nina." Rochelle smiled.

"Hey, how you doing, Rochelle?" Nina walked over and hugged Rochelle tight.

"Fine. We've got to do lunch, girl," Rochelle offered.

"Yes, we must." Nina nodded.

"If you want your hair done, get in line." Carla pointed behind her with her thumb. Nina grabbed her sister by the torso and pulled her into the kitchen.

"What?"

Nina held her tight. "He's mine, girl. I got the confirmation and I'm holding on to that promise."

"You go on, girl, and don't let nobody steal your seed."

"I won't. Don't I deserve it?"

"Girl, we are all sinners, we don't deserve nothing but hell and death, but I get what you're saying."

It was Nina's turn to ask her sister why everything was so hard for them.

"The more you say it, the more you make it true, Nina," Troi said.

"Okay, okay. Why are we being so blessed then?" Nina laughed. "He likes me how I am, sis."

"He's supposed to."

"I know, but how many men actually do? I mean, you know, they're always trying to fit you into some fashion-spread mold." Nina rubbed her hips.

"You got the real thing, sis, that's all. There are good men out there and then there are dogs. The good men are overshadowed by the dogs, so a sister is more likely to overlook the good ones."

"I know."

"But the dogs, they're everywhere. Littering the streets with their quick pickup lines."

"Ain't that the truth."

"Where's Shelby?"

"She'll be here, Martha, too."

"I appreciate all you've done."

"Don't thank me. You're my sister and I love you."

"I love you, too."

When Troi and Nina pried themselves from the kitchen, Carla was hugging Vaughn, and it seemed that they were back on speaking terms. Friendships were relationships, they took work, just like everything else. Troi appreciated the fact that Carla was her girl, a sister almost, and she cared to the core. When Troi hurt, Carla was there sharing her pain. Unconditional love.

At church on Sunday, Troi sang her heart out. She sang "His Eyes Are on the Sparrow." She knew that someone up there was watching over her. She knew that she couldn't have survived any other way. Troi grinned at Mother as she looked radiant in her freshly pressed church suit, foundation, mascara, and lipstick. Martha was content, and loving what Troi had done with her hair the day before. Shelby made a rare appearance in church, too, although she was spotted easing out the back door when they began passing the collection plate for the offering.

Daddy had made his usual appearance, wearing a tie, and he was alone for a change. And although he wasn't sitting with Mother, they were both in the house of the Lord, sort of together. Vaughn sat thanking God for every spare moment he'd have to spend with his family as the days passed and Troi knew her laughter made him realize that they all took life way too seriously.

"I'm going home," Troi announced after church. "I have six appointments in the morning."

Hugs were felt all around, and although Pastor dismissed the congregation, he interrupted the postchurch social to pray for the couple who had gone through the fire and still come out blessed.

"Vaughn, you cherish this good woman. Ain't many that would go through the fire, come out singed, and still stand by your side."

"I know," he said, hugging his wife.

"I love him, that's all, I do." Troi lowered her head.

Troi had realized sooner than not that God had promised her Vaughn, not total perfection.

The holidays would soon be approaching. The air was cool and a sweater today hadn't been enough. Vaughn had passed on his family reunion this year, which was fine by Troi. The streets were still cluttered with those who wouldn't forfeit summer. Soon the city would be clothed with the festivity of red and green mistletoe-clad doorways and dangling white icicle lights. The season would do as it always had, sneak in unaware.

"Daddee . . ." Dakoda called as Vaughn woke her from the backseat of the car.

Standing in the middle of their living room now, Troi didn't know how to feel. The pain of rejection had subsided, and the suspicions were following, although she couldn't determine how wise it was to allow them to.

"I thank God for my family. I didn't think that I would be here. I didn't know where I would be around this time of year," Vaughn said, looking around at his familiar things, which included his sofa.

"Well, I know that even in the midst of my fear, God kept my eye on Him, not you. Because if I had my eye on you, I'd be gone," Troi said, flipping on the coffeemaker. "I'd have been heavily medicated on a mental ward somewhere."

"I know. What can I say? I'm sorry, you know that already. And I love you, you know that, too."

"Yes, I know."

"I know you don't understand this whole thing about me, but all I can say is I get these thoughts, but I know that I don't have to necessarily act on them."

"Exactly."

"If I acted on every thought and impulse I ever had, I'd be on lockdown."

"Like Anthony?" Troi giggled.

"There's no Anthony, CeCe. I lied about that."

"I know. You think I didn't know? Deep down we always know."

"Troi, you are still beautiful, sexy, and I adore you."

"I know you do. Maybe not as much as you should, but I know you do." She hugged him tightly and kissed his head. "Let's take it one day at a time."

"Okay. My momma wants you to do her hair," Vaughn interrupted, his hand caressing Troi's back.

"Really?"

"Yeah."

"Great," Troi said, with Dakoda at her feet. She picked up her baby and smiled as her little girl cooed something that sounded like "mama and daddee," and Troi went to the kitchen to pour her husband a cup of coffee. Black, one sugar.

63

Vaughn's family was happy to have everyone communicating again. For a while it seemed as though they had lost him not only to the streets, but to death and all that lurked there. His momma was still feeding him like food was going out of style, and his father included him in conversations more and talked to the television less. Sam still hadn't returned any of his calls, so Vaughn was surprised when he surfaced at his momma's, willing to talk about things finally. After teary remembrances and revelations not far from his own, Vaughn had an idea why his brother had been so defiantly opposed.

"I never acted on it, though. And that's absolutely not why Brenda left," Sam explained.

This was his life, and he wasn't going to debate right and wrong with anybody. He knew in his heart what he needed to do for him and his family. Each new day found Vaughn enjoying the sound of laughter in his home again and arms that had hands that didn't hit, just hugged and embraced. His little girl was a month shy of turning three, and they were planning something really nice and colorful for her.

Troi and Vaughn had so much to give each other. They were learning to savor moments. No rushing. Just embracing the times that they spent together, never dwelling much on the fact that they'd nearly blown it all. Or rather, he did. But Troi had almost blown it by being too hasty and dwelling on all the unsolicited opinions. And Vaughn had almost thrown it all away because he had opened himself up to a seducing spirit that wanted to destroy his marriage and his life. "Once gay, always gay," the cynics said, but his thoughts didn't define him, his fruit did. God knew his heart, and with all he possessed that was good, he would conform to God and not expect it to be vice versa.

Vaughn couldn't promise his wife that he would never raise a brow at another man ever again, but he'd try. It was what was expected of him, and, more than that, it was what he wanted to do for his daughter. Vaughn couldn't get over Tracie's smirk and the grimace that had turned the face of someone he'd initially found attractive into someone who, in his opinion, was now as ugly as mud. Hatred did that to people. Resting his head in Troi's lap, Vaughn fought to imagine what it would feel like to have your entire being dispossessed from the heart of someone you loved. He couldn't conceive of it.

He didn't feel in the least threatened that people thought that because he felt something sexually for another man, he had to let it trap him. Everybody who had those feelings didn't necessarily want them. He refused to let a solitary thought affect the rest of his life. He knew his wife. Her wants, dislikes, and fears. He would never naturally feed into the things that haunted her most. He was sure that Troi would never allow herself to be overtaken by her childhood, her rocky marriage, or the demise of her shop. She would normally refuse to give the world's eyes the satisfaction. She always wanted to do what was right. Morality eluded most people.

Vaughn would not be the kind of man who boldly confessed that he had the right to decide his sexuality and then ended up naked in a hotel room, wrapped up in the sheets, staring out at the moon after an interlude and vowing never to do it again.

He couldn't speak for the others, he wouldn't dare. But he needed everyone to know that feelings were deceitful. Feelings weren't any more reliable than using a bedsheet as a parachute. Vaughn remembered feeling like he could fly when he was eight years old. He had a thing for Superman back then, but that didn't mean that he'd put on a cape, open the window, and jump out.

Something in him allowed him to love Troi. He thanked that part of himself repeatedly.

64

She anticipated his return. Quickly and creatively she made up her bed with a new vigor and determination that laid the path for him to walk through her heart. Nina and Tim found themselves on the telephone often, whispering to each other and making mental plans not only to be together, but for him chivalrously to rescue her and grant her the opportunity to be freed from the fortress of meticulously mapped knickknacks, which she had for six and a half odd years called home. There was no violent outburst that would douse this newfound passion, a passion that was electrifying and, at the same time, sent pulsing rays through their bodies that didn't need urgent quenching. There was more here than flesh; it was inevitable what the outcome would be.

She had managed to grasp onto the fundamentals, which revealed to her that Derek was the weak one, not her. He needed her to remain a victim so that he could feel superior. So many people in her life had. He had charged himself as her knight and had been protecting her from someone worse than himself, as if it were possible. Derek thought that Nina needed him. She had believed it, too, on occasion, but today there was an awareness. She was as worthy, and God would see her through. She also wanted to begin showing the brownstone. She hoped it would sell quickly.

One evening around eleven P.M. his time and two A.M. her time, Nina asked Tim, "Why should I trust you with my heart?" She made herself comfortable, as she was sure she would enjoy the creative way that Tim would woo her with words.

"Why should you trust me with your heart?"

"Yes."

"How many reasons do you want?"

"I dunno. Ten."

"Okay. Because I see the beauty in you that others overlook. You should trust me with your heart because to love means you have no other choice. You can trust me with it because I would never break it, harm it, or hurt it."

"That last one doesn't count as three, you know."

"Yeah, it does."

"No, it doesn't," Nina kidded.

"Can I get a break here?"

"Okay, all right. That's five," Nina snuggled under her blanket, pressing the telephone even closer to her ear.

"You can trust me with your heart because I need your heart to love you better, and because love starts with trust. Giving me your heart means trusting me with you."

"Yes, I do trust you."

"You can trust me with your heart because for me to love you, I have to love all of you, including your heart. The heart is a mystery, so for me to know your heart is to love you completely. And lastly, Nina, you can trust me with your heart because I trust you with mine."

"Ohhh, Tim . . ." Her voice cracked.

"What?"

"I can't wait to see you."

Sparsely clothed tree branches brushing together had a sedating effect as the old year made its exit without its winter whiteness and Valentine's Day inched closer, just days away. Like flowers, people were led to believe that they had no choice in who came by to pollinate them. Nina sat in the park. It was thirty-eight degrees. She was pondering how her survival instincts had kicked in, as ominous clouds dared her to make it home before they bombarded her with pelting showers. She didn't move.

The still winter rain soaked her to the bone. She sat motionless on a splintery park bench. She tried to read poetry, but the wet pages stuck together, and she fed herself grapes that weren't frozen, but were still very cold. She ventured home with a disregard for her comfort and took an intensely hot shower, then lounged about, kicking the sheets, finding no solace in being alone.

Five days and he would be there. He had requested her presence at Chez Josephine and wanted to see La Clemenza di Tito at the New York City Opera. She had never remembered a Valentine's Day that had ever given her much to look forward to. She knew that love was in the minds of people, a conquering game to others, where they wanted something just until they knew they had it, then they made room for it on a shelf; but this was different. He was. Although everything around her, including the shih tzu with the limp and the bus driver who dispersed two passengers at seven A.M., became less frequent, like a broken habit.

Her therapist had seen a change in her, despite the fact that she still talked to her plants and, on occasion, her fish.

"I think we can discontinue our sessions for a while. If you feel you need to talk, give me a call and we'll schedule something."

Nina didn't think she'd need anything as a crutch anytime soon. She sat fingering her shiny new red membership card for the local gym, which she believed she would use, especially since her membership was transferable. She was doing it for herself, not him. He was the only man who accepted her as is.

"I love my hips, I just want to tone my legs," Nina told herself.

Vaughn had called Nina two days ago, wanting Nina's blessing on him rededicating himself to his marriage. Renewing his vows.

"Sounds good. But what about your preference and what you feel?"

"I'll deal with that when the time comes. I've been praying now. I know that lifestyle isn't what I want. It's in me, I know, but I want to change. God can do anything. I love your sister."

"I love my sister, too, Vaughn. Be careful with her. We've had a hard life. You know what I mean?"

"Yeah. I'll be honest this time. No sneaking around."

Nina approached the house that she and Troi had called home for at least fourteen years. It was evident that Daddy loved Mother to a ruinous degree. No matter what she did, his love had always been there, nurturing her and trying to help her believe that her dreams didn't have to die. He didn't criticize her, he encouraged her, but she had no purpose, she had no goal. He had carefully laid her in bed at night when she'd fallen asleep slumped in the chair or on the floor in the kitchen. Even in the bathtub once. She just didn't have enough of herself to give to her children. She could barely care for herself day to day. Daddy had held it all together for years. He was tired. Everything had its limit. Daddy had been filled to capacity, like a tub that eventually overflowed and wet the bath mat. When Nina had asked Troi point-blank, "Is Daddy seeing someone else?" Troi had said, "Yes," confirming Nina's suspicions and exposing her daddy's lame excuse that the woman in church with him that day was the wife of one of the guys who worked for him.

Nina eyed the wall in the sky-blue bedroom that used to be hers when she was little. The nicks in the overplastered wall where she had thrown the jelly glasses, records, and all of her anger were still there as a telltale sign that not much changed, and that whatever you did could have lasting consequences. "Who would have known?" Nina spoke out loud in her room, which was empty now and no longer housed her childhood things or dictated the way things needed to be.

"I'll be there in a minute," Mother yelled from her bedroom.

"Take your time," Nina muttered.

Nina came down to the kitchen to find Mother neatly dressed, smiling, and still loving her new hairdo.

"Your hair looks good, Mother."

"You really like it?" Mother smoothed her hair.

"Yeah, I really do."

"You don't think it's too short?"

"Not at all. Are you ready?"

"Yes, I am."

"Okay."

"Nina? Guess what?"

"What?" Nina smiled.

"Your father called last night." Her mother grinned.

"What did he say?" Nina stood, hand on hip.

"He wanted to know if he could come back. Said some nice things to me. It's been awhile."

"Really?"

"I don't remember the last time I heard something nice."

"What did you say to him?"

"I told him I'll think about it."

Nina only nodded. "You'll be fine, Mother. See?" Nina grasped her mother's shoulders and turned her around to face the mirror that hung over the area that used to be a fireplace.

"What do you think?" she asked Nina.

"No, Mother, what do you think?"

"I like it. I think it looks good."

"That's all that matters then."

They moved quickly through Saturday-morning traffic, foraging for a parking space in a residential neighborhood. There was a woman they observed with a dirty orange wool ski hat, pushing a shopping cart full of empty cans and bottles. *She could have just as easily been my mother,* Nina thought. Homeless and wandering the streets of Brooklyn, looking for a handout or enough spare change to buy coffee and a buttered roll, yes, it could have been Mother. The winds were warm for February, and there was a boy doing wheelies on his shiny bike in the middle of the street.

Nina and her mother walked about six long Brooklyn blocks in silence. They came upon the church. The church was old dark brick. Tim would have appreciated that fact. Her mother reached for her hand.

"Help me, child," she said, never making eye contact.

The warmth of her mother's touch made Nina smile. Her lips trembled, and Nina bit her bottom lip.

Mother was dressed conservatively. After Daddy had left, she'd stopped performing for folks. Her reality was that she was alone. She honestly knew why Nina's father had left. He hadn't left her for someone else; he'd just gotten tired of her mess. But she had stood on her own, and now he wanted to come back to her, regardless of where he had been.

Mother might not have even remembered being sprawled face-down on the kitchen floor, one shoe on and one shoe off, when he'd have to roll her over and carry her to bed. His fear was probably that one day she simply wouldn't wake up. He didn't want to be around to see it.

Mother had on a pair of crepe slacks now and a printed top with a matching sweater. There was no visible evidence that two days ago she had been intoxicated. From the curb they could both see the sign that was taped on the wall in the entranceway of the church. Nina stood on the corner, admiring her mother, the building, the weather, and the thought of Tim. She deposited a Valentine's Day card in the mailbox slot and double-checked to make sure it had gone all the way down. Troi could use a whole lot of love right now, she thought.

There was an arrow scratched on the piece of cardboard that was taped to the church building, directing everyone to the right. At the bottom of the sign, in small letters, it said, ALL ARE WELCOME.

Nina and her mother made their way hand in hand up the stairs, and followed the arrow to the right. They looked up and around the room to find that there were approximately thirty friendly-faced people sitting around, appearing pleasant enough to welcome an unfamiliar.

"Come on, Mother." Nina tugged as her mother backed up out of habit. Life had caged her so effectively.

"Good afternoon," a soft-spoken woman said deliberately into the microphone. "My name is Janice, for those of you who don't know me. I'd like to welcome you all this afternoon. If you're here for the first time, we're glad you could make it."

They started off with a brief prayer. Some heads bowed, other looked around, some were just going through the motions. A man got up and shared his story about how he had almost lost his mind, not to mention his children.

"I'm sorry," he said. "Some people don't have anyone to apologize to. I could be dead right now. I could be six feet under, eating dirt, and rotting like something in a movie. I'm grateful and thankful. But I couldn't do this without my family. They forced me to see myself. I was in denial until I had given the word a new meaning. I'd just like you all to think of me and remember, you can do it, too, one day at a time."

"Thank you for sharing, Joseph, that was wonderful. We know how you feel, we've been there. Our families are the ones who suffer. I myself was too loaded to know the difference between judgment and genuine concern. But you all know my story. I'll let someone else speak if there's someone who wants to share."

Mother sat motionless and looked around the room at the faces of what could have been doctors, lawyers, and politicians. She gave Nina her purse, and Mother's eyes surveyed the room again. The woman next to Nina started applauding first when Mother rose to the invitation. Mother slowly and methodically walked to the front of the room. She didn't make eye contact. She was shaking and nervous. Her feet forgot how to walk. She stalled for a moment. She looked faint; then Janice stepped over from the front of the room and held Mother by her elbow until she reached where Janice had been standing.

Joseph touched Mother's shoulder, reassuring her that it would be all right. Janice handed Mother the microphone and stepped back, head bowed. Mother cleared her throat. She had always had something to say, mostly when it wasn't appropriate. This would be her chance to redeem herself. She wanted to tell them how she had never learned to be a mother and how her family life wasn't nearly an example. She wanted to say she was sorry. She wanted her husband, her life, and her beauty. She wanted the forgiveness of her children and her husband. She wanted to forgive herself for being just like her dad.

Mother had tears in her eyes. Nina could hear her sniffling from where she was sitting. She was thankful that she had accompanied her mother. She could see the sincerity. She really wanted to do this. She needed to do this. The applause had died down and the room was silent now. All eyes were on Nina's mother as if she were a game-show contestant. It was time to lose her demons.

Mother cleared her throat again, fumbling with the tissue crumpled in her hand. One of the friendly-faced women stood up and hugged Mother again for moral support.

"It's okay," she said. "You'll do fine."

Mother nodded, looking down at her hands, which were withered and drawn. She smiled weakly, gripping the microphone as if it might topple over.

"Hi . . ." she began, backing away from the sound of her own voice. "My name is Sadie, and I'm an alcoholic."